Unbridled Eye

A Penny Larkin Thriller

REBECCA JEAN DOWNEY

ISBN: 979-8-9926031-0-1

Table of Contents

"Four things greater than all things are,
women and horses and power and war."
Rudyard Kipling

The flames started with a whisper, tickling the edges of the stall before moving to the straw bedding of the quarter horse mare. It encircled the mare's ankles, causing her to prance as if she were competing in a show. Her steel horseshoes were hot. There was no relief except to keep moving. Her nostrils flared, giving smoke a grand entrance to her lungs. She threw her backside against the stall's wood door. It did not budge. She reared and drove her front hooves into the door's midsection, splintering it in two.

A trainer found the pregnant mare running from one end of the barn to the other looking for a way out. Her flank dripped with sweat. Foam oozed between her teeth and dropped onto the cement walkway. She whinnied and threw her head high as the trainer, pulling bits of burning straw out of her tail, led her to safety in a nearby pasture.

A fire truck screeched to a stop in front of the barn and a handful of firefighters rushed toward the flames, carrying hatchets and hoses.

"It's okay," the trainer reassured her, as he returned to the safety of the grassy pasture with two young geldings. They were snorting and stamping their feet, but the mare had no time for their antics.

She moaned and fell to her knees, where she gave birth to her foal in the comfort of the tall grass.

The chestnut colt's skin glistened in the light of the intense flames. When he opened his eyes for the first time, the clouds parted, revealing tiny candles of twinkling light—promises yet to be fulfilled and races yet to be won. The colt lifted his head and crawled toward his mother, tucking himself inside the mare's front legs. She whinnied and blew her warm breath over her newborn in a welcome gesture of hope.

Chapter 1

Penny Larkin drove north out of El Paso on Interstate 10 in search of the West Texas Gun Club. Her red Mustang convertible was still dripping water from the car wash. She too, was fresh out of her morning shower. There was something exhilarating about driving above the speed limit with the convertible top down and the wind blowing your face into a smile. Penny never tired of it, and perhaps, she mused, her late father's penchant for auto racing was truly in her blood.

It made perfect sense to Penny that a Texas firing range could be found in New Mexico. After all, Texas was so big, nobody really knew where the state began or where it ended. Penny chose to drive the Mustang today out of pure pride. She had only planned to be at the range for two hours and didn't want to spend the rest of the day in her SUV. Penny had promised to meet Sheriff Leo Tellez at his re-election party by 7 p.m. and had a very good reason for arriving there in style. Perhaps Leo's new love, Adriana, would be clinging to his side.

Penny, an agent with the U.S. Marshals Service, had shot and killed the last two fugitives she had been tracking. Even though both shootings had been in self-defense, Penny now faced a mental paralysis and an inability to even holster her weapon. She kept her Staccato 9mm Parabellum pistol, issued by the Marshal's service, in her glove compartment. It was tucked in there with her .38 caliber Smith and Wesson revolver, a gift of her former boyfriend, Sheriff Leo Tellez.

Today the plan was for Penny to meet Ollie Trejo at the gun range, get some tips and be gone by 4 p.m. Ollie was a well-respected competitive shooter, and mother of her closest friend, New Mexico State Trooper, Captain Johnny Trejo. While Penny had earned her rifle marksmanship ribbons as an agent with the Marshals service in the Southwest Sector, her recent kill shots had kept her away from the range. This had helped contribute to her loss her self-confidence and her courage.

While Penny would never want to be accused of being unprepared, she often lived life on the lip of the cup, waiting to take a sip before ever knowing what she had been served. And now she was forced to drive her beloved Mustang over a poor excuse for a road, with chunks of caliche pounding the undercarriage. And though her cropped blonde hair was tied with a scarf, there was nothing to keep the dust from stinging her eyes.

Penny had wanted to be a geologist when she went off to the University of Texas but eventually chose journalism because she was fascinated with criminal justice. To her law meant order. And order was something she truly craved. As she bounced through the Northern Chihuahuan desert, she knew there was no order here. Her tires were rolling through an ancient seabed and churning up dust from three-toed horses, flightless birds, and Mastodons. She couldn't help but wonder what had brought all these giants down? *Getting lost?*

Penny imagined the Mustang's fenders being swallowed up by the sand. Would hikers in a thousand years find the skeleton of her rusted car buried here and wonder what kind of dinosaur this was? Penny swore she heard the wind whistling the theme song from the movie, *Jurassic Park*. She was not amused.

As she passed the same hand-painted sign pointing to the gun club for the third time it dawned on her. "I'm driving around in circles!" Yep. And there was the same "Old Man" tree with its twisted limbs and wrinkled bark, holding a death-grip on the desert floor. If she kept going, perhaps she would discover a dead sign painter on the side of the road, too. She was ready to kill him, anyway!

A feeling of panic took up residence on the back porch of her mind. The Mustang's gas gauge and her confidence were hovering at a quarter tank. Ah, but she had been through much worse. Thoughts of a recent kidnapping by gunrunners came to mind.

"I'm going to raise the top." Penny said, thinking of her father's love of cars. She'd grown up around race cars and spent hours as a toddler learning to walk among the wrenches, sockets, and ratchets of his auto shop. As a racecar driver, who died doing what he loved, the once famous Johnny Larkin, would have had piston failure to see the leather interior of her Mustang being destroyed by the dust. She could hear his voice cautioning her: "You'll never be able to clean those vents or vacuum up all that grit from those seams in the upholstery."

The thought of her father's penchant for immaculate automobiles, made Penny smile. She remembered his strong hands, well-muscled from gripping the wheel during a race. She longed to be hugged once more by the father who always had engine oil under his nails.

Her mind focused back on the landscape. Surrounding her was a broad expanse of the Northern Chihuahuan desert which covered much of Southeastern New Mexico and West Texas. The desert was now inhabited by what Penny called *sneaky creatures*—the kind that sunned themselves by day and slithered under rocks at night. She shuddered at the thought of what might be lurking beneath her wheels but found reassurance in the 4,000 pounds of steel and four new tires separating her from the fangs of misfortune. Penny had no plans to get out of her car, anyway. And she was in no mood to become extinct!

Penny scanned the 10-foot drop-off on both sides of the narrow road. A slight turn of her wheels in either direction would catapult her car into a ditch. She focused her eyes ahead, refusing to let a little drop-off deter her. The road wrapped around a bank of sand sculptures, chiseled into haunting shapes by thousands of heavy rainstorms. She glanced at the sky, searching for a dark cloud. *Clear and blue*. Penny was relieved. A downpour could quickly turn to flooding and toss her car around like a Tinker Toy.

She blinked fast trying to clear her line of sight as sweat trickled down her forehead. The perspiration stung her eyes and turned the dust on her face into grit. She shifted into second gear. Her patience was a thin cloak in a storm of doubt. She revved the engine. The transmission jerked the Mustang over a hump in the road, ramming the front end into a deep pocket of sand. Penny's chin bounced off the top of the steering wheel, knocking her back against the bucket seat. The Mustang's motor, gasped. "You've got to be kidding me!" Penny coughed as the Mustang's exhaust pushed its way through the vents. She turned off the ignition and crawled out of the car. A whiff of fumes followed her. "My luck!"

Blinded by the sun, Penny stumbled over the uneven landscape and fell to her knees. The jagged stones under her legs tore the hem of her jeans. She was an unwelcome visitor on the desert floor. These days the place belonged to scorpions, tarantulas, and lizards, and for this Penny almost felt like apologizing. As she pressed the palms of her hands into the ground to get up, she heard castanets. As if on cue, a Diamondback slithered on stage from under a sun-drenched ledge of limestone. It had six or seven rattlers, and about three inches of zebra-like black rings on its tail. Penny watched as the rattlesnake lifted its head. A black tongue shot in and out of its mouth like a dagger. Its cat-like eyes glinted in the sun. Penny's feet were itching, sweat pooling between her toes. She gritted her teeth and held her breath.

Before she could exhale, the snake sank its fangs into the sole of her leather work boot. She tried to shake the snake off, but it was still hanging on tight, its tail searching for the safety of the ground. Penny jerked her foot until the rattler finally opened its mouth. *No luck.* Penny slammed her right foot several times into the dirt until the Diamondback released her shoe and dropped into the dust.

Penny took advantage of the snake's confusion and scrambled back to the safety of her car. Tears joined the sweat falling over her chin. She couldn't stop shaking. Her chest ached as she tried to take in air, but no number of breaths would reach the bottom of her lungs. She lay her head against the seat. Finally, she lifted her head and laughed.

"Get a grip, girl! You can get out of this mess, if you just inch your wheels to the left and the right, a little at a time."

Penny cranked the ignition, and the engine blew the sand from its fuel rail and roared back to life. She made a couple of small turns of the steering wheel to the left and then to the right, finally freeing her car from the pit of caliche. She spotted another badly executed sign. The way forward was hedged by a prickly pear cactus with longer arms than a sea creature. "Why not?" She shouted.

After a second hair-pin curve, she started wondering if the gun club members could shoot straighter than they could paint.

A little dust in her hair and lungs was just an inconvenience to Penny, compared to the insecurity choking the life out of her. She did not want her boss, U.S. Marshal Eugene Lujan, to know how insecure she was in handling a gun. A big question loomed in her mind, "Will I ever feel comfortable again?"

Penny had to try. And Ollie had promised her no self-respecting law officer would ever be target shooting at the West Texas Gun Club. But how much did a 65-year-old woman whose quilts won blue ribbons at the New Mexico State Fair know about guns anyway? It was a little too late to be wondering about that.

A foot at a time, the Mustang lurched past the sand sculptures and up to the crest of the road. The scenery at the top was just as desolate, punctuated by a few dust-weary mesquite trees and a scrum of Cholla cactus. *Have I made a wrong turn?* She saw no more hand painted signs pointing to the gun club. The compass on her dash pointed east.

The crack of a rifle pierced the air, repeated by the whistle of three more shots. Penny parted company with the road and drove toward the sound of gunfire. This brought her to the top of another hill, where she had a view of the range. Ollie Trejo was alone. Her rifle was pointed at a target some 50 yards away. She looked even shorter than her five-foot frame from this distance, but Penny could tell Ollie was handling the rifle like it was a third arm. *Crack!* Another bullet left the chamber. Penny's car crept down the slope into unchartered territory, crushing the desert's sharp teeth under its wheels.

Crack!

The sound of the repeating gunfire gave Penny chills. Her hands were shaking as she forced her car down the incline. The closer she got to the range, the more her body fought her progress. Her fingers gripped the steering wheel. Her head was an echo chamber as her protests bounced back and forth in her mind. "I can't do this!"

Penny had learned to shoot as a kid under the careful watch of her dad and even got consistent hitting the targets. But firing at static targets and aiming for and killing another human is a whole different thing. In the last two assignments as a Marshal, she had had to defend herself, and in the process, killed both suspects. But she had repeated this mantra of doubt over and over for months and desperately wanted to move forward. "I've come this far, and it might as well be today!"

Penny's Mustang rolled into the gravel parking lot despite her misgivings. Somehow, she had the presence of mind to put her foot on the brake and turn off the car. Through her dusty windshield, she could see Ollie waving and laughing. Penny blew out a long breath, slowly releasing her fears like a balloon hissing stagnant air. She unclenched her aching fingers and waved back.

Oh, how Penny wished she could start the day all over and have whatever Ollie had eaten for breakfast.

Chapter 2

El Paso County Sheriff Leo Tellez pulled his silver Tahoe into the Southwest Plaza parking lot. The day he had dreaded and longed for at the same time had finally arrived. In a few hours, Leo would know if he had been re-elected as sheriff, or if his badge would gather dust on his bedside table.

Leo perused the location of his re-election headquarters. The aging strip mall had several vacant storefronts, most of which were sprayed with graffiti. The shop selling clothing "per libra," was still open, and the neon sign at STAPLES, was all aglow, except for the letter "P".

Leo's stomach growled. He was tempted to stop at Freddy's, a few doors down. Herlinda Corchado was a legendary cook. He knew a bite of her food, or some reassurance from Herlinda's smile, was out of the question right now. The polls were closing in a few hours, and rumors were that Leo had lost most of his voters when he took a bullet during a shootout in Columbus, New Mexico and had been unable to campaign.

Would anyone be inside? Leo counted the cars in the lot. He recognized a few, and a sense of relief blanketed him with hope. He drove around looking for the best place to park.

Leo's opponent was wealthy businessman Francisco Parasea, a good-looking 36-year-old, whose naiveté and boundless energy had driven him to campaign fiercely for the sheriff's job. Even though Parasea had no experience in law enforcement, his campaign strategies were flawless. When he learned Leo was grounded from the campaign trail, he had pressed even more flesh and knocked on even more doors.

The *El Paso Times* editorial board had endorsed Leo Tellez for reelection, but the newspaper had declared his chances of winning were slim. Still Leo refused to give up on the voters, whom he hoped had appreciated his tireless devotion to the job.

It was late afternoon, and 40-mile-per-hour winds were holding a bag of trash hostage against the chain link fence that divided Leo's election headquarters from Julio's Car Wash.

Was this a sign of the times? Was his campaign all washed up? A gust of wind sprayed foam over the windshield of Leo's SUV.

Leo ran his wipers and scanned the lot for Penny Larkin's car. It was still early, but he hoped she would be there for him. He had begged her to come, even though he was guilty of manslaughter in the death of their relationship. He had seen his share of criminals who caused their own suffering time and again. Was he doomed to become a serial killer in his own love affairs?

A television reporter was camped outside the door of Leo's headquarters. He gripped a mic in his sweaty hands. "Sheriff, what plans do you have if you lose tonight?" Leo glanced to his right and noticed a cameraman hoping to catch him shedding tears, no doubt. The heat made it difficult for Leo to catch his breath. *How can this man have the guts to ask such a stupid question?*

Leo grimaced and brushed the reporter away just as the television camera dropped a halo of light over his shoulders. The sheriff cupped his hand over his eyes and ducked quickly inside. He was greeted by the applause and cheering of a couple dozen volunteers. "Leo! Leo! Leo!" The clapping and the chanting were almost unbearable to Leo who operated the sheriff's office in "There's no 'I' in team-fashion." But this was how the game was played, and he wanted desperately to be sheriff again. He waved and mouthed the words, "Thank you." Leo's reelection headquarters were Spartan, but this was the place he knew his volunteers would want him to hold his election night celebration. He was born and raised in the Segundo Barrio, and these were his friends.

Leo spotted Captain Paco Ontiverros at the serving table, busily arranging snacks and drinks for the campaign workers. *Thank God!* Leo had relied on Paco for everything to work smoothly at the Sheriff's Office, and now, here he was organizing the food.

"Leo!" Paco yelled across the packed room, motioning for Leo to join him.

Leo shook several hands and accepted two hugs in the time it took him to reach Paco. "You didn't have to do all this." Leo wrapped his arm around Paco's shoulders.

"You are my friend and my sheriff. I support you in everything!"

"Well, thank you, amigo."

"I haven't seen Penny yet. When will she get here?"

"I asked her, Paco. But you know Penny. She's got a stubborn streak."

"Leo, one thing I do know about her is she has a forgiving heart. Don't give up on her."

The last thing Leo wanted to do was give up on Penny, but he had suspicions she had already given up on him.

A tall, lanky cowboy around Leo's age stepped out of the shadows of the room. "Sheriff, I'm Ronald Becker, a friend of your brother."

"Thank you for your support."

"I can't vote here. I live in New Mexico."

Leo was puzzled. *Did Don send the guy all this way to volunteer?*

Becker cleared his throat. Leo could hear his heavy breathing. "I came tonight because I need your help. Don assured me I could trust you."

"He hasn't mentioned your name before."

"Don and I were roommates our senior year at New Mexico State."

"Well, this is an unlikely time to speak to me. I'm kinda busy."

"Sheriff, I'm desperate. We've got barn fires killing horses near Tularosa."

"You know I can't do anything. How about your own sheriff?" Leo shook his head in disbelief. *Is this guy nuts?* He rubbed the ache in his left shoulder recalling last time he stepped out of his territory.

"My barn is next." Becker wiped the sweat from his forehead with calloused fingers.

Leo took a few steps forward. *I should call Don right now and ask him to stop volunteering me for things!*

Becker pulled on Leo's shoulder. "I was hoping you could check into it in your free time."

Leo swung around. Small daggers of disgust shot out of his eyes. "Free time? Is it so well-known I don't have much chance of winning this thing?" Leo's fingers tightened around the brim of his hat, crushing its felt. Now he was angry. He needed to get away from Ron Becker.

The place was rapidly filling with people. Leo was happy the excited voices of his supporters made it increasingly tough to talk. Leo made eye contact with a volunteer and waved. He turned toward Becker indicating he had to go. "You should be asking Don for help, not me. He's got the whole El Paso Fire Department at his beck and call."

Leo took a few steps toward freedom. Almost every table was full, and several folks stood along the sidelines. He felt better. Perhaps, he had a chance, after all, if this many people had cared enough to show their support.

A waiter from Freddy's arrived carrying a large platter of hot empanadas. The volunteers cheered. Leo couldn't help but laugh. "Thank you, Manny!" The familiar young man, who regularly waited on Leo's table, turned and waved.

"I started with Sheriff Esteban," Becker said.

Leo jerked his heard toward Becker, who apparently refused to take no as a goodbye.

"Esteban laughed in my face. He said the fires were being caused by a bunch of bored teenagers and they would die down, soon. That's when I called Don, and he told me to ask you for help."

Leo knew Don was not into wasting anybody's time. If he asked Ron Becker to contact him on election night, something serious must be going on. Leo grimaced. Becker's eyes looked like the mist that gathers in the desert after a rainstorm. "Of course, Mr. Becker, if I lose tonight, I'll have all the time in the world!"

"Sheriff, whether you win or lose, please, help me. Sooner or later, more than horses are going to die."

Chapter 3

Ollie greeted Penny with a cold bottle of water. "You have no idea how much I need this! Thank you." Penny let the water rest on her lips, before swallowing it. She had not realized how parched her mouth and throat were. She tried to brush the dust from her jeans and out of her hair. She was embarrassed to discover rings of sweat under her arms.

"You look like you've been wrestling a jackrabbit. What in the world happened?"

Ollie placed her arm on Penny's shoulder. "You need to calm down. You're panting."

"I had to fight off a Diamondback, for starters. And then, well then, it was the desert versus Penny, and I finally won." Penny smiled, thankful that her lips were moist enough to show how much she appreciated Ollie's concern.

"A rattler attacked you in your car?"

"I got my front end stuck in the sand and had to jump out of the car to find out which way to turn my wheels. He sunk his teeth into the sole of my boot, but I was able to shake him off."

"Judging from the looks of you, I can only imagine how bad the rattler looks. I'll bet he doesn't get out from under a rock for a week." Ollie was laughing. Her brown eyes held a piece the sunlight, which reflected onto Penny's face. "Did you bring your gun?"

Penny crawled back inside her dusty Mustang, rummaging through the glove compartment until her fingertips located the 9mm, as well as her .38 caliber Smith and Wesson revolver. Even in this heat, the steel barrel of the .38 felt cool to the touch. The revolver had been a gift from Leo, and owned by his late father, an El Paso Police Officer for 30 years. Penny rested her chest on the console of the car and then pulled both weapons from the glove compartment. The 9 mm was assigned by the U.S. Marshal. The revolver, however, hadn't exactly been an engagement ring, but Penny always thought Leo would not have parted with it had he not intended to make Penny a permanent part of his life. *Boy was I wrong.* She had toyed with giving it back to him, but she just couldn't do it—not yet anyway. Penny tightened her fingers around the grip and backed out of the car and headed toward Ollie.

"Hey, let go of this thing!" Ollie pried the revolver out of Penny's hands. Ollie rubbed her fingers over the grip. Penny watched as Ollie's eyes twinkled with approval. "Every lawman worth his salt owned one of these in the 1950s. And they still do the job. No jamming like a semi-automatic pistol."

Ollie escorted Penny to a long table where she had positioned her arsenal. There were two rifles and two pistols. Penny knew that much. Penny handed Ollie her pistol and she laid both guns on the table.

"The first thing we're going to learn is a Winchester lever-action rifle. It's light and has little recoil. That's the worst thing women encounter. Recoil can knock us off our feet, you know like love's supposed to do." Ollie gave Penny a wink, and Penny got the message. If Ollie had it her way, Penny and Ollie's son, Johnny, would be more than good friends.

"Let's learn how to load it," Ollie said, as if she hadn't fired a shot of sarcasm at Penny. "We're using 30-30 caliber ammo, or as we like to call them in Spanish, *treinta-treinta*. This gun has a tubular magazine, which means we need to use round-nose or flat-nose bullets. If you use pointed nose bullets, one of them might jam in your gun, or worse."

"Or worse?"

"It might blow up on you."

Penny's chills returned.

"But as I said, we are safety first here. I brought round-nose bullets. Pull down the lever and you will see a tube. That is where you drop the bullets. I like to put in four or five at a time, because when you get going with the lever-action, you want to know there is another bullet waiting."

Penny tried not to shake. She wanted Ollie to believe she was braver than she felt. The box of bullets was heavy in her hands and smelled a little like the metal shavings in her dad's auto shop. She stared at them, amazed how these small cylinders could do so much damage. Of course, she already knew, having killed a child trafficker and a gunrunner. She blew out a breath of hot air and looked at Ollie, who was smiling. Ollie's assurance gave her a small sliver of confidence. Penny took another slug of water.

"What are you waiting for, Christmas? You've still got six weeks!"

Penny dropped one of the bullets into the gun barrel.

"You're not going to put more bullets in the rifle?" Ollie asked. "This gun holds up to 15 rounds. You don't want to be shy with a Winchester on your shoulder, girl!"

Penny could feel a heaviness in her chest. "Just let me give this one a go."

"Close your left eye and focus your right eye on the sight at the end of the gun. The Winchester is very accurate if your sight is right. Push the lever forward and load the shot from the tube into the chamber."

Ollie reached up and adjusted the rifle on Penny's shoulders. "Don't sag, Penny. Be bold! *Se audaz!*"

Penny's fingers shook as she pushed the lever forward. She could hear the bullet slip into the chamber. All she had to do was aim and pull the trigger. Carelessly, she yanked the trigger. The butt of the gun jammed into her shoulder. She stumbled backwards and dropped the rifle in the dust.

Ollie said nothing. She picked up the gun and wiped it off with an old towel. "We've got to make sure there is no dirt in the chamber." She found a tool in her bag that looked like a tiny broom and brushed it inside of the magazine tube and then blew in it. "Ok, *tienes esto.* You've got this!"

"You wish!" Penny threw her head back and laughed at Ollie's pep talk. It was the first time Penny had laughed today. She loaded the rifle with three bullets. This time she was as prepared as she could be for the wayward projectile. The first shot missed the target, but something had shifted in Penny's resolve. She knew she was going to learn how to hit the target this afternoon. Her adrenaline was running higher than her Mustang at full throttle. She loaded the rifle with 15 bullets. Learning to shoot a Winchester was not rocket science, she realized. It was physics.

After several turns at the bullseye, Penny began hitting it with accuracy.

"I'm impressed," Ollie said.

Penny nodded and eked out a smile.

"I've got a pistol I want you to try." Ollie reverently drew the gun out of her case. "This is a Browning Hi-Power. It's what I've used to win tournaments. I love it, and once you get the hang of it, you will, too."

"You win tournaments? I thought all those blue ribbons were for quilting."

Ollie shook her head and polished a spot on the pistol with the palm of her hand.

Penny's mind flashed back to the Mexican ranch where she had been held captive. She had been forced to load a semi-automatic pistol to defend herself. It was painful. The magazine had bruised the palm of her hand and pinched her fingers. She hated the thought of having to go through that again.

Ollie must have read Penny's mind. "Watch this. It's a classic 9-mm autoloader. Even with my small hands, I can push the casing up into the grip." Ollie shoved the magazine into the gun with relative ease. "Now you try."

Penny looked at her watch.

"You gotta be somewhere more important than learning to save your life?"

"Sorry, Ollie. Really."

"Penny, you are never gonna learn to hit a target if you are distracted enough to track the time."

Ollie was right, of course. But she needed to be back in El Paso in a couple of hours. Or at least she had promised to be. Paco Ontiverros, Leo's best friend, had called and begged her to come to Leo's reelection party. "He hasn't been the same since you guys split. I know he would love seeing you. Besides, he's not predicted to win."

Penny knew Paco was dealing her an empathy card. She would have to be careful how she played it. As disgusted as she was with Leo, she didn't want him to lose. He was a damn good sheriff. Besides, in a backhanded sort of way, she felt responsible for Leo being shot in the first place. Regret was rumbling around in her stomach like a bad batch of menudo.

"Earth to Penny!" Ollie was waving her hands in the air. "Are you with me today or not? I've got some where to go, too."

"Sorry." Penny straightened her shoulders and stared at the grip of the pistol. She loaded the magazine with six bullets and pressed the palm of her hand against the bottom of the casing. It easily clicked into place.

"Let's get the old Browning Hi-Power in gear and then we'll do some refreshers on the Chief. I can't wait to fire that one, myself."

Chapter 4

The door to Leo's reelection headquarters swung open, banging its doorknob against the wall. The windstorm blew in sand, a Styrofoam cup, and Penny Larkin. Leo rushed to Penny's side and slammed the door shut. Despite her frazzled look, Penny's eyes lit up her face, and she managed a smile. She ran her fingers through her cropped blonde hair.

Leo turned Penny around and held both of her arms in a distant kind of embrace that communicated, "Your text said you weren't coming!"

"You look good, Leo," Penny said. She could feel a tiny bead of sweat trickling down her back. She swallowed the words she wanted to say.

"Nothing's been quite right since we..." Leo's voice trailed off.

"It looks like you've got quite the crowd." Penny broke his grip on her arm and twirled around, taking stock of the whole room. Every seat was taken. "You've packed 'em in. Sure sign of a winner!" Her eyes remained focused on the helium balloons bouncing against the rafters. If she could have reached one, she would have pierced it, just like Leo had done to her heart.

"Thank you for being here. I'm worried about the outcome."

"You aren't going to lose. You've done a wonderful job as sheriff, and everybody knows it." Penny knew Leo had not been able to do much campaigning, but she figured El Paso County voters were smart. Leo was running against an inexperienced, an albeit, very handsome man whose focus had been all about taking control of the fentanyl epidemic spreading through county high schools. There was more to being sheriff than that!

Penny glanced at the television screens at the front of the room. The returns were just coming in and the race seemed even.

"Would you like something to drink?" Leo asked.

"Yes, please." Was it the garish light in the room, or did Leo look older? It had only been a few months, but Penny noticed deeper creases around his eyes, and threads of grey hair at his temples. His wonderfully long lashes blinked several times as he looked at her. With each blink, Leo's brown eyes seemed to deepen with concern.

He wasn't going to draw her in with those sad eyes. Penny would have none of that. She had only come at Paco's insistence. She had no patience even for small talk with Leo. Not tonight. Not ever again. *Where in the world is Paco, anyway?*

As if reading her mind, Leo steered her toward to refreshments, and to Paco, who was just carrying in a case of soft drinks from the back room.

Seeing Penny, Paco set the drinks on the table and rushed to her side. "I knew you would come!"

"It's so good to see you, Paco, I've missed you."

"How about some hot apple cider?" When he lifted the lid on the Crock Pot, the smell of cinnamon and cloves floated past Penny's nose. She breathed in the aroma and smiled.

"I would love that. Thanks."

Leo had disappeared in the crowd. Penny looked around the room for Adriana. *Was Leo looking for her too?* There was a rumor at the courthouse that Leo's girlfriend had returned to Los Angeles because her law partner was ill, but maybe she had come back for the election returns. Penny was in no mood to rub shoulders with Leo's lover in such a crowded space. Leo had left Penny a telephone message a month ago saying the relationship with Adriana was over, but Leo had deceived Penny in the past. She made a furtive scan of the room and saw no one with long black hair and a model-like silhouette.

"Penny, I'm so grateful you are here," Paco said. "I know it's hard to get over the crazy set of circumstances that caused Leo to fall for Adriana's charms. After all, he nearly died from a loss of blood. Certainly, you can understand how he might confuse Adriana for his dead wife—they were identical twins."

"Paco, I don't want to talk about it. What's done is done. You and I both know it. I do want Leo and I to remain friends, but that's it."

Paco pressed his lips tightly together and grimaced. "I was hoping you might reconsider."

"I'm here because you asked me. Nothing more." Penny clenched her hands, to reinforce her control over the situation.

Paco nodded. "I was afraid you'd say that." He turned to help another volunteer with a cup of cider.

Penny took stock of her clothing. She had grabbed an old green sweater out of the trunk to replace her filthy shirt. Her boots, however, looked like she had marched to the sea with General Sherman. Unfortunately, her jeans had a rip in the knee and near the hem. All in all, however, she felt she could pass muster. Penny drank the entire cup of warm cider. It brought some comfort to an already stressful, rattlesnake kind of day.

"Penny, there is someone I want you to meet." Leo had returned with a sandy-haired man, holding a black cowboy hat with both hands. Penny watched the tips of the man's calloused fingers circling the felt brim as if he were reading Braille.

"My name is Ronald Becker. I'm a horse rancher in need of someone to investigate some barn fires."

Even as he spoke, Penny could tell Becker was unimpressed with her. He barely made eye contact. Her small demeanor probably made her appear incapable of stopping even a pet canary from fleeing its cage.

Becker's eyes dropped his gaze to the cheap floor tiles, scuffed from overuse.

I am a waste of this guy's time. Penny looked at Leo, and then at the cowboy, whose eyes now perused the rest of the crowd, perhaps hoping for a better outcome. She was confused as to why Leo would even introduce them. This only fueled her animosity for Leo.

"I'm sorry, sir. But I'm here to support Leo in his reelection, not take on any new work." She flung her arm in the air and waved goodbye. She walked briskly away, her eyes burning with indignation.

Penny saw Leo trying to follow her, so she ducked into the women's restroom. She took refuge in an empty stall and sobbed. *Why did I come here tonight, anyway?* Her fingers wiped the tears streaming down her face. *I'm the big loser here. Even if Leo doesn't win the election, he can move on to some other law enforcement job. He is too good to be put out to pasture.*

As for me, if I must depend on Leo for leads, I might as well find something else to do with my life.

There was someone pounding on the restroom door. She stood and left the bathroom stall. She yanked the door open just as Leo had his arm poised for another round of pounding.

"Penny, please. Don't take your anger out on Ronald Becker. I don't know what he is doing here, but he has nothing to do with us."

"You set me up!" Penny shouted.

"He's a surprise to me, too. Don sent him over."

"Don?"

"For some reason Don thought it was a big enough deal to have Becker show up tonight in the middle of my election results. He's from Tularosa, so I can't help him. Could you at least listen to what the guy has to say, and then you can be on your way home? I know you just came because Paco insisted."

Penny looked at Leo's face. She had dated him long enough to know he was not fabricating a situation just to keep her close. Leo had a strained relationship with his brother, so for Don to interrupt Leo's evening, it must be urgent.

As Penny walked at Leo's side back toward Ronald Becker, she glanced at the television screens. Leo's opponent had taken a slight lead. Penny's heart flipped in her chest. Leo had perhaps not seen the latest results, because he was smiling at her, as if the world was falling back into place.

Boy is he wrong!

The cowboy leaned forward as Leo and Penny approached. This time Ronald Becker looked Penny straight in the eyes. "Miss Larkin, I'm desperate to find the people burning down barns in New Mexico and killing our horses. I learned this morning that my barn may be on the hit list for this weekend. These fires are costing Quarter Horse racing millions."

"I don't think I can be of much help." Penny knew very little about horses, and nothing about arson.

Ron Becker's right hand held a wad of cash. He waved it in front of her. "I'll pay you whatever you ask."

A few $100-dollar bills fell on the floor. Leo leaned over and gathered them up.

"It's not just helping me, Miss Larkin. It's the whole Quarter Horse industry of New Mexico. Horse racing is competitive enough without someone trying to kill our pregnant mares."

"I'll do my best, Mr. Becker."

"Your best may not be good enough but meet me anyway at the Cracker Barrel in Las Cruces at 7 am tomorrow." He handed Penny the cash.

Penny stuffed the money in her bag, not bothering to count it. Apparently, when it came to a man and his horses, money was no object.

Chapter 5

Penny stood by Leo's side as the final numbers came in. His supporters had moved closer to the television, forcing he and Penny to stand within inches of one another. He could feel the heat of her body. It was as intimate as Leo had been with her in months, and the regret showed on his face.

"Is everything okay, Sheriff? You look like you lost your best friend." A young woman in a t-shirt that read, *Badge Up! Tellez for Sheriff*, placed her hand on his arm.

Leo managed a big grin and shook her hand. "Sylvia, it's great to have you here. Thanks for hanging in there with me."

By now the crowd had worked itself into a frenzy, as they watched a popular television anchor calling other races from around El Paso County. Leo Tellez and Francisco Parasea were running neck and neck. Leo had been happy to have Ron Becker as a distraction, but now he had to face his voters in the homestretch. Whatever happened, however, he would stand tall and respond with grace.

Television reporters crowded around him hoping for an interview, but Leo's throat was dry, and he doubted he could say anything of value. Besides nothing he said now would change the outcome.

Penny and Leo remained silent as they watched the TV monitor. A reporter was interviewing Francisco Parasea at his headquarters in a swanky rooftop restaurant of a downtown hotel. The lights of Ciudad Juárez, Mexico, just across the Rio Grande, winked behind him. Seeing the television camera in front of their candidate, enthusiastic supporters began lifting their campaign signs and shouting, "Francisco for the future!"

Parasea's chin-length blonde hair swung left and right as he made a point to the reporter. His fair complexion and blue eyes qualified him as a güero, of Spanish descent. Parasea's parents had come from considerable wealth in Mexico before immigrating to the US in the mid-1960s.

Leo's family had also arrived in El Paso about the same time, but had remained on El Paso's southside, in a poor neighborhood only blocks from where Leo now awaited the election results. Leo reached down and grabbed Penny's hand. "Wish me luck!"

Penny squeezed his fingers. "You don't need luck, Leo. If the people of El Paso County are swayed by style over substance, then it's our loss."

XXXXX

A loud groan swept over the crowd. The numbers were in, and Leo appeared to have lost, even though the race had not been called. Gasps of disbelief were followed by a round of sighs that rolled across the room in waves as the realization set in among the volunteers that their beloved Leo Tellez may no longer be their sheriff.

A headline finally flashed across the television screen confirming their fears. *Legendary Sheriff Tellez falls to newcomer in nail biter.* A camera in the television studio focused once again on the evening anchor who remained behind the news desk. He had taken off his jacket revealing the rings of sweat under his arms. The hairdo of his female co-anchor was limp, and her makeup faded. Neither one seemed to care about how they looked. Everyone in Leo's headquarters, quieted down to hear. "Josie, it has been a long night. I know I speak for many voters who wish that Sheriff Tellez had been well enough to campaign."

A murmur of agreement floated across the crowd of Leo's volunteers. He watched as some turned to go home. Others busied themselves by cleaning up. No one, it seemed, wanted to stay for beans and brisket.

A dart of guilt pierced Leo's heart. He had let everyone down. He breathed out a deep sigh of regret. Volunteers began sweeping up confetti around his feet.

Penny's warm chest pressed against his. Leo's heart was bubbling over with joy even in his loss. He leaned into this delusion for a few seconds to bolster his courage. His cheeks were blood red, as if someone were holding a burning match to his face. Penny was not hugging him. She was waving goodbye.

Chapter 6

Penny found Ronald Becker sitting at a table near the window at the Cracker Barrel in Las Cruces. He had his back to most of the room, ready for her to arrive or maybe to ward off anyone, who might try to creep up on him. When he uncrossed his legs to stand, she could see a .38 caliber snub nose pistol tucked into the neck of his cowboy boot. "Thank God you're here," Becker said. "I wasn't really sure you'd make the trip."

"Of course, I like to keep my promises," Penny said.

They ordered breakfast, and while they waited for their eggs, Penny munched on a biscuit with honey and listened intently as Becker explained what he needed.

"I thought I'd better put this on the table right now. I didn't tell Sheriff Tellez, but there are rumors that the Betas Cartel has entered the horse racing business. I have no proof they are responsible for the fires, but if this information is going to put you off, I'll understand."

The word "cartel" hit Penny like a hoof to the side of the head. She dropped her biscuit on the plate and reared back in her chair. She'd had enough of the Mexican cartels to last a lifetime, and here she was possibly facing them again. She was determined not to show Becker she was afraid. She rubbed her sweaty fingers against the legs of her jeans trying to shake off her anxiety. "I'm not scared off yet," Penny lied. "Continue."

"In the horse business, we buy some of our racing stock at auction based on previous performances at small tracks, but mostly we choose sires for our mares because of their bloodlines. If the sire is a known winner, then his offspring can bring top dollar. Of course, the stallion's owner also must declare it if its offspring won a race using Salix, a powerful diuretic."

"Why would you give a horse drugs?"

"Most horses will have small amounts of blood in their lungs after a race. A drug like Salix is supposed to prevent it, though there is no real proof it does."

"Do you give your horses Salix?"

"No. Never. I don't think a horse that must get through a race on a diuretic will have the staying power over his racing life. Still some trainers use what they call a "milkshake", a concoction of baking soda, sugar and other stuff to boost their horse's performance. They also use mixtures like those to mask the effects of drugs such as Lidocaine, Procaine, and even cocaine."

Penny was stunned by the news that drugs played such a big role in horse racing. Even Becker looked tired after telling her. His shoulders fell forward. His broad fingers reached for his head, as if to keep it from falling face first on to the table. Beads of sweat soaked the collar of his denim shirt. Communication between them had stopped. It appeared to Penny that Becker was remembering something that was now paralyzing him.

A shadowy image appeared in her mind—an image of drug cartels hawking their wares inside a horse barn. A woman's slender fingers grasped a plastic baggie and pulled it to her chest. Penny strained to see the woman's face. Becker coughed, interrupting her viewing. Now she was back staring at her own plate of biscuits and honey. Goose bumps popped up on Penny's arms—a sure sign for her of imminent danger.

Becker straightened his napkin, smoothing it out over his lap. His face was pale, but his eyes brightened, as if hope had returned. "Yeah, cocaine for horses is a new cash cow for the cartels. But I didn't ask you to stop that, it's way too complicated. I need your help with the barn fires."

Was Becker trying to steer her away from the use of drugs in horse racing, or did he just not care? Penny wondered if agreeing to meet with the rancher had been a mistake despite all the money he was paying her.

Becker let out a big breath of air. The smell of alcohol drifted over Penny and hung between them like an uninvited guest.

"And like most horse breeders who don't stand a stallion," Becker continued, "I have most of my money tied up in pregnant mares. When they are about ready to foal, I protect my investment and move them from the pasture to the barn."

"So, a barn fire can be especially devastating to a breeder with a bunch of pregnant mares ready to foal?" Penny was shaken and confused. Something didn't feel right, but she had to keep talking or she might jump up and run out of the restaurant. She compensated by tapping her right foot against the floor.

"Of course! We're coming up on Christmas, and right after the first of the year, the foals start dropping. Breeders like to have foals early in the year. A filly born in January, for example, gets to compete against a filly born in June because all horses born in the same calendar year are considered the same age. If you're running in a race for three-year-olds, then the more mature the horse is, the better chance at the track."

"What proof do you have that a cartel is involved?"

"My neighbor down the road is an IRS agent. He told me a large amount of cash is being spent on Quarter Horses in New Mexico, Texas and Oklahoma with the paper trails leading nowhere. He suspects members of a Mexican cartel are laundering money. Who else has that kind of liquidity in today's economy?" Becker took a big bite of a corn muffin and washed it down with coffee.

"Why is the IRS involved?

"The IRS closely regulates racetracks, mainly for the winnings by horse owners, but they can also take part of gambler's winnings if your wager is large enough—even while you're standing at the ticket counter to collect."

She leaned back in her chair to make way for their meals, which had come steaming out of the kitchen. "Wow, I didn't realize that."

Becker placed his napkin on his lap, and picked up a pat of butter, lathering it on another corn muffin. "If the odds on the race are let's say, 300-1, and pay more than $600, then the racetrack reports your winnings to the IRS. The IRS also requires an automatic withholding from the racetrack on a payout that exceeds $5,000."

"It sounds like the IRS loves horse racing, because it's pretty lucrative for the U.S. government," Penny said.

"Horse racing can be good for everyone. It seems the drug cartels have discovered that, too. And now I'm in the center of the bulls' eye because I've got my best mare in foal to a champion Quarter Horse stallion, *First Edition*. I've sunk about a $100,000 into the breeding and care of Millicent, or Milly for short. If I lose her in a fire, I'm essentially out of business."

"How did you hear about your ranch being a target?"

Becker pounded his fist against the table. Penny jumped. She noticed a fellow diner eying them with suspicion.

"The workers at the stables all gossip. They think I don't understand Spanish, but I'm fluent. I like it that way. I can hear things I need to sometimes. I'm not an eavesdropper, you understand, but I don't like surprises."

"And you heard your help talking about a fire?"

He waved his right hand in the air as if he were swatting a horse fly. "Yeah. I was walking by the door of the barn on the way to my truck. I couldn't believe it. Pedro, my barn manager, was telling Jorgé, who was cleaning the stalls, not to hang around the farm too long on Saturday evening—that there might be fireworks."

"Did you do anything or confront Pedro?"

Becker twisted his napkin between his fingers and threw it on the floor. "I wanted to ring his neck right then, but I had to keep walking. I had to confirm my suspicions. And besides, if I move my horses, the arsonist will just wait until I bring them back to the stables. That's why I contacted Sheriff Tellez. His brother, Don, and I have been friends for years. I was with him when he filled out his application for the El Paso Fire Department."

Penny sighed. She was frustrated and yet intrigued. Could she overlook Becker's drinking? With her mother dying drunk, it was a bit of a risk. "I need to check out your barn."

"Anything you can do. I mean, what can you do?"

"I'm kind of a profiler. I examine a target, such as your barn, and then project what I see happening there. I've been successful."

Becker reared back in his chair, wiping his mouth with the palm of his hand. "Good Lord. Leo didn't mention this hocus pocus stuff. I need real help." Becker jumped up and shoved his chair with such force that it hit the empty table behind them. The couple sitting near the window looked up from their breakfast and shook their heads.

"Mr. Becker, do you want my help?"

He sat down. "I'm out of options! Darn it all. I tried to get my local sheriff to help but he said he didn't want to touch it. Said it was just kids with time on their hands."

"Give me a chance to get a feel for your barn and I'll get back to you this evening with my thoughts." Penny reached over and touched Becker's arm, hoping to overcome his rejection of her career as a remote viewer. The odor of alcohol dropped over her again as he sat, laid his hands on the table, palms up. His calloused, ruddy fingers had seen years of hard work. Penny's opinion of Becker ticked up a notch, even though his boozing before breakfast disgusted her.

"My wife, Georgia, died eight months ago, and Millicent was her horse. She loved Milly, and so do I. If I lose Milly, I've lost my life." Becker moaned.

Penny got it now. This was not just about money. She was being handsomely paid to save a barn because of something much more complex than just a man and his horse. That Becker might be drowning his sorrows over the death of his wife had a familiar ring to it. A fleeting vision of her mother's ongoing game of solitaire, scattered across the kitchen table, lingered in Penny's mind. The playing cards, stained with rings of whiskey glasses, were the stanchions of her mother's sanity. Penny was sure the never-ending shuffle of the deck had kept her mother from plunging into madness.

When Penny looked up, Becker was staring at her. He managed a smile, parting his chapped lips, and showing a mouthful of good teeth. "I don't want to draw suspicion, so when you come just tell the stable manager that you are with an insurance company, checking out the facilities. Pedro speaks English. Don't let him fool you. Here are the coordinates for my farm for your GPS. You've got GPS, don't you?"

"Yes, I do. Thanks. I'll be there in about an hour."

"Just look for the Becker Ranch sign out front. And thank you again."

Ronald Becker threw $30 in cash on the table for the check and strode out of the restaurant, leaving Penny to pay the bill and watch the daylight breaking over the parking lot. She hoped she could be of help because the thought of horses, or any animal dying by fire, would be an unbearable challenge for her remote viewing skills.

Chapter 7

Leo slept in. When his alarm went off at 4:30 am, he turned it off, flipped over in his bed and fell back to sleep. When his cell phone rang at 5:30, he considered ignoring it, but he was still sheriff for six more weeks.

It was Paco. Of course. Paco would be there for Leo, as always through the rough patches and lately, the potholes. "Mi amigo. What's up?"

"Leo, Marshal Lujan has called the office twice."

"This early?"

"Yeah. He asked you to call him ASAP. He's back on the job."

Leo rolled out of bed and walked right into the shower. There was no use talking to the marshal without first trying to scrub off the stench of losing the sheriff's job. Loss was like working up a sweat at the gym. After all your hard work, you stink, and the scars left on the muscles of your heart take forever to repair.

As a hot stream of water dropped over him, Leo kept asking himself, "What if I had only been able to knock on some doors?" Leo moved his toes in and out of the water that was gathering at the bottom of the shower stall. He would have to call the plumber soon and fix that drain. But for now, he would live with the clog.

Leo dried off and fired up the coffee pot before calling Marshal Lujan. He heard the phone ring in his ear as the coffee dripped into a glass carafe. "This is Lujan."

"Marshal, what in the heck can't wait until a more decent hour?" Leo coughed and looked longingly at the coffee pot, which was just completing its mission.

"Leo, how nice of you to call me back."

Leo heard the sarcasm in his voice.

"I thought I'd get a jump on any other Federal agency that might want to hire you."

"Oh, please, Eugene. I've barely opened my eyes. How can you be talking about another gig so soon after I embarrassed myself? I haven't even had time to mourn."

"Get your ass out the door and meet me at Starbucks on Sunland Park in 30. I'll buy the coffee. It's surely better than what you're brewing at home."

The marshal hung up before Leo had a chance to respond.

Chapter 8

Pedro Lopez washed down the aisles between the stalls with a garden hose. He liked to keep things neat, and even one blade of straw on the cement floor made him loco. Every halter and bridle hung at right angles in front of each stall door. He stopped before Milly's stall and watched Mr. Becker's prize mare munching on grain prepared for her in carefully weighed proportions on the barn scale. Since the stable used wheat straw for bedding when a mare was ready to drop her foal, Milly was now fed a mixture of oats, corn, and barley because Mr. Becker feared she'd develop an allergy to wheat. Becker limited Milly to just two flakes of hay a day.

It was two months before Milly was due to foal and she was still bedded down in sawdust, but Mr. Becker insisted, "You can't be too careful." Mr. Becker had been a renowned trainer in his day, and he knew all too well that a wheat allergy could cause water retention and bad digestion which could lead to colic.

The toughest part of the task of feeding Milly was crushing the corn to make it easier for her to digest. Every time he ground the corn, it reminded Pedro of his mother, who had made tortillas every day. That meant grinding the corn in a *molcajete*, a hollowed-out stone handed down to his mother by her mother. Grinding corn was a family tradition that every self-respecting Mexican family equated with an act of love.

Pedro didn't know if Mr. Becker loved Milly, but Pedro knew Becker wanted to make sure the foal had every break it could because he was counting on having a prize-winning colt. There was no talk of what would happen if Milly had a filly.

Pedro really liked Mr. Becker. He always treated Pedro fairly and paid him well. But Pedro still didn't make enough to live in town, where there was a bar that served hot food. Even though there was a hotplate and a refrigerator at the ranch, Pedro didn't cook. He had to sleep in the bunkhouse and drive five miles each way to buy his meals. But mostly, he chose instead to eat refried beans out of a can. A few years ago, he would have walked into town but at 35, Pedro's back ached from shoveling manure and throwing bales of hay down from the loft.

Ever since girlfriend, Lourdes left him, life had been one bad break after another. The worst break of all was learning his daughter, Maria, was sick. The doctor said it was her heart. How would Pedro ever pay for the surgery to save her?

He still had his pick-up truck, but it was a bucket load of problems. He had to spend almost all his wages just keeping it running. He couldn't sell it anyway. How would he eat?

Lourdes didn't seem to have the money either. He didn't think it was asking too much out of her to help pay for Maria's hospital stay. But then counting on a woman was a waste of time. His father told him the very same thing the day he left Durango, Mexico, and headed north. Pedro, who was 13 at the time, never saw his father again. And he wasn't surprised when his mother died soon after of what his aunt claimed was a broken heart. Pedro wasn't sure what a broken heart was, but he made a promise to avoid love at all costs. And maybe that's why Lourdes left him. Pedro still guarded his heart a little too well.

At 27, Pedro sold the family farm. It was yielding nothing but five acres of beans and three acres of corn. The sale was enough to pay a coyote to sneak him into the United States. He had dreams of heading to Los Angeles, but the smuggler had dumped him on the side of the road in southern New Mexico about a mile from the Becker Ranch. He got a job there because he had said he had experience working with horses—one horse. And this is where Pedro had remained for the past eight years. He had met Lourdes at a local restaurant in Three Rivers where she waited tables. Maria was born two years later, though he and Lourdes never married. At the thought of Maria, Pedro's heart ached, knowing he could not afford to help her get well without an influx of cash from the cartel.

But enough about his nightmares, Pedro had to get busy. He needed to have a plan ready before meeting his cartel contact that afternoon. The Betas had hired him to rig the Becker barn so that when anyone tried to fight the impending fire on Saturday, they would find the doors locked from the inside. He planned to padlock the doors and climb out a window in the loft, and crawl across the roof and jump into the pile of straw, which was always handy for providing bedding to pregnant mares.

Even though the barn would soon end up as a pile of burnt timbers, Pedro still wanted to keep everything as clean as possible for as long as it was in his care. Besides, Mr. Becker would surely notice if things were out of place. Pedro had spoiled him for far too long.

The birds flying in and out and dropping *la cagada* on the floor made his job *muy difficile.* He despised the birds and their constant chirping. He had set traps for the mice, but the birds were free to come and go as they wished. He would have to worry about it *por la mañana.* He had to get going.

Pedro stepped out of the barn and sat down on a bench to take off his work boots and pull on his cowboy boots, which he stored in a cloth bag in his locker. He was particularly proud of them. It took him two-weeks' pay to buy the boots. They were black leather, painted with turquoise roses intertwined with white vines and leaves. Gringos call them "cockroach killers" because of their long, pointed toes.

A shadow fell over the tips of his boots. When he looked up, Pedro saw a beautiful *señorita* standing before him. *Was he dreaming?* Where had she come from? What did she want?

"Hi, my name is Judy Rogers. I'm an insurance agent with the Quarter Horse Liability Company. I'm here to do an insurance appraisal for the farm. Do you have a few moments to answer questions?"

Pedro was on edge, but he tried not to show it. Regardless, his chest began heaving, as if he had been running after a horse escaping the exercise pen. He hadn't counted on being delayed. He had to be in Tularosa at the Rodeo Bar in 40 minutes. His daughter's life depended on him arriving on time. He would play dumb. "I'm sorry, *señorita.* No speak English so good."

She just stood in front of him like she didn't understand. *Get out of the way, lady!* How long could he remain polite? Nobody was going to stop him. It was his job to make sure little Maria could have the life-saving surgery she needed.

Pedro stood; his face so very close to hers. He wanted to slap this woman. Why wouldn't she step back? Who is she to walk into his world at such an important time? His nerves were brittle and ready to snap, like an old leather bridle, so weakened from constant wear that it could no longer control the horse.

"It won't take me more than 30 or 40 minutes. Is that okay?"

Pedro stepped back from her, breathing deeply. He could speak English as well as anyone who had been in the country for eight years, but he didn't want her to know that. "*Si, señorita.* I leave, go, *visitar my amigo ahora.*" What a mess of broken Spanish and English. Pedro was proud of himself. Only a trickle of sweat on his forehead showed how tense he was.

"Okay," the lady said. "*Puedo mirar por mí misma.*"

Whoops. So, she can speak Spanish, and she wants to look around by herself. That was fine with him. He couldn't be late. "*Bueno, señorita, usted puede ver todo. Gracias.*" He would leave her alone to do her work.

Pedro shoved his work boots in the cloth bag. The lady seemed willing to let him go. *Adios, Chica!* Pedro waved his hand, climbed in his truck, and fired the engine. It sputtered and died.

"No, not now!" Pedro slammed his fist against the steering wheel. It left the fingers on his right-hand stinging. He turned the key again, and the engine belched before finally turning over. Pedro wiped the sweat from his forehead, grateful he would make it to Tularosa on time. He gunned the engine, shoved his truck into first gear and spun his tires, leaving the good-looking blonde covered in a cloud of New Mexico dust.

Chapter 9

Leo beat Eugene to Starbucks. He stood by a table, tapping his boot against the floor. He was in uniform, but wore his sunglasses, hoping no one would recognize him and offer condolences. Losing was hard enough, but he couldn't bear to see pity in someone's eyes. A woman appeared to notice Leo's arrival and was headed toward him. He braced himself by clutching the table's edge. He would look like a fool running out of the coffee shop.

"Do you mind? Are you reading this?" The woman picked up the *El Paso Times*, which bore a large headline, "Sheriff Tellez is Sheriff No More!"

"Oh, no. It's all yours."

"Thanks!"

Leo's body collapsed into a chair. This was nobody's bad news but his and he might as well own up to the fact that no one else really cared.

By the time Eugene Lujan arrived, Leo was slumping over the table staring at his fists, imaging that his knuckles were eight tired soldiers surrendering in the war against crime. Leo looked up and laughed. Lujan placed his hand on his shoulder.

"Poor me!" Leo's laugh was a little too hardy. It did help, however, to joke about it. And it was always hard to be in a bad mood around the Marshal. He was as good at friendship as he was at law enforcement—steady and fiercely loyal.

"What can I order you?" Lujan asked as he was on his way to the counter.

"Just a black coffee." Leo still had trouble finding a reason to drink anything with a name that ended with an "o". He straightened up in his chair and watched the Marshal engage in a lively conversation with the barista. He was lucky to have such a good-hearted soul as Eugene for his friend.

The Marshal returned to the table bearing two hot cups of coffee and two blueberry scones.

For several minutes, the two men sat in silence eating and drinking. Leo picked at the crumbs of his scone, wondering how he was going to pick up the pieces of his life.

"Leo, God knows it hurts, but every Federal agency in the region is salivating over the opportunity to hire you, including me."

"I'm too old to become a foot soldier," Leo replied. He used his napkin to wipe the crumbs from his hands.

"I'm not asking you to spend time in the field," Lujan said. "But we will talk about this later."

Leo rubbed his forehead. "Send me an email about what you have in mind, and I'll weigh everything when the fog clears."

"Just remember I made the first offer!"

"I've got to go." Leo stood and shook Lujan's hand. The thought of heading into his department the day after his defeat was not something Leo relished. But the same kind of grace that made Leo a great law officer, would also give him the courage to act with dignity, win or lose. No doubt, though, Parasea would be hanging around, salivating over what designer color to paint his office.

XXXXX

Leo drove a little too fast out of the Starbucks parking lot and nearly crashed into a Prius. The driver waved an angry fist in the air and then noticed Leo's marked patrol car. The man shrugged and then mouthed, "It's okay, Sheriff."

Dear God, help me get control.

It would take Leo about 40 minutes to drive to the far east side of town where his department was located. It was just west of the Law Enforcement Training Center, and El Paso County's second jail. The east side jail held gang members and drug lords. The county tucked away the worst offenders in pod-like cells where they could be carefully watched.

Leo tried calling Penny, but her mobile went to voice mail. *So much for hugs.* Maybe that was just a transitory gesture to help him get through the evening. Then he remembered that Penny had an early appointment with Ronald Becker. He'd catch up with her later. And he had to remember to call his brother and find out why he was so interested in the New Mexico fires.

For now, Leo had to go in and face his team and apologize for letting them down.

Chapter 10

Penny brushed the dust off her jeans and shirt and headed into the barn. With Pedro being in such a hurry to get away, she entered cautiously, half expecting an explosion or flames to shoot out of nowhere. Instead, the barn had a calming effect on her. The sun streaming through the window in the loft was filtered by bales of hay and tumbled like a waterfall of pixelated light onto the barn floor.

The place was immaculate, except for a single black feather lying on the cement walkway between the stalls. A horse whinnied as Penny passed by a stall. She looked inside. A chestnut mare was heavy with foal. Penny wondered if she'd make it until January. She moved on, searching for the magnificent mare called "Milly." Penny found her in the end stall, the largest of them all. An open double window gave the mare plenty of fresh air, as well as a view of Ron Becker's two-story stone ranch house, sitting about 50 yards away, in a grove of pecan trees. The mare was a flea-bitten grey with hazel eyes, much like Penny's. She was standing in a floor of sawdust about a foot thick with her backside to the stall door.

Milly dropped her mouth of hay and moved toward Penny, pushing her muzzle through the bars of the stall. Hazel-met-hazel—the eyes of horse and human locked in a sensory communication more forceful than any words could ever supply.

Milly was a beauty. She could see why Ronald Becker loved her. If a horse had a soul, hers would be deep and wide and brimming with love and mercy. Penny could have spent the rest of the day in her presence, and she sensed, that Milly felt the same.

Without warning, however, Milly's ears flattened against her head. Her eyelids grew wide, framing her pupils like jewels floating in a sea of white foam. The horse kicked her legs in the air and jammed her front hooves against the wood door. A cloud of sawdust fell over Penny's face and arms. The blow shook Penny's confidence, but she held on tightly to the door's edge.

"Hey, Milly. It's okay. It's okay." Penny's fingers stretched tentatively toward the mare's face. The mare responded by showing her teeth. Penny yanked her hand back behind the bars and swallowed hard. Her mouth and throat were as dry as the flaking paint on the barn's walls.

Milly slammed her rump against the stall door, this time throwing Penny off balance. She grabbed for the stall's bars again, to keep from crashing to the floor. She did not want to leave Milly alone.

Penny's lungs were choking from the raging dust storm caused by the stamping of Milly's feet. The other horses began snorting and stamping their hooves, too. Should she make a break for it after all, if nothing more than for fresh air? What in the world had made Milly so angry?

Penny found a tissue in her jeans and placed it over her nose and mouth. The air in the barn was now so clogged with dust, she was beginning to regret her decision to remain in the barn. She knew a pregnant mare could be seriously injured jumping up against the door and throwing her weight against the other stalls. Ronald Becker would be furious if Milly was harmed in Penny's presence.

"Milly, I'm right here. I will protect you."

Milly moaned and then coughed. The raspy spasm emanating from her throat was painful for Penny to endure.

What was going on in Milly's mind? Was it possible to find out through remotely viewing it? "I've got to try!"

The pupils of Penny's eyes blurred into a kaleidoscope of wooden beams, bridles and hay bales, which flew passed her as the dust storm raged on.

Milly's legs, bearing the burden of a baby, quivered. Her back was covered in a heavy veil of dust. Penny watched as the rays of the morning sun transformed that veil into a halo of glitter. A hot blast of air scattered the glitter across the stall, forming it into a globe of molten glass. The shape of a woman's gaunt face was forming and playing out in stark contrast to her steely blue eyes. A second gust of air as hot as an ethereal blowtorch exposed the rest of the woman's body, and her long, brown hair. The woman's slender fingers reached for Milly's head.

Penny shivered. The woman's eyes glanced over at Penny whose own were riveted on this woman and concerned with her intent.

Milly reared, dodging the woman's grasp by backing herself into the far corner of the stall. The mare pawed the floor, digging her hooves into the depths of sawdust and churning up a cloud of dried urine which permeated the dusty air. The woman floated toward Milly, determined to touch her.

Milly yanked her head back. Her whinny began in the recesses of her throat, like marbles rolling across a steel floor. Her cry turned shrill and haunting, reverberating throughout the barn and rattling the windows in the loft. Penny was now shaking. The sight of a horse so troubled by this mysterious presence made Penny afraid, too.

Finally, the woman's floating image dissolved into the dust-laden air as mysteriously as it had come. Penny blew out a breath, grateful that this haunting sight had faded into the ether. This was not the kind of remote viewing for which she had hoped. And what did it reveal? Penny needed more substantive answers than this.

She pulled another tissue from her jeans pocket and mopped her face and blew the dirt out of her nose. Milly was calm now, and moved in measured steps toward her, no longer aloof, but rather, Penny thought, in full agreement, that in times of personal conflagration, we must carry each other's water to extinguish the flames of fear.

Milly's nose reached the tip of Penny's fingers and nudged her hand. Penny placed her palm gently over the mare's head, which was damp and hot to the touch. "We'll make this okay for you and your baby, Milly. I promise."

Milly's eyes closed and then opened halfway. Penny rubbed her nose and brushed some hay out of her forelock. Milly's ears fell forward. She nodded her head in recognition and then released a nicker from somewhere down deep in her belly. Penny watched as the horse shook her whole body. Her muscles rippled across her back, moving over the bulge in her midsection, and then she relaxed. Milly turned back to her meal as if nothing had happened. Penny listened to the mare chewing the flake of hay. There was a rhythm to it, like a guitar player strumming basic chords.

Penny could stand there all day listening, but she had to get busy. She had promised Ronald Becker some answers. She walked away from the stall and found a small stool on which to sit. Milly was the target, somehow the horse knew it, and was asking Penny for help. But Penny had also witnessed the translucent presence of a woman, trying to make peace with the mare. Milly would have none of it.

Penny would do everything she could to save this mare's life because she had given Milly her promise. But Penny knew there was more for her to do here than keep the barn from burning. She also would have to find out who this woman is and why Milly is so afraid of her.

XXXXX

Penny surveyed the inside of the Becker barn, which was framed with heavy timbers. She guessed the barn had been standing for generations because the wood had turned a ghostly grey and revealed several coats of peeling paint. There was not a nail to be found in its construction. As a sixth grader, Penny's grandfather had walked her through his 100-year-old barn and told her stories about itinerate craftsmen called "joiners". A joiner would travel throughout the countryside offering his services to build barns and houses. He would carve the end of a beam into a narrowed and rounded end called a "tenon", and then he made square holes or mortises on an adjoining timber. The joiner had to pound the rounded tenon into the square mortise. This ensured that the structure would stand for generations, if cared for properly. Her granddaddy swore this was how the term "round peg into a square hole" came into being, and to Penny, his word was the gold standard on which every man, including her own father, was judged.

Penny stepped inside the tack room, which looked as if it were right out of "*National Velvet*". She had watched the film so many times as a child she had Velvet's lines memorized. "Sometimes I see things," Velvet said. "As big as life, and I think they are real."

Like Velvet Brown, Penny could see things, too. But unlike Velvet, Penny was not so good at achieving her dreams.

Penny noticed a four-year-old calendar hanging over the tack room desk, as well as a bulletin board which held red and blue championship ribbons and two fading photographs of what looked like a younger Ronald Becker standing beside horses bedecked in blankets of flowers. A third photo featured an unknown man standing next to a beautiful woman with long brown hair. The man was lifting a trophy into the air. Had Penny seen the woman before? There were smudges of dirty fingerprints around the edges of the picture as if it had had lots of views.

The unidentified man in the photo was in his thirties and displayed a mouth full of white teeth—*perhaps a little too white*, Penny thought. She took the photo down from the bulletin board and stuck it in her bag. It wasn't as if she distrusted anyone with overly whitened teeth, but to her, it could mean there was some insecurity lurking under his skin. She would take the picture home and see what visions might appear after studying it for a while.

Penny continued her tour of the barn and with every step it was as though the spirits of dead horses accompanied her. It was reassuring, though to realize, that generations of equine athletes had been born and raised within these walls. It was heartening to know that champion bloodlines had been passed down from sire to mare to foal under the watchful eyes of those who had kept them from harm and believed in their futures. Why weren't human families as careful and as caring for their offspring? *Why didn't my mother care that much about me?*

Penny brushed off thoughts of the past and embraced the sense of peace surrounding her. Year after year, with the birth of a new filly or colt, the circle of life was an affirming reminder that there was a time to be born and a time to give your heart to something essential to your very being. These horses had been given that chance. Some sired the foals, some bore the babies, and some earned the blue ribbons, but in the end, everyone contributed to winning. Now that cycle of life was in jeopardy and Penny had a chance to change that. She relaxed as it dawned on her that as a remote viewer she could contribute to winning, too.

Penny walked out of the tack room and headed down the long cement walkway that separated the horse stalls. Penny watched a fly dancing across a thread of sunlight and weaving its way through the dust-laden air. She followed the light into the hayloft. She climbed the wood ladder and crawled across the floor. Bales of hay were stacked in neat rows. The floor had been swept clean. She walked over to the window and looked down on the piles of straw below. The sunlight bounced against something shiny tucked alongside the broken bales, near the foundation of the barn. "It's probably nothing, but I'll check that out when I get done here!"

From the purvey of the loft, Penny could see that there were six horse stalls in the barn with a cement walkway running the length of the structure. She knew that in recent years, farmers had gone to metal structures with metal roofs. Did the metal make a barn fire less of a threat? She would have to rely on her remote viewing skills to fill in the gaps in her knowledge about raising horses and raising barns because her grandfather had died years ago.

As a remote viewer, Penny used targets or items like photos as a way of finding clues to the past, the present, and with luck, the future. Penny wasn't a psychic. She used protocols developed by the CIA during the Cold War to help the U.S. Army spy on the Soviet Union and Middle Eastern dictators. Now remote viewers like her were hired by law enforcement to hunt down fugitives, locate kidnapped victims, and sometimes even help solve cold cases. This was Penny's first case that didn't require her to chase down a fugitive or find a lost child. *Am I out of my element?* She wondered if she had made a mistake in taking on an arsonist.

Chapter 11

The screeching of a raven brought Penny back from her reverie in the hay loft. The bird's black wings cast a shadow, making him appear much larger than he really was. He swooped through the barn, just missing Penny's head as he sailed over her. He landed on the top of the stall of the chestnut mare, letting out a high-pitched nasal call, followed by a clicking noise that reminded Penny of a gossiping old woman. Was it a warning of danger to come? Before Penny could answer her own question, the bird exited the barn through the window in the hayloft.

In most cases, to get her remote viewing to work, Penny used a set of protocols in a certain order. She had wasted many a viewing by failing to use the steps as they were prescribed, and now time was money. She tucked her bag between her feet and turned off her cell phone. She took a deep breath in preparation for her journey into her mind's eye.

Step one required that she relax and clear her mind. It sounded easy, but meditation experts say that the mind fights back. Penny had learned the hard way during her first viewing efforts to find a missing 11-year-old named Rosa Garcia.

Penny held her breath until the war of words and images bouncing around in her brain began to dissipate. She placed both hands on her stomach and began a pattern of deep breathing that forced oxygen throughout her diaphragm. Her breathing slowed until she wasn't sure she was breathing at all.

Step Two required that she abandon all personal desires in relation to the target. Penny had to throw out her images of horses burning alive in the barn. There was no room for emotional attachments during a viewing—in fact, it blocked the process.

Step Three ushered in harmony, where Penny looked for a perfect balance. She imagined using a skiff with clouds for sails, slipping through the horizon and churning up a froth of waves, as she circled a sphere where good prevails.

Step Four gave Penny the chance to use her secret weapon: God. She let her higher power take the lead and He lifted her on to a white stallion with a tail that touched the earth. She grabbed the horse's flowing mane, and it cantered through the universe until they reached the place of all knowing—a destination that no one discovers on their own.

Penny dismounted, and realized she was back inside the Becker barn. She saw Pedro wiping Milly's stall door to remove what looked like fingerprints. He kicked over a bucket at his feet, throwing him into a fit of despair. He ran into the tack room for a mop, and backed out of it just as quickly, for a large, overgrown bully was reaching for his neck.

"Don't hurt me! I've kicked over the bucket of kerosene in Milly's stall."

The dark figure with a drooping mustache and sweat laden cowboy hat, snorted. "Don't mess this up!" The thug handed Pedro what looked like a can of tuna fish.

"What's this? *¿Qué es esto?*"

"*Es fuego*. It's fire in a can, *idiota*!"

"It looks like sand." Penny saw Pedro trying to pry back the already opened tin.

"Kerosene is a big waste of time. It will take a lot to get these big timbers hot. Build a fire in the horse's stall. Keep feeding the can of sand with these chunks of paraffin. Don't worry, the sand will burn." The man handed Pedro a paper bag. Inside Penny saw a do-it-yourself kit for arson—chunks of paraffin, a lighter and another tuna can with sand.

She could also see that Pedro's neck was still red from the powerful grip of the angry man's hands. She grimaced as Pedro rubbed a sore spot on his spine. "Okay. Okay. If you think…I mean I know it will work, but how long will it take? *¿Por cuánto tiempo*?"

"Count on tending to the fire for about 15 minutes and then get the hell out of there! Someone will be watching you. When we see the barn go down, and hear that the mare is dead, you'll get the rest of your money!"

Penny saw the man wipe the kerosene from his feet with a handkerchief and stamp out of the barn. Pedro leaned against Milly's stall, tears dropping onto his jeans. He wiped his eyes and pulled his wallet out of his pocket. He found a milky looking plastic case holding a photo of a dark-haired girl with a missing front tooth. She had her arms around a grey horse.

"*Mija, cualquier cosa por ti*. Anything for you, Maria. Your *papá* must kill Milly to pay for your surgery. I know you love her so much. I hope someday you will forgive me."

XXXXX

The sound of a truck's engine driving up the lane to Becker Ranch shook Penny loose from her viewing. She stood and walked to the door where she saw Ronald Becker crawling out of his Ford 250 diesel and then struggling to stand. In his right hand was his pistol, which was swinging recklessly in front of his body.

As a child, she had seen this behavior before in her mother, a righteous alcoholic, with a habit that eventually took her life and sent Penny to foster care. She had to find a place to hide until Becker was gone.

Chapter 12

Captain Johnny Trejo was satisfied—a feeling that was all too often fleeting in New Mexico State Police work. He was returning from an investigation of *Colinas Blanco*, a boys' school, which had been part of the Three Rivers landscape as long as he could remember. In fact, as a teenager his father had threatened to send him to *Colinas Blanco* if he didn't straighten up. Johnny knew he wasn't serious, but the thought of going to a place like that sobered him.

Johnny had received information that nine boys were missing, and the news had gone viral. The public information officer for the New Mexico State Police was overwhelmed with calls from CNN, FOX NEWS and the *Albuquerque Journal*. Perhaps the uproar about the missing boys had made its mark on the American psyche after police in Florida used ground-penetrating radar to find 100 dead boys at a nearby reform school. It was all over the national news that authorities were still digging up the bodies from as far back as the 1940s and trying to match them with kids who had never returned home.

The truth was that the *Colinas Blanco* boys were on an annual field trip to Santa Fe which had been planned for months. The confusion started when the mother of one of the boys stopped by to surprise her son and found the school empty with only the housekeeping staff on duty. Not speaking good English, the mother thought she heard the head of maintenance say he didn't know where everyone had gone. Johnny had tracked the GPS on the school's van and found it in Santa Fe, where the boys were all enjoying a chuck wagon cookout. The school's director had turned off his phone to save his battery because he'd left his charger at home.

Most of Johnny's cases were protracted and all too messy. Happy endings were not generally a big part of police work, and it felt good to close a case so quickly. Johnny wondered if Penny might want to have dinner to celebrate. He had driven the three hours south and was nearing his headquarters in Las Cruces when he rang Penny's cell phone. It went right to voice mail.

Johnny was disappointed in not being able to touch base with Penny. "Call me when you get this. I see a steak dinner in your future!" He hadn't seen her for over a week and knew she had promised Leo she would come to his headquarters on election night. It was a shame that Leo had lost, but understandable in that he was unable to hit the campaign trail. Penny had reassured Johnny she wasn't going to restart her relationship with Leo. Had she taken pity on him after his loss and gone home with him? Ugly thoughts reared up in Johnny's head and mocked him until he became nauseous.

After her break up with Leo, Penny had sought refuge at Johnny's mother's house. It had been some of the happiest times in his life. He pulled off the road to collect his common sense and invest it in something better than worrying about Penny. His cell phone rang, and Penny's name popped up. "Hey, Penny, how are you?"

"Johnny, I need your help." Penny spoke in a whisper.

"What?" He could barely hear her.

"Ronald Becker, a rancher I'm trying to help, is firing his gun in his barn and scaring the horses. I'm hiding in one of the stalls, but he's so drunk, he may shoot me."

"Where are you?"

"I'll text you the coordinates." A blast from a firearm echoed in Johnny's ear.

Chapter 13

It was dark inside the Rodeo Bar and for that Pedro was glad. He waved at a couple of regulars whose silhouettes simultaneously turned to see who had let in a spear of sunlight now stabbing a corner of the room. A lone *Dos Equis* neon sign blinked out a greeting, as Pedro searched for his contact, a man known only to him as "Willie." In the farthest booth from the entrance, Pedro saw him. He was slouched in the bench seat, smoking a cigar and dropping ashes onto the sawdust covered floor.

The bar manager was wiping down a table and gave Pedro a quick nod. Pedro knew that vows of silence were the best insurance for keeping alive when it came to drug cartels—maybe even better than having a gun. But Pedro was no fool. He knew the manager, Ricky Knight, had a gun strapped to his ankle, and he hoped Knight didn't have to use it this afternoon.

As Pedro slid into the wood booth, Willie threw his cigar onto the floor and snuffed it out with the sole of his leather boot. A curl of smoke reached Pedro's nose as the burning ashes mixing with the sawdust, gave off a bitter stench.

Pedro coughed and cleared his throat. "*Hola*." He coughed again. He would have to keep himself together because Pedro could tell that Willie was weighing his resolve. There were plenty of guys just like Pedro who needed money.

Willie, who was not much older that Pedro, nodded and reached in the front pocket of his jeans. He pulled out an envelope, soiled from what appeared to be sweaty fingers. Willie's hands were clean, but badly bruised, as if he had been in a fistfight. Had the money come from across the border, Pedro wondered? He hoped it was American dollars and not *dineros*. He needed at least $5,000 right now because Maria was going to have surgery in the morning. He would have to make a practice of burning down barns to pay the entire bill. Pedro's hands were shaking so he hid them under the table. His work socks were much too thick for his beautiful leather boots. His ankles were damp with sweat.

Ricky brought Willie a bottle of beer and he sucked down three quarters of it with one toss of his head and wiped his mouth with his sleeve. Pedro shook his head at the bartender. Today was not a good day to drink and drive.

Willie threw the packet of cash at Pedro. "You do this right and there's something even better waiting for you."

"What?" Pedro asked.

"You'll know, when you know!" He slammed his fist on the table with such force that his beer bottle rose like a rocket and crashed onto the floor. Willie scooted out of the booth and kicked the bottle across the room. It stopped at the feet of a drunk leaning against the bar. The drunk picked up the beer and lifted it in salute to Willie and then pressed the bottle to his lips. The leftover liquid bubbled over his chin.

Willie rested one of his blue knuckles on Pedro's shoulder and whispered in his ear. "*Sabado*!" He jerked his body away from the booth and strode toward the exit. This time, as the door swung open, the sun's rays exposed the cash, which was still lying on the table. For a moment, Pedro feared the dirty little package might burst into flames.

He jammed the envelope inside one of his cockroach killers and scooted out of the booth. The door was still wide open and heating up the room. Pedro wiped his face and neck with his bandana and looked around. The drunk at the bar was dancing in circles, stirring up the sawdust, and making it hard for Pedro to breathe. *Somebody make him stop!*

Pedro gasped for air, but there was none to spare. Was it guilt or the dust choking him? He staggered toward the light, knowing the life of his daughter depended on him getting the hell out of the Rodeo Bar. He made a lunge for the open door, falling through it, and tumbling onto the gravel parking lot. His face hit the rocks, and he began to slide. He dug the toes of his beloved cockroach killers into the ground, trying to stop.

Pedro rolled on to his back, wheezing. When he was finally able to draw in a breath of fresh air, it smelled of clean laundry drying on a clothesline. Was he hallucinating? There was no such line and no such laundry. *Am I going mad?* Growing up in Mexico, his mother would hang the wash outside to dry. The wind would toss the clothes back and forth in the sun. He would be playing in the yard and run headlong into the laundry, burying his nose in the smell of crisp, clean clothes. It always represented security to Pedro, even when there was no security in his hometown.

There was nothing secure or clean about Pedro now. There was blood on his hands from pulling gravel out of the cuts on his face. His body was sore, but he could still move his arms and legs. He blinked and looked up at the cloudless blue sky. The sun was moving on, with other things to do. He had to move on, too. Daylight would be dipping below the Sacramento Mountains in a few hours. The hospital business office in El Paso, 100 miles away, would be closing at 6 pm and he had promised to pay the first installment today. If he couldn't, then Maria's surgery would be delayed until his good faith payment could be made.

Pedro was too weak to walk, so he crawled toward his truck. He was so low to the ground he could see oil dripping from beneath the truck's frame onto the rocks. He had never had the money for an overhaul, and now the oil leak had come at the worst possible time. Could he make to El Paso without burning up his engine? *I must make it!*

How had Pedro's life taken such a sour turn? He had always meant to make his mother proud by becoming a good father, unlike his own. Pedro was not his father. There was still time to make things right.

The musty odor of oil filled his nose as he crawled closer to the running board. For several minutes, he could do nothing but watch a little black pool collecting in the rocks. Finally, he grunted and pulled himself up by hanging on to the front fender and then grabbing the door handle. I can make it. "*Sí lo hare.*"

Pedro smiled, as he revved the truck's engine. It had turned over on the first try. It was running good for an old truck. He would have to be satisfied that he was doing wrong for all the right reasons. That had to be enough. Maria deserved to live, even if he did not.

Chapter 14

Leo trudged up the wood stairs to his office, preferring to climb rather than take the chance of meeting people on the elevator. All he had ever wanted was to be sheriff of El Paso County, and now that dream was ending. *Good things came to an end, right?* It had been his life's story. Good things gone like dust on the wind-swept plains.

He opened the door to the room where the dispatcher sat behind bulletproof glass. It seemed quiet, all too quiet. Was there a blue flu? He waved at the dispatcher and headed down the long hall leading to his office. He passed the break room and saw most of his officers and staff standing in there. When they saw him, they broke out in spontaneous applause. He walked into the room, and the clapping continued.

They were acting as if he had won. Lieutenant Josie Muñoz stepped forward. "Sheriff, we are so proud to be on your team. You could have easily given up and dropped out of the race, but you kept going. Regardless of whatever happens in the Sheriff's Department, we promise to hold you up as our example of integrity and perseverance."

The clapping ended. A couple of the staff members began passing out pieces of cake. Leo was handed a piece that had his badge number painted on it with icing. He took a bite of cake and immediately wished he hadn't because it lodged in his throat. Luckily Lt. Muñoz handed him a bottle of water.

Paco Ontiveros walked over and gave Leo a bear hug. "You can still be a deputy if you want. You know that don't you?"

Leo had not even thought of that. He had retired from the El Paso City Police Department to run for Sheriff four years ago. Did Paco think Leo would dare work under the orders of Parasea? He would have to choke down more than cake to keep working in the department. The Marshal's offer floated through his mind, and the thought of a way out brought a small smile to Leo's lips.

"Hey, he is smiling!" Paco said. Group laughter filtered throughout the kitchen.

Leo moved around the room and shook hands with some, and hugged others. He felt the festive atmosphere in the room temper and fall like the leaves from the tree outside the kitchen window. One by one the lips of the deputies straight-lined, their eyes focused on the doorway, just behind the sheriff.

Leo could feel Parasea's warm breath glancing off the left side of his neck. He must have taken the stairs, too, because he was breathing heavily. Leo turned and greeted the sheriff-to-be with a handshake—a welcome that only a gentleman like Leo could pull off under these circumstances.

"Welcome to your new home away from home!" Leo said. He managed to laugh, as he backed up and made room for Parasea. One of the deputies offered him a piece of cake, which he started to decline, but then appeared to think better of it.

Leo went around the room and introduced the members of his department, who were clustered at the back, near the only window. Streaks of morning light bounced off the officers' badges as they moved forward to shake Parasea's hand. The mood was tenuous, and Leo knew he had to guide his men and women into a new era of leadership. "Sheriff, you can rely on each and every one one of your team to execute your orders to the letter."

"Thanks, Sheriff. I am really looking forward to working with everyone. Would you give me a quick tour of the department?"

"Of course." Leo smiled broadly, a little too full for his team, which he knew they would notice. "Let's start with your new office."

Chapter 15

Johnny Trejo stormed down the highway, sirens blaring. What in the heck had happened with Penny? She hadn't mentioned taking a new case. *Is this Leo's doing?* Johnny's hands had been shaking when he punched the GPS coordinates into his onscreen computer. Now he was mesmerized by the little blue dot that represented his patrol car. Mile after mile, he seemed to be making little progress along the two-lane, Dona Anã County highway. He needed to make better time. He was worried about Penny's safety and wondered who had placed her in danger. *Of course, it was Leo!* He took his anger out on the sheriff rather than thinking about any harm coming to Penny.

Johnny's head was sweating as he drove his right foot into the accelerator. He threw his New Mexico State Police officer's hat onto the passenger seat and combed his wet hair off his forehead with his fingertips. He noticed the speedometer inching higher, but it still felt like he was crawling. He would never reach Penny in time.

Johnny glanced at the bottle of water in his console and wished he could take a swig. His tongue was dry. He reached for the water. Even with these few seconds of distraction, Johnny misjudged the width of the road. The wheels on the right side of his car hit the berm, churning up a barrage of rocks that sounded like bullets against the side of his car. He yanked the wheel sharply to the left, a mistake made by rookies. He was no rookie, but his determination to save Penny had warped his commitment to common sense. His patrol car shuddered as he drove back onto the lip of the road, slowing his speed to more respectable levels, until he was barely moving forward. His car stalled in the middle of the highway. "Whew, that was close!"

The International Harvester appeared at the crest of the hill. It was lumbering toward Johnny's car and hogging both sides of the highway. Johnny heard the driver pounding the brakes. The red tractor was roaring like an angry beast. Its tricycle-like front wheels skidded sideways, laying rubber on the highway. The Harvester's rear wheels were still shoving the tractor forward. Johnny's icy fingers fumbled with the keys in the ignition, trying to start the car. No luck. He had to get out!

He jammed his index finger into the red button on his seat belt, but the belt held tight. He punched the button again, but it would not unlatch. He threw his head against the headrest in surrender.

Johnny heard the grinding of the tractor's gears and watched in horror as the farmer's body was thrown into the windshield, shattering it. The Harvester slammed into the front of Johnny's patrol car, deploying the front and side airbags. Johnny's seat belt tightened like a vise over his chest, driving the air from his lungs.

Chapter 16

Leo had been polite for as long as he could stand it. He excused himself from his tour of the sheriff's department with Fransico Parasea and headed for his patrol car. He had work to do, and as long as he wore the badge, he would defend the citizens of El Paso County. When he was pulling out of the department's parking lot, John Randle, an agent with the Texas Alcoholic Beverage Code called him.

"Sheriff, you might want to witness this. In an hour, we're taking down members from the Barrio Norteño Gang who have been using the Red Marker Strip Club to distribute cocaine, as well as serve as a front for prostitution. It would be an honor to have you with us to take down these bastards."

"I'm on my way!" Leo used his flashing lights to head west on Montana Avenue, where he entered Highway 375, barreling south until he got to the entrance to I-10. At I-10 he switched off his flashers as the highway was surprisingly empty and he could make good time to the Eastlake Boulevard exit. The Red Marker was on the north side of the Interstate.

Leo pulled on to the concrete drive leading up to the strip club. The parking lot was jammed with cars. There were trucks, SUV's and sedans parked sporadically. It appeared the club's owners had not seen the wisdom in painting white lines on the pavement to facilitate order. A few trucks were also parked in an adjacent field. Business was good even in the morning hours.

Leo left the lot and parked on the side of the road. He didn't have to wait long. Agent Randle pulled alongside of Leo and motioned for him to follow. Leo drove behind Randle for about 400 yards, until they turned into another parking lot that served an unmarked building made of cement blocks. It was protected by a tall grove of pine trees to the south and west. If you had driven by the building, you would not have realized the place was there.

Both men got out of their vehicles at the same time. "Right this way," Randle said, as he ushered Leo inside.

Leo was stunned. Inside, the place was one big room, filled with desks. Agents were on the phone or crouched over computer monitors. "What is this?" He didn't bother to contain his surprise.

"We've been tracking the club's every move. Over there is Agent Hardaway. He's using keystroke logging to monitor the movements in the club's office. And Agent Castillo is using Web Watcher to track the club's email, social media and web searches."

"How did you get inside the club to install it?" Leo was intrigued by the ingenuity. Maybe Agent Randle's personnel could help train his deputies in this kind of information collection. Leo could feel a splinter of pain pierce his gut. He clenched his hands at the realization; he wouldn't need to do anything more for the Sheriff's office. In six weeks, he would no longer be in charge.

At the back of the room, a SWAT team of men and women dressed in grey uniforms and matching helmets were gearing up for the raid. They were wearing bulky bulletproof jackets. Each carried a semi-automatic rifle, most of them AR 15s, with backup firepower strapped to their belts and thighs.

"Listen up, everyone," Agent Randle yelled. "I think you know Sheriff Tellez, the best sheriff this county has ever had. He's here to help." This evoked an outburst of clapping, which embarrassed Leo, but he managed a smile and waved his thanks.

"Agent Donaldson will give us the signal when to head for the club." The SWAT team members nodded their heads and turned to face the back door. This highly trained team had just competed and won the SWAT Round-Up International in Florida last summer. Leo would learn a lot from them today. With or without the sheriff's duties, Leo would never leave law enforcement. Every case was a chance to strengthen his skills.

Randle escorted Leo to a coffee bar where he poured him a cup and pointed to the sweet rolls on the counter. Leo picked up a roll. It was about 11am and he was starving.

"Sheriff, have you ever considered joining a team like ours?"

Leo was not surprised at the question. The marshal had already given him a heads up about being recruited by other agencies, but it still seemed like he was being unfaithful to his deputies, many of whom were as close as brothers and sisters.

A scraping of chairs against the cement floor signaled that it was time to roll. Leo was happy he did not have to answer Randle. He was a very nice guy, but Leo wasn't ready to chat about what he would do next with his life.

The agents who had been sitting at desks stood out of respect for the SWAT team, as they left by the back door.

"I'll trade you a sweet roll for a flak jacket," Agent Randle said. He smiled as he helped Leo place the protective gear over his head. "And a helmet for good measure!"

Leo crammed a big bite of roll into his mouth and followed Randle to the back door, where the SWAT team was already moving through the field on the trek to the strip club. Randle and Leo ran to catch up.

"Let's stay back far enough so they can be the element of surprise we need."

Twenty minutes later, the group was in formation. The SWAT team split up with four members each surging through the front and back doors. Leo and Agent Randle stood near the back door hoping to stop anyone trying to escape. They could hear shouting and the grunting of men being forced to the floor. Three women ran out the back door. Agent Randle ordered them to get on the ground and stay there. "You will be safer here than running down the road without proper clothes!"

The women apparently agreed, because they leaned against the wall, awaiting their fate. One of the women began to cry. She wiped her face with her arm, which was covered with glitter. The row of silver spangles across her overexposed breasts drew Leo's attention. The tiny mirrors danced in the sunlight, throwing circle-shaped shadows across the side of the metal building.

SWAT team members began hauling the strip club's employees and customers out of the building. There were five men, all dressed in khakis and white polos with the club's logo—a slash of red marker—adorning the left side of each shirt. *They looked more like members of a yacht club than a strip club,* Leo thought.

The SWAT team made short work of handcuffing their prisoners and loading them into two 10-passenger vans that had just arrived to haul the workers and customers off to Federal lock-up in downtown El Paso. Members of the SWAT team pulled off their helmets and tossed their guns into a crate by the side of vehicle. They climbed on board, too, with one member riding shotgun. He was still dressed in full protective gear and carried his AR-15.

From his hillside perch, Leo watched the vans pull onto the access road that led to an entrance to the Interstate. He saw a black SUV exiting the interstate at the same time. It moved slowly up the road toward the strip club. At first, Leo thought the Feds had sent a third van as back-up. He slipped around the other side of the building to get a better look. The SUV passed the club's driveway and did a U-turn. As it got closer to the club once again, Leo could see there were no federal markings on the vehicle. The driver wore a baseball cap. *Were his three passengers wearing ski masks?*

A dome of dread fell over Leo's body. He wiped his clammy fingers across his face and then fumbled for his 1911 Sig Sauer pistol, secured in the holster on his belt. Not enough fire power, he knew. The gun battle in front of the Deming hospital spooled over and over in his memory like a bad movie trailer. It always ended with Leo taking a bullet.

Leo took quick, short breaths trying to suck in enough courage to act. For an instant, he wished he had never agreed to join Agent Randle for the raid. He was ashamed to even have such a cowardly thought. But he had to warn Agents Randle and Donaldson! There were only three of them to battle what looked like heavily armed cartel members out to settle a score. Leo found Randle still doing the inventory of weapons seized during the raid and Donaldson guarding the women until Leo's deputies arrived to take them to the county jail downtown.

"Take cover!" Leo was out of breath. "We've got men in ski masks moving up the driveway in a black SUV."

Agent Randle threw Leo an automatic rifle and ordered Donaldson to lock the women inside the building and return to help. *Where could they take cover?* Leo's mind was spinning. The entire back lot was an empty field of rocks and sand. They were like sitting ducks at the county fair arcade.

"Randle, I've got an idea. Let's head toward the opposite side of the building, and circle back behind them as they come up the hill."

Randle, Donaldson and the sheriff rushed toward the front of the strip club. The SUV had parked in the lot just below the club, and the gunmen were piling out of the vehicle. One of the men lifted his ski mask and wiped the sweat from his face. Leo knew it was over 90 degrees, and the midday sun could be brutal, especially if you were dressed to kill. Leo adjusted his helmet and his Kevlar vest. His chest was itching. He could feel the sweat boiling up under the vest and seeping into his underwear.

Randle tossed each man two magazines that held a total of 26 bullets. Leo jammed one magazine in the AR-15, dropped the other in his pants pocket, and unsnapped his holstered pistol. It was three against three, unless the driver got in on the act. The only advantage they had was the element of surprise, and that would not last more than a few seconds.

In the distance, Leo saw the El Paso County Sheriff's van exiting the interstate. Behind it was another patrol car. Leo shot a text to the county dispatcher to give the deputies a heads-up to prepare for an all-out assault.

Leo pointed out the van to Randle and Donaldson.

"I just hope they don't get here and find us lying in a pool of blood," Randle said.

"They've been brought up to speed." Leo said. "But we've got to start firing before they get near the front of the building, to protect the women."

Leo knew if they could hold off the cartel gunmen long enough, his deputies could take them from behind. Maybe they would get lucky. The hit men were adjusting their gear, but the driver stayed put.

"I'll give the signal, and we all start firing," Randle ordered. "Leo, you take the man on the far right. Donaldson, you've got the middle guy. I'll take down the jerk on the left."

Leo's phone rang. He jammed his hand in his pocket, trying to silence it. Instead, it tumbled on to the ground. He could see Penny's face lighting up the screen as his mobile continued to ring. He kicked the phone into a bank of scrub trees, but their element of surprise was gone.

The men in the ski masks fired first, as they ran up the hill toward the sound of the cell phone. A barrage of bullets bounced off the metal building, like pinballs in a gaming hall. Leo retreated to the back of the building. He had ruined the element of surprise, and he vowed to make it right. He grabbed another assault rifle from the inventory and ran down the driveway, weaving erratically toward the black SUV. The driver saw him coming and fired his pistol in Leo's direction. He missed. Leo reached the SUV without being shot. Outgunned, the driver jumped out of the vehicle and tried to run. Leo caught him by the arm and knocked him unconscious with the butt of his rifle. Leo jumped behind the wheel of the SUV and threw it into 4-wheel drive. Leo was angry, and the adrenaline in his veins drove him into a fire-breathing frenzy. He would have pushed the SUV up the hill by sure will power if it had been necessary. Fortunately, the transmission did the work for him. He left the driveway and dug his wheels into the manicured lawn in front of the Red Marker. Could Leo reach the hit men before they made a deadly assault on Agents Randle and Donaldson?

The three gunmen heard the SUV coming and turned around to hold Leo off. Randle and Donaldson dropped two of them with shots to the back. The other man had his laser site focused on the SUV. Leo watched the red line bounce off the windshield, but he roared upward, undeterred. Randle's bullet to the gunman's thigh did nothing to slow him down. The man lurched his body forward toward the SUV with his automatic rifle pointed squarely on Leo. Leo hit the gunman with the front bumper before he could fire a shot. He flew backwards and lay groaning in the grass. Donaldson ran over to contain him with a foot to the chest and then threw him on his belly and cuffed him.

The sheriff's van and the patrol car arrived just in time to help throw the third man, into the van. The deputies determined there was no need to call an ambulance. He could suffer a bit of pain on his way to the ER.

Chapter 17

Johnny regained consciousness as a bulging set of flannel arms freed him from his seat belt. The farmer carried him over to a small band of grass at the side of the road and laid him gently onto the ground. Johnny's head felt like it was a skein of wool being pulled tightly around his mother's yarn winder. The pain brought him fully awake. Out of his swollen eyes, he could see the face of his rescuer, a man about 60 years-old, with shards of glass hanging from his whiskers. Blood dripped from his nose and ears, but his blue eyes were as clear as the New Mexico sky.

"You okay, officer?" The farmer's voice was gruff, but sincere. "I checked you over before I moved you. Saw no need to get us both hurt worse by stayin' in the middle of the highway."

Johnny could not answer. The air bag had punched him in the throat and chest and left him too winded to talk. He nodded his aching head.

"My name is Drake. Joseph Drake. I was working a few acres of winter wheat and headin' home for lunch, when I hit you. Dang it!" Drake pulled a blue bandana out of his back pocket and wiped his nose. The collar of his shirt was soaked with blood. "I've got OnStar in my rig. They should be sending someone our way any time now."

Drake withdrew a flask of whiskey from his other pocket and unscrewed the cap. "Take a drink. You look like the scarecrow in my wheat field!" He chuckled, as he tipped the flask toward Johnny's lips.

The heat of the aged bourbon burned all the way down Johnny's throat, but by the time it landed in his stomach, he did feel like he would live. Then he remembered Penny's call for help and tried to sit up.

"Whoa. You shouldn't move, Officer. You took quite a hit."

The sound of the oncoming siren reverberated against the ground where Johnny lay. He would undoubtedly know the EMTs and feel like a fool being hauled to the hospital. As if that weren't enough to frustrate him, Johnny could hear his mobile phone ringing from the recesses of his totaled patrol car. Good luck answering it. It was probably Penny wondering what in the hell had happened to him? Would she call Leo instead? His body twitched and jerked at the thought. He made another attempt to get up. A pair of pudgy hands kept him on the ground.

The infusion of oxygen to his lungs by the EMTs brought life back to his vocal cords. Johnny choked out a "thank you" as a medic cleaned his face with an alcohol swab. He could smell the vapors of the disinfectant mixing strangely with the bourbon and kicking his fanny. Johnny could see another EMT picking bits of broken glass from Joseph Drake's beard. Traces of blood on his nose and ears were almost gone.

Gratefully, the two medical techs were new on the job. They recognized Johnny only by his uniform and his rank. "Captain, we're going to transport you to the hospital, just as a precaution. From the looks of your car, you took the full force of that tractor."

Johnny shook his head. "I've got to respond to a distress call at the Becker Horse Ranch." He moved his legs and arms. Nothing hurt so much that it would keep him from getting to Penny before Leo did.

"Sir, I can't order you to go with us to the medical center, but I would recommend it, out of caution."

"Drake!" Johnny called out to the farmer who was now walking around the battered red Harvester, trying to assess the damages. "You got a vehicle I can borrow?"

Chapter 18

Penny's cell phone had gone to voice mail for the fifth time and Leo had given up dreaming she needed him, now or ever. He sat opposite his brother Don Tellez, in the Good Coffee Shop on East Montana Street. The place had been around El Paso forever, and it was an easy drive for Don, whose house was just a block away. Don, a well-respected arson investigator with the city, was often called upon for his expertise throughout Texas. Leo was determined to find out what Don's relationship with Ronald Becker was and why he had referred Becker to him. But most of all, he wanted reassurance that he had not sent Penny off an assignment that would put her in danger.

"Leo, I know it sucks losing the election, but you've got a good future in front of you. You're only 50 for God's sake." Don reached out and patted Leo's clenched fist, just as the waitress topped off both their cups. The steam from the coffee rose between the two brothers, a visceral vapor uniting them, much like the blood in their veins.

"Don't talk to me about losing. Everything I have ever worked for or dreamed of is gone." Leo punched his fingernails into the palms of his hands.

"Are you talking about the election?"

"Now Leo's hands were aching. He tightened his grip on the edge of the table until his knuckles were as pale as the peaks of the White Mountains. He rubbed his hands together trying to get the circulation going and then picked up his phone to look for any missed calls. *Nothing.*

Leo took a small sip of coffee. It was hot and burned his throat. "So, I talked with Ronald Becker. What's so urgent you needed him to bother me on election night?"

"You remember that multiple homicide last summer where we found three bodies in the charred ruins of that warehouse over by the airport? One of the dead men was a Quarter Horse trainer. A big-time trainer at that."

"Why wasn't this shared with my office?"

"The DEA asked us to keep a lid on it until DNA confirmed their suspicions. They just sent us the results on Friday. And besides, the city's forensics is just coming back on track. You know that. Our new medical officer has been scrambling to review cases and trying to remove the glut that piled up for the eight months, when we did not have a coroner on staff."

The waitress brought their eggs, sausage and pancakes, and the conversation stopped while the brothers dug into their meals.

After a few bites, Don continued. "Out of the three men killed, we were able to ID only two. The second man is Fernando Del Rio, a known messenger for Juan Uribe Fuentes, the heir apparent of the Betas Cartel. Del Rio must have been killed in some sort of gun battle because the gang left him to burn in the fire they set at the warehouse. The horse trainer was Sonny March. He had worked for several ranches, but most recently for Ronald Becker."

"Does Becker know he's dead?" Leo grumbled in disbelief. He stabbed his sausage and took a big bite. He'd had his fill of the cartel madness.

"I didn't tell Ron. Not yet. I wanted to talk with you first and see if you could help him, and me. And now that you're free…" Don's voice trailed off and he stared at his plate, moving his coffee cup further from his fork.

"Thanks. I'm free all right, but you didn't know that on election night." Leo wrestled with the thought of getting up and leaving the restaurant. Was it public knowledge that Leo was not going to win because he was too crippled to campaign?

"The Texas State Fire Marshal is forming a task force to investigate how much the state is being impacted by the arson fires, and if the cartels are responsible. So far most of the damage to barns and horses has been centered in New Mexico and Oklahoma, but this fire in El Paso has rattled a few cages. Now it involves my department. I was hoping you'd join us."

Leo ignored Don's question. "Ron Becker is a good friend of yours?"

"Ron is a good man. I met him at New Mexico State. He was studying animal husbandry, and of course, I majored in business. He lost his wife last year in a weird accident. She fell in the stable and was trampled by her own horse. He came to me a couple of days ago complaining that the sheriff in his county wouldn't give him the time of day. You know Sheriff Cerillo is gutless. So, I sent Becker to you."

"I turned him over to Penny."

Don chuckled. "How did that go over? Becker's as narrow-minded as they come. I can't see him agreeing to work with a psychic."

"Penny doesn't consider herself a psychic, don't ever say that to her face." Leo took a sip of coffee and wiped his mouth with his napkin. He felt his breakfast climbing up his throat.

"I don't know what else you would call claiming to see things that aren't directly in front of your eyes." Don reared back in the booth and laughed.

"To her, controlled remote viewing is a science, and I'm inclined to agree." Leo swallowed hard and reached in his pocket for a roll of Tums.

"You still pumping antacids? Good grief, bro'. Go to the doctor."

"It's getting better," Leo lied.

"Regardless of what she thinks she is, I'd like to talk to her." Don took a last swig of coffee and pulled some cash out of his front pocket to pay the bill.

"You that desperate to pull in someone with skills you doubt?"

"Look, I know you well enough that you wouldn't waste your time on Penny if she didn't have the goods. And besides, I knew you would never agree to help us, and we are out of leads."

"Penny called me earlier when we were taking down some cartel hit men at the Red Marker, and I couldn't get back to her. Now, she doesn't answer her phone." Leo shook his head and watched as his younger brother handed some cash to the waitress. Don didn't look like he had aged at all since college. He was the *handsome* Tellez brother—the Homecoming King at Bowie High School, the football team quarterback, the Texas debate champion, and on and on.

Both brothers were over six feet tall, but Don's eyes were almost black, where Leo's were brown. And Don's darker complexion, unruly black hair and engaging smile drew everyone in. Leo was more of a brooder—or as Leo believed—more of a deep thinker. Lately though, Leo hadn't been drinking from the well of deep thinking, and it was costing him everything he loved.

Both men stood and walked to the front door of the restaurant. From a dark corner of Leo's mind reared a terrible scenario—one he knew well from high school. If he arranged a meeting between Don and Penny, she would be taken in by Don's charms. And even though Don was skeptical of Penny's skills, he could get her eating out of the palm of his hand. He was the master of charm.

Leo's intestines tightened and he thought his eggs might revolt. He shoved the door to the restaurant open with such intensity that it slammed into the outside wall. His legs were cramping, and fingers of sweat were gripping his calves. Could he get to his car without making a fool of himself?

"I'm not sure she'd want to have anything to do with the cartels, again." Leo looked Don in the eyes, hoping his warning would change his mind.

Don laughed and pounded Leo on the back. "Bro', what do you think she's doing right now? If you sent her to check out barn fires, then she's stepping into a great big pile of cartel manure. She'd better watch where she walks."

Chapter 19

Joseph Drake's 1960 red Ford pickup truck rattled through the back roads of New Mexico with Johnny Trejo at the wheel. He was now limping toward Becker Ranch at 40 mph. Drake had been kind enough to fill up the gas tank at his farm, and Drake's wife, Dorothy, had thrown in a cooler with two egg salad sandwiches and a Thermos of lemonade. According to the wrinkled New Mexico map the farmer had shoved into Johnny's hands, the ranch was just eight miles due east of the Drake's house. Those eight miles, however, were made up of hardscrabble roads bearing the ruts of heavy-duty farming vehicles. Johnny was so grateful to be alive, he hardly noticed when a wheel found a chuckhole and caused the whole truck to shake. He leaned his head against the seat and placed his left arm on the ledge of the open window. The warm desert air blew over his face and the sun warmed his throbbing eyes. His uniform was torn, and his hat had disappeared in the crumpled aluminum frame that had nearly become his casket. He had no cell phone and no police radio, and yet, Johnny felt strangely at peace and yet still connected to the world. The kindness of the Drakes reminded him of why he loved serving the people of New Mexico so very much.

Chapter 20

"Pedro, I know you're in here! Show yourself." Ronald Becker's shout was followed by a ping of a bullet bouncing off a metal surface somewhere in his barn.

Not taking any chances, Penny had hidden in one of the barn's stalls. Becker may be aiming for his barn manager, Penny thought, but a drunk never can shoot straight. From her place of hiding, her roommate, the chestnut mare, bellowed and stamped her feet. Her bulging belly swayed like a bulldozer with a full load.

From Penny's crouched position, the massive animal appeared even larger than she recalled. She blinked back tears, knowing probably what had to come next. Penny fumbled around in her bag, finally locating her revolver. She had left her 9mm in the car. The revolver was still formidable, as if its weight alone could save her. But firearms needed human hands to work. Penny hated becoming an unwilling partner to violence again, but Ollie's lessons had given her some real confidence. Now the gun felt at home, lying in the palm of her hand. But she would do everything she could to keep from firing it.

Penny heard the angst of wood and metal rubbing together. Becker was either opening Milly's stall or leaning against the mare's door.

"Milly. Milly! Do you miss Georgia?"

Penny heard Milly blowing air from her nose and responding to Becker with a refrain of soulful nickers. She was surprised when Becker began singing a Lyle Lovett song that Penny knew well:

"When I was a very young man
I was a cowboy,
The best in the land.
But then she settled me down
With a touch of her hand.
Now I'm begging you mister,
Tell me if you can,
Which way does that old pony run?

Which way does that old pony run?"

Penny decided it would be a good time to run, as well. She stood and unlatched the stall door. Hearing the squeaky hinges, the pregnant mare lumbered toward freedom. Penny slipped out of the stall under the cover of the big-bellied mare, which whinnied and threw her head in the air, tossing her mane like a sail over her neck. Penny remained safely out of Becker's sight until the horse made an unexpected left-hand turn and headed toward the closed double doors that led to the pasture. The mare slammed her body into the doors, trying to escape.

Penny saw Becker's head jerk toward the sound of the horse crashing into the wood doors. He was inside the stall with his arms around Milly's neck. His gun was resting on her withers. Becker saw Penny standing on the cement walkway, in the line of his fire. She took off running.

Outside the barn, Penny scanned the gravel lane for Johnny's car. *He should be here by now.* She shouted into the horizon where the morning sun was flirting with the Sierra Blanca Peak to the east of the ranch. "Where are you?"

Penny opened her car door, which was thankfully unlocked, and jumped inside. She looked back and saw Becker stumble out of the barn, falling face first into the gravel. She locked the car, placed her revolver in the passenger seat, and dropped her arm down on to the floor, engaging her fingers in a sweeping search for her keys. Sweat poured down her face. Or were they tears? At last, the tips of her fingers touched the keys. Her hands were shaking as she grabbed for them, but they slipped out of her grasp. She dropped her head below the seat again.

Finally, she got a firm grip on the keys, but as she straightened up, her head was spinning. Her eyes did not focus. Her fingers were damp with perspiration, and her chest was heaving from breathing so hard. Penny jammed the key in the ignition and tried to start the car. The key wouldn't work. Frustrated, she tried to turn the key again and pressed her foot on the gas. Still nothing. She pounded her fist against the steering wheel. Was the battery dead? Her throat ached from panting through her mouth. She yelled. "Dear God, save me from this idiot!"

Penny glanced out the car window. Becker was advancing toward her car, gripping his gun with his right hand and swinging it like a pendulum in front of his legs. Penny brushed her sweaty hands on her jeans and held the keys tighter. She tried to engage the key in the ignition, again and again—but still no luck. Then it dawned on her that these weren't her keys. These were the keys to Leo's Ford truck. She had hidden them there months ago when she used it to take a load of trash to the dump.

"Darn it!"

Penny's face was hot and sticky. Her head ached and her mind was in overdrive. She pulled her revolver from her bag as she jumped out of the car and ran toward Becker at full speed. The element of surprised threw the drunk backwards. He fell into the gravel. Penny placed her foot against his stomach.

"Becker, it's me, Penny Larkin. I'm not Pedro."

Becker raised his .38 in his right hand. He didn't seem to hear her. A chill shot up her back and she shivered. Penny cupped her hand over her mouth, stifling a scream. *I can't shoot him!* Her heart was thumping in her chest, drumming up an anger that surprised her. She pointed her gun at Becker, anyway. *Anything to make him stop*!

Mercifully, a ricocheting signal from a nearby cell phone tower had reached Becker's mobile phone. It buzzed in the holster on his hip. He swatted at the annoying hum at his waist, as if a hornet were aiming to sting him. Whoever was calling Becker had saved Penny from shooting him.

Sweat dripped down Becker's face, collecting in the dimple of his chin. His eyes were puffy and consumed with fear. Penny waved her revolver in a wordless move to have him drop his gun. She watched as Becker released his grip on the pistol, one finger at a time, until it fell into the dusty driveway. He lay moaning in the dirt.

Penny was not in much better shape than Becker, but she managed to scoop up his gun and throw it as far away from both of them as she could. Her fingers were like ice, as if she was enduring a bitter winter storm. She realized her fear of guns had been precipitated by a blizzard of memories about loss—loss of her parents in such a short amount of time, a loss of innocence after a failed foster home experience and an inability to hold onto a love relationship.

In the last two times she had held the revolver, two men had died. As bad as their behavior had been, they were gone, and their families felt the pain of it all. She placed her .38 back in her bag. This time, she had killed no one. Carrying a gun was not a death sentence for any one she pointed it at. It was a deterrent, and she was thankful she had handled herself with restraint.

Penny heard the red truck before she laid eyes on it. She watched in disbelief as the ancient looking vehicle lurched up the lane, belching blue smoke and stirring up a ghostly wake of dust and sand. Whoever this was, Penny thought, she was well prepared to defend herself again.

Chapter 21

Pedro leaned against the wall in the hallway outside of his daughter's hospital room at the Sierra Providence Children's Hospital in El Paso. He couldn't get the awful smell of the place out of his nose. The pine air freshener gagged him. He was used to the smell of real life—the sweet breath of his horses, the fresh sawdust in the stalls, the pungent odor of manure. He knew what real pine trees smelled like, for God's sake, and this wasn't it. *Who are they fooling?*

He had made it to patient services just minutes before the payment window closed. He forked over the $2,500 in $100 bills—enough for the down payment on Maria's open-heart surgery—something Dr. Roberto Santoscoy called "*Tetrology de Fallot.*"

"If we don't fix it," Dr. Santoscoy had said, "Maria will die." There was no way Pedro would ever allow that to happen.

Pedro was now standing near the nurse's station, waiting for Lourdes to leave Maria's room so he could slip in and give her a hug and pray with her. She was very weak, and he knew she still needed more than a surgeon could provide. That's where the Rosary he planned to give her would help. He rubbed the tiny pink hearts on the silver strand and whispered the Lord's Prayer, before bringing the beads close to his face. Tears poured from his eyes, soaking the hearts that linked the Crucifix and the oval crest of the Virgin Mary.

His daughter, who was named after the Virgin, was the only person left in the world who loved him. She accepted him just as he was—a simple man with a simple plan—to give her all the chances at life that he had never had because he was in the country without papers. Born in the U.S.A., Maria was a citizen!

"Please God, if I could, I would take Maria's place. I want her to know beautiful things. *Es mi regalo para ella.*" Pedro dropped his hands and shifted his hips. He looked up at the ceiling. A string of pearl lights winked back at him, mocking his thoughts.

What time is it? His watch showed that 30 minutes had passed since he had arrived on Maria's floor at the hospital. It seemed that Lourdes was never going to leave Maria's room—not even to go to the bathroom. Pedro was angry that Lourdes refused to be seen with him. All this waiting could be avoided.

"She will think we're still together," Lourdes had said. "I want her to concentrate on getting well, not worrying about us."

Pedro had been leaning against the wall for too long and his back hurt. He tucked the Rosary in his pocket and stretched his body, throwing his arms upward in surrender. "I give up!" He headed into the patient waiting room, where he plopped into an orange plastic chair. *Could the hospital make these things any more uncomfortable?*

He was angry that he had to wait his turn. He shoved his chair into the wall, banging his head against the windowsill. He moaned, rubbing the back of his head. A large bump was forming.

From his seat, he could keep an eye on Maria's door—the second one on the right side of the long hall, whose pattern of green and white tiles went on forever. *How many people are sick in this place, anyway?*

The rays of the late afternoon sun spilled through the bank of windows behind Pedro's head, heating up the waiting room and making him drowsy. He rubbed the knot on his head again and looked over at the coffee pot in the corner of the room. It smelled bad. The coffee was burning and grafting to the inside of the pot. No sense trying to choke down a cup of the sludge.

Pedro had hoped if Lourdes saw how he had stepped up to save their daughter, she might reconsider coming back to him. It had been a year since she left, but there was always a chance. Pedro lived on hope. It was the only thing he had left.

He pulled his bandana out of his back pocket and wiped his face. The sweat stung his cheeks as the salt seeped into the cuts caused by his slide out of the Rodeo Bar. He winced and dropped his right hand over his eyes, hoping to block out the daylight. He left a small space between two of his fingers, framing a window where he could still watch the entrance to Maria's room. He leaned back in his seat and yawned. Exhaustion was massaging his brain. He thought about the warm towels he used to rub down his horses after they had worked up a lather in the exercise pen. A warm, wet towel on a mare's skin, was the best way to calm a horse before leading her into her stall for a drink from a bucket of cool water. Oh, how he longed for one of those now.

XXXXX

Pedro's snoring jerked him awake. He caught himself before he fell out of the plastic chair. He sat up quickly, making his head swim. He gripped his chair, hanging on until the rolling waves before his eyes were gone and he could focus on the string of orange chairs wrapping around the waiting room like a cheap necklace. His throat ached from sleeping with his mouth open, and his tongue was sticking to his teeth. He needed water.

Pedro stumbled toward the nurse's station, hoping someone could direct him to the water fountain. He got there just in time to see the backside of a law enforcement officer, dressed in an olive drab uniform, walking in the direction of Maria's room.

"Are you here to visit somebody or to arrest him?" Pedro mumbled under his breath. *After all, when is a cop up to anything good?*

The cop stopped in front of Maria's door and knocked.

Pedro's body twitched in response as if he'd taken a whip to the midsection. *Who the heck is this? Has something happened to Maria?* "Oh, no, please God!"

The door opened and the officer stepped inside Maria's room. Pedro ran after him but resisted the urge to barge inside. He would listen first. He could hear Maria's voice and then her laughter. Pedro felt a wave of relief rush through him. Maria was still okay. She was giggling just like when Pedro used to chase her through the pasture with Milly running by her side. It was Milly who kept Maria going as she slipped further and further into her sickness. Sometimes Pedro could see the blue around her lips as she gasped for air, and he would have to look away. When she could no longer go to school, and Lourdes was waiting tables in Tularosa, Pedro would roll Maria's wheelchair into Milly's stall, and the mare would nuzzle her and often kneel so Maria could kiss her nose. Pedro swore the paleness in Maria's cheeks would all but disappear whenever Milly was nearby.

He leaned closer inside the doorway, which the cop had left partially open, giving Pedro a chance to check out the middle of the room. He could see the officer standing at the foot of Maria's bed. Lourdes was standing on the other side of him.

They are holding hands! This was no official visit! *Who is this guy?* Pedro's heart was stomping the life out of his chest. *Have I lost Lourdes for good?*

The officer's mobile phone rang, jolting Pedro back from his pity party. The cop turned toward the exit, hoping to talk in private. Pedro saw his face and his badge. It was Otero County Sheriff Estefan Cerrelio. Pedro's heart sunk to his feet, paralyzing him.

"I'm on my way," the sheriff said. Pedro was still standing at the door, in shock. He could not move.

"Don't go!" Pedro heard Lourdes begging the sheriff to stay. Cerrelio turned around and gave her a hug, before releasing her and waving at Maria. "God bless you, Maria!"

The blood pumping through Pedro's head felt like a mountain of hot lava ready to erupt. His eyes bulged in anger. He forced his feet to move. He took one step and then another. He didn't want the sheriff to see the rage on his face, or to be tempted to punch the cop's lights out. Pedro grabbed for a doorknob on the first door he came to as he stumbled down the hall. It was locked, as was the second. His entire body was on fire. He resisted the urge to scream. Instead of lava pouring down his head, it was sweat. It soaked his undershirt. He grabbed for the third door, but his sweaty hands kept him from getting a good grip. He fell to his knees but finally managed to grasp the door handle. It was unlocked. The sheriff was just exiting Maria's room, but had his head down, looking at his phone. Was he too distracted to notice the weird man groveling on the floor? Pedro finally wrenched the door open and crawled inside, pulling it shut.

A single bulb dangled from the ceiling of what appeared to be the janitor's closet. Pedro was at ground zero for the putrid odor of artificial pine trees. There were bottles and bottles of the greenish-yellow liquid on the shelves and spray bottles of something that smelled just as bad. Pedro placed his hand over his nose and slid onto the sticky floor. He lay his head on a cotton string mop that smelled like urine.

It was still damp, but what did it matter? His life was in the toilet anyway.

Pedro decided he would rest there for a while—at least until his heart stopped pounding against his ribcage and he regained the courage to see his daughter. He pulled her Rosary from his pocket and began to pray. "*Creo en Dios, Padre Todopoderoso, Creador del cielo y de la tierra; y en Jesucristo ...*" He stopped in mid-sentence and dropped the Rosary onto the floor. He was not worthy of the Rosary and no amount of reciting it would make any difference. He was doomed to keep on sinning. Sweat was pouring down his face again, soaking into the strings of the mop and making his face itch.

If only he could offer Maria his own heart. His kept on beating regardless of all the horrible things he had ever done, and in this case, was about to do. How was this fair? What had Maria ever done to deserve this?

He lay there for several minutes, weighing his options. Pedro would rather die in the fire at Becker's ranch, than to have to tell Maria he had killed the horse she loved. The coward's way out would be to die in the fire, of course. But he had to remain alive, at least long enough to finish paying for Maria's surgery. He still owed more than $50,000. That meant Milly must die and so must other horses like her.

Pedro had always promised Lourdes he would never gamble at the races, even when he went with Mr. Becker to help the jockeys. He had been true to his word, and yet, here he was, gambling with his own life and Maria's. His odds were not good, but he had to try and save her.

Pedro was so very tired, and for an instant, he nodded off. But he jerked awake. He must not fall asleep or the same nightmare that had been chasing after him at bedtime would return. He didn't understand the dream, but it filled him with fear every time it occurred. Pedro decided he would shut his eyes, though, for a few minutes. He would just rest. After all, there wasn't much chance of him falling asleep in this putrid closet.

As a dark curtain fell over his mind, Pedro heard the familiar sound of the tractor pulling the starting gate onto the racetrack. He watched as a dozen jockeys mounted their horses and one-by-one, entered their assigned stalls. The steel truss overhead groaned, as each gate locked behind the skittish horses. There was no backing out now; the horses and riders were committed to the race before them. They waited for the blast of the starting pistol to bolt out of their gates and into victory circle.

There was an explosion, but it did not come from the starting pistol. Flames were darting like fireflies across the sky. The racetrack official tried without success to release the starting gates, but all the locks were jammed. There was a chorus of whinnies and the stomping of hooves against the metal walls. Jockeys were calling out for help, but help does not come. It never does.

The black cloud of smoke rolled across the infield, like a raging herd of tumbleweeds, forcing its way into the tunnel that led under the track to the barns. Pedro saw himself crouching there, like a coward, with a bandana over his mouth. Smoke is sucking every inch of fresh air out of the tunnel. Pedro groans, knowing he is about to die.

Chapter 22

The brakes of the red pickup truck squealed to a stop just a few feet from Ron Becker's gun, which was lying in the grass, near the berm of the gravel driveway. With a stranglehold on her own revolver, Penny was ready for whatever happened next. Certainly, if she had to confront the person in the pickup truck it would not be any worse than facing Becker's alcohol-fueled rage. She watched, however, in disbelief as Johnny Trejo jumped out of the truck, his handgun aimed at Becker, who had not moved. Johnny's eyes focused on Penny for an instant, giving her a reassuring smile, before he went to work securing the scene.

Penny gasped in relief. She released her grip on her own firearm, placed her gun back in her bag and wiped her sweaty hands on her jeans. She watched Johnny pull Becker into a sitting position.

"Ouch! You're hurting me!" Becker yelled.

She watched with alarm as Becker used his girth and height as weapons, knocking Johnny to the ground. Penny ran toward the fight.

"Ronald Becker, you are under arrest for attempted murder," Johnny called out the order, even as he remained on the ground with Becker hovering over him. "You have the right to remain silent. Anything you say can and will be used against you in a court of law. You have the right to an attorney…"

"I know my rights! Enough, already." Becker waved Johnny off, before turning his back and lumbering toward the barn.

"Mr. Becker, stop where you are!" Johnny jumped to his feet in pursuit.

Penny reached Johnny just as he was brushing the dust off his pants. Together, they charged after Becker. They managed to grab him from behind and drag him back toward the truck. Becker lost his footing and fell on his rear end.

"Get up, Mr. Becker. I am going to cuff you to the side of my truck until I find out just what is going on here."

Becker tried to stand, but collapsed in Johnny's arms, like a balloon losing air. Tears were streaming down his cheeks. Johnny and Penny hoisted him into a vertical position and held him upright. "I'm sorry. I wasn't going to shoot anybody. I was just trying to keep Pedro from killing my horses. Did you catch him?"

Penny watched as Johnny grabbed Ron Becker's shoulder. "We will sort that out later, Mr. Becker." The three of them took the last few steps to the truck, locked arm-in-arm. Johnny cuffed the horse breeder to the door handle, as he had promised. Becker's huge frame slid down the side of the truck, until his backside landed on the running board. His right wrist, constrained by the steel cuffs, halted his fall onto the driveway. Becker's head fell back against the door, where he remained staring at the barn.

Johnny turned his focus on Penny. He wrapped his right arm around her shoulders and drew her close. "Are you okay?"

A tingle of reassurance found its way into her heart. "I am now." Penny shifted her stance until she was facing him. She remembered the constant look of uncertainty in his eyes. She knew that look. It was the remnants of grief over the death of his father, a New Mexico State Police Officer, who had died in the line of duty a year before. It was then that she also realized the State Police officer's hat that Johnny always wore on duty was gone and so were his sunglasses. His shirt was ripped. His eyes were swollen, as if he had taken blows in a boxing match.

Penny gave him a questioning look and asked, "What in the world?" She ran her fingers over a slash in the fabric of his uniform and then lightly stroked the bruises on his cheeks and chin. Johnny pulled Penny close. Her body caved to his touch.

"You will never believe what it took to get here." Johnny's voice sounded like a simmering pot on the verge of a rolling boil. His mouth was quivering as he moved his lips gently over hers like feathers in the wind. His body was hot. She felt the perspiration soaking his uniform as he held her close.

In all the months they had known each other, and through the many sunsets shared on his mother Ollie's front porch, nothing physical had ever come between them—until now. The gesture was so sweet that it left Penny begging for more.

"OUCH!" Ronald Becker had twisted his arm behind his back. He was yelling for help.

Johnny and Penny broke their embrace and returned to Becker who was pulling on the door handle and had pinched his fingers on the cuffs, trying to free his right wrist. "Let me go!" Becker sobbed.

Penny knew it was Johnny's intention to haul Ronald Becker off to jail, and at first, she agreed, but when she saw tears running down Becker's cheeks, she weakened.

"Fell off the wagon," he moaned. "Been sober for 10 years. Got my ten-year chip in my pocket. He tried to reach in his pocket, but realized his right wrist was still contained. "Why did you go and do that, officer?" Becker looked at Johnny with the eyes of innocence.

"Keep his gun and let him go home and sleep it off." Penny pleaded with Johnny.

"I can't do that! He was trying to kill you."

"Not trying to shoot me. He was aiming for Pedro." Penny was as surprised as Johnny at her defense of Becker. She had endured years of name-calling from her seldom-sober mother, who had never aimed a pistol at her, but had fired off bullets of abuse like a professional gunslinger. Never once did she hear her mother declare she wanted to quit drinking or get help of any kind. And most importantly, she had never carried any AA chips in her pocketbook.

Becker was different. Penny had enough history to know this. She had not sensed any loathing in Becker's heart—only desperation. She touched Johnny's shoulder and pleaded. "Please. I don't want to press any charges."

XXXXX

Johnny and Penny escorted Ronald Becker to his house. It was a rambling, two-story post and beam custom home, with green shutters and a welcoming circle of limestone steps that led to the front porch. Two wooden rockers, painted yellow, sat near the entrance—a double oak door, which was decked with six vertical panels of beveled glass. Penny watched the trio's reflection in the patchwork of glass as they helped Becker through the door.

Penny inhaled in appreciation as they entered the great room. Her eyes ran up to the 30-foot ceilings, which were secured by large oak beams that shouted, "We're not going anywhere!" At the end of the room was a massive stone fireplace that had as its centerpiece, a jagged flagstone embedded with a giant Trilobite—a tribute to the many pre-historic creatures who called New Mexico home.

Over the fireplace was a painting of a beautiful woman with blue eyes and long brown hair—her arms hugging a gray horse. They stopped in the middle of the room, each of them captivated by the artwork in which the woman seemed to pull the energy out of the air. Becker looked up and waved his arms.

"There she is. There is my lovely Georgia."

Penny felt a draft of cold air blow past them. She shuddered and swore Georgia's hair ruffled with the movement of the air. Did they leave the front door open? Penny blinked, trying to blot out the memory of the blown glass beauty who had hovered over Milly in her stall. This was the same woman whom Milly had despised. Nothing made any sense.

Johnny made the first move toward the staircase that led to the bedrooms. "I'll take it from here," he said to Penny. "Come on, Mr. Becker. Let's get you into bed."

Penny was flabbergasted by the staircase, which was carved from a single piece of hardwood, perhaps a birch tree. Penny was, of course, just guessing. Her grandfather had been a woodworker. He had taught her how to choose good furniture, which from the stores, he told her was mostly junk. "Make your own," he would insist, and then laugh, when he saw his eight-year-old granddaughter's confused look.

This staircase was not bought in a store. It had been commissioned by a spectacularly, talented sculptor. Penny marveled at its intricacy. The handrails were carved into long reins, which appeared to drop out of the ceiling and flow down the stairs until they reached the bridle of this magnificent horse. The animal's amber-colored mane was flaring upward while its tail was draping the floor.

If the staircase made an impression on Johnny, he didn't show it. Penny could tell he was concentrating on getting Becker up the stairs without either of them falling. He could admire the stairs later. She also noticed that Johnny was in pain as he helped Becker up the stairs, his right hand securely entrenched in Becker's armpit.

With Penny alone, she would have time to check out the rest of the house. If the staircase were this elaborate, what else was in store? She rummaged through a few drawers in the dining room but found nothing of interest, except some embroidered tea towels.

Penny found her way into what looked like Becker's office. But it wasn't what she had expected in a horse trainer's place of business. The entire wall facing the barn was made of glass. Becker would miss very little of went on in the pasture or the exercise ring. He also had four television monitors on the opposite wall that were tuned into various parts of the inside of the barn including each horse's stall. She could see Milly's tail swishing back and forth as she munched on some hay.

A blanket of dread dropped over Penny. She brushed her hair out of her eyes and shook her head in disgust. *Becker could have been watching my every move.* Sweat dropped from her forehead onto her cheeks. She was having a hard time catching her breath. Maybe he had been trying to shoot her, after all.

How could she keep working for the man if she didn't trust him? Her hands shook, as she considered her predicament. The afternoon sun was permeating the wall of glass, making the room stifling hot. How did a big man like Becker survive in this room? Penny made a useless attempt to wipe the sweat from her face with her sleeve. She remembered how welcome Becker's cash had been to her waif-like bank account. Now she would not be able to return his money. It had already found its way into her mortgage payment, her mobile phone charges, and her past-due electric bill.

Penny yanked open the drawers to the desk, rummaging through them, one by one. She resisted the urge to throw everything she found on to the floor, like a burglar, searching for something to sell. But she wasn't stealing anything. She was just trying to do the job Becker hired her to do.

In the bottom drawer, she found some faded blue ribbons and a few yellowing newspaper articles on wins that the Beckers' had taken at a track in Ruidoso. She found some personal checks, which had the name Georgia Becker printed on them. She also found some notes written in a female's handwriting. Penny took a second look around the room and realized this was not Ron Becker's office. This had been Georgia's.

Penny dug deeper into the drawers where she found a half-used bottle of French perfume. She lifted a pile of files out of the drawer and dropped them on the desk. Mixed in with these files was Georgia's will and inside of that was a folded newspaper. A front-page headline, dated eight months ago, jumped out at her. "Tularosa Woman Dies in Tragic Accident." Penny plopped down in Georgia's wing-back leather chair to read more.

"Georgia Becker, wife of renowned New Mexico horse trainer, Ronald Becker, was killed by a kick to the head from her own horse at the Becker Ranch, just south of Three Rivers, on Tuesday, March 6. The freak accident was discovered by Maria Lopez, the five-year-old daughter of Pedro Lopez, the barn manager.

"Maria Lopez displayed a tremendous amount of bravery and presence of mind to place the horse in an empty stall to keep Mrs. Becker from further injury," said Otero County Sheriff Estefan Cerrelio. "She then ran to find her father, who called 911. Pedro Lopez tried unsuccessfully to revive Mrs. Becker with CPR. Georgia Becker was pronounced dead at the Gerald Champion Regional Medical Center at 6 pm."

"He's all tucked in," Johnny said. Penny jumped at the sound of Johnny's voice. The chair rolled out from beneath her. She staggered and reached for the edge of the desk. "You frightened me!" She had been so deeply engrossed in the story of Georgia's death that she had forgotten all about Johnny. She ran her fingers over her eyes, which were aching.

"Would you like to have a picnic lunch on the front porch?" he asked. "We should wait around for a while and make sure Becker is no longer a danger to himself, or anyone else."

Penny and Johnny sat in the wooden rockers and ate egg salad sandwiches and drank lemonade from the Drake's Thermos. The intense rays of the sun flickered over their faces as it journeyed toward the White Sands Missile Range, 25 miles to the west. Hues of red and gold were trapped in the dusty air and hung like a chandelier over their heads. The wind had stalled, it seemed, because the Becker Ranch was for the moment, a silent, peaceful place. Penny was grateful.

"I think this is much better than a steak dinner," she said, smiling at him. She reached over and touched Johnny's shoulder and let her arm drop over the side of the chair. He grasped her fingers and smiled. The sun was reflected in his brown eyes. She could see the rings of sweat under his arms and could see dark blotches on his face, where the bruises were already turning color. It had been a difficult day for Johnny, and she truly loved him for coming to her rescue, and for agreeing to let Becker sleep it off.

Johnny began massaging the palm of her hand with his thumb. The rhythm of his thumb moving over her palm and up through her fingers, was more sensual than Penny had been prepared to experience. She squirmed in her chair. Penny wanted so much to be closer to Johnny—to fall into his lap and breathe in his essence. Instead, she leaned back in the rocker and gripped the armrest with her left hand so tightly that her fingers were in pain.

Johnny's fingers were now caressing her arm, stopping only briefly at her elbow, before lingering on her wrist. If he had been feeling for her pulse, he would have found it raging. Penny crossed her legs and pulled her hand away.

The sun moved beneath a solitary cloud, robbing the moment of its passion.

Johnny stood. "I probably ought to get the truck back to the Drake's before it gets too late."

Penny could still feel the blood pulsating from her fingertips and into her wrist. She sighed, hating to let this moment go. Why had she been so hasty?

Johnny pulled Penny to a standing position, wrapping his arms securely around her shoulders. "I'm not letting you off that easily." He kissed her forehead, her cheeks, her chin and then her lips.

Johnny's kiss—bold and warm—was everything she had hoped for, and she found herself buoyed by feelings of joy. But she must not get carried away by the glow of the lingering day. She was not a child. At 35 years-of-age, she knew the outcome of this relationship was as sure as darkness follows the day. Johnny would find a good reason to leave her. Everyone left in due time. Everyone.

Penny forced herself out of his embrace, hiding her tears by turning her face toward the mountains. She blinked as the last threads of sunshine snapped and dropped below the curvature of the earth. Her hands were shaking, even as her pulse still battled for her attention.

"What's wrong?" Johnny turned her body toward him. She could see the passion in his eyes, and she wanted so much to return it, but she would not be hurt again.

"Nothing is wrong," she said. "That's the problem."

Chapter 23

Pedro Lopez walked alongside the gurney carrying Maria to the operating room. The two male orderlies who had the task of rolling the patient to surgery did not make eye contact with Pedro, nor with one another. Maybe one of them had a daughter Maria's age, Pedro thought, or maybe this was just another day, another body. One thing was for sure, Pedro knew these guys wanted no part of the "goodbyes." Maria's mother had not been able to handle the stress. Lourdes had told Pedro to be strong for both of them and then had departed the hospital in tears.

Maria was clutching the Rosary with the tiny pink crystal hearts. She smiled at him and whispered the word he loved to hear, "Daddy." Pedro could hardly keep it together. The doctor had promised him that Maria had a good chance at a normal life if they operated now. Pedro had staked everything on that promise. No more blue lips or breathless walks across the ranch. No more having to stay home from school because she couldn't keep up with the other children. No more heartless kids who made fun of Maria because she struggled to climb the steps to the school bus.

The orderlies stopped at the swinging doors to the operating room. It was time to go. Pedro took a deep breath and leaned down and kissed Maria on the cheek. "I'll be here when you wake up, Mija."

"Daddy, will you take Milly a carrot—a great big one? And tell her not to forget about me."

Why in the world would she be asking me this right now? Pedro's gut tightened with the guilt. He took another gulp of air and stared at Maria's big brown eyes. They glistened with tears. Her words, with the precision of a surgeon's scalpel, were slicing into his own heart. He could feel the blood draining from his body, one beat at a time. The green and white tiles on the hospital walls were fluid, melting before his eyes. Pedro steadied himself on the edge of Maria's mattress. He felt sick to his stomach—just like when he rode on the back of the hay wagon at the horse ranch. He swallowed hard

"Of course, Mija. Of course, I will bring Milly all the carrots she wants."

The cart banged against the double doors. Maria grabbed at Pedro's arm again with her tiny fingers. "Promise me, Daddy. Milly is my best friend. She will wonder where I am."

Pedro wiped away a tear that had trickled down her face. "*Mi promesa si siempre tuyo.*"

The hospital aides rolled Maria into the room for surgery. The refrigerated air from the operating room rushed over Pedro, raising goose bumps on his arms. His little girl would be lying in that cold place with her lips turning blue. He prayed the doctors could keep her warm enough and that they could fix her beautiful, but broken heart.

He shivered and hobbled away from the operating room doors. She was in the surgeon's hands now. A father could only do so much when it came to the life and death of his child. But God knows, he had tried.

Pedro kept wiping away tears from his cheeks with the back of his hand. As he stumbled onward, he could not stop sobbing. He hoped he could make it to the waiting room, filled with those dreadful orange plastic chairs, before he collapsed.

Chapter 24

Penny twisted in her seat at the Good Coffee Shop, no doubt polishing to a shine, the red vinyl cushion beneath her. Don Tellez was 25 minutes late, and to kill time she was listening to The Guess Who singing *American Woman* via the buds linking her iPhone to her ears. She drummed her fingertips on the table keeping time with the music. For the past few months, the lyrics of this venerable oldie from the 1970's had served as a reminder that love doesn't last.

She mumbled the words under her breath. "I got more important things to do, than spend my time growin' old with you." Its relentless beat reminded her that there were few men or women these days who were willing to commit to a lifetime with anyone, let alone with her.

The world was different now and she had better get used to it. Penny yanked the earbuds off her head and threw them on the table. It was all over with Leo, but this fact had been hard for Penny to accept. Like a fool, Penny had rushed into the relationship with him on a rebound from her eight years with Porter Jenkins. Porter had abandoned her for a job in China and Leo had eventually chosen his dead wife's twin sister as a substitute for his grief. She couldn't even compete with a dead woman. How bad was that?

Besides being irritable over Don's tardiness, Penny was also exhausted, having fallen into bed last night just before Midnight. Penny had followed Johnny to the Drake's farm where they left the red truck in the driveway. She drove Johnny to Las Cruces, where he lived with Ollie, and then headed 40 miles south to her home on El Paso's west side. When she finally opened the door to her rambling adobe house at 11:30 pm, there was a message on her home phone from Leo asking her to meet Don at the Good Coffee in the morning. It had been too late to get out of it.

Now she was waiting for Don who had still not arrived. Penny's annoyance at him was only making her more irritable. She considered tardiness as a lack of respect for her and her profession. Finally, Penny saw the door to the restaurant swing open. Even this early the glass on the front door was smudged with the hands of its many customers. Don Tellez was a steady customer it seemed because he waved at the waitresses. Even the cook came out from behind the counter and shook his hand.

Penny had always appreciated Don's good looks, but this morning he appeared taller and more muscular than she remembered. He had Leo's curly hair, and angular cheekbones, and straightforward gait. Don was scanning the room for Penny, but she did not wave in recognition. Why should she? She was doing him a favor, and he could find her without her having to pretend she was happy to see him.

Penny had chosen a table at the very back of the room, away from the traffic of those lining up to pay their checks at the cashier near the entrance. People waiting to pay for their meals always had prying eyes. And besides she wanted to keep her distance from Don and all four-top tables were in the rear. She looked down at her phone, covering up her annoyance that she had been cooling her heels for almost 30 minutes. A shadow fell over Penny's shoulder. Don had apparently found her hiding in the back of the room.

Instead, she saw a weary looking waitress standing at her table and holding a green order pad in hand. "What'll it be, Ma'am?" The waitress frowned but finally broke into a giggle. Don was hiding behind the woman, whose apron looked like it had been painted with scrambled eggs and a dash of blueberry syrup.

"Linda, bring Penny and me some coffee and a couple of your morning specials. Rush me out an extra side of bacon. I'm starved. Thanks, doll."

Penny stared at Don in disbelief.

"It was the only way I was going to get you to look up from your darn phone," he said. "And I figured you weren't too excited to see me. The Tellez family isn't on your Christmas list, I'm sure."

Penny couldn't help but laugh. She simply could not pull anything over on Don or Leo. There was no sense pretending to be disgusted with any of the Tellez boys. They were just too charming and way too smart.

Don's long legs folded under the table. He sat in the chair closest to hers instead of directly across from her as she had hoped. He was neatly dressed in freshly ironed khakis and a white, button-down shirt with his monogram "DJT." His brown leather boots were polished and scuff free. He was sitting close enough that she could appreciate his aftershave, a mixture of cloves and freshly washed, cotton shirts. Penny took in a deep breath and fidgeted in her chair.

"Did Leo tell you why I wanted to talk with you?"

"He said something about a local fire."

"The city has given me permission to hire you to help with our investigation of an El Paso warehouse fire that killed three. Fernando Del Rio, a gopher for the Chihuahua Cartel and Quarter Horse trainer Sonny March were both ID'd through dental records. A third body could not be identified."

Penny's stomach twitched at the mention of a Quarter Horse trainer. She pressed the tips of her fingers into the vinyl cushion on her chair. This time she would collect everything about the case before accepting it. The Ronald Becker fiasco was a perfect example. She had been so happy with Becker's $5,000 that she had abandoned her good sense. She had almost died from that mistake. It wouldn't happen again.

"Whether you accept the job or not, I want you to know that the last place Sonny March worked was at the Becker Ranch."

This plate of bad news arrived at the table with as much heat as the platter of hissing bacon the waitress was now placing between them. Both were too hot to touch. What in the world was going on? She should have insisted that Johnny haul Ron Becker off to jail when they had the chance. She rested her arms on the table and leaned forward. "How long was he employed by Becker?"

"About two years. He apparently left suddenly in the middle of last March."

Penny's wrists ached where the edge of the table's linoleum was pinching her skin. She was nauseous. She moistened her parched lips. If only she could reach for her glass of orange juice. Her arms seemed paralyzed with fear, or maybe it was anger. This news about the dead horse trainer had stunned her. Sonny March had left the Becker Ranch just about the time Georgia died. Maybe it was just a coincidence. But as Leo always reminded her, "There are no coincidences when it comes to solving a crime."

"I'll take that plate from you, Linda," Don said.

Penny looked up to see the waitress balancing two plates of eggs and a pile of pancakes. Don took Penny's plate and placed it on the side of the table. "Thanks. It looks delicious." He then gently tapped Penny's arm. "It's okay. You'll feel better after a hot meal. Would you like some maple syrup?"

"Yes, thank you." Penny twisted her paper napkin between her thumbs until it was in shreds.

"We're not asking you to work alone." Don continued. "The Texas State Fire Marshal is forming a task force, and you would be a member of an excellent team of arson investigators. Of course, I am one of those." Don's eyes rolled toward the ceiling, and a tiny smirk pierced his lips.

Penny leaned back in her chair and managed to eke out a professional question. "What would you expect from me?" Her hands were shaking as she poured the maple syrup over her pancakes. She hoped she wouldn't have to examine the burned bodies to find a lead. She used targets to inspire her viewings, and with burned victims, she would have to draw the line.

"Don't breathe a word, but we don't have a single clue to this fire, and we need your insight. I saw what you did for Leo in finding Rosa Garcia, and then tracking down that gunrunner, Juan Rico. I admit I was skeptical at first, but I've seen your success and want what you've got."

"I'm not sure I would be much help." Penny's stomach growled as she stared at her plate of food, trying to avoid eye contact with Don. Her stomach was starved but her mind was stuffed with doubts.

"We're prepared to pay you $2,500 a month until the case is solved."

"That sounds like a full-time job. I can't devote that much to it since I've already agreed to work with Ronald Becker. And then there's my contract with the U.S. Marshal." *Whatever good it will do now*, she mused.

"That's just it, Penny. Isn't there a possibility that both cases are related?" His inquisitive eyes, as dark and deep as the table's maple syrup, pierced Penny's hazel ones with an intensity that made her squirm. She reached for her fork and jabbed at the eggs on her plate.

Don pulled a photograph out of the front pocket of his shirt and handed it to Penny. "This is a photo of Sonny March."

Penny's eyes widened in recognition. She had seen this man's picture on the wall in Becker's barn. In fact, a similar photo was now in her bag, hanging on the edge of her chair. "What do you want to know?"

"I'm hoping you'll take this with you and see if it brings anything to mind."

Like some controlled remote viewers, Penny used photos such as this to envision clues to a victim's background, or in some cases, to determine their location. This could be a dangerous pursuit when the suspect is still alive, as Penny had recently discovered. In this case, Sonny March was now lying on a marble slab in the morgue. She was going to need some help.

"Whatever it takes, Penny. We're desperate. I don't think we've seen the last of this arsonist."

She tapped her fingers on the table with a rhythm of fear. "I already know this man."

Don reached over and laid his hand over hers. The warmth of his touch rattled her more than her encounter with the snake in the desert. She tried to pull free, but he wouldn't let go. She was being gamed—and she knew it. Don was dropping quarters in the slot and aiming the pinballs straight at her heart.

"Penny, your involvement could save lives. We're concerned that the Betas Cartel has greater plans than just burning down barns. That's bad enough, but now that folks have died, we're real interested in stopping these guys."

Penny yanked her hand away from Don's. Her sudden move knocked over her coffee mug, which bounced against the plate, shoving her stack of pancakes and maple syrup into her lap. A stream of coffee followed, causing a burning sensation to spread across her thighs. "Ohhh," she groaned, and reached for her paper napkin, which was so twisted out of shape, it was useless.

Don grabbed a towel out of a hovering waitress's hands, and placed it on Penny's legs, soaking up the coffee and protecting her from the additional liquid that continued to drip from the table and on to his own pants. He was so very close that his breath blew down her blouse. She tamped down the memories of Leo holding her close and telling her how much he loved her. Penny had to get away, but to do so she would have to move her face toward Don's.

"Bring me another towel, Linda." He shouted, as if he were in triage on the front lines. Penny remembered that Don had served in Iraq as a medic. Even his voice reminded her of Leo, and his face was just a younger version of him. For a fleeting moment, Penny halfway appreciated Leo's own dilemma with Alejandra's twin sister, Adrianna. But unlike Leo, Penny was not going to cave into Don's chivalry despite the many fine characteristics that both brothers shared. And that meant she could not work with Don, regardless of his threat that more people might die. That's how she got entangled in these barn fires in the first place. And besides, the link between Sonny March and Ron Becker was just too much to absorb right now.

Despite her growing anger, she allowed Don to help her stand. The pancakes fell to the floor, the syrup still dribbling between her legs. Penny nodded her head in agreement when he insisted on walking her to her car. Her jeans had soaked up much of the syrup and coffee, making Penny self-conscious about her sticky thighs which rubbed together. *How embarrassing!* She looked straight ahead, as nosy patrons waved to Don and chuckled. He and Penny exited the restaurant through the greasy, fingerprinted front door and headed for the parking lot.

Chapter 25

Leo was just wrapping up a meeting of the regional task force on drug enforcement at the County Courthouse. He had survived the inevitable handshakes, backslaps, groans and head-shaking that the male officers had provided to console him. The lone woman, Sylvia Hernandez, the commander who ran the City's drug enforcement efforts, held back and took him aside after most of the members had left the room. "Losing sucks, Leo. You are a fine sheriff, but it does not and should not define you."

"What dictionary are you using, something by Dr. Seuss?" Leo laughed.

"This isn't green eggs and ham, Leo. I've been in law enforcement for 30 years and sometimes wish I could have had a window of time to consider who I am and how I like my eggs. This loss is a gift."

XXXXX

The morning sun violated his sunglasses as Leo turned onto Justice Avenue, the road leading to his office. He had never found losing to be all that helpful regardless of Sylvia's thoughts on it.

He pulled down his visor and a photo of Penny fell into his lap. The picture had been snapped four months ago, on the day she had been flown out of Mexico after her successful rescue by the U.S. Marshals Office. She was standing near the Sikorsky Jayhawk Helicopter that had carried her to safety. The movement of the blades was blowing her short hair like a swift breeze through grass. She was wearing black sweatpants and a sweatshirt, both torn to shreds, revealing good portions of her arms and legs. Her legs were bloodied, and her face was bruised and swollen, but her smile displayed the pure joy of getting out of Mexico alive. Leo's heart ached knowing that just a few hours after this photo was taken, he had made Penny cry.

Leo parked his car and rang Don's office phone. Like his mobile, there was no answer, only a bland message from his brother promising to return his call. He was anxious to find out if Penny had agreed to work with Don.

Penny had heard Leo grousing about Don's reputation with women. She had always just laughed it off, telling Leo he was exaggerating. "I can't see how he has anything on you, Leo. I would never be attracted to a guy like Don. Even in high school, I could have seen right through him."

Certainly, Leo had to take Penny at her word when she went on to say, "I'm not into players."

Knowing his brother, if Penny had agreed to a breakfast meeting, Don had already convinced her that he not only believed in her skills as a remote viewer, but he also endorsed them fully. Don had probably accomplished this even before they had finished their first cup of coffee. This was a lie, of course. Don had been one of Penny's biggest naysayers when Leo had hired her last year to help find kidnapped eleven-year-old Rosa Garcia.

"You're going to end up looking like an idiot," Don had chided. "Nobody can find Rosa using voodoo tricks, no matter what the lady calls it." Leo had been dumb enough to fire Penny when she didn't find Rosa right away. She had taken on the task of finding Rosa by herself, and had done so successfully, and killing the leader of a Russian child trafficking ring. So much for voodoo.

And despite all her success, Don continued to harass Leo about Penny. What he had against Penny Leo just did not understand. Penny was beautiful and smart, and Leo simply loved and admired everything about her.

Leo shook his head and took his cell phone out of the leather pouch on his belt once again. All Don needed was a half-truth to ignite a spark with Penny. And Leo knew that when it came to sparks and fires, Don was the arson expert. He punched in Don's number once more.

"Hey, Leo. Can I call you back? Penny has had a slight accident, and I need to give her some assistance."

"What kind of accident?" Leo yelled back into the phone. He noticed his brown eyes in the rearview mirror. His pupils were wide with rage.

"We've got it under control. It just involved some hot coffee and the waving of arms. I'll call you later. Bye.

Chapter 26

Leo entered the Sheriff's Headquarters from the back stairs. He was still too embarrassed to engage anyone in another round of "I'm sorry, Leo. Things will be okay." Thankfully, he found his office void of Francisco Parasea. Paco had called an hour ago and complained that Parasea kept hanging around, getting in everyone's way.

Leo was relieved that Parasea had finally taken the hint and left the building, perhaps to find the nearest television station and crow about his victory. It seemed strangely quiet for the normal bustling activity of the El Paso County Sheriff's Department. Maybe Parasea had chased everyone out of the office. Leo dropped his car keys on his desk and stepped into the hall in search of his friend, Paco. His office was empty.

Leo walked into the public waiting room, thinking Paco might have gone to the gym in the basement via the elevator to get some time on the treadmill. As he glanced back through the glass that separated visitors from the inner workings of the sheriff's office, Leo noticed that the dispatcher was missing from her post. Then he saw a man in the squad room pointing a pistol at Paco's head.

Leo dropped to his knees, hoping he had not been seen. How in the world did he get past the dispatcher who worked inside the bulletproof glass? And where was she?

No visitors were allowed in without the dispatcher buzzing them through. Leo buzzed himself back in with his key card, and dropped onto his knees once again, keeping his profile below the windows while crawling toward the dispatcher's desk. He found the dispatcher lying in a pool of blood. Leo felt her pulse. She was still alive, but he would have to get her help fast. Did he dare call 9-11 yet without the gunman hearing him? He had to risk it.

"This is Sheriff Tellez," he whispered. "I've got an officer down in headquarters. She's been shot. Send an ambulance ASAP and law enforcement back-up. The suspect is holding another deputy hostage."

Leo crept into the squad room, taking cover behind one of the metal desks that held piles of old paperwork, waiting to be shredded. He rested his hands on the tower of paper, yielding years of hard work by his officers trying to do the right thing for the county. He noticed that his own hands were calloused, and his fingernails were rough and brittle from so many years in the field. Would this be the last time he got a chance to make a difference?

He took a good look at the suspect. He was about 45 years old, with dark skin and black hair that had recently been cut. He smelled of Old Spice aftershave. His hair was neatly trimmed around his neck. Leo could tell that a barber had nicked one of the man's ears.

"I am only going to say this one more time. Call the jail and have my brother Victor Grasso set free. We will head back over the border with no more trouble. I promise he won't be bothering anyone in El Paso again. *Ese idioto*!"

"I can't do that," Paco said.

The man hit Paco in the head with the butt of his gun, knocking him to the floor. The gunman leaned down toward Paco and pointed his weapon at his chest. Leo charged the suspect, throwing the full force of his 175 pounds against the man, dropping him onto the tile floor. Leo could feel the residual pain from his shoulder wound, as he shoved his body into the suspect. Leo lunged for the man's gun, but not before the man squeezed the trigger. A stray bullet ricocheted off the glass wall and lodged in a poster announcing the next SWAT Team competition in January.

Paco, wincing from the blow to the side of his head, staggered toward the man. Leo had his right hand on the butt of the intruder's pistol but could not gain control. Paco kicked the man in the back, knocking the air out of him. The gun flew across the squad room.

"It's all over." Paco yelled. He pulled the man off the floor. The suspect, who was trying to get his breath, managed to wrench a switchblade out of his boot and slice Paco across his chest.

Paco stumbled forward and collapsed onto the floor.

Leo pulled his 911 automatic out of the holster and blew the knife out of the man's hand with a single shot. The suspect, eyes wide with rage, gazed at his bleeding fingers, the tip of one of them dangling. He lunged at Leo. Leo dodged his blow, causing the culprit to crash onto the tile floor, hitting his head against the wall and knocking him unconscious. Leo cuffed the suspect to the leg of the metal desk and ran for the squad room phone.

Leo called two ambulances. "We've got two officers down." Paco's blood was spreading across the front of his olive drab uniform. His face was grey, and the pupils of his eyes looked like marbles. "Hang in there." Paco moaned and threw his arm over his face. "He's right. I am such an idiot." Paco tried to get up.

"Don't you dare move. That's an order!" Leo pointed his index finger at him and shook it as Paco tried to get up again. Then Leo laughed. "You never change, *mi amigo*."

Leo ran to check on the dispatcher, who remarkably had regained consciousness.

"We've got an ambulance on the way, Dorita." Her real name was Doris, but everyone lovingly called her by her nickname most of the time. He squeezed her hand, which was cold. Doris gave Leo a sliver of a smile and pulled at the Sheriff's arm. "New sheriff down."

"Sheriff Parasea isn't here yet…not until January."

"He hid on the stairs."

Leo's eyes widened as he considered what Doris was telling him. He ran to the emergency exit door that led to the front stairwell and shoved open the door. Francisco Parasea had been shot in the back and had fallen headfirst down the stairs. His long, blonde hair was caked with blood. Leo felt for a pulse. Blood bubbled from his nose. *He is still alive!*

Leo yelled into his cell phone. "We need another ambulance. We've got a third officer down." He turned Parasea onto his back, then used his hands to clear the airway around his nose. Parasea coughed, and blood trickled out of his mouth. He felt for a pulse again, and now there was none.

"You're not leaving me this way!" Leo couldn't wait for the medics to arrive. He began compressions against Parasea's chest. He heard Parasea's chest pop, like his ribs were breaking. No matter how many times Leo had done CPR, a cracked rib always took him by surprise. Leo tilted his head, pinched Parasea's nose and used mouth-to-mouth resuscitation, counting to himself. Still nothing.

Leo repeated everything he had been taught and carried out a dozen times along the side of the road. He repositioned Parasea's head and tried again. He compressed his chest, this time with more force. Finally, Parasea gasped and drew a rattling breath of air, before coughing up blood.

EMT's spilled out of the elevator, along with a couple of reporters from the El Paso Times and the local ABC news station. They infiltrated the squad room like a gaggle of geese and soon found Leo and Parasea in the stairwell. The lights from the photographer's camera lit the darkened staircase, exposing the pool of blood and the badly wounded Sheriff-elect. Leo paid no attention to the reporters. He helped lift Parasea onto the pallet as a medic was making sure he was still breathing. "We've got him, Sheriff. Thanks to you, I think he's still got a chance." One of the EMTs placed his hand on Leo's shoulder and looked him in the eyes. "You're one heck of a sheriff. Thanks."

As Leo followed the EMTs out of the stairwell, he saw another team of emergency medical personnel taking Doris to the elevator, and a third team heaving Paco's six-foot-five-inch frame onto a stretcher. And it was no easy task. Paco's burly arms and bare feet dangled over the edge. He was bare-chested, exposing a wide girth of white bandaging covering the knife wound to his stomach.

When Paco saw Leo moving toward him, a tear rolled down his face and he took his fingers and wiped his cheek. "Sorry, boss. Real men don't cry."

"Yes, big men—real men, do cry," Leo said. "And you, *mi amigo*, are as real as they come."

Chapter 27

Johnny's lower back was aching from trying to cram his lanky body into the twin bed of his childhood. The room was hot, and the late morning sun pierced the pea size holes in the yellowing, paper window shade. He had not turned on the tabletop fan at his desk before he fell into bed last night. Now, when he tried to inhale, the stale air seemed to lodge in his throat like a day-old Mexican Concha.

Johnny had moved back in with his mother, Ollie, after his dad had been shot and killed. He knew she would probably be okay without him there, but it was just the two of them now, and it gave them both a sense of wellbeing to watch after each other. He had sublet his furnished Las Cruces condo for a year and planned to move back in when he could see that his mother was smiling more than crying. That was eight months ago and still counting.

He sat up in bed and then regretted it. His bare chest looked like it had been beaten with a hacksaw. He noted a nasty slash across his midsection and cuts and bruises on all four limbs. Johnny had been afraid to look at his face in the mirror last night, hoping a good night's sleep would make it all better, and not cause his mother needless worry. She had been in bed when Penny dropped him off, so Ollie did not get to see her careless son, who had narrowly escaped his demise on that backcountry road.

It was now 7:30 am, and he needed to try to get ready for work. He was shocked at how long he had slept. Johnny placed his bare feet on the handmade rag rug and used the bedside table to help him stand. For an instant, the room flipped and fluttered like an old black and white TV screen. The color had drained from his world. It was grey and scratchy. Johnny rubbed his eyes and tried to refocus. He shuffled his feet forward in the manner of a man twice his 35 years and made it as far as the mirror hanging over his chest of drawers. Just below his left eye was an ink-blotch injury of purple and yellow, which reminded Johnny of the birthmark on the back of his neck. Both of his cheeks were pockmarked where the EMT had removed bits of tar and gravel with tweezers. Now all he had left was a little road rash. He could deal with that. But slender red threads lined the landscape of his eyeballs. He made the decision right then; he would not go into work today. Johnny Trejo was a loyal captain of the New Mexico State Police, but his current condition would result in too many questions. And besides, it was time he realized he was not Superman. The Harvester Tractor had been his kryptonite, and he was no match for 15,000 pounds of forward-moving steel.

Johnny opened the door to his room and slipped down the hall to the one bathroom in the house. He saw that his mother's bedroom door was already open. An early riser, she was probably in the kitchen making breakfast or in the backyard filling the birdfeeder. She was as predictable as sunrise, and as welcoming as a brand-new day. Ollie Trejo was a gentle spirit who collects friends like nectar attracts hummingbirds.

A quick shower turned out to be a bad choice. The hot water peppering out of the shower head felt like poison darts piercing his already compromised skin. Even after the water stopped, it continued to hollow out little places in his epidermis. Johnny stood in the shower stall, hoping he could drip dry. The thought of a towel against his naked body was unthinkable.

He opened the shower door and made a wet path of footprints back down the hall to his room. He fell back into bed, knowing full well he was soaking the sheets. He would have to regroup before his mother came tapping on his door and wondering why he had not gone to work.

The desert air of New Mexico was happy to soak up the dampness of his body, and in about 20 minutes, Johnny was dry enough to dress. He found a pair of shorts and a clean white T-shirt and then slipped on his flip-flops. He took one more glance at his image in the mirror and shook his head. It was time to face his mother and tell her about his foolishness. She would not be pleased.

He found her singing as she stood in front of the stove making an omelet. He recognized the song. "*A la puerta del cielo.*" It was a tune his mother had sung to him as a small child. She would rock him to sleep in the late afternoon, especially whenever he had a hard time going down for a nap, which was often. Johnny stood quietly listening to her voice, which brought back those magic mirrors of innocence, shattered years ago.

A la puerta del cielo
Venden zapatos
Para los angelitos
Que andan descalzos
Duérmete niño
Duérmete niño
Arrú arrú

"Good morning, Mama."

Ollie turned around at the sound of her son's voice. She saw his face, and Johnny could read her mind. *What in the world has happened to my only son?*

"I'm okay, Mama."

She flew to the table and pulled out a chair. "*Siéntate!*"

Johnny did as he was ordered and sat. She always spoke in Spanish when she was upset with him. She leaned over and brushed his hair out of his eyes. "*Que te ha pasado, Mijo*?

"I was in an accident with a tractor."

"*Que paso*?"

"I was rushing to help Penny, who was trying to fend off a drunk firing his gun at her."

"*Oh, mi Dios. ¿Está de acuerdo*?"

"Yes, Penny is fine. She was a little shaken, but she will be okay."

"*¿Puedes invitarla más por un plato de enchiladas*?"

Johnny knew his mother equated healing with a plate full of enchiladas. And she was probably right. Many a problem in a Mexican household was solved over a meal smothered with Hatch green chilés and melted cheese.

Ollie finished making the omelet and placed it on Johnny's plate. She passed him some *pico de gallo* and sat across the table from him. At first her face looked troubled. The few wrinkles she had, were trying their hardest to compromise her beautiful olive skin, but without much luck. Finally, she smiled, and her youthful appearance returned. His mother understood that this was all in a day's work as a New Mexico State Police officer. The backroads—as hazardous as they are—were part of the public service contract you had with the citizens. You would not let them down, if possible. His mother had lived and breathed the dangers of the backroads for thirty years, right until the day when her husband was cut down by a drug cartel's AR-15.

There must be a special place in heaven for the wives of those in law enforcement, Johnny thought. Maybe that was why he wasn't married. How could he put a spouse through such torture?

Johnny watched as his mother took the receiver off the green wall phone in the kitchen and then hung up just as quickly. "As soon as we're done here, I'm calling Penny and inviting her for dinner. She needs a big plate of my enchiladas."

Chapter 28

Penny's right hand was still stinging from the dousing of hot coffee during breakfast. The syrup just served to heap more sorrow on her belittled state of mind. She could feel the moisture wicking through her jeans and into her underwear now, as she had walked with Don Tellez to her car. She was embarrassed, and all she could think about was getting away from him. She could only imagine Don and Leo getting a good laugh at her expense.

Then she remembered, she could not go home. Penny had left her house so quickly that she had forgotten the exterminator was going to be there applying chemicals to both the inside and outside of her home. He had asked her to stay away for most of the day so that everything would be good and dry when she returned.

"Penny, why don't you let me help you," Don said. "My place is just around the corner."

"I'm going to need a set of dry clothes, and I'm not sure yours will fit me!" Penny looked up at Don who was at least a foot taller than her five foot-four-inch frame. His hand was placed on the small of her back as he ushered her through the parking lot. She shuddered a little. Perhaps from the shock of the burn to her skin.

"I'm pretty sure I have something that will fit. I promised my neighbor I would drop off a bag of clothing for her to Goodwill. I remember seeing some jeans in it."

If this were true, Penny thought, it would save her a great deal of time. She could forgo her fashion sense for one day. Returning home and trying to get in the house when she had promised the exterminator she would not enter, was risky. And besides, she lived more than 30 minutes away. She had justified this meeting knowing that from the Good Coffee it would be only a 40-minute drive to Becker's ranch. She needed to get back to Tularosa and check on Ron Becker. And now, with the latest knowledge about his dead trainer, it seemed more urgent than ever that she find out who was behind these fires and snuff out their plans.

Penny arrived at her car, and remembered she had a towel in her gym bag in the trunk. She placed the towel over her leather front seat, sat down, and started up her Mustang. Don leaned in and gave her directions to his place, but she looked confused.

"Just follow me," he said.

True to his word, Don's place was nearby. It was tucked behind a large, two-story stone house, which Penny estimated to be at least 4,000 square feet in size. He waited for her to park on the street, and then walked with her down a leafy, brick-lined path around the side of the house. She stepped over a half-eaten dog toy, the leather ripped around the edges.

Don lived in a quaint cottage, built of the same stone. There were green painted shutters on the windows, and a bed of red and white geraniums planted on either side of the wooden Dutch-style front door. She fully expected to see Red Riding Hood's grandmother come out of the house to greet them.

"This is not what I expected," Penny said, as he opened the door. The living room opened straight away into the dining room and kitchen. Everything was well-decorated, with a comfy floral sofa and a leather side chair facing the stone fireplace.

Penny took a breath and let the air out slowly. Where in the world was she? This was nothing like Leo's house, a Spartan affair. Leo chose to spend most of his time at work or the cemetery and paid little attention to his décor.

"The bathroom is just down the hall. If you want to shower, there is an extra set of towels and a washcloth hanging in there. I'll go retrieve the jeans, and maybe a top or two, and you can choose for yourself."

Penny was still bewildered, but she did as she was told. She entered the bathroom, which was as clean and modern as the cottage was charming and quaint. She pulled off her sticky jeans, which felt like they were glued to her thighs. She let out a lungful of air. How dumb could she be to talk with her hands? It was a bad habit she had to stop. Her underwear was like a second skin. She peeled them off and stepped into the shower.

The rain shower head was designed to drop water right from the tiled ceiling. She let the lukewarm waterfall cascade over her body. Slowly, she added more heat. The stinging on her hands and right thigh were easing, and so were the bad feelings she had for Don. Whatever she had thought about him before, she now knew that some of what Leo had told her had been through a lens of brotherly competition.

The shower watered her spirit, which had been feeling dry and parched since last night when she had turned away from Johnny's embrace on Becker's front porch. She had wanted desperately to be with Johnny, but she had to protect herself from the pain of losing people she loved.

She heard the door to the bathroom open. Through the clear glass shower door, she saw Don dropping some clothes on the seat of the toilet, before stepping out as quickly as he had appeared. She was grateful for his kindness, and she would make sure Leo knew his brother wasn't the monster he had painted him out to be.

Don had been correct. The jeans were her size. He had left her two tops. The first top was a simple white V-neck, T-shirt and the other was a turquoise filigree top that flowed from the bodice and covered the waist of her jeans. Everything looked practically new. How could anyone give these clothes to Goodwill?

Penny chose the turquoise blouse. And unbelievably there had been a pair of white cotton underpants tucked inside the jeans. With the jeans and her tennis shoes, she appeared pretty much put together. In fact, better she looked better than when she had arrived at the restaurant.

She stepped back into the living room, but it was empty. She sat on a bar stool at the island, which had a polished, cement countertop. This place was a puzzle. Certainly, on an arson investigator's salary, Don Tellez could not afford this cottage.

Don appeared, newly dressed in jeans and a white cotton golf shirt. "The coffee and pancakes took a toll on my slacks, too" he said. He smiled and ran his fingers through his curly black hair.

"I'm sorry for talking with my hands. It's a bad habit of mine."

"How about some coffee and a cinnamon roll? I bake as a hobby."

Penny looked bewildered. This man was full of surprises.

"I know you are wondering how and why I live here. Jessica Armand is the owner of the big house. About five years ago, I needed a place to live, and I rented this cottage. Jessica is a widow in her 70s and wanted to feel safe. So, she made me a deal. She would fix up the cottage and turn the deed over to me, if I would stay and provide protection to her while she was in town, and to the house, when she traveled."

"And the clothes? They look too nice to give away," Penny said.

"Four months ago, Jessica lost her granddaughter in a drunk driving accident. Elisabeth lived with her grandma while she was in college. She was just 20 years old and a junior at UTEP. Those are her clothes."

Penny's shoulders collapsed at the news.

Don was pulling the cinnamon rolls out of the cabinet. They were lathered with caramel icing and pecans. He popped the rolls in the microwave for a nanosecond. Penny's stomach growled as the sweet aroma floated across the room. Her pancakes had gone the way of the trash bin, and she had hardly touched her eggs. Don ground some coffee beans and placed a pot of coffee on to perk.

"Jessica just got the courage to clean out Elisabeth's room this past week. I told her not to worry, I would find a good home for her clothes. And I think I have. The jeans and top look wonderful on you."

Don placed one of the cinnamon rolls on a plate and pushed it in front of Penny. "Here's a napkin. They're sticky!"

"Thanks. I'll try to keep them out of my lap!" Penny smiled at Don and licked the top of the roll. The icing was perfect. It wasn't too sweet. As she took her first bite of the roll, she let the icing linger on her tongue. It was so good.

Don was leaning against the kitchen counter and eating a roll, too. The coffee pot beeped, and he took down two big mugs, and poured them each a cup.

Penny took a sip of the coffee, which was some of the best she had ever had. "I'm not sure why you eat at Good Coffee when you can cook this well," Penny said.

"I do that for the company. I don't like to eat alone every day. It's no fun at all."

Chapter 29

Leo waited outside the surgery unit at University Medical Center. Francisco Parasea was on the operating table where doctors were trying to save his life. Leo hated hospitals. He had had terrible luck in them, and he certainly didn't want to lose the new Sheriff of El Paso County on his watch. As much as he despised Parasea's tactics during the campaign, he felt sorry for him. Hiding in the stairwell during a crisis was not the best way to make a good first impression with the public.

Paramedics had asked the sheriff's office for his next-of-kin, but no one knew a thing about Parasea's relatives. So, Leo felt obligated to wait in their stead. With any luck his office could locate someone soon who claimed to be related or at least cared about him. Leo hoped that the new sheriff never found out that he had save his life. It would certainly be a source of embarrassment for Parasea, knowing the man he had beaten in the election had provided CPR until the EMT's could arrive.

Doris was still in surgery, but doctors had given Leo the good news that nothing vital had been touched with the perpetrator's blade. For this he was very grateful. Leaving office and losing Dorito would be too much to bear.

Paco was on the next floor, recovering from what ended up being wounds the emergency room surgeon was able to stitch up quickly. Paco was headed for a full recovery. As soon as Parasea was out of surgery, Leo would head upstairs and visit with Paco, who was in a private room big enough to accommodate his large family, including his parents, wife and five children. Leo knew he would not be missed.

He reached for a pot of coffee in the waiting room. It was cold, but he poured himself a cup anyway. His throat was dry, and it ached. It hurt to swallow. He took a sip of the cold brew and licked his lips.

He had given Parasea mouth-to-mouth resuscitation which had fallen into disfavor with the medical community, but Leo knew it worked, and he would continue to practice it when a life depended on his help.

Leo sat in an upholstered armchair that looked like it had held the tears of many. And it was badly stained with coffee. There was even a burn mark from a cigarette. Stress, Leo knew, brought out the very best and the very worst in people. And from the looks of it, the weight of the world had come to roost in this one chair.

A 30-something woman, with long auburn hair entered the room and took a seat a few chairs away. He could tell she had been crying, but for now the tears had stopped. Her eyes looked red, bewildered and lost.

"I would offer you a cup of coffee, but it is cold," Leo said kindly.

She looked at him as if she had seen a ghost. The blood drained from her already pale face. "Sheriff Tellez?"

"Yes."

"I'm, Lonnie, Francisco's ex-wife. Your office called me, as he has no other relatives living nearby. Everyone in his family has moved to California, or back to Mexico City."

"I'm so very sorry this has happened," Leo said.

"I'm surprised you are here." Lonnie looked down at the floor. Her long hair rested on her shoulders, giving her a look of innocence and reflecting a picture of someone too young to have ever been married.

"I didn't want him to be alone," Leo replied. He stood and carried the lifeless Styrofoam cup over to the sink, emptied it and tossed it in the trash.

Lonnie looked down at her lap, where she held a badly torn tissue. He watched her continue to pull on the tissue until it had the consistency of feathers. It covered her lap like a wounded bird.

Leo took his own handkerchief out of his pocket and handed it to her. "Here, you might need this."

"Thank you." A single tear fell down her cheek. She wiped it away with the clean linen.

A doctor appeared at the door to the waiting room. He was dressed in green operating scrubs, a matching cap and white paper footies. His face was peppered with perspiration, and he was out of breath, as if he had run a mile to get there. The doctor leaned on the casement and waved at Leo. He and Leo had exchanged passing hellos when Parasea was rolled into the operating room.

Both Leo and Lonnie stood at the same time and approached the surgeon.

"This is Sheriff Parasea's ex-wife," Leo said.

"Dr. Forbes." The surgeon shook her hand. And when he did, the handshake revealed a large band of sweat under his right arm. "I'm still not sure Mr. Parasea is out of the woods. His injuries were worsened by his fall down the stairs. He has a bad head injury. We had to operate anyway because of the internal bleeding. We removed the slug, a .45 caliber, which is the good news. The bad news is that there may be some side effects from the head injury, but we just won't know until he comes around."

"How long will that be?" Lonnie looked even more frazzled than when she had entered the waiting room. The woman rocked slightly toward the wall. Leo resisted the urge to steady her.

"Why don't you return to the hospital in about four hours? By then, we will have a better idea of his long- term prognosis." Dr. Forbes spun on his heels, not waiting for a reply, and ran back toward the recovery room.

Lonnie swung her arms down toward the floor and howled. "I can't believe it. His life was turning the corner. And now this!"

Out of instinct, Leo tugged on her arm and tried to calm her. "It is a waste of your energy to think the worst."

"Francisco spent years in rehab, trying to kick heroin. And he beat the odds. As a kid he was running with a scary crowd in Mexico City. His parents moved north to El Paso to get away from them, but the drugs came along. They were too deep in his veins to give them up overnight."

"Where are his parents?"

"They died several years ago, a few months apart. Their deaths set Francisco straight. He kicked heroin, an amazing feat in and of itself. Francisco started an import/export business between the U.S. and Mexico, with his inheritance, and has done very well. He hated how drugs had almost destroyed his life. He spends his off-hours talking to kids in the city's rec centers. And that is why he decided to run for sheriff. He truly wanted to make a difference."

Leo looked at Lonnie's frail frame. Her face was gaunt and grey. She looked like she could use a meal. "Could I buy you some lunch in the cafeteria? Leo asked.

"I'm not all that hungry, but perhaps I should eat something. It may be a long day."

Leo and Lonnie got in the elevator and headed to the basement where the cafeteria was located. The journey downward in that small, moving box was a silent one. Leo could hear Lonnie breathing a little too rapidly. Finally, she let out a long sigh, just as the doors opened.

The cafeteria was packed with men and women in scrubs of every color and style, from the traditional surgery green to Disney cartoon characters. The noise was an assault on Leo's senses. Everyone was chatting and laughing, as if the floors above them were part of an amusement park, and each person had just exited their favorite ride. Leo knew that the human psyche could only handle so much stress and observe only so much grief. It had to spill out somewhere, and amid the cafeteria cheer was just the place to land.

Both he and Lonnie chose a small cup of soup and whole wheat crackers on the side. They sat quietly, looking down at the table. The noise was like a wall of protection. They did not need to interact with others or with each other. Finally, though, Leo broke the silence.

"Why did you and Sheriff Parasea get divorced?"

Lonnie sucked in a pocket of air. Leo's handkerchief covered her eyes, but it was not enough to hold the deluge of tears pouring down her cheeks.

Leo felt a hand pressing on his shoulder and he looked up. He recognized George Archuletta, a reporter from the *El Paso Times*.

"Sheriff, I'm wondering if you could give us a statement about what has happened to Francisco Parasea since you saved his life?"

Leo noticed Lonnie's eyes widen. She wiped her face and blew her nose. Her hands were shaking.

"Let's not worry about who did what to get Sheriff Parasea here. What's most important is that he is here and he's in good hands."

A camera flashed in their eyes.

Lonnie blinked and jumped up from the table and ran toward the restroom.

"Who is the woman with you? Is she related to Parasea?"

"You'll have to ask her. I have no other comment."

The reporter and his photographer shuffled toward the women's bathroom. Leo cringed. Hopefully, they would not confront Lonnie as she came out.

Leo finished his soup and then munched on his crackers. Lonnie's cup of soup was barely touched. Still hungry, Leo stole one of her crackers. It had been ten minutes and Lonnie had not reappeared. He threw his napkin on the table and walked over to the hovering reporter and his photographer.

"Just how long does it take a woman to pee?" Archuletta laughed.

Leo moved past the men, knocked on the door and then headed in the women's restroom. He found Lonnie lying on the floor, blood seeping from her left arm. She had sliced her wrist with something very sharp.

Leo shouted for medics. A woman in pink scrubs entered the room and rushed to help. She pulled a roll of bandages out of her pocket, wrapping it around Lonnie's wrist several times, just above the laceration. "What's the chances of me having this? I just came from a class where I was training newly graduated nurses about the real world."

The nurse placed three fingers on a pressure point inside the fold of Lonnie's elbow, to slow the blood loss. Leo had seen this technique done by paramedics before. Confident that the nurse knew her stuff, Leo walked outside the restroom and rolled a trashcan in front of the door.

George Archuletta, and his photographer were still leaning against the wall. They would earn their wages today, Leo thought. They were in a prime spot to capture a photo of a stretcher rolling out of the bathroom, carrying a bleeding young woman who had tried to take her own life. Leo wondered if they felt any responsibility for Lonnie's desperate act. *Probably not.* And from the looks of Lonnie's bleeding body, divorce papers were just that—papers. Leo knew love could not be regulated in a courtroom nor from the depths of a graveyard.

Chapter 30

Penny trailed her fingers over the photo of the warehouse fire. She had reluctantly agreed to give Don a few minutes of her time before taking off for the Becker Ranch. Don stood behind her and pointed out some of the gruesome details, including the mummified body of the horse trainer, Sonny March. He was lying on the cement floor, face-up. His eyes were partially open, giving Penny the impression, he was looking at her. His arm was elevated, and his fingers appeared to be pointing at something. Penny felt a tingling sensation as if ants were doing a victory dance on her arms. Sonny March was communicating with her, even from the depths of this one-dimensional photograph.

"Is he trying to tell us something?" Penny asked.

"Oh, you mean his hand? I wouldn't put much stock in the position of the arms or hands on a burn victim."

Intrigued, Penny couldn't help but want to know more. "Could we go to the warehouse and look at where March was lying?" The words tumbled out of her lips quicker than she could grab them by their syllables and pull them back. *Don't do this, Penny!* Common sense told her, if she left right now, Penny Larkin could make a clean break from the Tellez brothers. But her questions about this warehouse and Sonny March's presence, were flashing in her mind like a neon sign and blinding her to her own pain.

"Sure. I'd have to clear it with the team, of course. When?"

"I could meet you tomorrow about 6?"

"AM?"

Penny laughed. "Sorry it's so early, but I've got a full day planned."

Don feigned distress, wiping his brow with the back of his hand. "I'll bring the coffee." He smiled and winked one of his very dark eyes.

She remembered Don had not been exactly punctual today, and for her, time was money. "Promise to be on time."

Don laughed. "Sorry about that. I didn't get a chance to apologize. Jessica's bathroom sink overflowed, just as she was getting ready to head to the Humane Society, where she volunteers."

"Does she have animals? I didn't see any running around the property, but I did see an old toy."

"Jessica's dog, Reckless, was in the car when her granddaughter got hit. She was returning from a visit to the vet. The German Shepherd was killed, too."

Penny rubbed the arms of her new turquoise top, feeling the very breath of life slipping through her fingers. She needed fresh air! She rushed toward the front door to escape the winds of death encircling her and tripped over her own feet. Don caught her, and she fell against his chest.

The steadiness of his heartbeat encouraged her to remain there, even though she knew better. Don's warm breath, holding only a hint of cinnamon, blew across her face. His arms encircled her in a gentle embrace.

Once again, old film reels played in her mind. She saw herself as a sixteen-year-old hiding in a neighbor's barn, having fled her foster father's grasp. She watched the tears rolling down her young face— badly scratched from burrowing out a hiding place in the bales of hay. How long could she stay hidden from the world? It had been more than two decades, and Penny was still afraid. She wasn't any more alive than the corpse lying on the scorched floor of the warehouse. Even eight years with Porter Jenkins had not healed her. Maybe that is why he left her. She just could not love anybody.

Don slowly turned Penny's body toward his own. He lifted her chin until his eyes looked directly into hers. "You've got some healing to do," he said. "We had better get started on that, or you will always be wondering why love never stays."

Penny's cell phone buzzed from the confines of her purse. Her head jerked toward her bag, as heavy as a millstone on her shoulder. She hoped it would stop. She wanted to hear more about what Don had to say about love. No one had ever talked to her so frankly.

The phone continued to ring. She took a breath, but never broke eye contact with Don. She fumbled around inside her bag, until she located her phone.

"Hello. This is Penny Larkin."

"Penny. This is Ollie. I'm making enchiladas tonight and want you to come for dinner."

Chapter 31

Penny drove north toward Tularosa with her windows open. Her right arm was resting on the ledge of the driver's side where the November air blew over her, ruffling the sleeve of her turquoise blouse. She needed the coolness of the midmorning to collect her thoughts. Her chest felt twisted and tight, as if she had spent the past week operating her grandmother's wringer washer, and it had mangled her heart.

Penny had been in the arms of three men this week, and each of them had shot little darts into the target of her resolve to keep from getting hurt again. There was the reoccurring assurance, however, that no one can leave you, if you aren't together.

And she couldn't help but think of her own father, Johnny Larkin. He was her hero, even if he had been away from home a lot when she was growing up. She could watch him on television because he was competing almost every Sunday at one of the racetracks around the world. He always tried to find a cameraman who would let him send her a secret signal—the peace sign—two fingers in the air.

"When you see me, my dear Penny, remember I will always love you." Her father talked in the past tense, perhaps because he knew that on any given day at the track, it could be his last. And finally, it was. She had watched in horror as his open-air race car blew a tire. His speed, more than 200 mph on the straightaway, made him a human missile. She hung on to the photograph of his mangled car, a sculpture of twisted metal and resins, crushed against the wall of the Sonoma Raceway in northern California. As morbid as it seemed to her teenage friends at the time, the photo comforted her. And it still brought her solace tucked away in her dresser drawer.

Penny felt the closest to her father when she was driving her own car. It was there that she most often heard his voice, his reminders of how to drive safely, and other idioms that spoke to the core of his being. He was the bravest person she had ever known, and so kind. How had he been so courageous, while Penny lived life at the curb? And how could she ever learn to be kind and caring when her heart was a twisted wreck?

She looked down at the top Don had given her. The teenage girl who owned it would never have the chance to love fully. Couldn't Penny at least give love a try in honor of this young life cut short by drunkenness? Of all people, Penny knew that alcohol could rob you of life at any age. You didn't have to be on the highway. It could kill you right at your kitchen table. "One last drink before I die." That was her mother's mantra. She said it every night before heading to bed.

The memory of her mother's sad eyes faded from her thoughts as Penny came upon Rodeo Ridge, the road that led to Becker Ranch. She made a right turn and used the next couple of miles to prepare for a confrontation with Ron Becker. She had called him along the way and told him she would be there by Noon. She was right on time, and she wanted to send him the message that she was a professional and would not tolerate any more desperate ploys to take matters into his own hands. He either wanted her help or he did not. If he did, he would have to stay away from the booze. If he did not, she wasn't sure how she could return the money, since it had already gone to pay bills.

Ron Becker was waiting for her at the main entrance to the barn. He looked freshly scrubbed, and his hair was parted on the left and slicked down, as if he expected a high wind. A black Stetson hung from the fingertips of his left hand. His right foot was tapping to a rhythm that only he could hear. He stopped moving when he saw Penny step out of her Mustang.

She approached him, cautiously. Her eyes rolled left to right, scanning the driveway, hoping Becker was not setting her up in some way. She could now hear a country western tune playing on the radio in the tack room. She'd seen enough cowboy movies to know that the man in the black hat was always the bad guy. Becker could easily have a loaded rifle with a trip-switch hidden out of sight. A single tug on a string tied to the trigger could blow her head off. She had watched Westerns with her father for years while they lived in Indianapolis, where her father's racecar team was housed. She knew how things went down in open car racing, and sometimes you hit the wall.

Penny kept her eyes focused on Becker's body and particularly on his boots, where he kept his .38 tucked out of sight. Becker tossed his hat into the air and caught it with his right hand, before placing it on his head and adjusting the brim so that it threw a shadow over his eyes.

He smiled at Penny and blew out a long breath that turned into a whistle between his teeth. Penny did not return his smile, choosing to wait and see what he would do to make amends. Becker breathed in deeply again and reached in his shirt pocket. Penny's back stiffened. She stopped in mid-step, as he pulled out a white handkerchief and wiped his eyes. "Penny, can you ever forgive me for being so stupid? I could have killed you." His eyes were like little pools filling from an underground spring. A single tear tumbled onto his shirt.

From the front pocket of his jeans, he retrieved a small object and tossed it to her. She caught it and turned it over in the palm of her hand. It was a brass recovery coin from Alcoholics Anonymous, with an "X" on it for ten years sober. Under the X were the words, "To thine own self be true."

"I want you to have it, Penny. I blew my ten years sober because I didn't trust you to help me. It's an ongoing issue for me. My father was an alcoholic, too, and I grew up fearing that others would let me down because my dad always did."

Penny took a few steps closer to Becker. His words rattled her. They sounded vaguely familiar, like those that haunted her mind on sleepless nights.

"I can train horses like no one's business, but I can't train myself to love and be loved. Georgia tried so hard to earn my love, but I could not give it to her fully. In the end, she turned to horses and finally, to other men." His voice trailed off into the horizon where his gaze also landed.

A small, dark cloud, dense with moisture, slogged across the otherwise sterile sky. Penny wondered about the storm clouds hanging over her own life and wished for a clear day when she would not be afraid of anything. She rubbed the recovery coin between her fingers and then tucked it in her jeans pocket. She would carry the coin as a reminder that sobriety was more than a lack of alcohol or drugs. Living sober means living free, and her mother had never been free. And frankly neither was she. Every weekend, Virginia Larkin had lived in fear of losing her husband. This fear had ruled her life with such force that Penny was sure it eventually caused Johnny Larkin's race car to spin out of control and smack into a wall. Thoughts have power. Of all people, Penny, as a remote viewer knew that. It was time for her to start some positive self-talk, and it would begin today.

"Let's get to work!" She shook off her earlier fears and headed for the side of the barn, where she had seen something shiny while exploring the loft. Becker's drunken antics with his gun had sidetracked her and she had almost forgotten about it until she was on her way back to the ranch. Becker trailed her, asking no questions.

Penny pushed the straw around with her feet, searching for something that did not belong. At the edge of the barn, tucked partially under the cement foundation, she found a metal device on a key ring. Attached to the key ring was a piece of red plastic, with a rod jutting out of it. This was not a key. She held it in the air so that Becker could see it, too.

"That's a high-heat fire starter!" Becker grabbed the item from Penny's hands. "This is a magnesium alloy stick. I use them for camping in the mountains. At least I did before the drought made campfires illegal. It produces a spark that is hotter than 5,000 degrees Fahrenheit." Becker pounded his fist against the side of the barn. "What kind of beast would do this?"

Penny took the fire starter from Becker and put it back where she found it.

"Aren't you going to take it with you?"

"I don't want to alert the arsonist that we're on to him."

Becker leaned down and ripped the fire starter from her hands. "I can't take any chances. I don't care what Pedro thinks."

"Please put it back." Penny tried to pull the fire starter out of Becker's grasp.

He moved away from her and headed back to the front of the barn but stopped suddenly. "Sheriff Cerillo's SUV is pulling up the drive. I can see the bubble lights on top." Becker tossed the fire starter to Penny. "You win!"

Penny placed the starter back where she had found it and joined Becker, who was now standing in front of the barn. Penny noticed that the Otero County Sheriff's insignia on the side of the silver Ford Explorer was painted with gold and dark grey stripes which ran the length of the vehicle. The name SHERIFF in all caps emblazoned both the driver's and passenger doors. It was hard to miss.

The tinted, automatic window lowered and revealed the Sheriff's tanned face. "*Hola*, Ron. I'm just making a routine check on your ranch. I know you don't think I care about your barn, but I've ordered round the clock patrols for this weekend."

"I've taken matters into my own hands, Sheriff. This is Penny Larkin, a private investigator. Penny, this is Sheriff Estefan Cerrelo."

Penny always joked she could read people like a book, and Sheriff Cerrelo was a novel she would never check out of the library. His eyes were small and set a little too close together. His long, narrow face and high cheekbones reminded her of someone who had lived their early years without good nutrition. She guessed the sheriff was in his early forties, but he appeared much older. His skin was wrinkled and dull, hastened by a lifetime in the New Mexico sunshine and maybe a little too much whiskey. There was a flicker of light in his eyes—perhaps from a candle of hope still burning inside his heart. The glimmer did little to diminish his look of disdain for them both.

Finally, the sheriff smiled, showing a mouth of yellowed and misshapen teeth. "So, this is the famous, Penny Larkin. I've read about your escapades with the drug cartels. You really do like to take on the big boys, don't you?"

Penny did not answer him. *He was taunting her.* A nagging shiver of irony chiseled away at her spine, hoping to break her new-found courage into tiny little pieces. Instead, Penny laughed, pushing fear back into its proper place. "Sheriff, if you call working for law enforcement 'play', then, yes, I was playing with the big boys."

Penny could see that her remark did not endear herself to the Sheriff. She could care less. She wasn't sure how regular patrols around the ranch would help all that much, but it was something. Her plan was to hang out inconspicuously Saturday evening and try and catch Pedro, or whomever, in the act.

It was obvious that the Otero County Sheriff's Office was not interested in preventing anything, only dispensing an artificial pulse to Ron Becker's heartfelt plea for help.

The Sheriff revved the engine of his SUV. "Gotta' head home. The wife has lunch waiting for me. Miss Larkin, it was lovely meeting you today." The sheriff tipped his hat and drove away from the barn. At the end of the driveway, he gunned the engine and made a left on to Rodeo Ridge. Within a few minutes, the sheriff was only a bad memory, although a shroud of brown dust still hung in the air.

Chapter 32

Penny sat across from Johnny at Ollie's kitchen table. Both were waiting with much anticipation for the chicken enchiladas, smothered in green chile sauce, to come out of the oven. The sweet ambrosia of melting cheese and Hatch green chiles permeated every crevice of the small room. Penny inhaled and smiled at Ollie, who was scurrying around the kitchen, and putting last minute touches on the chopped lettuce and tomato salad.

Penny preferred to watch Ollie, rather than stare at Johnny, whose face was a patchwork quilt of bruises and cuts. Even a small shift in his position caused him to wince. He never once reached for a tortilla chip. It did seem ironic to Penny that two of the most valued men in her life were named, "Johnny." And both pursued dangerous careers. Was this the reason Penny had been reticent to move her relationship with Johnny Trejo beyond just being friends?

Penny felt awkward chomping on a chip and savoring the salsa on her tongue, when Johnny was not eating anything. With each bite, the crunching was so loud in her head, she was certain it was causing Johnny a headache.

It had been a long day, which ended with Penny and Ron Becker agreeing on a plan to surprise the arsonist and scare him away from setting the fire. They had no other choice. They didn't have enough information to call in law enforcement, and having met Sheriff Cerillo, Penny was sure asking him for help was a lost cause. For some reason the sheriff had little interest in saving Becker's barn. What he had against Becker, Penny couldn't begin to guess. And Ron Becker couldn't supply any reason for it either.

"So why are you wound up as tight as our mantel clock?" Johnny asked Penny.

Penny's body jerked at the sound of Johnny's voice, but she didn't answer him. His words broke the silence that hung over the kitchen like the steam from Ollie's kettle, which was always simmering on the stove for endless cups of hot tea.

Instead of speaking, Penny focused her attention on the ticking of the clock above the fireplace. It had been a gift to Johnny's father from the New Mexico State Police for 25 years of service. Now it was a constant reminder that life should be measured in minutes not years.

Johnny laid his hand on Penny's arm. "Are you okay?" He managed a smile—which Penny knew was no easy task. There was a slice in his skin just above his upper lip that looked like it needed stitches.

Penny let out a deep breath and smiled back. Looking at Johnny in any condition made her happy. "I'm good."

"So, what's the plan for Saturday?"

"Ronald Becker and I are going to lay in-wait and try to surprise the arsonist. We really don't have a choice. Sheriff Cerillo dropped by the ranch today and seemed totally disinterested in helping Becker. I'm not sure what that's about."

"You can't do that alone!" Johnny slapped his hand against the kitchen table and looked like he immediately regretted it. The pain brought tears to his eyes.

Penny tried to ignore his outburst. "I've got my gun." Penny said.

"These people are pros. They don't care who gets in the way."

"Becker paid me big to protect his horses and I'm going to do so."

Johnny shook his head in disgust and struggled to his feet.

"Sit down, son!" Ollie yelled. "You've got no right to judge what Penny does. You've got yourself in such a mess you can't even help her when she really needs you."

Johnny did as his mother said, scooting his chair a little closer to the table.

Ollie brought the piping-hot casserole dish out of the oven and set it on the counter.

"Can I help you, Ollie?" Penny asked.

"No. I've got this under control. You just relax." Ollie cast another sour look at her son.

Penny looked over at Johnny who was smiling at his mother. There was something special between a mother and her son—an unspoken bond of mutual respect and exceptional tolerance for weak-hearted behavior.

Ollie served Penny and Johnny and then placed a small plate of enchiladas for herself at the third-place setting. She poured herself a cup of hot tea and bowed her head, in reverence for God. No one spoke, waiting for Ollie to pick up her fork.

Penny's stomach growled. She was embarrassed, but no one seemed to notice. Everyone was entrenched in their own set of reveries—thoughts of a very personal nature it seemed—because the silence remained even after Ollie began eating.

Five minutes into the enchiladas, Ollie put down her fork. "Penny, since Johnny can't go with you Saturday night, why don't I go along?"

"Mama, you can't do that!" Johnny raised his voice in protest. His eyes were black with regret.

"I'm one of the best shots in the Doňa Ana County, and you know it! I even outscored your father a time or two." Ollie jumped up from the table and left the room.

"My goodness, what have I done?" Johnny rubbed his fingers through his already rumpled hair and then looked at Penny. "Don't go along with any of her ideas, Penny. Please!"

"What do you expect me to do?" Penny had already seen firsthand how proficient Ollie was with a firearm. And besides, Penny knew better than to get in between mother and son. Both people were dear to her heart. Instead of placating Johnny, Penny folded her hands under her chin and waited for whatever Ollie had in mind.

The banging in the hallway, and the groans that followed, conjured up visions for Penny of a tiny woman wrestling rifles, tactical gear, and ammo, and dragging them toward the kitchen. She would not be disappointed. When Ollie appeared in the kitchen, Penny could tell Ollie had come ready to rumble. So, in support, Penny strapped her pistol on her belt.

Chapter 33

Leo found his way back to the cafeteria two hours after being assured by hospital staff that Doris and Paco were going to live.

He sat at a corner table, and ordered a bacon, lettuce, and tomato sandwich with lots of mayo. He had called his headquarters, and things were mercifully quiet. In fact, his deputies had encouraged him to hang around and call them as soon as there was more info about all four patients. They were particularly curious about Parasea's health. Apparently, the Sheriff's office was abuzz about the Parasea's capacity to serve. And the dispatcher told him, there was wishful thinking that Leo might get to remain in charge.

Leo was happy to share with his team that Doris would thankfully recover but would have to remain in the hospital the rest of the week. Paco was the best of the four. "You know you can't keep a good man down," Leo laughed "His doctor has given him a thumbs-up to go home on Friday." Leo had watched everyone in Paco's hospital room laughing and celebrating, as if it were Christmas. Life couldn't give you too many gifts, and Leo was grateful to still have Paco's friendship as one of his.

The Sheriff was just taking a bite out of his sandwich, when a tall, slender nurse in red scrubs, entered the cafeteria on a mission. She found Leo sitting at the back of the room.

"Sheriff. Lonnie Parasea is asking for you."

Leo dropped his BLT on the plate and grabbed his hat.

"She's been moved to an ICU annex on the fifth floor. I'm heading to lunch, so can you find her on your own?"

He nodded, and soon found his way to the ICU annex, which was tucked around a corner at the end of a long hall. If Leo hadn't known better, he would have guessed the hospital had made a janitor's closet into a patient care room. It was that tiny. But its small size did nothing to make the petite woman lying in the hospital bed look any larger. Her diminutive body was connected to a superhighway of tubes and wires.

Seeing Lonnie lying there alone in this windowless space brought back a wreck of memories about losing his wife, Alejandra and infant daughter, Marta. His stomach lurched, and he swallowed hard, hoping he would not be sick.

The ICU nurse moved in and out soundlessly, checking Lonnie's vitals. After 20 minutes of listening to Lonnie's heart monitor and watching her IV drip slowly into her veins, Leo saw Lonnie's eyes flicker open. Her eyes were the color of the autumn leaves in the cemetery where Alejandra and Marta were buried. A chill ran up Leo's backside and he squeezed his shoulders together, trying to bury this memory in the graveyard of his mind.

A small, shaky hand, inching out of a bandaged wrist, reached for Leo's fingers, which were clutching the bed rail. "Sheriff, I'm so sorry." Tears welled in Lonnie's eyes. The glistening moisture accentuated the color of her eyes, which were indeed, auburn, just like her hair.

"There will be plenty of time to be sorry," Leo said. "Right now, you need to marshal all of your willpower to heal."

"I just couldn't bear to have those reporters find out about me."

"They aren't around. I think they felt badly about causing you so much distress. I'm sure they won't bother you again."

"I can't be sure."

"I can protect you."

"Sheriff, no one can protect me."

Leo's face reflected his skepticism. "Lonnie, you are safe."

"You don't understand. My real name isn't Lonnie. I'm in the..." Lonnie stammered, searching for words that seemed to catch in her throat. "I'm in the U.S. Marshals witness protection program. Since 2009."

Leo was stunned. The muscles in his face were quivering. He fought to control his reaction by swimming in Lonnie's amber eyes and then diving into her deep well of honesty. *Why were people so quick to be honest?*

Lonnie's were not *Lyin' Eyes*, as the old Eagles' song goes. How could a young woman find her life in such an upheaval? She was the kind of person every man longs for—someone for whom he can protect and be strong—someone he could love.

"Did Francisco know this when you married him?"

"I finally had to confess to Francisco, but only right before we were married. He promised never to work in the public eye. When Francisco wanted to run for Sheriff, I filed for divorce. I couldn't afford to have my photo in the news."

"Who are you?"

Lonnie scanned the room, apparently expecting danger in every corner. Her hands were shaking so hard, she placed them under the blanket. "I'm from Buffalo. I was placed in witness protection after I testified against one of the Falzone brothers, who headed a huge extortion ring. I was dating Gino, one of Arnie Falzone's grandsons."

"How did you get called to testify?"

"I would have never told anyone about Gino's grandfather taking bribes and shooting a man who wouldn't pay. But, when he killed Gino, too—his own grandson, who threatened to turn him in—I knew I was next."

"You still haven't told me your name."

"Sheriff, I'd like to keep it that way." Lonnie's cheeks were bright red and dimpled with perspiration. Her breathing became shallow and fast. He could hear her heart monitor picking up speed.

Leo found a small washcloth and ran it under the faucet in the bathroom. He swabbed her face, trying to cool her off. Was it possible that she had a fever? He felt her forehead. She still felt hot. "I'll be right back."

Leo headed to the nurse's station and asked if someone could take Lonnie's temperature.

The thermometer revealed the worst. Lonnie had a 102-degree fever.

"Sheriff, I'm going to ask you to leave now. Miss Parasea has a raging fever, probably caused by the self-inflicted cuts to her wrist, not today, but last week."

"Can you help her?" Now Leo was shaking. Was he a bad luck charm for hospital patients? *Should he leave now?* Why had he ever come in the first place?

The nurse placed her hand on the Sheriff's shoulder and whispered. "If we can get an antibiotic that isn't resistant, we may be able to contain the infection. But I am not holding out hope, as her fever is so very high."

Leo slumped out of the room and made his way to the waiting area where he had first met Lonnie. The lyrics to "Lyin' Eyes" ran through his head again:

"My, oh my, you sure know how to arrange things
You set it up so well, so carefully,
Ain't it funny how your new life didn't change things,
You're still the same old girl you used to be..."

Leo leaned against the wall, preferring to stand rather than sink into one of the coffee-stained chairs. As if on cue, Leo could see Francisco's surgeon taking quick steps toward the waiting room.

"Sheriff, we have good news. Mr. Parasea has come out of surgery and is now resting comfortably in ICU. Could you please tell his ex-wife, he is expected to recover?"

Chapter 34

Penny was shivering as she waited alone in the dark alley. It was barely 6 am and the air was brittle, as if a sudden move could break a bone. The stink of the burned-out shell of a building was an early warning for what lay ahead, and it was already nauseating her. She swallowed hard. *Where is Don?*

Penny stamped her feet, partly in frustration and partly because her toes were numb. She sighed, and wrapped her wool scarf tighter around her neck, wishing she had remembered her gloves.

She heard Don whistling. The notes bounced off the walls of the narrow alley lined with aging brick buildings. Penny watched two white paper coffee cups moving like spaceships in a sea of black. "A little peace offering, for being late, as usual," he said. Don handed her the cup. His eyes were as dark as the coffee. She hadn't remembered them being that black. She took a sip and smiled. It was just the way she liked it.

"How did you know?"

"Give me some credit. Oh, and I did give Leo a call to jog my memory."

Penny stared at Don in disbelief.

"I'm just kidding! Have you forgotten coffee at my place, already?"

Penny grimaced and took another sip and let the steam roll across her face. It mingled with the moisture collecting in her eyes. The pain of her break-up with Leo still stung. *Who am I kidding?*

Don handed her a paper mask to place over her nose. "I'm used to the smell, but you may not want to keep the stench in your memory bank the rest of the day."

"Thanks." Penny hooked the band around the fingers of her left hand and drank more of her coffee. The warm liquid wasn't courage, but it did help her feel a bit calmer. "Did you bring the photos?"

"Yes, but I left them in the car. I'm not sure how much they will help us at this point, but I'll be right back." Don handed her both coffee cups and ran back down the alley. She watched Don disappear into the nothingness that was neither darkness nor light. Penny stood there balancing a paper cup in each hand. It reminded her of the scales of justice. Life was a balancing act, she knew, and so was the law. Mother Justice was blind-folded, but Penny swore she peeked now and then, delivering verdicts that favored some over others.

There was movement in the dark alley. Had Don returned so soon? A cloud of heavy smoke drifted toward her. In the haze, she could see a human form—a man—but he was much shorter than Don. Penny's back tightened, pinching her spine like a rod in a vise. Was Sheriff Cerillo haunting her? The figure looked strangely like him. A pistol dangled from his right hand. His brown hair, thin and receding, was lacquered against his skull and rose up in unison with every step he took. She was ready to drop the coffees and pull her revolver from her handbag, but he did not seem to notice her. In fact, the man floated above the filth of the alleyway, looking beyond her to what was left of the entrance to the building where Penny and Don were headed, too.

A hand gripped her shoulder. Penny jerked around. This time the cups of coffee splashed onto the alleyway. "*Señorita*, this is no place for a lovely woman like you." The man's lips were curled above his poorly trimmed mustache. He smelled of too many cigars, and old leather tanned with urine. Her only defense was the look of fearlessness in her eyes. *Don't mess with me!* She wasn't sure how far an attitude would get her. A glint of a badge emerged from his black jacket.

"Who are you?" she asked, refusing to back down.

"He's a security guard, Penny." Don appeared just in time. She was ready to slug the man with her handbag, or worse.

"This *señorita* is with you, Mr. Tellez?"

"Yes, Ricardo. She's with me."

"No problem, miss. I'm sorry if I made you jump." He laughed.

"We're going to be taking another look at the building."

"Not much to look at, except cinders and cement floors," the guard replied.

"Thank you, Ricardo. We'll take it from here." Don placed his hand on Penny's back and ushered her toward the door of the warehouse.

"Watch your step, Penny." Don did not remove his hand from Penny's back but rather pulled her closer. "The first few feet are a jumble of wires and trash. The firemen had to push the debris away from the center of the room to get to the bodies."

Penny's eyes were riveted to the floor. Don was right. The rubble was several inches deep. She watched as her shoes and socks accumulated the pervasive grey dust with each step she took.

Don handed her the "first-on-site" photograph—one that the City's arson photographer had snapped. It was standard procedure that only one investigator initially enters a burnout, to record anything that might otherwise be disturbed with the movement of team members across the crime scene. In the photo, one body was tucked under a metal desk and had remained largely free from any serious burns. The other two weren't that lucky. The first was barely recognizable as a human form, and the other was that of Sonny March. She pointed her fingers in the air, trying to replicate March's pose.

"Don't be alarmed." Don was peering over her shoulder. "Mr. March was probably in shock before fire consumed the place. The other guy has yet to be identified, but his fate was like that of March.

"How about the guy under the table?" It looked as though he was just taking a nap.

"The smoke got him. And miraculously, because he was hiding under the well of the metal desk, the fire missed him. But he was shot, too, and wouldn't have lived long."

Don handed Penny the second picture. It was the close-up of Sonny March. His right arm was raised, and his finger pointed at something or someone.

"Where was he lying?" Penny asked.

Don took the photo out of Penny's hand and walked several paces away. "Right about here."

Penny looked at the location where March had died and then raised her eyes. The roof had been hacked open in spots by the fire department, which had fought the blaze with a ladder truck. Penny could see bits of early morning sky stabbing the otherwise murky room. The rays of light accentuated the dust that floated all around them. She could see Don's face more clearly now. Penny cleared her throat and adjusted her mask.

A web of perspiration was penetrating her blouse. She closed her eyes and waited for any images to appear to give her an idea of what had happened here. She saw what looked like Sonny March pleading for his life, without any luck. She could only see the back of the man waving the pistol. She watched as March dropped to the floor rolling on his side, while his assailant popped three bullets in his torso.

"Don, I think March was turned over onto his back. Somebody was looking for something and I wonder if they found it. He must have still been alive because he lifted his arm to show us something."

"This place has been worked over pretty good."

"Do you mind if I take another look?"

Penny took the photograph of March, and walked the area of the room, where most of the killing had occurred. There were places where a broom had been used to uncover the floor, leaving striations, like tiny evenly placed fingers running through the dust. She stepped carefully to the location where March had been lying and cast her eyes upward to where March had been pointing. It was a corner, piled high with garbage.

Penny's eyes scoured the area and then focused on a cement pillar that bore the weight of part of the building. She blinked. She thought she saw something shiny reflecting in the sun's rays, which were now injecting a little more life into the room.

"Can you see that?" Penny pointed at the girder.

"I can't see anything. Don't let your imagination carry you away. Besides, it's time to go. I've got a meeting at 8 am." Don pulled Penny toward the door.

"Don, there's something up there. I can tell."

"Penny, you've got to let this go. Write up a report on your initial thoughts. I do think you're right, though. March may have been turned on his back by the killer searching for something, but we've got nothing else, and we certainly can't prove it."

Chapter 35

Penny drove to the Starbucks two blocks away and went inside to order an iced latte. Perhaps she would gain some inspiration after a little more caffeine. She took a sip. The espresso was a little too bitter today. She wrinkled her nose at the barista, who knew her well and threw up her hands. Penny walked out the door and into the parking lot. The sun had paid its dues, driving the temperature to bearable levels. Her car thermometer read 50 degrees. It would take a cold day, however, to make Penny drink her non-fat latte hot, bitter or not.

Her next stop was the hardware store, where she asked to see a tall ladder. At $70, it was well beyond her budget. She had to find out what was hiding on the ledge of that girder some other way.

Penny headed to the sporting goods store where she purchased a heavy-duty rope for $15. "Perfect for climbing," the salesman had told her. "Can I interest you in a safety belt? If you're heading to the Hueco Tanks, you can't be too careful."

"No thanks."

She returned to the hardware store and bought six long nails and a rubber-tipped sledgehammer. Another $6. Her hair-brained idea was costing her. This make-shift rappelling gear would have to do. Hopefully, she would not run into Ricardo again.

It was 9:42 am when Penny returned to the place she had parked earlier that day. She left her gun in the glove compartment and gathered her gear and walked down the alley. Daylight exposed the alley's sins. An old wine bottle and a paper bag lay next to an abandoned sweatshirt that looked like it was covered in vomit. She stepped over fast food wrappers, cups, straws, and even an old boom-box. The odor of urine stung her nostrils., causing her eyes to tear. Penny stopped at the door to the burned-out building, leaned in and yelled, "Ricardo! Are you in there?"

She moved quickly, regretting that she had forgotten her mask, which lay on the front seat of her car. She gagged, and spit on the floor.

Penny dropped the rope on the ground, throwing a cloud of dust into her airspace. She coughed again and wiped her face. Why hadn't she thought to buy leather gloves? Penny took two of the nails and hammered them into the cement block wall. It was not an easy task. Her fingers were cut and starting to bleed. She managed to secure the nails at an angle. She would step on the first two nails and hammer her way to the top.

Pulling the rope up with her, Penny pounded as she went. Her chest was aching, and the dust was making it hard to breathe, but she was determined to keep going. At last, she made it far enough to throw the rope over the metal girder that ran the length of the room. All she had to do now was pull herself up the rest of the way. Without gloves, her damp hands could not get a firm enough grip on the rope. She lunged at the rope again with her right hand, but missed, bumping her head against the cement and burning the palms of her hands as she slid down the rope to the floor. She crashed into the slide of the wall, screaming as she fell.

Her head darted back and forth, looking for Ricardo. Had he heard her? Penny struggled to her feet. She had to hurry. Penny placed her feet on the nails again, one by one. She would not be defeated by a few rope burns and a bruised backside. Grunting and panting, she pulled herself up to the top of the pillar. Her heart was pounding. She was so excited to have finally mastered the climb. She peered over the top of the girder. But she saw nothing. *Nothing.*

Ricardo had heard her after all. "*Señorita,* what are you doing here, again? Can I help you?"

"I'm just checking on some things the fire inspector might have missed."

He grabbed her legs, trying to force her to the ground. "Come on, amiga, don't get yourself mixed up in something you can't solve."

"Let me be the judge of what I can solve."

Penny wrapped both arms around the steel beam. "I guess you didn't hear me. Let this be, chica."

Ricardo kept pulling on Penny's legs. In response, Penny kicked Ricardo in the chest. He fell backwards, stumbling onto the cement floor, where his wide body generated a Mahmood of dust.

She reinforced her grip on the metal beam, and when she did, her fingers touched a groove in the metal surface. There was something resting there, and it felt very much like a key.

Ricardo was on his feet. He reminded Penny of an old bull that should have never been allowed in the ring. He was dangerous when angered, even in his overweight state. He staggered and then charged at her again. Penny knew she couldn't hang on for very long. She grabbed for the key and dropped on top of Ricardo. As her shoes hit his midsection, she noticed that his eyes were bloodshot, and his stringy mustache was stuck to his teeth. Ricardo rolled on his side, groaning like a wounded animal. He spat on the floor and cursed her in Spanish words she did not understand.

Penny left the rope and nails behind and dashed down the alley, her discovery tucked safely in her pocket. She slammed her car door and locked it. She fired the engine and rocketed away from the curb. She would call Don later. Now she had to hurry.

Chapter 36

It was almost 11 am. Maria had been in surgery for four hours. Pedro was getting nervous. He did not want to leave the hospital until he knew Maria was out of the operating room and doing well in recovery, but he had a job to do. It would take him two hours to drive back to the ranch, and another hour to get everything ready for the fire. He thought about what tomorrow would bring. He would be out of a job, of course. He had gambled everything on saving Maria's life. Maria would be alive, and Milly would be dead. It was a trade-off he had to make. He would get hired at another stable and find Maria another horse to love.

His butt was hurting from sitting in the plastic chairs. Why did the patient and the visitors in the surgery waiting room both have to be in pain? He stood and stretched his body. He was tired and achy, as if he had fallen off a horse. He leaned over to rub his thighs, which were both asleep. As he looked up, he saw Sheriff Cerillo and Lourdes entering the waiting room.

"Any word on Maria?' Lourdes asked.

"*Nada*," he said. Seeing his girlfriend with the sheriff was not a surprise, of course, but he was still not prepared for how it made him feel looking them both in the eyes. He fought back the anger churning in his throat and the knife-edged words ready to force their way to his mouth. Instead, he turned away from them and looked out the window. He swallowed the bitterness and stared at the Franklin Mountains. Even they were looking dry and brown.

The Southwest had seen little rain the past year, and the fire danger was very high. If a brush fire swept through the Becker barn, it would free Pedro from the act of terror he was going to force on his horses. *His horses?* Yes, they were his! Becker seldom came into the barn anymore. Pedro had loved and cared for them like they were his own, especially after Georgia died. She had been kicked to death by Milly, shortly before

Becker's trainer, Sonny March, had left the ranch in a hurry. No one knew why he quit, but Pedro had his suspicions.

When Georgia died, Maria took over care of Milly as much as she was able. When she visited the ranch, Pedro let her feed the mare, help bathe her and walk her in the lunging pen. Maria would sit in Milly's stall and sing to her, at least until Maria's lips turned blue.

Pedro looked around the waiting room. He had yet to hear a word. If Maria wasn't out of surgery in the next 30 minutes, he would have to leave. At least her mother would be there for Maria when she awakened.

And if things didn't go right with the fire, he might soon be a memory. *Little girls grow up and forget, don't they?*

Dr. Santascoy walked in the room, saving Pedro from his growing anger at having Lourdes and Sheriff Cerillo standing with their hands nearly touching each other. "Maria has made it out of surgery. She will make a full recovery. I'm confident of it."

Pedro rushed to the doctor and shook his hand. "*Muchas Gracias, el doctor.*" The tears blew out of Pedro's eyes like an old faucet that hadn't been used in years. "*Gracias, María, Madre de Dios*"

Lourdes joined Pedro, and the tiny circle of love and approval settled over them. Sheriff Cerillo remained standing near the window. Pedro could see a look of satisfaction in the doctor's eyes. This must be the reason you become a doctor, Pedro thought, for moments like these when a life has been saved.

Knowing Maria would live a normal life, put the iron back in Pedro's spine. He knew he had stepped up and became the man his father never was. The first payment for starting the Becker fire would cover one-tenth of the bill, but still, Willie had promised him something bigger, if he was good at this job. He would be very good.

"When can we see her? Lourdes asked.

"The nurse will come out and tell you. It will be about two hours."

"*Gracias. Gracias.*" Lourdes began to cry, too.

"I'll leave you to celebrate. I've got another surgery in an hour. *Adios.*"

Pedro was a man of his word. It was time to leave his little girl with her mother and the man who wore a badge. He ran from the waiting room, heading for the elevator and to his truck, parked on the street. He had just enough time to get to Becker Ranch.

Chapter 37

Leo had dozed off in the hospital chapel. He had gone there to pray and figure out what to do next. He woke to the creak of the heavy, stained-glass door. He saw Chaplain Brian Dougherty's tall, broad frame filling up most of the small room. Then he remembered why he was here. Lonnie was fighting for her life, and Francisco Parasea was going to live. Parasea would still become sheriff. *Nothing seemed fair.*

"Howdy, Sheriff. Can I be of help?"

Leo's brain was still in a fog. He waited a few beats for his mind to clear before answering. He stretched his arms above his head. His right arm was asleep from leaning against the wooden pew. He rubbed it trying to get his circulation going.

"Yes, you could be a tremendous help to Lonnie Parasea in room 333. It's touch and go with her. A suicide attempt. I can't stay at the hospital any longer. She has no family. Could you keep an eye on her?"

"Certainly."

"Brian, here is my card with my cell phone number. Please call me if things get worse for her. I'll come right back."

"Leo, is there something I can pray with you?"

Leo turned away from the chapel door and looked at the chaplain. He knew he couldn't tell him the truth. "Life is way too complicated right now to list everything. Perhaps you could just pray for God's guidance as I move on with my life."

"I will do so, Leo. You are a good man, and God will provide."

Chapter 38

Penny was not far from a tack shop on Doniphan Drive. She decided to drop by there on her way back to Becker's Ranch to meet up with Ollie. She didn't have much time, but she had to know just what this copper bead was used for. She had a suspicion it had something to do with horses. She fought off a weird wave of nausea as she crawled into her Mustang and headed to the Bridle and Bit Shop, a mile down the road. She never felt sick, so just pushed off this feeling as not enough sleep.

The place was a simple, stand-alone feed store with tack and a few saddles. She had driven by it many times. The bell jingled on the door, letting the non-visible shop keeper know someone had entered. Penny felt comfortable in stores such as this. She could be at ease here regardless of who she was, or what she was wearing.

A tall, blonde man, in his 30's, greeted her as she handed over her phone with the photos of the cylinder. "What is this?" She asked.

"It's an Argentine Dog Bone Bit."

"It's for a dog?" Penny asked in disbelief.

"No, see this snaffle with the copper roller. There are twin double-looped links that attach on either side of the bit. For some reason, they are missing, but I can easily recognize it as a product from Argentina. Some trainers around here use them. It holds the horse's tongue down with less pressure. It's good for young or intermediate horses, or maybe a mare that an owner likes to ride."

"Do you know of any trainers who do use them?"

The clerk opened his computer and tapped a few keys. "Yes, here are three for starters—Randall Richards, Gonzalo Alvarez, and Sonny March have bought them from me."

The name Sonny March rattled around in Penny's brain before it dropped into her gut where it began burning a hole in an already upset stomach. She pressed the palm of her right hand against her midsection trying to extinguish the pain. "Do you have the date when Sonny March last bought one?"

The man tapped a few more keys on his computer. "Yep. It's been almost a year. The last purchase was in December. Now that I look at his record, it seems like he must train a bunch of young horses, because he has purchased more than a dozen in the last two years."

"Thanks."

"No problem. Do you mind if I ask why you want to know?"

Penny handed the store owner her card. "Could you call me if anyone comes in to purchase another one? I'm investigating a fire for the City of El Paso. It may be helpful to know about who buys them and why."

"Absolutely! By the way, my name is Ken. Ken Whatley. Is there anything else you need?"

"Not now, Ken, but I would appreciate using you as a resource."

"Of course." Ken wiped his blonde hair back from his forehead, accenting his eyes that were so blue, Penny thought they surely needed to be outlawed. She remained motionless for a moment. Ken cleared his throat, and this brought Penny back to her business. She shook her shoulders and reached in her bag for a business card and handed it to him. "Thanks, but you already gave me one."

Embarrassed, Penny laughed it off. "It's been one of those days."

"It might help for you to know that each of these guys train quarter horses for the track. I don't know if that means anything to you." He smiled broadly, revealing a mouthful of well-cared-for teeth. His button-down denim shirt was neatly tucked in his Levi's. There was no need for a belt because his jeans rested easily on his slim waist. Ken leaned forward, laying both hands on the counter. He was comfortable in his skin, Penny thought. And she felt comfortable enough to share the case with him, which was very odd, since Penny trusted few, very few men.

"My cell number is on the card. Don't hesitate to contact me if these guys, or anyone else, for that matter, purchases an Argentine Dog Bone Bit."

Ken took the card and put it in his jeans pocket. "I know this may sound forward, but would you be interested in going to the Rio Grande Racetrack at Sunland Park? We might run into the trainers, and I could introduce you. It would be just to advance your investigation, of course."

Penny leaned back on her heels and considered his offer. *Why not*? She needed first-hand knowledge of racing, didn't she? "That's a great idea."

"There's racing at the track on Sunday. You want me to pick you up?"

"I can meet you there. What time?"

"How does 1 pm suit you?"

"You're on! Thanks." Penny hung around the door to the shop, debating whether she should tell Ken more. "Oh, just to place this case in perspective, I want you to know that Sonny March is dead."

Ken's head rocked back. His eyes widened as he took in this information.

"Are we still on for a visit to the track? You can still back out."

Ken rested his fist on his chin and then looked Penny in the eyes. "Yes, count me in!"

Chapter 39

Penny was sitting inside Starbucks, again, and drinking another coffee. She needed a fresh perspective on this case. She allowed the coolness of the iced latte to move through her hands and into her fingertips. She was delighted to know that Ken Whatley was so willing to help her solve this case and meet up with her on Sunday. Would she finally get the answers she needed about what Sonny March had really been doing at the Becker Ranch?

The chatter all around her was comforting. Even though the coffee shop community of strangers didn't realize it, they would help prepare her for the Becker Ranch confrontation that would soon come. Their voices and laughter were instilling her with courage.

The plan was for Ollie to meet up with Penny a mile from the Becker Ranch on Rodeo Ridge. There was an outcropping of rocks that held a fresh spring where ranchers often stopped to drink water. Penny and Ollie would follow each other from there and park their cars at Ron Becker's house. Becker would join them and show them the best places to hide and not draw the suspicions of Pedro, the barn manager.

Penny was counting on surprising the arsonist. She hoped he was not armed. Why would he be, when the assignment was to burn the barn down, not to shoot the horses? Although, killing the horses first would be kinder. The urgency to save these amazing animals pumped adrenaline through her bloodstream more than caffeine.

Penny leaned her elbows on the table, closed her eyes and breathed in deeply. For this plan to work she needed extra insight. That meant calling upon her remote viewing skills. It was the extra edge she had over other detectives—whether anyone wanted to believe in it or not. She did, and this skill had saved her and others several times. She would not give up on her ability to see beyond what was right before her eyes. The question was, could she conduct a remote viewing in the middle of Starbucks? In the essence of time, she had chosen to be immersed in a crowd of chatter. This would be the real test of her capacity to concentrate.

Penny pulled the Argentine Dog Bone Bit out of her jeans. She held it in the palm of her hand. *What did a horse bit have to do with burning down barns?* And why would Sonny March hide it, but then point to its location once he knew he was a dead man? She rolled the copper bead over and over in her hands until the bead and the links attached to it, were warm to the touch. The heat relaxed her hands and then her arms. She fixated on the copper bead; the two stainless rods had once been attached to the horse's bridle.

She used her thumbs to roll the bead around in the palm of her right hand. Rays of light streaming through the window, bounced off the sphere as she twirled it with the tips of her fingers. Round and round the copper bead orbited in her mind's eye. It was now hanging over the horizon like the sun—surrounded by streaks of purple and turquoise. The vision of it thrilled her! *It was magical!*

The heat of this copper cosmos repelled the violence trying so desperately to penetrate the atmosphere. Evil had been banished to the remotest part of the universe and then shoved down a black hole.

Penny breathed in and out rapidly embracing the pure joy she felt. She gripped her prize and drew upon its energy, holding it close to her face. Bursts of yellow and red joined purple and turquoise, lighting up her brain—like fireworks.

Her eyes watered. And then they were burning like hay on fire. Penny squinted, shielding her eyes. Relief came as a shadow fell over the world. The darkness morphed into a figure—a small man—embracing the sun. *How was this possible?*

The man pulled out a hypodermic needle and inserted it inside the sphere, causing a cloud of powder to burst forth. It was hard to see his face because stardust had fallen all over his hands. He licked his fingers and then picked up a towel and polished the metal pieces to a shine. A whinny pierced the air, jerking the man to attention. His head was on a swivel. He looked all around as if danger lurked somewhere in the forgotten sky. His gaze fell upon Penny.

It is Sonny March! Penny had been doing remote viewing long enough to know that while March could see her, he could never hurt her. And besides, wasn't he dead?

It was the same pattern each time she viewed someone remotely. They would stop what they were doing and look straight at her, as if acknowledging her skill. But that was as far as it went. She was safe.

She watched in wonder as March carried the Argentine Dog Bone Bit to a bellowing horse. He lay the piece on the horse's tongue and attached it to the bridle. Penny could see that the horse was a gray one, much like Milly. It groaned and whinnied and nodded its head. Penny knew it was Milly, speaking to her across the cosmos. *What has he done to her?*

Penny was sweating, as if she had run a mile up Transmountain Road. Her hands were shaking so hard she knocked her latte to the floor. A man at a nearby table, picked up her drink. It had barely spilled a drop.

"You, okay?"

"Yeah, I think so. Sorry. Something strange is going on, like someone slipped something in my drink."

"What can I do for you?" he asked.

She dropped the mysterious horse bit into her handbag and used both hands to hold her head. "I'm not sure. Could you just stay close 'til this wears off?" Penny's shaking hands rocked her head back and forth. Her nose was running and dripping onto the table.

The gentleman handed her a tissue.

"Thank you. Can you help me? I'm not sure what is happening. Help me." She knew she was repeating herself. Her fingers would not stop shaking. She was freezing. Her whole body shook until she fell forward and dropped to the floor. Penny's body was wrenching in pain.

When she came to her senses, paramedics were lifting her into an ambulance. She sat up and yelled. "I've got to get out of here!"

The EMT would have none of it. "Look miss, I know a drug overdose, and you've gone on a bender. We'll get you some help at the hospital."

Penny rolled off the cart and fell onto the floor of the vehicle. "I've got to go!"

"Strap her in!" the medic shouted to his colleague.

The EMT pulled out two straps and wrapped them around Penny and rolled her back on the stretcher. Her arms were pressed tightly to her body. She pulled on the straps, but her wrists were unable to release her arms. She could hear the ambulance driver revving the engines.

"Hey, are you okay?" The same kind gentleman from inside the coffee shop was leaning inside the back end of the ambulance.

"I would be okay if I could just use the bathroom."

"Sir, get out of the way. We've got to get this woman to the hospital!"

"Sir, I'm Dr. Obregon, this woman's doctor. I would like to release this woman into my care."

The EMT looked down at Penny and then back at the doctor. "Are you sure? She seems out of control."

"I'm pretty sure what has happened will soon pass," the doctor replied.

"Kill the engine, Miguel!" The EMT took in a deep, doubtful breath and began unhooking the straps that confined Penny to the gurney.

"You're sure?" The medic asked again, while shaking his head in disbelief.

Penny used Dr. Obregon's arm as a crutch, as she stumbled back into Starbucks and headed to the restroom, which was mercifully open. "Thank you so much. Can you wait for me?"

The doctor nodded his head.

She locked the door and stood in front of the mirror. Her face was pale, as if the blood had drained out of her head and landed in her feet, which were on fire. Her hands were splotchy and swollen. Penny leaned over the sink and threw water on her face. The wrenching of her stomach dropped her head over the sink, where the dry heaves rippled through her body like a train hauling box cars full of coal.

When the heaving stopped, she lay her head against the rim of the basin until her breathing slowed. She pulled a couple of paper towels from the dispenser and soaked them with water. Penny wiped her face and arms and then rinsed her mouth out from the faucet. Tears were streaming down her eyes, and they were stinging, as if she had been running through acid.

Penny was no fool. She had never taken an ounce of any kind of illegal drugs, but she knew she had been exposed to some bad stuff. She wiped the tears and perspiration from her face and wondered what to do about this new knowledge. *Run*? She considered it, but she was no quitter. And then it sunk in. Something was inside that copper bead!

When Penny exited the bathroom, Dr. Obregon was leaning against the wall in the hallway. "Thank you so much for waiting for me." She pulled the copper bead out of her bag and showed it to the doctor. "There is something inside this thing that has made me very sick."

"I was on my way to the hospital. I could run some tests in our lab, if you thought it would help."

Penny managed a smile. "I'm a U.S. Marshal and I need to get to the bottom of this. Lives are at stake."

"I'll take this directly to the hospital and rush it through." He took a napkin and wrapped the bone bit inside. "You should hear from me within a few hours."

Chapter 40

Leo hated hospitals. People he loved died in hospitals and Lonnie was still fighting for her life. He cared deeply about what happened to Lonnie, but he could not control the outcome. It would be best for him to stay as far away as possible. Leo still had six more weeks as sheriff, and he would do the best he could to finish out his term with class. He had left the chaplain in prayer. What more could he do?

Leo pulled out of the hospital parking lot and blended into the traffic on Mesa. It was bumper to bumper heading east since the entire westside of El Paso was under construction. Paisano Drive was closed, and I-10 was limited to one or two lanes. Even Transmountain Road, the mile-high highway through the Franklin Mountains, was a victim of the sledgehammer. El Paso leaders were never much for planning, and this time, simultaneous highway and road construction projects had placed a strangle-hold on the city's westside.

Leo looked to his right and saw workers tending to the installation of the trolley planned for downtown. *Good grief!* It might be nice in a few years, but for now, it was a nightmare for his deputies trying to get from one side of El Paso to another. Commuters were angry. And no one had even considered that these roadblocks could put a serious dent in the security of the whole county.

Keeping El Paso County residents safe was doubly hard on the Sheriff's office, thanks to the daily arrival of 60,000 Mexican nationals who lived in Ciudad Juárez and worked in El Paso. Each morning, they crossed one of the city's six international bridges to get to their jobs or to school. The wait times going back and forth across the border could run into hours. It was not an easy commute, and all the construction only exacerbated the issue. But today, perhaps it wasn't just the traffic that was making Leo angry. After all, it would not be his problem much longer. He pushed his patrol car toward the middle of town and finally pulled over and parked. Leo had Penny on speed dial.

"Hello, stranger," Penny answered. "How are you?"

"I was wondering how your meeting with Ron Becker went?"

"Oh, it was very interesting! And you would appreciate this. Ron Becker's former trainer, Sonny March, was one of the casualties in Don's arson investigation. You always told me there was no such thing as a coincidence in law enforcement."

"How are things going with Don?"

"Don, is not the ogre you made him out to be."

A small shiver rippled through Leo's body. This was not the news Leo wanted to hear, but he was not surprised. Don was great at impressing women, and most people, for that matter. He was disappointed, however, that Penny had fallen for his charms. Should he warn Penny off, or leave the situation alone? He ground his teeth together, until his jaw ached.

Leo lied. "I agree. Don's a good guy." His stomach tightened.

"I found something at the building, but I haven't told Don about it yet. He doesn't know I went back after our visit. I'm chasing down a lead before I fill him in."

"Do you have time for coffee?"

"No, unfortunately, I've got to get to Becker's ranch. We are planning to surprise the arsonist tonight, and at the very least, hold him off from burning down Becker's barn."

"You are doing this yourself?" Leo was stunned. Beads of sweat gathered on his forehead. The midday sun was pouring through the car window. "How about Johnny Trejo? Didn't he offer to help you?" Now Leo's stomach churned like it was filling with wet cement. The pain was excruciating. He rubbed his midsection with his left hand, trying to stave off the inevitable dose of Gaviscon. Heat was building up in the car without the air conditioning on. He started the engine, hoping a dose of cool air would keep his head from exploding.

"That's a long story. Let's just say that Johnny is laid up for a while with injuries from a meet-up with an International Harvester. His mom, Ollie, is going to be my back-up."

Leo was shocked. He didn't know Ollie, but how much help could she be? He looked at the digital clock on his patrol car and wondered if he had the time, or the authority to join her. "Penny, I can't let you put yourself in such a dangerous position. This is my fault."

"Ollie is a crack shot and knows her guns. She gave me a quick lesson with a rifle and a pistol, and I've got your dad's revolver. We are ready to rock and roll. Trust me!"

"I'll contact Sheriff Cerillo to provide you back up."

"No! Please don't. He's bad news. He came to Becker's ranch yesterday, and he expressed no interest in helping. I'm not sure what he is up to, but it's not anything good."

"Penny, I'm begging you not to go."

"Too late, Leo. I'm almost to the ranch."

Leo remained on the side of the road wondering what he could do to help Penny. This was his fault. He had encouraged her to take the case, thinking he could somehow stay engaged with her. And now she was heading for trouble.

He looked up Sheriff Cerillo's number. Penny might think the sheriff didn't care, but Leo was certain he would. No law officer who took the job seriously would look the other way when a crime was going down.

After a few short rings, the sheriff picked up. "Hi, this is the Sheriff."

"Estefan, this is Leo Tellez in El Paso."

"Hey, Leo, *que pasa*?

"I've got a big favor to ask you, and I know you will want to help resolve it."

Chapter 41

Pedro's engine stalled about five miles from the Becker ranch. He jumped out of his truck and lifted his hood. The massive clam shell of steel wouldn't stay up on its own so Pedro ran along the roadway until he found a stick that would keep the hood propped open at least half-way. He felt like a hermit crab forcing his body inside the compartment, which was so dark, he could barely see the engine. Sweat soaked his forehead and stung his eyes. He needed a flashlight. Pedro backed out of the compartment, but not before cracking his head on the edge of the hood. "OUCH!" Blood was dripping down his face, and he wiped it off with the sleeve of his shirt as he climbed back out in search of a flashlight. Pedro finally found one under the seat and clicked it on. It had just enough juice to generate a wavering stream of light. It was better than nothing!

Pedro crawled back on top of the bumper and once more squeezed his body inside the engine compartment. It smelled like oil and dirty rags. The fluttering light hovered over the engine, offering just enough light to see a crack in the oil pan. The pan was covered with black goop and spilling its guts on to the engine. Pedro was surprised there was any oil left.

Pedro figured that even if he was able to drive his truck back to the Becker Ranch, his chance of getting the truck to start still another time, was slim. there would be little chance for an escape once he started the fire. His truck could not run without oil So Pedro would have no choice but to die with the horses. Pedro shuddered at the thought of never seeing Maria again. He would never brush the sides of a quarter horse nor hear the soft nickers of satisfaction coming from those in his care. And he would never have another chance to win Lourdes back. His body shook. He dropped his shoulders and cried. There was no turning back now.

Pedro returned to the cab of truck and climbed in. He turned the key, but the engine still would not turn over. He dropped his sweating forehead onto the steering wheel and cried. "*Mi Dio. Por que me estas haciendo esto*?" Pedro sobbed. He was at the end of everything.

The honking of a car horn jerked Pedro's head up. He could see the flashing lights of a police car in his rearview mirror. A feeling of dread dropped into the depths of his gut—just like a rock caught in the stomach of a horse which was always bound to cause colic. The dark shadow of Sheriff Cerillo fell over his passenger window. He could see the sheriff's badge in the sunlight, burning a hole in his shirt. *If only it really would.*

The sheriff was knocking on the window. Pedro cranked down the window and looked at the sheriff with a blank stare. *Now what? What else could go wrong?*

"Pedro, this is your lucky day. I normally don't take this backroad—too many rocks, you know? What's the problem?"

"My truck is dead. It needs major help, which I don't have the time or the money to handle right now."

"Can I give you a lift?"

"Sure. That would be great. I'm headed to Becker's."

"I'll call for a tow truck and have it hauled to the ranch. You can deal with it from there. The tow is on me."

Pedro was puzzled. *Why would the sheriff be nice to him? Because he now possessed the love of his life?* "Thank you, Sheriff." He would not let the sheriff see the pain that was gutting his heart. Pedro slipped into the passenger side of the patrol car and slammed the door. Fighting back the tears, he turned his face toward the window. The patrol car roared onward, gathering rocks and grit in its undercarriage. Pedro imagined his body falling under the wheels of the car, crushing his lifeless form into the earth.

"I'm about to confide in you, Pedro. It is important that you tell no one else."

"Of course." What in the world could the sheriff want to tell him that no one else would even care to know? *That he loved Lourdes? That he loved Maria?* The combination of fear and guilt grabbed at his gut and churned his stomach into knots. His swollen feet, crammed in his cockroach killers, were killing him.

"I've got the rest of your payment for burning down the barn." He tapped his fingers on a package that lay between them. "Willie gave it to me."

Pedro was confused. *The sheriff is in on the barn fires*? He turned in his seat and looked at the sheriff, who had his eyes on the road. They bumped along knocking them both into the car doors. A rock flew in the air and bounced off the driver's side window.

"Darn these gravel roads!" The sheriff pounded his fist against the steering wheel.

"You have my money?" Pedro asked this in disbelief and crippled by fear. He gripped the side door handle, knowing it was too late to escape.

"Yeah. Ain't that something? I didn't know who the Betas hired to burn down Becker's barn. But then I saw you leaving the Rodeo Bar, just as I was getting there. I went to meet Willie, too. He didn't say who was doing it, but I knew by the way you ran or rather, skidded out the door, that it was you!" Cerillo laughed and wiped his mouth, where his mustache had collected some saliva.

"I'm paying for Maria's surgery. No other way to save her." Pedro thought he owed the sheriff an explanation for committing such a horrible crime.

He noticed that the Sheriff went quiet. He didn't say anything else as they rode along, but just continued tapping the fingers of his right hand on the steering wheel. Pedro stiffened his back, preparing for what might come next.

The sheriff pulled up in front of the barn. The large black crow screeched his welcome. Pedro knew it was the bird that was always dropping feathers and pooping on his barn floor. He cursed the bird under his breath, grasped the handle to the door, and jerked it open.

"Look, Pedro. Now that I know it is you, I can offer you some protection. For a price, of course. How about 10% of your take?"

Pedro knew he had no choice but to agree to the deal. He shook his head. The Sheriff peeled off several one hundred-dollar bills from the top of the stack.

"I was gonna' take half of your score, but now that I know it is for Maria, I'll cut you some slack." The sheriff handed him what was left of the money, and Pedro looked at him with an emotionless stare. "*He hecho un trato con el diablo.*"

The sheriff howled with laughter at the joke of making a deal with the devil. He slapped his neatly manicured fingers against the steering wheel.

Pedro jumped out of the SUV and stumbled into the gravel driveway. The only good thing to come of this day would be his own death by fire. He deserved it. But he felt terrible for Lourdes. She didn't deserve a life with this horrible man.

Chapter 42

Penny entered the Flowing Well Park at 3:30 pm. She saw Ollie deep in conversation with one of the local ranchers. She waved at Penny.

"This is Sampson Dales. He lost a couple of horses in a barn fire last spring."

"Howdy, ma'am. Ollie tells me you are going to take on these killers." Instead of giving Penny a mocking look, he seemed genuinely appreciative. "Could you use my help?"

"Sir, this could be very dangerous." Penny said.

"Danger and I shook hands years ago. I served in 'Nam as a sniper. The experience leaves you numb and fearless."

"Thank you so much for your service." Penny knew it would be foolhardy to invite another person into the mix of protecting Becker's barn. "But I can't ask you to do that."

"I live up the road a piece. I'll get my Springfield M-1A out of the closet. It's been lonely and needs some love." Sampson chuckled, gathering joy as his voice moved up his throat and out into the light of the New Mexico sunshine.

"If you are sure," Penny said. There was hesitation in her voice, and Sampson caught it.

"Believe me, there would be no greater satisfaction than finding the guys who killed my mares."

Penny and Ollie shook Sampson's hand and left him to fill up a five-gallon water jug. He agreed to meet them in front of Ron Becker's ranch house at 6 pm. This would give Penny time to explain to Becker what the new plan now entailed. He should be thrilled to have reinforcements.

Ollie decided to ride with Penny to keep the number of cars at the ranch house to a minimum. As they drove down Rodeo Ridge, Penny saw a tow truck loading what looked like Pedro's truck onto a flatbed.

Penny pulled in front of the Becker home and shut off the engine. The air was surprisingly still. There was no wind howling across the high desert, stirring up the dust. The tranquility of the day did not offer a clue as to what might lie ahead. She glanced at the yellow rockers on Becker's front porch and remembered the picnic she and Johnny had enjoyed there. The thought of his hands running over hers gave Penny a chill. She shook herself and groaned, "Ohhh."

"Are you okay?" Ollie asked.

"Yes, just thinking about Johnny."

"I hope they were good thoughts." Ollie winked.

"Always." She reached over and touched Ollie's arm. "Thank you, again, for being here for me."

Ollie blew off the compliment. "Let's get this show on the road!" She opened her door and jumped out.

Penny popped the trunk and headed to the back of the car, where they had stashed Ollie's weapons. It was 4:00 pm and there was no sign of Becker. His truck was not even on the property. "Could it be a planned distraction?"

"We will have to plan carefully where we hide," Penny said. "I noticed Pedro's truck on the side of the road. Perhaps we caught a break. If he can't drive, he can't escape either."

Ollie was focused on the guns and yanked the first two rifles out of the back of the car and carried them to Becker's front porch. "Distraction? I'll give him a distraction!" Ollie yelled and took long, purposeful strides back to the car, where she pulled a portable gun safe out of the trunk.

Penny searched the horizon for any sign of Ron Becker's truck rumbling up the driveway. *Nothing.* She looked over at Ollie, intent on setting up an arsenal of weapons on Becker's porch. *Were they fools?* Had Becker chickened out? She took a big breath, trying to gather the clarity to consider how Ollie and she could confront the arsonist without Becker. The promise of Sampson Dale's help was looking more and more welcome.

In the distance, she saw an SUV pulling onto the road that led to the barn. Penny soon realized it was a sheriff's vehicle. She watched as Sheriff Cerillo rolled to a stop in front of the barn's double doors. Pedro hopped out of the sheriff's car and waved goodbye. She was thankful they had decided to hide their cars at Becker's house.

"Follow me," Penny whispered. She helped Ollie carry her guns on to the porch, and then through the front door, which was thankfully unlocked. They house was empty of life and yet, the place was full of departed thoughts and fears. Georgia Becker's portrait still hung above the fireplace but today she seemed angry, as if even she knew their plan would fail. The afternoon heat had stagnated the air. Penny wasn't sure how long she could last inside. Not a window had been opened for circulation. *Where is Becker?* It felt like he had abandoned his home.

Penny took Ollie into Georgia's office, where the television cameras were still operational. She switched on a fan to get the air stirring in the room. The heat was almost unbearable.

Ollie was amazed she see Pedro walking around inside the barn. "Well, isn't this handy!"

Pedro's work appeared to be routine. He strolled down the aisle of the barn. He didn't seem agitated at all. Perhaps Becker had been exaggerating the risk. Or maybe he didn't understand Spanish as well as he thought he did.

Penny opened a bottle of water and handed it to Ollie, and then uncapped one for herself. "We may be in for a long night." She looked out the west side window where a shadow of the sun hung tentatively in the overcast sky. Would it set tonight or not? "Ha. Ha. Ha!' Penny laughed out loud at the thought of the sun not doing what it had always done for thousands of years. Penny's ill-conceived plan to stop the arsonist, however, appeared to be unraveling as the day grew older. Her driving ambition to succeed sometimes got the best of her. Was this one of those days?

"Is anybody here?" Penny and Ollie turned at the sound of Sampson Dales' voice. Before he wandered too far afield, Penny headed to the front door to greet him, with Ollie following her.

"Ah, there you are. I felt weird entering someone's house, but I had been hanging out in the driveway for ten minutes."

"Sorry about that," Penny said. "I wasn't sure you were serious about helping out."

"I never joke around about bullets." Dales said, patting his magazine case strapped to his belt. He rested his rifle on his hip and broke into a smile, which immediately put Penny's concerns to bed. The heat of the room was already taking its toll on his skin. Dale's complexion glistened. A drop of sweat trickled down the side of his face.

"I need a high point for getting a bead on this guy." Dales switched his stance from relaxed to stiff. Penny noticed that his fingers were twitching.

"Let's try the second floor," Penny suggested, trying to avert any emotional reflex from Dales.

"I'm going to keep an eye on the television cameras," Ollie said.

Penny led Dales up the curving staircase.

"Whew! My wife, Jan, was right. This place is over the top." Dales stopped on the staircase and rubbed his hands across the flowing mane of the carved horse. "Who thinks this stuff up?"

"Your wife has been inside the Becker home?"

"Yep. Jan used to visit Georgia all the time to play bridge and to buy her riding competition outfits. She competes in the Amateur Quarter Horse shows."

Penny was confused. "What did Georgia Becker have to do with riding clothes?" They had arrived at the top of the staircase, which gave them a view of a long hall, with doors on either side.

"I know Georgia Becker used to keep her competition apparel business upstairs somewhere," Dales said. "My wife always bought clothes from her for her horse shows."

"Really?" Penny said. "There is much more to this woman than I gave her credit for."

"She was pretty well known in Quarter Horse circles across the country."

They passed two bedrooms, one of which Penny surmised was Ron Becker's because she noticed the large, unmade bed and a pair of men's pajamas tossed in a heap. She had not followed Johnny upstairs when he put Becker to bed. The other bedroom was more pristine and looked like it was seldom used. Finally, they arrived at the end of the hall where there was a hand-carved wooden circular staircase that mimicked the large banister on the first floor, only in greatly scaled down proportions. Dales shook his head, before following Penny up the steps which opened into a huge room that stretched the length of the house. There were several wall-to-wall hanging racks full of costumes, in a variety of colors, and sparkling jewels.

"Wow. I didn't realize that riders were so competitive," Penny mused.

"You've never seen anything quite like the world of horse shows. I know that the Arabian owners are over the top, but Quarter Horse riders are pushing the limit, too."

"How much does one of these outfits cost?"

"They can run into the thousands. Of course, I never let my wife spend like that, but typically to get decked out for a competition could set me back several hundred dollars."

Penny ran her fingers over a line of shirts, with jewels that looked like real gemstones but on closer look, she saw they were made of highly polished glass. Her eyes looked up, resting on a row of helmets. "Do all riders were helmets?"

"They should, but most choose a cowboy hat, unless, of course, when you are competing in dressage. Not too many Quarter Horse riders go that route, though. The Quarter Horse Association in New Mexico is pushing for protective helmets for adults in competition as well as while workers are around the barn. Kids fourteen and under are already required to wear a helmet in competition, but it differs from state to state."

"Did your wife know Georgia well?"

"In their younger days, they were best of friends, but Jan said Georgia started acting strange and withdrawn, so they gradually grew apart."

"Did Jan ever mention that Georgia looked like she might be using drugs?"

"Funny you should say that. Jan did tell me sometimes Georgia's eyes looked like they were on fire. Or she said Georgia would shift her eyes left and right. Jan just couldn't take the bizarre behavior. It wasn't all the time, but when Georgia did act that way, it was hard to be around her."

"I wonder if Georgia had on a helmet when she got kicked by Millie." Penny's eyes made a circle of the room, as she considered that. She noticed a large window that appeared to look out over the barn. "How about this?"

Dales checked out the window and opened it with ease. He got out his gun, which was slung over his right shoulder. He rested the butt of the rifle on the windowsill and crouched on one knee. "Just like I like it!"

"So, we can stay in touch, what is your cell phone number?" Penny was pulling hers out of her jeans pocket, as she asked.

"Don't have a cell phone," Dales mumbled. "But I did bring Jan's."

They exchanged numbers and tested them to make sure they could communicate, even out in the middle of nowhere. "Success!" Penny cheered.

"Where's Ron Becker?" Dales asked.

"I'm not sure," Penny answered. "We may be all on our own with this. Is that okay?"

"A sniper is a lonely job. I'm used to it, so don't you worry about me."

Chapter 43

Leo did the unthinkable and called the New Mexico State Police headquarters in Las Cruces. "Hello, this is Sheriff Tellez in El Paso County. Is Captain Trejo in?"

"I'm sorry, Sheriff, but Captain Trejo has taken the day off. Can I leave him a message or can someone else help?"

"How about his mobile phone? That would be a big-time saver."

The dispatcher obliged and rolled off a string of numbers that Leo wrote on a note pad and golf pencil he kept in his shirt pocket. He pulled out his cell phone, stopping short of pressing in Johnny's number. If he called, Leo would be admitting defeat. But he loved Penny and that meant making the right choices for her. He couldn't help Penny, but he could do the next best thing, and that was finding someone who could. Captain Trejo could be his backup plan in case Sheriff Cerillo's help was a bust.

The phone was growing warm in his hands as he sat in his car, suspended in thoughts of what he had given up by playing house with Adriana. She had since left El Paso and returned to Los Angeles where she was a partner in a law practice. Apparently, Adriana was only practicing, and their relationship was just one of convenience. By the time Leo had returned to his senses, Penny had refused to even meet him for coffee until she had joined him on election night.

He pounded his phone against the steering wheel. "Idiot! You idiot!"

Tears were falling down his face, joining the sweat soaking his uniform.

The thought of Penny trying to take on an arsonist without professional help was foolhardy. The guy would certainly be desperate to get the job done, and Penny would be a small obstacle to this end. She might die in the fire, too. Leo pressed in Johnny's number and waited. It rang and rang, and finally Johnny's voice mail clicked on.

"This is Captain Trejo with the New Mexico State Police. If this is an emergency, please dial 911."

This was an emergency for sure, Leo thought. *Johnny, why aren't you answering your phone?* No self-respecting law officer would let a call go to voicemail. Leo remembered that Penny had mentioned something about Johnny being injured. He punched in the numbers again. Once again, the call went to voicemail.

"Captain, this is Leo Tellez. Penny is in real trouble and could use some back up. She said something about getting help from your mother, but you know she will need more than that. No offense, but cartels play for keeps. Please call me back and let me know if you can get there to her in time. Thanks."

Leo pounded his fist against the steering wheel. Desperate to give Penny back up, he called Don.

"Hello, Leo. You, okay?"

"Don, Penny is in trouble. She is trying to take on Becker's arsonist alone. Could you leave now and get to the Becker Ranch?"

"I'm just finishing up in the office. I can be there in 90 minutes. Is that too late?"

"Late is better than nothing. I'll send you the GPS coordinates. Bring your Glock."

"Are you coming, too?"

"No, I need to stay close. We've got an issue here I should tend to. Besides, I've learned my lesson about interfering in Penny's cases when they are in New Mexico."

Leo ended the call. There was nothing more he could do now. He had sent in the Calvary, and unfortunately, he wasn't mounting for the charge. Leo leaned his head against the bucket seat and shut his eyes. His life as El Paso County Sheriff would soon be over, and now his chances with Penny, seemed doomed, too. The tears returned. He had told Paco that real men cry, but he wasn't feeling all that grown up. As a kid, Leo recalled running into the house when he had skinned his knee after falling out of a Mesquite tree in the backyard. His mother took him in her arms and rubbed his back and shoulders. After he had calmed down, she carefully treated the wound with antibacterial cream and wrapped his knee in a bandage. She wiped his tears and told him, "It will heal, Leo. Everything heals with time."

Chapter 44

Johnny slipped out of bed and pulled on a pair of boxers, sweatpants, and a sweatshirt. They were the softest things that his skin would tolerate. He looked in the mirror one more time, and almost laughed, except that he caught himself, because the muscles in his face really hurt. He looked more like the walking dead rather than a man of the law. He would never watch those shows on TV again.

He picked up his cell phone and noticed there was a message. It was Sheriff Tellez telling him something he already knew—that he was an idiot for letting his mother do his work for him. He clenched both fists and pounded the wall, an act he immediately regretted.

He grabbed the keys to his Jeep and walked through the kitchen. On the table was a note from his mother. "Johnny, there is a sandwich in the fridge." He opened the refrigerator and pulled the sandwich out and placed it in a brown paper bag that his mother had also left on the table. "Come if you can," she had also written. She had underlined the word, "can." It was his mom's way of saying she could sure use his help.

It was now 5:15 pm. He could be at the Becker Ranch in 40 minutes. He hoped that was enough time to provide back-up for the two women in his life he deeply loved. He had floated the word "love" out there. Johnny had no idea if Penny had feelings for him. He thought she did, but the way she acted every time he tried to hold her, she shrank back inside herself. It didn't matter if the love went just one way. Johnny would be there for her.

As he climbed into his Jeep, he thought about Leo again. It must have taken some courage for Leo to call him. His estimation of the man rose above loathing. Maybe Penny was still in love with Leo. Johnny couldn't blame her. He was everyone's hero.

Johnny had even considered joining the El Paso County Sheriff's Department because Leo Tellez was recognized as one of the best lawmen in the nation. Who wouldn't want to work with him? But Johnny's dad had been a state trooper, and he felt an allegiance to his father who had worked his way up the ranks until he was a commander. Johnny was now on his way, too, as Captain in charge in Las Cruces. And besides he would have never met Penny on that windy stretch of I-10 where her car was stranded, and a dead man lay in front of her grill.

Johnny punched in her number on speed dial and listened to it ring before Penny's voice came on asking him to leave a message. "Penny, I'm on my way. Tell my mom. Don't take any chances, please."

Johnny climbed in his Jeep and turned the key. Nothing. The battery was dead and so were Johnny's chances of reaching Penny and his mother in time.

Chapter 45

Leo was still laying his head against the steering wheel when the call came from the hospital. "Sheriff, this is Chaplain Dougherty. You asked me to call you if there was a change in Lonnie Parasea's condition. She has fought back from a near death encounter. She's asking for you."

"I'm on my way. Thank you."

Leo looked at his face in the rearview mirror. His eyes were red from weeping. It didn't matter anymore. He had already sacrificed his pride in the name of recklessness. If folks thought he looked weak, so be it. He was a broken man, and he had to deal with it. For the first time, Leo began thinking about retiring from law enforcement. Without being Sheriff, the passion was not there. While he was flattered to be courted by Federal agencies, his commitment ran deeper than a federal job would allow. And besides, as a Fed he might be transferred away from El Paso, and that was not acceptable. He had some money saved. And perhaps his pension from the El Paso City Police Department where he had served for almost fifteen years might be enough to carry him through. Four years as sheriff were not enough for the county to pay him anything on the retirement front, but with careful planning he could live frugally. He would have to.

As he drove to the center of the city, Leo began thinking about Lonnie, and how much he enjoyed being around her. He was thrilled to learn she had pulled through this horrific suicide attempt.

Perhaps he could play a more important role in her life. Heaven knows, she could use a friend. And so could he.

By the time Leo pulled into the hospital parking lot, he had made up his mind to ask Lonnie out to dinner when she had fully recovered—as friends, of course. Leo would have a difficult time justifying anything remotely close to a romantic relationship at this point. Penny Larkin was still front and center in his heart, but it was time he looked at life beyond her. In his temperamental gut he felt Penny wasn't coming back. Maybe losing the election was a gift. This was a chance to take a closer look at his life. One thing was certain. He did not want to go on living without someone special in his life. He had spent too many hours at the gravesite of Alejandra to realize that memories were no substitute for the warmth of the human touch.

Leo found Lonnie sitting up in bed and sipping on a glass of water. She smiled at him. "Thank you for coming."

"You look so much better," Leo said.

"I am doing so well. The doctor was very surprised."

"How can I help you, Lonnie?"

"You've already done so much, but I have one more favor to ask. Could you forget everything I told you about— you know—my secret?"

"I would never divulge what you told me in confidence."

"Well, I was pretty sure you wouldn't, but Francisco came by to see me, and we are going away together."

"What about his being sheriff?" Leo stared at her in disbelief.

"He told me he isn't cut out for it. He just wants to be with me. He asked for you to come up to his room once you've talked with me. I think he wants to thank you for saving his life and to tell you in person about his decision."

Leo's eyes moistened, and he blinked, trying to keep the hot tears from burning his eyelids. "Francisco is one very lucky man. To give up this victory for love is beyond comprehension for most folks."

"Just go see him. He's been moved to room 452." She took Leo's hand and squeezed it. Tears dripped down her cheeks.

Leo felt the warmth of her touch. Francisco was indeed a very lucky man. He leaned over and kissed Lonnie on the forehead and wiped away her tears. "You have my card. Call me if you need me for anything."

"Thank you, Leo. I don't think you'll be hearing from us again. We are heading to Mexico, to his family's ranch. We can have a good life there."

Leo turned away from Lonnie and moved quickly out the door, but not before banging his bad shoulder against the casement. His heart was pounding in his chest, as if he had lost something precious to him. His steps quickened and his arms moved up and down in a pendulum fashion, propelling him toward Francisco's room. Francisco had fought like a warrior to beat Leo in this election and now he was not only giving it up, but he was also taking Lonnie with him and leaving Leo unemployed. This news was a splinter in Leo's soul, and he knew the solution was to yank it out as fast as possible. He picked up speed.

Leo reached the fourth floor via the stairs, taking a moment to catch his breath. His shoulder still ached, and his chest felt tight. Was he having a heart attack or was this how losing really feels? *Oh, yeah. This is how it feels.* He remembered losing Alejandra and the pain was similar. It buzzed through his midsection like a chain saw. The loss of Lonnie even before the relationship had a chance to bloom, accentuated the pain of losing Penny. Up until this very moment, he had refused to admit that Penny was really gone. This realization was his Black & Decker moment. The chain saw was ripping his heart right out of his chest.

Leo found #452 with little effort. He knew these halls, as if he owned them. He had witnessed so much sorrow in these rooms. Perhaps soon, the memory of Lonnie would turn out to be a happy time. He had, for certain, saved both her and Francisco. *How ironic is that?*

Leo knocked on Francisco's door.

"Come in, *por favor*. Ah, Sheriff. Thank you for coming to see me. I wanted to thank you for saving my life. My doctor told me it was you who did CPR until the EMTs could get there. You are a true hero in my book. I will never forget your kindness and courage."

"There is no need to thank me. It's just part of the job." He immediately regretted those words, realizing that Parasea could not measure up to the responsibility. He had sworn on the Bible to preserve and protect. It was apparently not in Parasea's DNA and that was okay. Law enforcement was not for everyone.

"That's just it, Leo. May I call you Leo?"

Leo nodded his head.

"I realized that God is giving me a third chance at life. First, He saved me from drug addiction, and second, thanks to you, He kept my heart beating. Now I am having a third chance with Lonnie. I am not cut out to be a lawman, and I plan to resign."

"Francisco, this is premature. I know you are reacting to a weakened state from being shot, but you will bounce back."

"Lonnie has told me all you have done for her, and thanks to you, as well, I will still have her in my life. But the only way to be with her is to leave the country. My family still has a ranch in Mexico. It's isolated and away from the eyes of Mob bosses. She told me that she shared with you, her circumstances. I was foolish and only thought of my own selfish desire to have a bigger impact on the drugs moving across the border. But at what cost? Getting shot was the best thing that has happened to me. I finally woke up to the fact that I need Lonnie in my life and nothing else matters."

Chapter 46

Leo shoved his feet forward—his knees aching —as he inched his way to the hospital exit. His legs were lead pipes. His blood felt like it was pooling in his ankles. He searched for his pulse. His fingers were cold and damp as they ran over his wrists chasing after his heartbeat. He could see the green illuminated sign directing him to make a right turn. Instead, he found himself at the doors to an oncology lab. Why were hospitals always a labyrinth of passageways to clinics and laboratories and never to the place you needed to be?

Leo knew if he could just get into the sunlight of the parking lot, he would feel better. His mind was a mangled state of anger and loss. And still the exit alluded him. Being disoriented in a hospital he thought he knew so well was only deepening his feelings of frustration. Gone was the chance to get to know Lonnie better. Gone was his life with Penny. Gone was his career as Sheriff. And to make matters worse, Leo had lost the election to someone who didn't want the job. Now the County Commissioners would likely appoint one of their cronies. Leo had seen that happen many times. The office of sheriff was now a political football to be kicked over the goal post by the highest bidder.

Leo pulled on to I-10 and headed to the northeast side of town. He would clear his head amid the tombstones and talk this feeling of loss over with Alejandra. She always understood him best.

Chapter 47

Pedro gulped water from a tin cup. It was good and cold coming from the well feeding the barn and corrals. He had not realized how thirsty he was. When had he had anything to eat or drink? He refilled his cup and sat on a wooden bench trying to figure out how to solve one big problem. He now had the last wad of cash for Maria's surgery in his pocket. It was much more money than he had expected, and this was a reason to celebrate. With his truck out of commission, however, he couldn't just hang around while the barn burned. The best thing, the only choice he had left, was to die in the fire. But that didn't get the money to the hospital to pay Maria's bill.

If Pedro had been thinking straight, he would have asked the sheriff to take the money to the hospital for him, but there was no guarantee he could trust him. And the thought of Sheriff Cerillo coming to Maria's rescue made him furious. Pedro took another swallow of water and decided on a plan. He would give his truck another try. If he could get it started, he would leave it running, get the fire going, and then head to the hospital before anyone knew the barn was burning. November was making short work of the day, and Pedro needed to get ahead of it. He had made a big decision. His goal to avoid dying in the fire if possible. He wanted to be there for Maria, and being dead, he realized, was not the best option. Having Sheriff Cerillo raise Maria would be unthinkable! Besides, Maria relied on him, and with her mother thinking more about Sheriff Cerillo and less about her daughter, made it even more important live!

Pedro yanked off his dress boots and laced up his pair of work boots. He brushed the dust off the turquoise roses winding around the shanks of the boots, admiring them perhaps for the last time. But he couldn't bear the thought of them getting roughed up or burned up in the fire. He coaxed his beloved cockroach killers inside the soft cloth bag and carried the bag out to his truck. Just looking at the shoe bag made him sad.

He pulled one of the boots back out of the sack and traced his fingers across the black leather again and wiped more dust off with his sleeve. Other than his daughter, these boots were the only things he prized in his life. A Mexican man is known by his boots. They bring him respect and dignity among his friends and family. There was no way he would ever risk even the possibility of dying in a fire with these boots on his feet. His worn-out work boots would suit him. Somehow knowing that his boots might have to live on without him brought him some comfort.

Pedro slid into the driver's seat and turned the key while shoving his foot against the accelerator. Maybe through some stroke of luck, he could fire the engine. His truck groaned as the gas searched for the spark plugs. The motor sputtered and died. The smell of fuel reached his nose and spread through the cab. Pedro knew he had flooded the engine, but this was a good sign.

As he waited for the engine to cool, Pedro decided on what must come next. In all his planning, Pedro had relied on his truck. *Que estúpido!* It was the one major key to the success of his plan to get away from the fire and get back to the hospital. He had promised the hospital he would have the second payment there before Maria left the hospital, which was in a few days. He reached for the boot bag and tucked the cash inside. His writing was not very good, but in case he didn't make it out of the fire, maybe he should leave a note so that whoever found the money could take it to the hospital. Maybe. He searched in the glove compartment for a pencil and paper and found an old envelope and a pen. He wrote: "Por Favor. Take this money to the hospital to pay for Maria's surgery. Gracias."

Pedro wiped the sweat from his forehead and placed his fingers on the key to the ignition. Would God grant him this wish to live, or would he have to stay at the ranch and die?

Chapter 48

Leo pulled into the Morningside Cemetery on the northeast side of El Paso. He parked on the roadway by Alejandra's tombstone. It sat on a small knoll overlooking the stone marker for Marta, who had died when she was only 72 hours old. Leo rested his hands on his knees and gazed out of the windshield, starring at a fog of regret. Why was regret so infinite and joy so fleeting?

His cell phone jolted him out of his despair. "Hello. This is Sheriff Tellez."

"Leo, this is Don. You, okay? You sound like an old hound who lost his duck in deep water."

"Oh, good, Don. Thanks for calling. Are you on your way?

"Yes, but you never sent me the coordinates. I'm just passing through Las Cruces."

"Sorry. I'll send them now. I haven't been to the Becker Ranch, but Penny was to meet him at his house."

"Thanks. Becker and Georgia were always asking me to dinner, but I never made the time. After his wife's death, we used to meet in Las Cruces for a drink and dinner."

"Don't take any risks that would endanger Penny," Leo said.

"What about endangering me? Don't I count?" Don was laughing.

Leo chuckled, but the laughter caught in his throat. He coughed. "You're killing me, Don. Remember, your charm might light a fire, but it won't stop one."

Chapter 49

Sampson Dales assured Penny that he was in the perfect spot. From the vantage spot of the third-floor window he could keep watch on the driveway leading into the ranch and get a bead on anyone who might enter the barn from its double doors. Penny cautioned. "Don't move from this spot!"

She planned to use Dales as a last resort. He could observe the perimeter of the ranch so that no one could sneak up on them, but she wanted to take on Pedro herself. "Shoot only if our lives depend on it." Dales responded with a grunt, which Penny could not be sure meant an affirmative or what.

Penny had not found any firearms in the barn after an earlier search of the office and tack room. Her gut told her Pedro was not armed with anything except his insanity.

She felt for her own revolver which she had tucked in the side pocket of the windbreaker. Ollie wanted her to take the Browning, but Penny wasn't secure in handling it.

Penny headed down to the first floor of the house where the air was still very hot.

She searched for the air conditioning controls and switched them on. Almost immediately she felt the cool air reaching the living room. Hopefully it was powerful enough to reach the third floor where Dales stood watch. Although when Penny had complained about the heat to Sampson Dales as they had checked out Georgia Becker's handiwork, Dales had laughed. "This ain't nothing compared to the rice paddies of 'Nam."

When Penny returned to Georgia's office, Ollie was sitting at her desk. Tiny beads of sweat rested on her nose. "I've been tracking Pedro's movements since you left," she said, pointing to a note pad before her. "While it appears he is cleaning up in the barn, he has a pattern which he keeps repeating." Ollie pointed to where Pedro had stopped by Milly's stall three times. The first time he scooped up the manure and threw it in a three-wheeled cart. The second time, Ollie had watched Pedro grinding up corn in a wooden bowl and carrying it into Milly's stall. In the third instance, Pedro brought two or three carrots and fed them to Milly, one by one. "This doesn't seem like the behavior of somebody who is on the verge of killing horses," Ollie said.

"You're right," Penny said. "And he is paying particular attention to Milly."

"Maybe he's not our culprit." Ollie stood and stretched her legs. She reached for a handkerchief in her back pocket and wiped her face.

"Becker is certain it is Pedro. But where is Becker now?" Penny wondered if she had been set up. The memory of drug cartels lingered in her mind. She had had her share of confrontations with them, would they go to this extreme? She shivered, and then shook off her concern. She had too much to do to wait around for the answer.

Ollie sat again and renewed her study of Pedro's behavior. "He's slumped over on a stool. Take a look."

Penny watched as Pedro dropped his head into his hands. He wiped his eyes with his sleeve, and then stood. Penny and Ollie saw him walk over to Milly. The horse was hanging her head over her stall door. He rubbed her face. She reciprocated with a nudge to Pedro's chest. Tears fell down Pedro's face.

Penny was confused. Her gut tightened. Doubt grew and fear began feeling at home in her head. She had to know what was going on. "I'm heading over to the barn," Penny said.

"Not without me." Ollie grabbed her gun and shoved it into a leather holster strapped to her belt.

Penny called Sampson Dales to let him know they were on the move. He told Penny he could track their whereabouts with his night vision goggles. "I can watch you until you enter the barn. Then you are on your own."

It was now almost 6 pm and a bank of clouds had dropped a veil over the stars, making it difficult for Penny and Ollie to find their way. Penny cussed Ron Becker's absence. "It's not going to be easy to get to the barn without breaking our necks. I had counted on Becker to give us cover."

Headlights from a vehicle bounced down the driveway. "Get down!" Penny motioned for Ollie to crouch down behind a clump of trees. An automatic floodlight clicked on, spreading its wings across the parking lot and exposing what looked like a police vehicle. Penny could see the bubble lights on the top of the car. Penny's phone vibrated. She could tell it was Dales. She had to answer it, or he might call again. "Hi Sampson," she whispered. "We see the car. Thanks. Hang tight."

The dark figure got out of his car with his gun drawn and moved around the side of the barn. Penny's fears were confirmed. She heard Ollie gasp behind her, as a motion-activated light illuminated Sheriff Cerillo, creeping down the driveway. He made a turn at the corner of the barn where the straw bedding was stored. *He's searching for the Firestarter!*

Penny motioned for Ollie to follow her. Both women had their own firearms loaded and ready for what might come next. They crept up to the entrance of the barn. Feeling exposed by the flood light, the two women instinctively shoved their bodies into the side of the barn where a slight shadow gave them some protection. The barn light flickered off. Penny could hear Ollie breathing hard.

"Be ready to run if the sheriff heads back to his patrol car," Penny cautioned.

"My husband never trusted that man," Ollie whispered. "He always thought the sheriff might have been on the take. But no one could ever prove it."

"What if we sneak inside the barn and hide?" Penny thought it might be best to find better cover than the shadows. And it was a much safer option than running. She motioned for Ollie to follow her. She knew there was one empty stall. She figured they would be safe inside it because Pedro had no need to clean it, as he incessantly did everything else.

"Follow me!" Penny waved her arm at Ollie.

"Are you sure you want to go in there?"

"We can't risk having the sheriff see the barn light flare on again if we try to retreat to the house. He'll know there is someone else here. We can get out easily enough. The main barn door is just 20 feet from the empty stall."

"Didn't we see Pedro inside? He will know we're in there."

"Come on, Ollie. I know where we can hide, and Pedro won't know the difference."

"I don't feel good about this." Ollie was grumbling under her breath. Penny knew Ollie had good instincts, but she ignored them. The adrenaline buzzing through her bloodstream inspired her to stop this fire at all costs. Even if Becker had failed to show, she would not let Milly down.

Penny could hear Pedro in the work room grinding more corn for Milly's dinner. Penny ran her hands along the bank of wood stalls, until she reached the empty one and motioned for Ollie to follow. The door opened without a sound. She took Ollie's hand and guided her inside.

"Now what?" Ollie asked.

"Shhh. Let's wait to see what the sheriff's doing here. Maybe I misjudged him."

Chapter 50

Leo was still hanging out at the cemetery. A ragged piece of moon hovered over the corner of Alejandra's tombstone. Clouds sifted through the stars, casting intermittent streaks of light across the gravesites, as if flirting with death. He looked out the window and bemoaned, as he had many times, about how Alejandra had waited too long before letting the doctor to do a C-section. Her blood pressure had been rapidly on the rise, and yet she refused help. "It will give the baby a better chance," she kept saying.

"Why did you wait?" Leo raised his fist. His years of grief were entangled with lingering anger. Countless visits to her gravesite had not eased his pain. "You chose Marta over me."

At last, he had put his voice to the truth. Alejandra loved Marta more than she loved life. She loved her child more than she loved Leo. This is why he had been unable to forgive her and move on.

Alejandra had a stubborn streak. It was one of the things he had always loved about her. When she made up her mind, she was generally successful in everything she touched. In this case, she had called it wrong. Waiting, only killed her and eventually took their daughter. In the end, waiting had destroyed any hope of Leo having a normal life.

Now he had also lost his other love, serving as Sheriff of El Paso County. He might as well bury his badge in this place, too. He jumped out of the car. He ripped his Sheriff's badge from his chest and laid it at the foot of Alejandra's marker.

Leo blamed himself for not getting out of bed to campaign. Of course, he could also place the fault at the feet of Alejandra's sister. Adriana had come to his rescue in the hospital when he had been gravely wounded. He had even rejected Penny's requests to help. That decision now appeared to have been insanity, or heavy drugs talking. Why else would he give up someone he loved, for someone who reminded him of someone he had lost?

Adriana had insisted he stay home and recuperate. "Nothing is as important as your health, Leo." He had agreed, secretly enjoying the time he shared with her, and revisiting his life with Alejandra. He stayed away from the campaign trail, hoping this relationship with Adriana would restore the years that Alejandra's bad choices had stolen from him.

Two months into his physical therapy on Leo's bullet-riddled shoulder, Adriana had announced she had to return to Los Angeles. The partner in her law firm was ill, and she had to take on his cases. "I'm sorry, Leo, but I've got to head back. I'm counting on you spending time with me when you are out of therapy."

She had leaned down and kissed him on the lips, and hung her arm around his wounded shoulder, as if it were an albatross to her happiness. And then just like her sister, Adriana left Leo alone to stare at his linoleum floors and sip chicken noodle soup out of a can.

Adriana had been wrong, of course. Something was more important than healing from a bullet to the shoulder. Being sheriff sent oxygen to his lungs, blood to his bones, and a song to his soul. Now his very existence was being shredded. What is living to serve others if you are dying to yourself?

Leo's cell phone vibrated on his belt. He fumbled to unsnap the phone holder from his waist and dropped his mobile on the floor. By the time he had retrieved it, the caller had hung up. He saw the phone go to voicemail. It was better that way. He had few words left to share with the world. He just listened to the message. "Sheriff, this is Sergeant Stemple. I thought you should know. Francisco Parasea has resigned. It's all over the news."

Chapter 51

Johnny tried to start his Jeep a couple more times, but the battery was just as dead as the last time he tried it. His mother's car was gone, so there was no chance of jumping his Jeep. He ran back in the house and called his headquarters.

"This is Captain Trejo."

"Captain, how are you feeling? I heard about your accident?" The dispatcher was Linda Fortillo, an old friend. She had known Johnny's dad well, too, having worked at the department for almost 30 years.

"I'm pretty ripped up, but I'll mend. Thanks, Linda. Listen, is there anybody who could run me over another patrol car? I need to answer a call."

"Are you sure you're up to it?" Johnny could hear Linda breathing heavily. She had had her own bouts of bad health, including COPD. "You want me to send another officer to go with you?"

"That is a great idea. Yes. You are the best, Linda. Thanks for helping me think straight."

"I'm not sure who will show up, but I'll have them there in about 45 minutes."

"Awesome. Thanks so much."

Johnny hung up the phone and headed to the coffee maker. He measured out the coffee and watched the water seep into the carafe. He had planned on getting his mom a new coffee pot for Christmas, and this dribble-by-dribble effect had confirmed it. He watched the black liquid plop into the pot, killing ten minutes of his time. He found a Thermos™ in the cabinet and poured the coffee inside. He made another sandwich to match the one his mother had made for him. Whomever Linda could find would need some nourishment because they would probably miss their dinner. He pulled two bags of chips from under the counter, threw in another apple and packed everything in the bag.

Johnny sat in a kitchen chair tapping his fingertips on the table. Waiting provided his mind with some unwelcome free space for thought. He made it a practice to fill his day with so much activity he seldom had time to think of anything meaningful, but now he had the gift of time. *Some gift.*

He was 35 and still had not made a serious romantic commitment. Like his father, Johnny had discovered being a state police officer was commitment enough. Serving the state of New Mexico wrestles everything else out of your life. Johnny's mother could testify to that. Why she had stayed with his father, always amazed him. Volunteering to help Penny was a big risk for his mother, but she knew someone had to help Penny and his mom had the gun skills to bring to the fight. Johnny felt like a chump having his own mother do his job.

Johnny had been engaged once, but Judy had grown tired of waiting and moved on. Now he had high hopes for a life with Penny, and so did his mother. Ollie loved Penny. Why else would she risk her own life? He knew his mother well enough to understand that while she was an expert with guns, she abhorred using them against another human being. She had shared the emotional upheaval her husband, Johnny, Sr., had gone through when he had to shoot someone in the line of duty.

News reports would have the public believe that taking a life has no effect on a law officer—as if they shoot and kill someone on purpose. Nothing could be further from the truth. More than anyone, a law officer understands the concepts of life and death. They are the first on the scene of an auto accident. They try to revive the mangled body of a father who has been thrown from the car. They carry a small child to safety after her parents are killed in gang crossfire. They knock on the doors of countless homes to give the bad news about the loss of a loved one and experience the agony in those faces.

Johnny looked up at the clock. He had killed another 15 minutes. Good. He got up and went to the bathroom and threw well water on his face. Nothing would help his bruising, except time, but the coolness of the water being pulled from the depths of the earth did help a bit. The mirror revealed a scratched forehead and two eyes turning a queasy shade of yellow. The cuts on his cheeks had swollen in places, making him look more like a prize fighter than a law officer. This was a face only a mother could love, he thought. And this time he was pushing his luck with her.

The honking of a horn broke his line of thinking. It was time to go.

Johnny grabbed the lunch bag, his badge, hat, gun and his coat, and headed out the door. Nobody locked their doors in rural New Mexico, and he wasn't going to start now. He ran to the passenger side of the patrol car and jumped in.

When Officer Norma Soto smiled, she revealed two rows of wayward teeth, wrenched into place by metal braces. Inside the car, illuminated by the overhead light, Johnny found the 30-something New Mexico State Police officer, freshly scrubbed and in full uniform. Soto's dark hair, a tangle of short curls, was still damp. The air was filled with the scent of jasmine.

The sweet aroma relaxed him at little. He had not been expecting this. "Thank you, Sergeant. Thank you. I thought you were headed on vacation."

"It can wait another day. You are more important, than a trip to Santa Fe." Norma smiled again. This time he noticed that her eyes were moist. She turned her face to the windshield. "Where to, sir?"

Chapter 52

Penny had positioned she and Ollie inside an empty horse stall so that they had a view of the double doors to the barn. If the sheriff was heading inside the barn, they would duck down, before he could them. Simple enough.

"Penny," Ollie whispered, "I'm allergic to sawdust. I hope I don't sneeze." She placed her hand over her mouth and nose, as she moved around in the stall trying not to stir up the three inches of wood chips gathered around her legs. She finally sat on a stool tucked in the corner. Ollie's breathing sounded husky. "Damn. It's my asthma!"

Penny motioned with her hand to keep quiet. The sheriff was inching his way into the barn, his gun drawn. She couldn't imagine what he had in mind. Perhaps he planned to surprise Pedro and stop the fire by himself? She stood on her tiptoes trying to see where he was headed. When the sheriff walked toward the work room, Penny resisted the urge to follow him. She would love to be there when he arrested Pedro. Perhaps they were on the same side, after all.

"Pedro, why in the hell are you grinding corn for a horse you are going to kill? I don't think you're up to burning down anything. I told Willie you had no guts. I'm here to make sure the job gets done."

Penny could not hear what Pedro was saying. He was doing more moaning than talking. There was a scuffle. She heard what sounded like the workroom chair break against the wall. "Where's the money I gave you?"

"I can do this."

"I asked you where's the money?"

"*No señor. No!*"

The shouts coming from Pedro sounded desperate. Penny wondered if she and Ollie could overpower the sheriff. Not likely. She looked at Ollie, who was reading her mind, and shook her head.

"The money. Now!"

"No."

"No, you can't give me the money, or no, you can't burn this place down.

"No, señor, por favor, no hagas esto."

"It's just like I thought. You love these horses too much, Pedro."

"Don't take my money, *por favor. ¡Sabes que María lo necesita!"*

The tenon and joinery rafters reverberated with the sound of a pistol. And then a second shot blistered the air. Pedro was moaning. *"No, Maria. Mijo!"*

"Maria and Lourdes belong to me, now. Pedro. You aren't man enough to be a father or a husband."

The door to the workroom slammed shut. Penny held her breath as the sheriff ran past their hiding place. She heard Milly whinny and stomp her feet. Was he inside her stall? *Is he hurting her?*

Now Penny was angry. It was all she could do to keep from attacking the sheriff. She clutched her gun. *I'll kill him if he does anything to Milly.* She was surprised at her anger but swallowed hard. The dusty stall had left her tongue parched.

Milly's cry echoed throughout the barn. *He is hurting her!* She could hear Milly stomping in her stall and calling for help. She had promised Milly nothing would happen to her, and now something was. She wanted to rush out and take the sheriff down, but she held back, knowing this was a dangerous man.

She saw Ollie pushing a magazine of bullets into her pistol. The sheriff passed by their stall again, his black hat covered with the dust of the barn. He headed out the double doors.

"Good!" Penny said. "He's leaving." There was sound of the doors rolling closed and then being bolted.

"What has happened?" Ollie asked. "Did the sheriff shoot Pedro? Are we locked inside this place? I warned you not to go in here!"

Penny opened the door to the stall and headed for the work room with her revolver drawn. Milly was beating her hooves against the stall door, but she would have to wait. Ollie followed. She could hear Ollie jamming a cartridge into another pistol.

The women found Pedro lying against the wall with gunshot wounds to both thighs. He couldn't get up. He was mumbling and crying. Tears rolled down his face, which was streaked with saw dust and grit. "I'm sorry, *Mija!*" He was delirious.

"He's going into shock!" Ollie said. She found some work shears and cut strips of cloth from an old work apron hanging on the door. She secured tourniquets above the wounds. Pedro was pale and moving in and out of consciousness. He needed help quickly or he would bleed to death.

Penny sniffed the air. She thought she could smell something like melted wax. She ran toward Milly's stall. There was a tuna can smoldering in the sawdust. A few sparks flew through the air, landing near Milly's feet. Milly stamped her feet in response to the heat. Penny could not grab the can because it was hot. Melted paraffin was spilling out of it and heating up the area surrounding it. She grabbed Milly's grain bucket and filled it with water. She threw it on the paraffin, but the fire was too hot. She needed more water.

She ran to get Ollie, who was rubbing a wet cloth over Pedro's face. "Ollie, we've got a fire in Milly's stall. I need your help."

Before they could get back to Milly, Penny smelled smoke coming from somewhere else in the barn. "The tack room!" Penny dashed down the cement walkway to find out what else was burning. The room was almost consumed by the flames. She watched the blue and red ribbons flare into a pillar of fire. The cork bulletin board was scorched, and its calendar and photographs curled in the heat.

"See if you can find a way out of here," Penny said. "I'll try to put this fire out.

"We're trapped in here!" Ollie yelled. "We need to get Pedro and carry him out of this." Smoke billowed around them, as Ollie forced her tiny body against the bolted double doors. The doors were solid oak. They did not give.

As the dust and smoke swirled in an uneven tango around the barn, Penny scanned the roof, looking for the best way out. Even if they could somehow hoist Pedro up into the loft and jump into the straw bedding, she would have to throw him off the side of the barn. He would suffer grave injuries without being able to fall to his feet. And, most importantly, she would not leave Milly or the other horses to die.

Chapter 53

Leo had a bad case of indigestion. It was as though he could not breathe. His chest hurt. He had not eaten a thing for hours. What in the world was wrong with him? He grabbed his arms, which were increasingly growing numb. He looked across the cemetery at the rows of tombstones, some of which had eroded with wind and time. Perhaps they were now only a record in someone's ancestral tree. *Am I going to die here?* It served him right. He had logged so many hours at Alejandra's tombstone, maybe death was finally calling him home.

Pain wrapped around his body like a straitjacket. He had the presence of mind to punch in Don's number. Heart attack or not, Leo needed to make sure that Don would get to Penny in time. He knew she was in trouble. He could feel it.

"This is Don Tellez."

"Don, it's Leo. I'm having a heart attack."

"What? Where are you?"

"In the cemetery." Bile was creeping into his raw throat like a venomous reptile. He coughed trying to keep the monster at bay.

"Of course, you are!" Leo could hear the anger in Don's voice. His brother had cautioned him many times to move on, but he just could not.

"I'll send an ambulance. I'm almost to the Becker Ranch."

Leo heard nothing on the other end of the phone. It would serve him right if Don never called for help. That would leave only one Tellez brother to care about Penny's future.

Chapter 54

Ollie had found two more aprons. She handed one to Penny. "Tie this around your nose and mouth." Penny had no time to regret her mistake of making them both victims of this fire. If she survived, she would never again corner herself in the pursuit of a suspect. Lesson learned, perhaps too late. She tied the apron over her face, as Ollie had instructed and ran throughout the barn looking for a way out. She passed a large piece of sheet metal tacked on the wall to protect the barn wall from the collection of pitch forks and shovels, leaning there. She saw her reflection. She looked like a marauding bandit or even worse like windless sail on a sinking ship.

When she returned, she had a plan. "Ollie, I need you to climb up to the loft and crawl out on to the roof and jump into the straw. Then look for a way to unlock the door."

"I'm not leaving you here." Ollie shouted. Her face was red, and a line ran across her cheekbones, where she had tied the apron over her nose.

"And I'm not going to let Johnny's mother die in here."

"And I am not going to let the woman who Johnny loves, die either," Ollie shouted in anger.

For an instant Penny let Ollie's words prick her heart. What does love have to do with her? She let out a big breath and shouted. "Go check with Pedro and see if he knows any other way out of here."

Penny ran to Milly's stall. The fire was now flitting through the sawdust, but it had not flamed up. She guessed the sheriff knew he only had to bide his time before the saw dust would catch fire and spread throughout the barn. *Very clever.*

She remembered seeing a metal box marked "work gloves" hanging on the door of the tack room. Could she get to them? Penny grabbed a bucket from the empty stall and filled it with water. She could see the flames consuming nearly all the room, and smoke was rolling out into the main part of the barn. Penny ran toward the smoke and flames anyway. She could see the metal box on the door. She threw the bucket of water on the flames. The steam hissed and spat hot sparks back at her. The metal box gave off a red glow. Unbelievably, the lights to the tack room were still working. She used her apron to protect her fingers and opened the metal box and pulled out the gloves.

She immediately covered her mouth again and ran back to Milly's stall. The other horses were nickering and whining and stamping their feet. She heard one of the mare's rear up and shove her hooves against the stall door. Sawdust and bits of straw flew in the air, rushing toward an untimely end.

She donned the gloves and grabbed the tuna can, dropping it into Milly's grain bucket. She held the bucket in front of her as she left the stall and placed it on the cement walkway. The residue of water in the bucket confronted the hot paraffin, causing steam to rise and mix with the smoke.

Penny then ran to the work room, where Ollie and Pedro were talking in Spanish with such a crescendo, she could not keep up with what they were saying.

"Pedro says there is a trap door at the end of the hallway that leads to a tunnel. It was dug to drain out excess water from the barn, in case the water lines froze and flooded the place."

Pedro was pointing north. Ollie and Penny picked up Pedro and placed his arms over their shoulders.

"*Dios mío. Me duele tanto.*" Pedro yelled.

"I know it hurts" Ollie said. "*Sé valiente. Sé fuerte.*"

"Yes, be strong," Penny said.

By now the smoke was blinding the women, as they hauled Pedro down the walkway. "Feel with your feet," Penny told Ollie. "The cement leads all the way to the end of the barn."

Pedro pounded on Penny's arm. "*¡Aquí está! ¡Aquí está!*" He pointed to a square door, painted yellow.

In the middle of the chaos, Penny's cell phone rang. It mercifully lit the darkening space where they stood, about to embark on a journey into the unknown. "Hello."

"Penny, this is Dr. Obregon. I got the results back from the tests on the copper bead. It's a mix of cocaine and Clenbuterol."

"Doctor, can you send help? I'm trapped with a couple of other people in a burning barn at the Ronald Becker Ranch near Tularosa."

"Of course. Yes, of course. Stay as low to the floor as you can!"

Penny replaced her cell phone in her pocket. It was probably too late for this news, but if Georgia was giving this stuff to Milly, no wonder she despised her and launched out in defense.

Penny opened the yellow door and looked inside. It was total darkness but she was able to feel what appeared to be a narrow cement-lined ditch—just large enough to carry water out of the barn. "Hold Pedro for a minute." Penny said. She ran back to the work room, now dodging small fingers of fire creeping down the walkway. She had seen a gardening spade there. She grabbed it and returned. "I'll go first and dig a wider track if I can."

Penny crawled inside the tunnel her body squeezing inside the trough like a sausage. She looked back and realized they would need something to transport Pedro through the tunnel. She handed Ollie her apron. It was made of sturdy, waterproofed canvas. It might just work. "Use this under Pedro, and tie it around him, so we can slide him along.

Ollie made a sling out of the two aprons and threw the strings of one apron to Penny. "This canvas is heavy duty stuff. Great idea. Let's give it a go."

Ollie put Pedro's head inside the tunnel and Penny pulled him forward. "You are going to have to crawl, too, Pedro."

"*Si. Si. voy a*!"

Ollie came behind Pedro, pushing him forward on to the canvas sling. When he lost his strength, he began to cry in pain. Penny stayed the course, and for a few moments the smoke followed them inside, although Ollie had shut the door. She grunted and shoveled her way forward. She could feel the heat from the barn's floorboards. They must be passing under the tack room.

"We've got to speed it up!" she shouted.

Penny pulled Pedro and Ollie pushed, inching their way to a point where they both could smell the night air. Penny's lips were caked with mud, from shoveling a path through the tunnel. Her nose twitched as the smoke greeted her like a fickle friend. "I think we're close."

"I hope so," Ollie said. "Pedro has passed out. We'll have to drag him the rest of the way.

Finally, after several minutes of shear willpower, the trio reached a dead end. "There is no way out!" Penny cried out in despair. She could smell the smoke gaining density in the tunnel. Did she lead them to a certain death by asphyxiation? "Can you see anything?" She hoped that Ollie's eyes, three decades older than hers, had a better view.

Penny watched as Ollie ran her fingers over the roof of the tunnel pushing upward. "There must be an exit. Perhaps someone blocked it?"

The arsonist had thought of everything. Penny's hope crumbled. She realized that if Sheriff Cerillo had blocked this ditch, this was grounds for murder, not just killing horses. She thought of the photo of Sonny March, now burned to a crisp. Penny shuddered. She could feel her eyes filling with tears, realizing she might soon be a statistic, and fodder for a team of arson investigators.

Refusing to give up, Penny joined Ollie, shoving on all sides of the ditch. Finally, her fingers jammed against something hard. "Feel this?"

Ollie moved her hands across the area, which was solid. She confirmed their suspicions that someone had pounded a large rock into the caliche. It did not want to budge.

"Help me push on this thing!" Penny slammed her shovel upward against the mud-caked ceiling. The smoke was now threatening them. Ollie started hacking uncontrollably.

"Hang on, Ollie!"

Ollie crawled over Pedro and placed her hands against Penny's. The women pushed upward with unknown strength, Penny stuck the end of the spade into the crevice between the ceiling and the boulder, managing to move it a few inches at a time. Fresh air was seeping into the tunnel. Penny breathed in a cocktail of mud, grass and smoke. "One more shove," Penny urged. Penny shoved her garden spade against the lip of the boulder, lifting it slightly. Another thrust, and the rock tumbled away from the opening. "We've got it now!"

Penny and Ollie pulled Pedro out of the hole by grabbing the belt loops of his jeans and the apron ties. He was still unconscious. "He's got a heartbeat," Ollie said.

They arrived at the pasture, where Becker had thankfully installed a drain for excess water to flow into the grass. They sat in a circle of dampness, gratefully soaking in the night air. Penny could see the barn's shadow across the driveway. She heard sirens.

"I've got to get those barn doors open and rescue Milly and the other horses."

"I'm going with you!"

Ollie and Penny left Pedro in the safety of the pasture.

As they reached the double doors, a volunteer firetruck rolled up in front of the barn. The search lights from the truck exposed Penny and Ollie, blinding them. The barn's automatic motion-activated light also flared on, bringing all the players on stage front and center. Two firemen ran toward them with hatchets. A female firefighter was unrolling the hose and attaching it to the water pumper on the back of the truck. Water began gushing out of the hose.

Penny and Ollie stepped back to let the firefighters do their jobs breaking apart the bolted doors. Hatches made short work of the oak doors, too. As they entered the barn, Penny ran past them. "There are horses in here!"

"Hey, get back out here!" A fireman yelled. His eyes were amber, reflecting the flames in the whites of his eyes.

"Please. We've got to save these horses. There are three mares in here."

The firefighters followed Penny and Ollie. Each one led a mare out of the barn, amid the blinding smoke. The fireman had a mask, but Ollie and Penny, who had long ago ditched their aprons, were wheezing. Water poured over the group— horses and helpers—as they moved toward the pasture. One of the mares was moaning as she rolled in the grass at the entrance of the pasture.

"She's ready to foal," Ollie shouted.

The female firefighter ran over and handed Ollie and Penny masks, offering a jolt of oxygen to their parched throat and lungs. "Dispatch, can you send a vet to Becker Ranch. We've got a mare ready to have her baby."

Then, the firefighter noticed Pedro lying in the grass. "I'll get help." She ran back to the flames and her job as the pumper for the hoses, trying to save Ronald Becker's barn.

Thirty minutes passed in what seemed like an eternity to Penny. A siren blared in the night sky, bouncing off the stars and reverberating in her ears. Headlights of two cars were moving in tandem up the driveway. An ambulance swerved around the other vehicles and pulled in front of the barn, just behind the firetruck pumper. EMT's ran toward Penny and Ollie. "Are you okay?"

"We've got a man shot. He's lying in the field." Penny pointed to the gated pasture. The medic did not wait for another explanation. He dashed toward Pedro with life-saving intensity.

Penny's attention reverted to the cars, whose four headlights were bouncing off the front of the barn and making the scene appear more like a three-ring circus than a three-alarm fire. A man got out of the first car and ran toward the barn. Penny watched as a firefighter held the man back. She could hear him shouting. "No, sir, you can't go in there!"

"I've got to find Penny Larkin."

It was Don. He had come to her rescue! Penny did not know what to make of it. She ran toward him and threw her arms around him. "Don, I'm okay."

Don pulled her away from the smoldering barn and wrapped his arms around her. "I thought I had lost you!"

Penny looked in his eyes. This was not Leo. This was a person independent of any other man she had ever known. That he would come to help, meant that Leo had called him. But the important thing was he had come. Penny lifted her face toward his and gave him a kiss on the cheek. He pulled her closer to his chest and kissed her on the lips.

Lights from the second vehicle flickered over Don and Penny's shadows, casting a bigger than life silhouette against the side of the barn.

In disbelief, Penny saw Johnny jumping out of a patrol car— another woman on his tail. Johnny was hobbling toward Penny and Don.

"My God, Penny, are you okay?" He slid into them as he stopped, knocking Don backward. He stared at Don and did a double take. For an instant Penny could see he was confused, and then maybe a little bit angry.

"Johnny. Oh, my goodness." Penny broke out of Don's arms and wrapped her arms around Johnny. From over his shoulder, Penny could see a female police officer, dressed in full uniform and regulation hat.

She stood silently behind Johnny, frowning. Penny looked from Johnny to Don, and then back again. *What's happening*?

Ollie ran up to the group and shoved her small frame in between them all. "*Johnny, hijo mío, gracias por venir a salvarnos.*"

"Mama. Are you okay?"

Penny looked more closely at Ollie. The barn light showed her body covered from head to toe in mud. Her eyes were all that were recognizable, but they twinkled as bright as stars. Penny glanced down at her own body and saw more of the same. Don and Johnny's shirts were also covered with muck. She laughed out loud. "We may be covered in mud and horse manure, but we are alive!"

For an instant, a spirit of relief filtered through the eclectic group, but Penny realized her work wasn't done. "We've got to find Sheriff Cerillo. He set this fire. And he meant to kill Pedro, as well as the horses."

Chapter 55

The ambulance arrived at Sierra Providence Hospital in record time. Sheriff Leo Tellez was on board, and the medics wanted to make sure they were the heroes who rescued El Paso County's favorite son. Leo was still conscious as they wheeled his cart toward the emergency room door. He had vomited on the way over to the hospital and the smell permeated the confines of the emergency vehicle. Thankfully, the air conditioning blew over him when the hospital doors swung open. The cool air which was in stark contrast to the overheated ambulance, brushed over Leo's face and arms and made him feel a little better.

The ER Medical team was ready for him, cutting off Leo's shirt, and tearing off his white t-shirt, too. They placed his gun and belt in a cubicle behind them. An attending nurse stuck an electro cardio button on his chest. Leo could hear his heart beeping loud and strong.

"Are you still in pain, Sheriff?" The ER doctor was not taking any chances with this precious cargo either. Leo noticed it was Carlos Arce leaning over him. He had been there when Leo had brought his wife to the hospital for the birth of their first and only child. There were no strangers in this emergency room. Everyone loved Leo and he knew it. He had been thanked many times for saving accident victims on the side of the road, applying medical treatment like one of their own before the ambulance ever arrived at the ER.

"I'm not in any more pain." He ran his fingers over his face, which was sticky with puke.

A nurse washed his hands and face with a warm, wet cloth. "Thank you." He looked at her as if she had given him the most valuable gift in the world.

The nurse smiled and lay her fingers on his. "You are my sheriff. Always will be."

"I could run more tests," Dr. Arce said, "but after listening to your heart, I think you had a panic attack."

Leo was mortified. The great Leo Tellez in a panic? He hoped his prognosis wasn't spreading around the hospital like a bad case of diarrhea.

Dr. Arce leaned in closer to Leo. "No mind, Sheriff. I'll not report it as panic. Just a bit of food poisoning."

"Thank you, Doctor."

"I'm going to ask the nurse to roll you into a treatment room so you can rest. I've given you a sedative to help you sleep. When you awake, I've put in orders to take you home."

Chapter 56

Penny yelled at Johnny. "We have to stop him!" Johnny couldn't believe that Sheriff Cerillo had started the fire and shot the barn manager. It seemed far-fetched even though he'd never known Penny to exaggerate. Johnny was reluctant to head out after the sheriff without proof and without back-up. Chasing after another officer of the law got complicated.

Johnny took a summary of his feelings. He was angry, relieved, agitated, and happy, all at once. Penny and his Mama were both safe. *Couldn't they be satisfied with that?* "Are you sure it was the sheriff? Did you *actually* see him light the fire?"

"I watched him enter the barn," Penny explained. "He was carrying a Firestarter in his right hand. I heard him fighting with Pedro and then firing two shots.

"I heard the shots, too," Ollie said.

"Then I watched him head to Milly's stall," Penny continued, "where, I am certain, he started the first fire. Then he went to the tack room and set it on fire, too. Who else could it be?"

This information was incredulous to Johnny. He knew Sheriff Cerillo had a bad reputation, but murder was way over the line.

"I didn't see him," Penny said. "But there was no one else in the barn."

Johnny looked at Officer Norma Soto, who was lingering behind the group.

"Officer Soto, this is my mother, Ollie, and Penny Larkin, a U.S. Marshal."

Johnny watched Penny as she reached for Officer Soto's hand. "Thank you for getting to the ranch so fast," Penny said. "You are a lifesaver."

This brought a sliver of a smile to the officer's lips. "It was just my duty, ma'am."

"Officer Soto, I need you to call headquarters and put an APB out for Sheriff Cerillo. He is armed, of course."

"That won't be necessary!" A bodiless voice drifted over them. A tall, aging man appeared as if on stage, from the depths of the darkness. He was lumbering toward the group.

Johnny saw an older man in his late 60's, carrying an assault rifle with a knapsack, looped under his arms. He felt for his own pistol.

"I've got the sheriff tied up in the corral," Sampson Dales said. "I got a bead on him as he was leaving the barn. I could see smoke and figured Penny and Ollie were in trouble 'because they weren't anywhere in sight. I also called the fire department."

"You shot the sheriff?" Johnny asked in disbelief.

"I just clipped his knee with a bullet, and that took him down."

"From what vantage point?"

"Penny set me up in Ron Becker's house, on the third floor. He was easy pickins' at 150 yards, when he ran out of the barn and headed for his patrol car."

XXXXX

"Johnny, this is Sampson Dales. He was a sniper in Vietnam." Penny knew she had better be the one to offer the explanation before Ollie blurted out that she had befriended Dales and asked him for help.

Penny watched as Johnny took control over the crime scene. "Officer Soto, place the sheriff under arrest and call an ambulance. Set up a security detail 24/7 outside of his hospital room."

"Yes, sir." Soto took off running to the corral, her flashlight scanning the path before her.

"Don, would you mind calling the arson investigator in Otero County and get someone out here right away? And could you stay here until they arrive?"

Penny looked at Don, who seemed eager to oblige Johnny, but he appeared unhappy about having to stay behind. He reached over and squeezed Penny's hand. "We're not finished with this."

XXXXX

Johnny insisted on driving his mother home in Penny's car. He hobbled over to the Mustang and helped his mother into the front seat. "Penny, you sit in the back." He flashbacked to the time he had ordered Penny to sit in the back of his patrol car. It had been during a dust storm on the side of Interstate 10, and it had led to her temporary arrest for murder.

This time Johnny wasn't going to let Penny out of his sight. He wished he could lock her up after what he had just witnessed. But he knew he was somehow responsible. How in the hell had Don Tellez made his way into Penny's life? Johnny knew he was an arson investigator and Leo's brother. Had she called on him for help? *Certainly not.* Penny had often laughed about Don and Leo's rivalry as brothers, and she usually came down on Leo's side.

Johnny felt justified in taking over the investigation. After all, Don Tellez had no jurisdiction in New Mexico. He had been a gentleman and thanked Don profusely for taking the time to show up on Penny's behalf. He would, however, purge from his memory the embrace between Don and Penny. He was no fool. Don was trying to move in on Penny, and he had to protect her. And that also meant protecting himself.

Police officers live their lives in compartments and Johnny was no different. When he arrived home every night, he kept what happened at work locked in a box. It had to be that way, or he would go insane. Johnny would place the embrace between Don and Penny in his lock box and move on.

Johnny had half expected Don to protest when he asked him to stay on the scene. He was waiting for Don to explain how it would be more convenient for him to drive Penny home since they both lived in El Paso. But he did not.

The fire chief walked over to Johnny as he was opening Penny's car door. "We got lucky, Captain. We were able to save this barn, believe it or not! We got to the large beams and joinery before they were damaged. Scorched, yes. Compromised, no."

"That is so wonderful!" Penny said from the confines of the backseat. "Thank you so much."

"I would like to speak to Ron Becker. Has anyone seen him?" The fire chief asked.

"No," Penny responded. "He was supposed to meet us here tonight, but he never showed. But he will be thrilled to know his horses are safe and his barn can be salvaged."

"It takes a lot more than a few sparks to bring down an old barn like this," the fire fighter said. He wiped patches of soot from his neck with a bandana. "You can tell Becker it was an honor to save this old place. It means a lot to the people in our county to keep it standing."

Johnny realized he had to make one more call before taking off. He picked up his cell phone and punched in the numbers. "Mr. Drake. This is Johnny Trejo. I could use your help. I've got three pregnant mares that need a place to spend a few nights."

Chapter 57

Penny tumbled into bed without washing her face or brushing her teeth. She had dropped her jeans, top and filthy socks in the hamper. Everything was covered with mud and reeked of smoke, but she didn't have the energy to do more. She lay the photograph of Sonny March on her bedside table. She would take a good look at it tomorrow and see if any other images came to her about this case. It certainly wasn't over, but her body argued that she should be done with barn fires. The sheriff was in custody, and things could be sorted out with Pedro. He wasn't going too far with gunshots to the thighs.

Penny pulled the blankets over her shoulders. The night was chilly. She heard the furnace kick on, and the fan blowing warm air. "Good. I'll sleep well," she reassured herself before shutting her eyes.

Penny's cell phone buzzed on the table. She would let it go to voicemail, nodding off to a blissful slumber. Her phone buzzed again. In the darkness, she reached for her phone. "Hello. This is Penny."

"Penny, this is Dr. Obregon. Are you okay?"

For a blink of an eyelid, Penny wondered who this was. Of course, she was okay. She was lying happily in her own bed on a comfy mattress. And then the tumblers of the previous 18 hours fell into place. "Oh, Doctor." Penny answered. "Yes, I'm home. Thank you for sending the firetruck. You saved three lives, three horses, and a horse barn."

"I want you to come to the hospital right away. I'll meet you here. You should have a blood test to make sure you haven't caused yourself any permanent harm from holding that copper bead."

"Harm?" She asked, as if the word was foreign to her lips.

"The mix of cocaine and Clenbuterol is highly addictive and dangerous for your heart."

"I am so tired. Can it wait?"

"No. I don't want to take any more chances. I should never have let you go on your way after your episode at Starbucks. It was irresponsible of me."

"I feel fine."

"I'm sending an ambulance. What is your address?"

Penny dutifully gave him her address but still felt compelled to insist on driving herself to the emergency room. "Doctor. Please. I'll meet you at the hospital."

"No. The medics are already on their way."

Chapter 58

Pedro Lopez awoke to the smell of iodine. He noticed a dark figure hovering over him. He wanted to escape, but he was strapped down. And there was something stuck inside his nose. He tried to pull it out. It was pinching his face.

"Whoa. You aren't getting up, sir." A disembodied voice came from the bowels of the tunnel under the barn. Or was he in prison? He lunged again, trying to move.

"We've got to go faster. This guy is moving in and out of consciousness."

What are you talking about? *I'm right here.* Pedro was confused. Was someone trying to save him or kill him? In his world, both acts had the same benefits.

The sirens ripping through the New Mexico countryside jolted him into high alert. He was in terrible pain. *"¿Dónde estoy? ¿En el infierno?"* Pedro asked.

"No Señor. You are not in hell. You are in an ambulance. We're headed to the hospital in El Paso where the surgeon is waiting to pull a couple of bullets out of your legs."

The wheels of the ambulance responded to Pedro's questions by digging into the pavement and causing his gurney to bounce back and forth. He could feel the ride now. He was moving, and he hoped it was in the right direction. Did these guys know he had been trying to burn down Mr. Becker's barn? They didn't seem to be concerned about that.

"Can I see Maria?"

"What? You are going to the hospital, not to your home."

"My daughter. She is in the hospital."

"This guy is delirious. We've got to make it snappy."

"Maria!" Pedro began to cry. Tears dropped down his face, faster than the medic could wipe them away.

"Hey, Ernie. Do me a favor," the EMT called to the driver. "Call the hospital and see if there is a Maria Lopez registered as a patient or maybe she's an employee there."

Chapter 59

Penny managed to rinse off in the shower and pull on a fresh pair of jeans and a sweatshirt before the ambulance arrived. Her eyes were gravelly from the smoke, mud, and lack of sleep. She prayed the ambulance would not wake her neighbors and cause them to worry.

"Now, what's happened to Penny?" Mrs. Nordant was a busybody, though a very nice person. She brought Penny banana bread whenever she baked a loaf for herself. She didn't want her 70-year-old neighbor spreading rumors that Penny's remote viewing had finally driven her off her rocker.

Thankfully, the ambulance pulled into Penny's driveway with only its lights flashing. She was waiting at the front door, greeting the medics as they walked up the driveway.

"I don't need to lay down on a gurney. I'm fine." She tried to explain that Dr. Obregon was only sending them out of precaution. And then she looked at one of the guys standing at the back end of the vehicle and realized it was the same medic who had tried to help her earlier in the day.

"Yeah, we knew we should have insisted you go to the hospital," he mumbled. "We know our stuff."

"Thank you for coming. Can I ride in the back without lying down?"

"No. Fool us once. Twice, not happening!"

Penny lay down on the cart. She was compliant as they strapped her down—a little too tight—but she knew it was best to remain quiet. However, the chill of the night air mingled with the air conditioning inside the ambulance caused her to shake.

"You guys have this place freezing in here."

"It keeps our patients humble." The medic laughed as he pulled a pre-warmed blanket over her.

"Thank you." Penny lay her head on the tiny pillow and tried to relax. She was in no position to complain any further. Perhaps she could get a few minutes of sleep. The ambulance had not turned on its sirens, so the road to the hospital would be swift and silent.

The Sierra Providence Hospital on the Westside was just ten minutes from her house. She had barely nodded off when the EMT woke Penny. "We're here. Dr. Obregon is waiting in the ER for you."

The EMT's wheeled Penny inside the hospital. It was a new building, and the lights all had a glow that favored the skin. Hopefully, the doctor would think she looked great, prescribe her some aspirin, and not order her to be admitted for further tests.

An ER nurse approached to take Penny's vitals. "Dr. Obregon will be with you shortly."

Penny nodded her thanks. An orderly moved her to an alcove with just a curtain blocking her from other patients-in-waiting. She had not spent a great deal of time in emergency rooms, but she did know they used a triage system. Certainly, she would not be high on their priority system, with other more serious injuries demanding their time. She might get a few winks in, after all.

She shut her eyes, but even with them closed, the overhead lights were distracting. She placed her arm over her eyes and whispered into the chilly room. "Please, God. Get me out of here quick!"

A nurse arrived and began applying cardio nodes to her chest and arms. "The doctor has ordered an EKG. It's painless."

"What will this test show the doctor?" Penny asked.

"The EKG measures the electrical signals that control your heart's rhythm. These impulses move through your heart, which is a muscle, of course, contracting and relaxing. The doctor will look for spikes and dips in the waves."

Penny looked closely at the digital screen to see if her heart had any irregular beats. If there was a spike, Penny did not see it, but then who was she to know how to measure electrical impulses of the heart? She couldn't even measure her capacity to love. She was sure there were enough scars on her heart to keep her from feeling much of anything. And certainly, no EKG could detect the depth of her heartache with much accuracy.

The nurse removed the nodes from Penny's skin. "I'm sending a digital report of the test to Dr. Obregon," she explained. He will be right with you. She waved goodbye and wheeled the EKG cart to another lucky shopper.

Penny tried to sleep, thinking this would be the best way to make the time go more quickly. It was a tough job, though. The ER was noisy. Carts rattled passed her alcove, blowing open her privacy curtains and revealing the frenetic behavior of the ER staff. "Give him a shot of NTX!" someone yelled.

"He is coding. Somebody give me some help."

Penny heard grunting and punching, as if they were beating up on a patient. Within a few minutes she could hear a heart monitor beeping. "He's back! Great job, everyone."

Penny turned on her side. She was grateful she did not have to work in such a volatile place. Her heart would be experiencing spikes for sure. She slowly drifted into a state of relaxation. She placed her hand on her heart, and could feel its steady, sure beating. She would be okay. She was certain of it.

"The sheriff is awake. Dr. Arce has orders to send him home."

Penny's eyes popped open. The sheriff? What sheriff? Sheriff Cerillo? Certainly, he had been taken to the hospital in Alamogordo. She sat up and dropped her bare feet on to the cold tile floor. "Excuse me, sir." The orderly who had moved her into the alcove was within earshot.

"Can I help you?"

"I heard the nurses talking about a sheriff. What sheriff?"

"Oh, you mean Sheriff Tellez? He came in a few hours ago with a case of food poisoning."

Leo is in the ER. Penny was in disbelief. She trotted off to find him. "Where is Leo Tellez?" She asked at the nurse's station.

"I'm right here," Leo said. "Thank God you are okay!"

Penn spun around in the direction of the familiar voice. Penny couldn't believe it. Leo did not appear to be sick. He looked as well rested as she had ever seen him.

Chapter 60

Leo insisted on staying with Penny. He walked her back to her bed and helped her back up on it. "Are you cold?"

"A little."

Leo found a blanket above the cupboard in her area and laid it over her. He tucked it around her shoulders and then ran his fingers lightly over her face. "Looks like you got a scratch running from your ear down to side of your neck."

"Yeah, it was quite an ordeal. Ollie, Johnny's mother and I, got trapped inside Ron Becker's barn. Sheriff Cerillo shot the barn manager and then set the place on fire, while we were hiding inside. He locked the doors for good measure."

Leo was stunned. He had called Sheriff Estefan Cerillo despite Penny asking him not to. Leo hoped Penny would never find out he had contacted him. Leo had broken her trust, and it nearly cost Penny her life. Cerillo had never been one of his favorite law enforcement officers, but still, how could the sheriff be involved in attempted murder?

He gave Penny a closer look. Had she been injured any place else. "Is that why you're here? Did you suffer any injuries?"

"Ollie and I got out of the barn, thanks to Pedro knowing there was a ditch to funnel excess water away from the barn."

"Did Don make it in time?"

"Don got there just as we were pulling ourselves out of the tunnel."

"Did he just leave you alone to fend for yourself?"

"No, Johnny showed up, too. He had been badly injured in an accident with a tractor, and he had a trooper drive him to Becker's place. He showed up around the same time."

"Then, why didn't Don bring you home?"

"Johnny asked Don to call the arson investigator for Otero County and wait at the scene until he got there."

"How did you get home, then?"

"Johnny insisted on driving me to his house in my car. His mother was with us. He wanted me to stay the night, but I refused and headed home on my own."

Leo was confused. "So, what are you doing here?"

"Remember, I told you I found something in the burned-out warehouse, I hadn't had a chance to share with Don. And I still haven't had a chance. But what I didn't tell you was that what I found was an Argentine Dog Bone Bit. It was laced with cocaine and Clenbuterol. I had a reaction to it, and my doctor wanted me to come to the ER to have my heart examined."

Leo was furious. His lips quivered, as he tried to keep his composure. Penny had exposed herself to two deadly drugs. Either one could make her sick, but mixed, he knew they could cause permanent damage to her heart. This was his fault.

"Hello, Penny." Leo noticed a tall, good-looking doctor, parting the curtains in the alcove.

"Hi. Dr. Obregon. This is Sheriff Leo Tellez."

"I know who he is. I'm truly sorry for your loss, Leo. But did you hear that Francisco Parasea has resigned before he even began the job?"

Leo looked over at Penny, who he was sure had been too preoccupied trying to save Becker's barn to hear the news.

"What?" Penny asked. "How can that be?"

"I'll wait outside while Dr. Obregon checks you over."

"Are you leaving the hospital?" Penny asked.

"No, I'll be sitting in the waiting room. I can get a patrol car here and drive you home as soon as you are released."

XXXXX

Penny was bewildered. So much had happened in such a short amount of time, she wasn't sure she could process it. "Well, doctor, let's get this party started."

"Penny, I know you say you feel fine, but the effects of Clenbuterol can be subtle. Your EKG looks normal, but I want to dig a little deeper. The drugs can marginalize the pumping power of your heart. I will check for any swelling of the heart muscles, too."

"And I am going to send you home with a Holter Monitor."

"You're doing what?". Now Penny was worried. What in the heck was a Holter Monitor?

"It doesn't weigh much. I'll have the nurse attach another set of electrodes to your skin, and for the next 24 hours, the monitor will measure your heart's activity. It's like an EKG on wheels!"

"Are you sure I need to go home with something, doctor? I feel fine. I'm a little tired, but then I've been through hell. Being trapped in a burning barn is no party."

"I want to make sure there was no aortic rupture."

"Rupture of what?" Now Penny's breathing began picking up speed.

"Penny, I am being cautious. Clenbuterol can weaken the walls of the heart. I am just making sure you are okay. Trust me."

"And what about the cocaine. You said it was mixed with cocaine."

"You lucked out on the cocaine. It was cut quite a bit with baking soda."

"Yuck." Penny was angry. What kind of sicko would try this on themselves, or on horses?

"Penny, report back to the hospital in 24 hours," the doctor ordered. "In the meantime, I'll leave you in the hands of Sheriff Tellez. He looks like he would be a pretty good babysitter." Dr. Obregon laughed at his own joke. Even Penny saw the humor in it and laughed.

"Oh, and I almost forgot. I've packed the dog bone bit in a plastic baggie. Be careful handling it. You'll want to get it to law enforcement in New Mexico. That appears to be where all the trouble began."

Chapter 61

Pedro did not have to stay long in the emergency room. Orderlies were on hand to wheel him directly to the operating room. In his confusion and perhaps delirium, he thought he saw Penny Larkin in one of the rooms, sitting on a bed and pulling on her boots. Maybe it was just wishful thinking because he had never had the chance to thank her for saving his life.

The orderlies were picking up speed as they moved down the hall. The wheels of the cart were turning so fast that Pedro could feel the rush of air passing through their green medical scrubs. They smelled as fresh as laundry on the line. This immediately calmed him. They rode the elevator to an uncertain floor. Lying flat, Pedro could not see what the game plan was. He would just have to trust the hospital team. Trust was not his strong suit. And besides, how in the world would he pay for his operation, when he was still trying to pay for Maria's?

He strained his neck trying to watch where he was headed, but it was useless and only drained his energy. The elevator doors parted, and the medics slowed down a bit as they entered another hospital wing. "It's Room #223, I believe." The black man with the short-cropped hair pointed to the next room on the right side of the hall. He could see those same green and white tiles lining his path. Pedro thought the man looked a little too serious. Was he going to die, after all?

"Here it is. We're making a short pit stop, Pedro."

The orderlies wheeled Pedro's cart inside the room. He first saw the Crucifix, with the pink crystal hearts hanging on the side of an IV station. Then Maria came into view. She was sitting in her bed, playing with a toy horse, and galloping it across the bedsheets. She looked up as the orderlies entered the room. "Where's my daddy?"

They maneuvered Pedro's gurney as close to Maria's bed as they could. She leaned over and gave Pedro a big kiss on his nose. "I love you, Daddy. Is Milly doing okay? Did you give her the carrots?"

Pedro was silent. Tears welled up in his eyes.

"Daddy. Don't cry. It won't hurt a bit. The doctors are very nice."

Pedro shook his head. He was dreaming. But then, he watched in disbelief as Maria took the Crucifix off the pole and laid it on his chest. "Daddy, this will make you okay."

"I know, Mija. I know."

Chapter 62

Leo was only too happy to take Penny home. They pulled up in her driveway, just like before when he spent the night at her house. He hated to let her go. He idled his car, trying desperately to think of something that would heal his relationship with her.

"Would you like to come in for coffee, for old time's sake?"

"Aren't you beat?"

"I haven't talked to you for so long, Leo, and I could use some sound advice on what to do next with this arson fire. It's not over."

Of course, Leo was well rested, and his stomach had settled down, but he hesitated to take advantage of Penny's state. He knew she was exhausted.

"Thanks. I could use a jolt of coffee before driving home."

When they entered Penny's house, the emotional toll on Leo's heart vacillated from joy to anger. He felt so at home here. Penny had excused herself to use the bathroom and had asked Leo to make the coffee. He walked into the kitchen, turning on the lights as he went, and headed right to the round oak table. He got out the placemats, napkins and a couple of plates. Leo had sat here with Penny many times talking about their future. And now the future was as dark as the night outside the kitchen windows.

He looked in her pantry and spotted the coffee beans. Beside them was a jar of peanut butter. Peanut butter sandwiches had been there first meal together. He had hired Penny to find Rosa Garcia, an 11-year-old who had been kidnapped for the second time. He and Penny had broken up a Russian child-trafficking ring operating out of Mexico.

Leo pulled the peanut butter out and some bread. He ground the coffee beans and placed the coffee on to brew, before making two sandwiches. He found some dill pickles in the refrigerator, and place one slice on each of their plates.

When Penny walked in the kitchen, she smiled. She was adjusting a Holter monitor, which was clipped to her waistband "It's the latest fashion accessory!" Penny laughed until tears fell from her eyes.

Hearing her joke about her circumstances made Leo as happy as he had been in weeks and weeks. "You always look beautiful to me." He did not regret laying it on the line. He loved Penny.

"Thanks, Leo. I'm starved. And I'll bet you are, too." She got two cups out of the cabinet and poured the coffee. Both liked their coffee black. She placed a steaming cup in front of him and looked in his eyes. "You are the best lawman I will ever know, Leo. And you are the most decent man I know, too. Never forget that, regardless of whatever happens between the two of us."

"Penny, I am—you know how sorry I am over what happened."

"Leo, I didn't really understand it until I worked with Don. And now I see how you could get confused. You needed to cling to Alejandra, and you did so through Adriana. I get it, even though it still makes me crazy."

"Something has happened between you and Don?"

"Nothing has happened, Leo. At least, nothing I can't handle."

Leo's heart sunk to his feet. His coffee stung his throat as he swallowed it without thinking of anything but his love for Penny and his frustration with Don. He choked and reached for his napkin.

"You okay, Leo?"

For the sake of his pride, he moved forward. "So, what kind of questions did you have about the Becker case?"

"I need your help with a little side investigation."

"Of course! Whatever you need, Penny."

Chapter 63

Johnny felt well enough, and more importantly had healed enough, to return to work without embarrassment. Before heading off on vacation, Officer Soto had briefed his team, so there was little need to spend time repeating the fact that Sheriff Estefan Cerillo was in protective custody at the Gerald Champion Regional Medical Center in Alamogordo.

Sampson Dales had also been brought in for questioning, and pending any other inquiry, he was released. He did, however, promise not to leave the state of New Mexico. "I'm never leaving this place," he had told Johnny's officers. "I've had enough of Vietnam and other places in hell to last a lifetime. I don't need to fly on a plane to feel better."

Johnny had called Penny a couple of times, but her cell had gone to voicemail. She was no doubt getting her rest. It had been a grueling couple of days. Even his mother slept in until 7 am. At breakfast, he had noticed that Ollie had a bruise on her right cheek and a few scratches on her arms. She was lucky nothing got broken, like a hip! But then his mother was one tough cookie, and she seldom crumbled except for the day her husband was gunned down by the Barrio Norteño gang.

When his cell phone rang at 9 am, he saw Penny's face light up the screen. "Hello, Penny. How are you doing?"

"I slept in this morning."

"I would expect you to rest."

"I had to go to the hospital last night. I was exposed to some bad drugs yesterday."

"What are you talking about? You never mentioned that in the car heading home."

"I had other things on my mind, Johnny."

"What in God's name happened to you?"

"When Don and I visited the warehouse, I found a horse bit. In fairness to Don, I never told him about it. I wanted to check it out first. It was stuffed with a mix of cocaine and Clenbuterol. Of course, I didn't know it and I kept rolling it around in my hands trying to figure out what it was. I got a bad reaction."

"Oh, my God. Don't tell me the Betas Cartel is doping horses?"

Yep, it's more than fires, Johnny. We've got a cocaine and Clenbuterol racket among horse trainers. I suspect that the Sheriff Cerillo is in bed with the Betas Cartel. He's probably their main contact, I'll wager. They've been doping racehorses, and using the same stuff on pregnant mares, trying to get them to abort."

"He never let on about any doping. In fact, the sheriff has said nothing. But I would expect nothing less. He's in danger and he knows it. But thanks for this info. I've got to call the New Mexico Racing Commission."

"Another thing. Pedro, Becker's barn manager is involved, too." Penny added.

"I'll ask Leo to set up a security detail at Sierra Providence."

"You might want to do that, but I would like to know more about what motivated Pedro to agree to burn down Becker's barn in the first place. He loves those horses as much or more than Becker. And, while your mom and I were hiding, he did not give us any indication he was planning on setting the fires."

Johnny's cell phone had an incoming call. He hated to hang up with Penny, but duty called. "Penny, can I call you right back?" Johnny disconnected the call.

"Hello, this is Captain Trejo."

"Captain, this is Don Tellez. I got a call this morning from Ronald Becker."

"Where has he been?"

"He admitted himself to a rehab center yesterday after nearly drinking himself into a stupor. The police in Three Rivers picked him up but recognized him and asked if they could give him a ride somewhere. He said, 'Yes, send me to rehab.' They took him to Alamogordo."

"So that's why he never showed up to help Penny. She will want to know what happened to him."

"I can call her if you want," Don said.

Johnny's first reaction was to yell in the phone, "Hell no!" But he really had appreciated how helpful Don had been. The Otero County

Arson Squad had responded quickly and had given Johnny's office a full report. The fire was sparked by sand and paraffin, using a high intensity Firestarter. It was just as Penny had told him.

"Why don't you give Penny a call," Johnny said. "I know she will really be interested to learn about Becker." Johnny could hardly believe he was speaking *nice* to Don Tellez.

Chapter 64

When Pedro Lopez was transferred to his hospital room after spending several hours in ICU, he thought he noticed a uniformed police officer stationed outside of the hospital room. Right now, it meant nothing to him. He was in too much pain to care. His eyes were blurry from being under the knife pulling the bullets out of his legs. He shut his eyes and thought about his beautiful daughter who was also in the same hospital, getting better by the day. Pedro would find a way out of this mess, but for now he needed to get well for Maria.

The nurse gave Pedro a sip of water through a straw and used the electric controls to move him into a sitting position. "You need to keep in motion, Mr. Lopez, but the doctor hasn't given us permission to get you up out of bed yet. In the meantime, you've got a visitor."

Yes, Pedro thought. No doubt, if the police were outside his room, then being handcuffed to the bed could not be far behind. He blinked trying to focus his eyes. They were weak from losing so much blood. At least that's what the doctor had told him. But he had also told him he would pull through.

At first, when his visitor entered the room, Pedro thought had lost his mind. If his legs were bullet ridden, then so was his brain. It was Lourdes walking over to the side of his bed. She leaned down and brushed Pedro's curly hair out of his eyes. "*Mi amor. ¿Cómo pudo hacerte esto?*" (My love. How could he do this to you?)

How could Sheriff Cerillo shoot him in the legs, she asked? Easy. He had a pistol pointed right at his heart, but fired at his legs, instead. "*Es un hombre malo, Lourdes.*" (He's a bad man, Lourdes.)

"*Lo sé. Lo sé. Lo siento mucho.*"

She was saying she was sorry. Did Pedro hear that right? Pedro watched in amazement as Lourdes pulled a chair up next to his bed. She placed her hand on his arm and rubbed it gently. He saw a tear dripping down her cheek. His beautiful one. "*No llores, querida*. No crying, *por favor.*"

"*Nunca te dejaré de nuevo*, Pedro."

She is not going to leave me again? He must really be wild with a fever because Pedro had long ago given up on ever having Lourdes in his life. "*Te quiero, Lourdes. Yo haré lo que sea necesario para mantenernos juntos.*" Yes, I love you. I will always love you, Lourdes."

A New Mexico State trooper stood in the doorway to Pedro's room. He recognized the black uniform and the cap with the gold braid and gold leaves spreading across the brim.

"Mr. Lopez. Are you up to me asking you some questions?"

"Sí." Lourdes moved away from his bed and sat near the window. Pedro smiled at her and gave her a look of assurance. "*Está bien, Lourdes.*" It will be okay.

"Mr. Lopez, my name is Captain Johnny Trejo of the New Mexico State Police. Is it true that you took money to burn down Ronald Becker's barn?"

Chapter 65

Penny used her GPS to find the White Sands House of Sober Living, on Rochester Street in Alamogordo. She wanted to see Ronald Becker in person and give him the good news about his barn and his horses. She also wanted to break the bad news about the doping and the death of Sonny March. She was sure what she had seen during her remote viewing in the barn, was Georgia and Sonny March trying to give Milly drugs. But why?

Penny pulled into the parking lot of the rehab center and headed to the main desk. She had called ahead and asked for permission to visit, and Becker had agreed. He was sitting in a large leather chair near the window. She could tell from his view that he had been watching her walk from her car into the building.

"Mr. Becker. You look pretty good," Penny said.

"Penny, you know how much I wanted to be there to help you, but I couldn't." His eyes drifted to the window, and then looked back at Penny.

"I know that. And that night is behind us now. I came with good news. Sheriff Cerillo started a fire in your barn, but your local volunteer fire department saved most of it. The only real damage was in the tack room, and a bit of smoke and burned timber in Milly's stall."

"Milly! Is she okay?" Penny watched as Becker squirmed in his chair and gripped the arms until his knuckles grew white.

"Milly is fine, and so are your three other mares. They are happy as clams at Joseph Drake's farm. Although, one of the chestnut mares had her colt early. She was under a lot of stress; the vet told me. I'm sorry. She dropped her foal last night. But she and your new colt are doing great."

"And what about Pedro?"

"I do believe Pedro took money from the Betas Cartel to start the fire, but I don't think he had the heart to follow through with it. Sheriff

Cerillo caught up with him in the barn, shot him, and took the money the Cartel had given him."

"Is he alive?"

"Pedro? Yes, he is in the hospital in El Paso. He received some wretched wounds to his thighs. But he will be okay."

"I never could understand why Pedro would do such a thing. He and his daughter, Maria, loved Milly so much."

"Well, that is the other thing I wanted to share with you. We believe Pedro took the money to pay for Maria to have heart surgery, which was yesterday. I checked with the hospital's business office, and he had paid the first half of the amount he owed, the day before the fire."

"I wish he would have told me Maria needed help. I knew she did not look good. But why he didn't ask me for the money, I don't know."

"Perhaps that is something you can ask him for yourself."

Becker stared out the window, as if lost in another place and time.

Penny walked over to the window to see Becker's view. There was a small pond, where three swans were moving in tandem across the water. Penny always thought a swan could get trapped in a small pond if there weren't at least 30 yards of clearance for a takeoff. Were they trapped there, forever swimming in circles? *Am I running in circles, too?*

Penny couldn't delay her questions for Ron Becker any longer. But she needed to broach the next subject carefully. The counselor had told Penny on the phone that Becker still had three more weeks of rehab and months of recovery at home. She had been warned about mentioning anything that might make Ronald Becker take a backward step.

"Do you mind if I sit down with you?" There was another chair close to the window, though not as large or as sturdy.

"Oh, please. I apologize for not asking you sooner."

"Mr. Becker."

"Please call me, Ron."

"Thank you, Ron. I have some other news I think you should know, but I need to be assured that you can handle it."

"You've got my ten-year sober chip. Get it out of your bag and give it to me. I'll hold it, and that way you can tell me anything, and I'll be okay."

Penny searched around in her bag until she found the chip at the bottom, close to the secret pocket where she hid her revolver. She handed it back to Ron. "I know you suspected that your wife was having an affair. And you probably already realized it was Sonny March. Was that why you fired him?"

Becker's chest swelled as he took a huge breath and blew the air across the room. Penny was relieved to smell peppermint and not alcohol as it passed by her face. She waited for Ron to answer, hoping he could face the truth. Truth was not an alcoholic's strong suit. Denial was the king of spades in every alcoholic's deck of cards.

"Yes, that is why I sent him packing!"

"Well, there is more to this story, I'm afraid. For some reason, Sonny March and your wife, were doping your pregnant mares."

Becker stood and pounded his fist against the wall, rattling the nearby window. "No!" he shouted it so loudly that an attendant came rushing into the room. "No!"

"Are you okay, Mr. Becker?"

"Yes, thanks, Hector. Truth is never the cocktail of choice in my life. It's hard to drink it in."

"Do you want this woman to leave?"

"No, no. She needs to stay, and I need to face the truth. Finally."

The attendant helped Becker back into his chair and left the room. Penny caught a glimpse of him standing just outside in the hall.

"Ron, do you have any idea why they would try to dope these horses, especially Milly? I thought Georgia loved her?"

"I had suspected for several months that March was doping my racehorses. But I had no proof. Testing always showed them to be clean. But I think March must have figured out a way to disguise it at the track."

"Where are those horses now?" Penny wondered.

"I sold them at auction after Georgia died."

Penny continued her explanation of the doping. "The cocktail of cocaine and Clenbuterol is particularly hard on pregnant mares. Besides causing them to hallucinate and go lame in their stalls, it can cause them to abort their foals."

"How do you know they were giving my mares this stuff?"

"They used an Argentine Dog Bone Bit for training these select mares. I got proof that March regularly purchased these bits in El Paso. When he took a mare out to exercise, March would attach the bit to the mare's bridle and feed her the drugs under the tongue. It was injected in the copper roller in a powder form. I had the misfortune of having a reaction to it myself."

"Oh, my God. I am so sorry to put you through this."

Penny pointed to the monitor, hidden under her jacket. "As bad as my overdose was, it led me to find out how your horses, and others in the state were being harmed." Fires were just the last straw, so to speak.

"How can I repay you?"

"Ron, you already paid me very well, although on another day, I'll tell you the story about being trapped inside the barn when the sheriff set it on fire. You can buy me breakfast at Cracker Barrel. It's a two-biscuit kind of story."

"Oh, my God!" Penny watched Becker twist in his leather chair and bring his calloused hands over his eyes.

"In case you ever need to escape, you can get out of your barn by crawling through the tunnel you installed to bleed excess water out of the barn's stalls. I'm grateful."

Ron Becker dropped his hands into his lap. He rubbed his ten-year chip in his palms, turning it over and over. "A chip can motivate you to stay sober," he said, "but it can't buy happiness. Only facing the truth, gives you any chance at happiness."

"Was Georgia unhappy?"

"I was a cold son-of-a-gun sometimes. I just couldn't find it in my heart to love Georgia as much as she needed. When we were first married, she was beautiful and loving to me, but my drinking drove her away."

"Ron, I know how that feels. My mother did her best to drive me out of her life."

"Is your mother still alive?"

"Funny you would ask. It has been ten years ago this week that she died." Penny had thought she would never forget that anniversary, but here she was nearly forgetting the exact date.

Becker stood and handed Penny the chip. "I want you to keep this chip. You've earned it."

"Thank you. I will cherish it, Ron. It means a lot to me. I know this may be hard to tell me, but did Georgia love Sonny March?"

"I suspected that Georgia was in love with him, yes. And I did worry she was making plans to leave me. She had her own inheritance from her family, which would make it easy to do."

"Do you think they were planning to launch out on their own? Maybe taking drug cartel money to take out the racing competition was just too tempting."

"That was my thought," Becker said. "But then Milly kicked Georgia, and she died."

"Ron, I also wanted to tell you that Sonny March is also dead. He died in a fire in an El Paso warehouse. It was arson, and we believe March was murdered. Maybe by the Betas Cartel, which we suspect is also behind the barn fires in New Mexico."

"Where did you hear about this?"

"You can thank Don Tellez. He also hired me to investigate the El Paso fire, and that's how I learned about March's death. I suspect that Georgia and Sonny March were trying to cause Milly to abort, and then perhaps convince you to sell her to a silent buyer—them. It's just a guess. I also believe Milly was trying to keep Georgia from giving her those drugs. She knew it was bad, and she fought back in the only way she knew how, with her hooves."

"I wish there was some way I could make it up for all the misery I have caused," Becker said.

"Would you consider keeping Pedro on as your barn manager? I think it's time he knew what real love is."

Chapter 66

Johnny was uncomfortable asking Pedro Lopez such direct questions with his girlfriend in the room, but it had to be done. And besides, Pedro had yet to tell him the truth. Johnny asked the same question from another angle. "So, is it true, you took money from the Betas Cartel to pay for your daughter's surgery?"

This got an immediate response. Pedro's eyes lit up and his head fell back into his pillow. "*Sí, Capitán. Tomé el dinero. Estaba tan desesperada. Mi hija iba a morir sin la operación.*"

Lourdes moved closer to Pedro. "He was desperate to help our daughter!" She leaned down and held him close. She was crying loudly and making Johnny even more uncomfortable than he already was. He changed positions in his chair.

"Why did the sheriff shoot you?"

"He didn't think I had the heart to kill my horses."

"Your horses?"

"Yes, they are my horses! I take care of them. I wash them, feed them, brush them down, and love them. Mr. Becker hasn't done any work in the barn since…"

"Since what?" Johnny asked.

"Since Georgia died."

"So, it was Sheriff Cerillo. Right? You didn't have the guts to start the fire?"

"I am a father, first, and a coward, second. I was torn in two with grief. Maria loves Milly, and I did not want Milly to die. And I also did not want Maria to die. The doctor told me she was going to if she didn't have the surgery."

Johnny leaned back in his chair and contemplated what he was about to say. Did he have the authority to make such promises? He would risk it.

"The sheriff lied to me," Lourdes said. She leaned over and held Pedro's hand, massaging it and crying. Tears rolled down her cheeks.

Johnny pulled a tissue from a box on the side table and handed it to her. "If you would be willing to help us track down the sheriff's contacts with the Betas, we could go easy on your sentence. You did, of course, break the law."

Pedro smiled. "Of course, I can help you. Find Willie. He works for the big boss, *el jefe*."

"Thank you, Pedro." Johnny placed his hand over his heart as he spoke. "I will see what I can do to work things out for you. I cannot promise, but I know in your heart, you were trying to do the right thing."

Pedro pointed to his blue jeans, which were hanging on a hook. "Willie's phone number."

Johnny reached inside the jeans, which were worn through in places that he knew were not done out of a sense of style. They were all Pedro probably owned. He pulled out a small piece of paper which a phone number printed on it.

"*Muchas Gracias, Pedro.*"

Johnny left the hospital. He had to get in touch with Penny. He couldn't wait to share this news.

Chapter 67

Leo drove home after a wonderful hour with Penny, sharing coffee and peanut butter sandwiches. How could he have been so dumb giving up such a beautiful woman? When he unlocked his front door, he was struck by how cold and drafty his house was. Why had he never noticed that before? Penny's place was warm and inviting. He felt so at home there, and so out of place in his own home. He needed new windows. They rattled every time the wind blew. He turned up the heat and headed to the kitchen for a cup of coffee. Leaning against the counter, he contemplated his next steps. In six weeks, he would be an after-thought in the world of law enforcement. He would no longer lead anything. Was he ready to work for the Feds? Leo knew his style was a bit more off the books. And he was so darn stubborn, preferring to solve cases his own way. The Federal government always made life, and solutions to big problems, complicated.

Leo walked from room to room in his house, each of which was tattered around the edges. He had never bothered to make it feel like a home. He had moved here after Alejandra and Marta had died. It was a small bungalow with only a couple of bedrooms. He made the second one his office, although he seldom spent any time in it. He was either on the road, in his department headquarters, or at Alejandra's grave.

Leo was meant to be a loner. He was satisfied with that. He sought out loneliness like a good friend. Now he had time to deepen this friendship. He knew he had not prepared for such a destiny. He had had so many great dreams, but year by year they all arrived dead or barely breathing.

The buzzing of his cell phone stung him with the truth. *Damn!* Technology was still trying to connect him to the world. He would not answer. He would learn to love being alone. His cell phone buzzed again, from the safety of his belt, where it hung in good company with his gun, his Taser™ and some bullets. He yanked the mobile from its leather case and answered. "This is Sheriff Tellez." His voice was hollow and strained.

"Sheriff, this is Ricardo Delgado. The County Judge wants to meet with you this afternoon. Can you make it at 4?"

Chapter 68

Penny shoved Ron Becker's AA chip in her jeans pocket and gave him a hug around the neck. Love showed up in the most unexpected places. Penny needed to know that she could care about another person and so did Ron.

"It wouldn't hurt you to do the 12-Step program, Penny." He smiled and patted her arm.

"Yeah. I'm sure you're right." She returned his smile and looked back through the window. The swans were gone. Only the cattails shooting out of the pond remained, and they were releasing their seeds to the wind.

"You just have to take the first step," Ron said. "Admit you are powerless, and your life is unmanageable."

"You've got that right, Ron. But I've still have to find who hired the arsonist. My work for you isn't done."

"Don't get in harm's way. You've done enough."

"These fires won't stop. You were lucky this time."

"Then, have Don Tellez help you."

"Thanks. I'll give him a call. Be well, Ron. I'll keep you posted on my progress."

Penny walked out of Becker's room and out of the House of Sober Living. Perhaps the first day of her own sober life was just beginning, too.

Chapter 69

Sunday morning dawned bright and hot. Penny drove as fast as the law would allow—well maybe a bit faster—to get to Sunland Park, New Mexico, which was just a stone's throw from El Paso's city limits. She had promised Ken Whatley, she would meet him at the Rio Grande Racetrack by 1 pm. She had no other leads unless Sheriff Cerillo coughed up his contacts. And she guessed, the sheriff's lips would be sealed even after a hard-nosed interrogation by special investigators with the New Mexico State Police. The Betas Cartel had no doubt already threatened the sheriff's wife. And they didn't bluff. That much Penny knew from personal experience.

Much like the Sicilian Mafia in poor Italian neighborhoods during the 19th century, Mexican drug cartels had moved into underfed and underserved regions of Mexico in the 20th century. Penny knew criminal enterprises like these always filled a hole for the hungry and the oppressed. Having lived on the border for almost a decade, she soon realized that poverty, greedy politicians, and the Roman Catholic Church were the only constants in Mexico.

Penny pulled into a parking lot jammed with cars. She had to park about a football field away from the front door to the casino. She opened her trunk and did a quick change of clothes. She looked at the heart monitor clipped to her belt, and then tossed it in the trunk. She would put it back on after her meeting with Whatley. She owed Dr. Obregon that much.

Penny donned a pair of khaki shorts and a t-shirt and slipped on a pair of Skechers sandals. She grabbed her bag and fumbled around to make sure her gun and cell phone were hidden and secure before making the trek inside. She also saw a tired canister of pepper spray. *Wouldn't hurt to keep it with me.* She had learned some time ago that parting with protective gear made for a very bad time.

Going through the casino to the racetrack meant she would have to pass through the rows and rows of one-armed bandits with attendant gamblers armed with lighted cigarettes and large plastic cups to catch their winnings. She didn't relish it, as it always made her feel sad. Plus, how long could she hold her breath?

But Whatley had told her to look for him in the lobby, and she hoped he would be on time. The smoke always gagged her, and she would not be able to remain there for long. It took Penny five minutes to make the walk to the front door. By then she was dripping with sweat and longing for a cool glass of water. To her surprise and delight, a casino employee handed her a bottle of cold water as she opened the door. "Welcome to Rio Grande Casino," he said. "Enjoy your time with us and good luck!"

Penny had little hope of enjoying her time, but she did hope her luck was about to change. With her client, Ronald Becker, in rehab, she was even more determined to solve this case. Perhaps if she could talk with a trainer who had used the Argentine Dog Bone Bit, she could get a sense of what was going on. Certainly, not every horse trainer who used this kind of bit, had evil intentions for pregnant mares. However, it was probably a much bigger picture than she could see now. It always was.

She saw Ken Whatley standing off to the side of the lobby smoking a cigarette and talking with a beautiful dark-haired woman, dressed in a cream-colored suit with matching three-inch high heels. Penny chugged down the rest of her water and tossed it into a recycle bin, as she walked toward the pair. Whatley waved at Penny. He snuffed out his cigarette in an ashtray and said goodbye to the woman. Her eyes were black, perhaps accentuated by her choice of the light-colored suit. Her gaze burned a couple of holes in Penny's chest, which was still heaving from the hike from the parking lot. She gave Penny an insincere smile, and left the lobby through double doors that read, "Do not enter. Alarm will sound."

The perspiration running down Penny's arms, made her skin tingle. Her sunglasses were fogging up from the smoke and the heat. She threw her glasses in her bag and wiped her eyes with her sweaty fingers. Penny moved toward Whatley who was still trying to weave his way around the gamblers. As he moved closer to her, she could see in her mind's eye that beyond those double doors was a backroom where men were playing cards. The cigar was the smoke of choice. It curled around their heads like crowns of mischief. Every man had a mustache and a crop of curly brown hair. Beads of sweat danced on their chins. Glasses of whiskey stained the green felt-lined table. Penny watched as one player reached forward to scrape in his winnings and spilled his drink. Another player took offense and stood. Penny noticed both men had guns strapped to their belts. One of the angry poker players was stretching his fingers, as if they were stiff from holding the cards. His fingers moved slowly to his waist where they fluttered over his pistol like a bird of prey.

"Hi Penny. I am so happy you made it. I wasn't sure you would bother to come."

Penny jerked her eyes toward Ken Whatley. It would take a few seconds to adjust from what she had just viewed in the shadows of her mind. Whatley had his hand extended toward hers. She could see his hand reaching toward her, but she still could not lift her own arm to meet his. Penny knew she did not have the luxury of time to process what she had just witnessed. She had to stay in the present moment and go with her gut. The problem was that her gut sensed that something didn't feel quite right.

Whatley reached for Penny's right hand which was still hanging at her side. If he had been up to no good, it was not apparent in his smile. He gave off that same air of youthful innocence he had displayed at the tack and feed shop. He shook her hand vigorously, as if trying to shake some sense into her. Finally, Penny blinked into awareness.

Did she dare ask who the woman was that had just left by the double doors? She thought better of it, already knowing what was happening in that back room. She would be safer keeping her mouth shut. She wiped the hair from her eyes, and a whiff of smoke passed over her face.

"Sorry we have to walk so far to the racetrack from here, but I thought it was easier to meet in the Casino," Whatley said, as he coughed. "Normally, we could enter the barns from a gate behind the building."

"No problem. This was the best way, I'm sure. Thanks."

Penny followed Whatley through the crowds of gamblers, security guards in black suits, and cocktail servers, who carried their trays of drinks above their heads. That would take a special skill, Penny thought. She could probably master cocktailing if she could keep an oxygen tank and a mask near the bar to whisk the smoke out of her lungs.

"Right this way, Penny." Whatley led her through a long hall, and down a wide ramp toward fresh air.

Before them stood several long white barns, with beige trim around the windows. "This is beautiful." Penny said. And she meant it. A gentle breeze carried the aroma of hay and horse feed passed her nose. A horse whinnied.

"Step back!" Whatley moved his arm in a protective motion in front of her, as the horse and his trainer tromped passed them.

The Quarter Horse glistened with sweat flowing off his flanks. His mouth was foaming, and his nose was wet and congested. Penny watched as the handler guided the animal adroitly passed several other people who were also standing in the way.

"The second race just ended. The horses will be returning to their stalls. Maybe a couple of trainers will have time to talk," Whatley said.

"What color is that horse?" Penny had never seen a red horse.

"That would be a red roan or a red dun. I'm not all that certain. After a horse has finished a race, his colors deepen."

"What a peaceful place." Penny said, even as she wondered how the criminal mind could ever foster plans to harm these beautiful animals. She could easily understand, however, the lure of being around them. "How did you get started in this business?"

"My father owned the store, and I took over when he retired five years ago. I was raised doing my homework on hay bales and figuring out my math problems by counting bags of feed and inventorying the tack."

"It must have been a wonderful way to grow up. What was the biggest lesson you learned?"

"Like humans, horses have a fight or flight instinct. A horse can never win a race without learning to trust humans."

"Wow. My dad was a race-car driver. He relied on his pure grit, and his love of speed to win races. He wasn't long on trusting others."

"A horse who has promise must be started at a young age to learn to work with humans, and to believe that the handler has the best in mind for his future."

"Maybe everybody should be required to spend a year working with horses, to learn about building relationships and learning to trust."

"I couldn't agree more." Whatley smiled as he led Penny into the depths of a second barn, along a walkway that was lined with a rubber-like floor. "A horse's hooves are hot after a race. Many tracks have installed a rubber liner to keep the horse from injury as he walks back to detention."

"To what?" Penny asked.

"The winning horse must have his blood and urine tested. The horse is then taken by stable hands to a hot walker to cool down. Come this way. There is someone I want you to meet. And we're late!"

Whatley's stride picked up speed, as if he were preparing to sprint out of the barn. Penny quickened her step to keep up with him. As they walked into the depths of the barn, the hallway grew darker. It was tough to see where to step with black rubber floor beneath her feet. There were no windows for natural light, and the overhead lights were off.

Whatley stopped abruptly at a door on the right side of the hallway. "Here we are!"

Penny tripped and fell forward, grabbing Whatley's shoulders to keep from winding up on the floor. Whatley turned and took her in his arms. He massaged her shoulders and leaned his face into her neck. His breath was hot and smelled of cigarettes. He took Penny's head in his hands and used his index finger to trace the shape of her face, winding up at her lips. He held her, perhaps a little too tightly. His eyes were now dark gray, and his long lashes fluttered.

Whatley's mouth was warm and moist. His tongue penetrated the back of her throat. Penny's adrenaline raced through her bloodstream, encircling her breasts. The neurons of her brain lit up like neon, flickering in as many colors as a racetrack full of jockeys' silks. Whatley pressed his chest hard against hers, pinning her to the wall. Penny had never been so shocked and yet so willing to let him continue. Maybe it had to be this way. She was panting like a horse searching for a water trough.

"You are a good-looking pony, you know that?" He kissed her again, running his hands over the length of her body. Whatley opened the door, and flicked on the overhead lights, revealing an office with a large desk, empty of paperwork. He moved her toward the desk, sweeping her up in his arms and laying her on the desk. Penny's eyes were darting from Whatley to the lights and back to Whatley. She was dizzy and confused.

She tried to keep from breathing so fast. She could feel her eyes filling with moisture. She blinked back tears.

Whatley lunged at her, and by instinct Penny rolled out of his way. His chest took the full force of wooden desktop. She could hear the air rushing from his lungs. She took advantage of the opening and tried to dash for the exit.

Whatley managed to rear up like a bucking horse and grab her leg. He lifted her body, which she made stiff and heavy as an anvil. He shoved her against a coat rack hanging on the wood paneled wall. She cried out, but he refused to let go. His mouth fell against her neck. He was breathing heavily and moaning as he slammed her against the coat rack again.

Penny's legs buckled from the stabbing pain in her back. He released her, letting the weight of her body take the full blow on the cement floor. She braced herself for what this angry man had in mind because she had no more energy to fight with him.

But Ken Whatley did not try to hurt her again even as she lay nursing her hip, which had taken the brunt of the fall. Instead, she watched his highly polished, brown boots make a 180 degree turn and march out of the room, slamming the door behind him.

Penny could hear the lock on the door clicking into place.

Chapter 70

Penny remained panting on the chilly cement. It hurt to move and to breathe. The tenderness in her back and hip were bearable. After all, she had suffered worse when she had to jump over a barbed wire fence in Mexico. But her chest was throbbing from breathing so hard in her struggle with Ken Whatley.

She rolled her head side to side, which filled her lungs with the rancid smells of sawdust and manure. Penny saw the boot prints of trainers or handlers who had walked in and out of this office. There were bits of straw clustered in the corners of the room, too, where someone was careless with a broom.

Whose office is this? Will they be coming back soon? Penny realized she had to be ready to defend herself regardless of who walked through the door. At the thought of Whatley's return, Penny tried to pull herself up by gripping the legs of the desk, and then hanging on to one of the drawers, which was partially open. As she moved upward, she fell into the drawer, pinching her fingers. She dropped back, rubbing her hand. It was her shooting hand. She winced, as she wiggled her fingers. Thankfully, nothing was broken.

Penny knew her bag had fallen behind the desk. In Whatley's haste, he had not seen it or had forgotten she was carrying one. She inched her way under the desk and pulled on her bag, which was wedged between the desk's legs and the back wall. One big tug brought the purse flying straight at her head. Penny pulled the bag close to her chest. This was her lifeline out of this dismal hole, and no one was going to take it from her.

She rummaged inside, trying to pull the mobile phone free of its hiding place. It was wedged securely inside the conceal-and-carry portion of her bag, along with her guns. She had ordered the bag on Amazon, and it had saved her bacon a few times. She finally freed the phone from the bottom of the bag and shut off the ringer. She did not want to draw the attention of anyone walking by the office.

She noticed that she had missed a call from Don. She pushed redial.

"Penny, where in the hell have you been?"

"Don, I need help."

"Where are you?"

"I'm locked in an office in one of the barns at the Rio Grande Racetrack."

"Which barn? There are 30 or more."

"I don't know exactly."

"Do I dare ask what you are doing at the track?"

"I've got a bunch to tell you, but I was locked in here by Ken Whatley, who owns Bridle and Bit on Doniphan. You know the place?

"Yes, sort of. Who is this guy?"

"I asked for his help on tracking down some trainers." Penny was afraid to confess she had not given Don all the evidence he needed for the warehouse fire.

"I can explain later. Can you send help? I don't know how much time I have before Whatley returns."

"Leave your phone on, and I'll see if we can get a tracker on it. I'll be there as soon as I can."

"Don, I need more than you. This is big. Can you call Johnny and have him send in the cavalry?" There was no response on Don's end. Either the connection was lost, or he had hung up in disgust.

Penny rolled over on her good hip and brought her aching body to her knees. She used the chair to pull herself to a standing position. She opened one of the bottom drawers, and tucked her cell phone deep inside, under a pile of papers. Then she took her revolver out of her bag and placed it in the left-hand drawer, which was filled with pencils and pens, and a pair of scissors and a stapler. She tucked her pistol in another drawer out of caution. The scissors might work in defending herself, but she doubted she could wrestle her way to safety with them. Ken Whatley could no doubt overpower her. Scissors as a weapon were just plain stupid, she thought. She hid them in the back of the drawer, just in case he thought to use them against her.

Penny opened her makeup kit and looked at herself in her compact mirror. Out of habit, she powdered her face and rubbed some pink lipstick across her mouth. Why are women so vain? She shook her head. Did she need makeup to cover her fear?

The door to the office swung open with such force that it banged against the paneling. Penny still had her compact in her hand. Ken Whatley was laughing. He appeared in good spirits, as if nothing had occurred between the two of them. His arm reached down and grabbed Penny's bag, knocking the compact out of her hand. It fell to the floor, breaking the mirror in two pieces.

"I realized I forgot to get your purse before I was so rudely interrupted in our little rendezvous." He reached inside Penny's bag.

She could hear him rustling through her personal things. It made her sick. Penny knew what he was looking for, but he would not find it.

"You don't have a cell phone?" Whatley's eyes were like question marks. His pupils were large and dotted with contempt.

"I already looked for it. I must have left it in my car, plugged into the charger. My mistake."

"Your mistake, and my lucky day!" Whatley's voice was increasing in volume. He leaned in closer. Penny smelled the fragrance of whiskey on his breath. It was so powerful that is dominated the smell of nicotine on his fingers, which were wrapped around her arm. "Let me help you to your feet, my dear."

Whatley kept yanking on her arm until she stood next to him. He shoved her into the chair, spinning her up against the wall. "I have to leave you now. Sadly, I cannot stay and play." He smiled and tossed her bag on the floor. His face looked different. His youthful innocence had fled, along with his integrity. He saluted Penny with his right hand, and left so quickly, she did not have a chance to make a break for it. Heck, she didn't even try to bang Whatley over the head with her purse when he had thrown it on the floor.

Chapter 71

Johnny saw the phone call coming in from Don Tellez, and for a nanosecond, thought about not answering it. After all, it probably had something to do with Penny. Johnny would rather not have Don and Penny linked in the same sentence. If he had been an English teacher instead of an officer of the law, he would diagram Don right out of her life.

"Hi, this is Captain Trejo."

"Captain, this is Don Tellez. I just spoke with Penny. She's locked in one of the barns at the Rio Grande Racetrack. This is your jurisdiction, and I thought you would want to know. Besides, she told me to call you and have you bring the cavalry."

"Did she say exactly what barn?"

"No, she didn't know for sure. But she's locked inside one of the offices."

"I can try and put a tracer on her cell phone."

"Yes, I told her you would try that, too."

"Thanks, Don. I'll get on it."

"I want to join you."

Johnny, hesitated, knowing this was police work, not arson, but something in his gut told him it was the right thing to do, even though it wasn't the legal one. "Give me 30 minutes to contact Penny's cell phone provider."

"It's Verizon?"

"Yes, I believe it is," Johnny said. "I remember talking to her about it one day last summer. She likes it because she can get cell phone service almost every place in New Mexico, except for a few spots between Deming and Las Cruces." Johnny knew this all too well, having found Penny six months ago stranded there on the side of the road in a dust storm.

"I'll be waiting for you to call me back," Don said. "I don't have to ask you to hurry."

"I know. I'll do my best."

Johnny regretted, as he often did, the lack of funding to the state police in New Mexico for high tech equipment like a cell site simulator. But, with a bit of time, he could generally work around that by contacting the cell phone provider and asking them to provide tracking. With the carrier's help, he would be able to get close enough to where Penny was being held. He was sure of it. The question was, would it be in time?

Johnny dialed his contact, Judy Farnham, at Verizon, who quickly helped him set up a tracking system. "This is going to take us every bit of 30 minutes to ping off our cell phone towers. Then, with any luck, I can get you within 100 feet of your suspect."

"I'm going to move in the direction of the racetrack," Johnny said. "You've got my cell phone number. Call me on that. I've got to get going. And many thanks."

"No, problem, Captain. We are happy to help."

Johnny ran toward the parking lot, choosing an SUV with a full tank of gas, and the most modern equipment, including a GPS screen, like the one that got him into trouble the last time he was on his way to rescue Penny. He was going to have to give her a lecture about staying out of harm's way. He chuckled, at the thought of Penny doing any such thing. She wore *harm's way* as a badge of courage.

Don Tellez answered his phone immediately. "Hi, Captain. I'm just a few steps from my car."

"Meet me at the parking lot near the backside of the racetrack, near the barns. You will probably beat me there but stay put until I arrive."

"Will do. Are you sending backup?"

Johnny took in a breath and slapped his leg with his hand. He had been so determined to find Penny he had forgotten her request for more help than just he could provide.

"I'll take care of it. Thanks." Johnny called dispatch from his car and asked for back up for the racetrack. "Bring the hardware," he said. By hardware, his team knew he meant automatic weapons. Something told him if a cartel was involved, then state police would have to respond with guns as big as theirs.

Johnny kept an M828A3 Barrett automatic weapon in his trunk. He drove past his vehicle and grabbed the gun and threw it on the front seat of the SUV. He felt more secure with it since his days in the Army. He surely hoped he didn't have to use it, but then that is why he carried it. It was his "just in case." And this was a classic case of *just*.

His cell phone rang, and Penny's face popped up on the screen.

"Johnny, did Don call you?"

"Yes, I'm on my way."

"Hurry, please."

"Can you remember anything about the barn?"

"I know we walked the length of at least two barns from the casino, but I can't be sure in what direction. The floors are covered in rubber, to protect the horses. Does that help?"

"It's something. Keep your phone on."

"I will. The battery is running low, so I am going to hang up now."

"Penny, I'm on my way. Don't worry! Verizon is pinging your phone now." Johnny wasn't sure she had heard him. There was nothing but silence on the other end, which was some 35 miles from his location heading south on I-10. Had her battery gone dead? He prayed it was still bouncing off the Verizon towers.

Chapter 72

Leo took the stairs to the third floor, where the El Paso County Judge had her office. There were two banks of elevators, but all were painfully slow. The stairs gave him some time to ponder what could possibly have occurred in the chambers of county government that needed his immediate assistance? Judge Patricia Achio was a well-respected and well-educated leader, with her law degree from Stanford University. El Paso County probably didn't deserve her, but Leo figured they were lucky to have her for the time. She was young and would no doubt find more satisfying things to pursue in the future. But now is now, and he was grateful for today.

The double glass doors leading to the Judge's office were open. Two of the El Paso County Commissioners were holding them as they chatted, waiting for the entire bench of eight elected officials to arrive. They shook the Sheriff's hand and pointed him toward the conference room.

Leo poured a cup of coffee from a stainless carafe and sat in one of the side chairs. He wasn't sure where he should sit, but the places bordering the wall seemed appropriate. When the Judge walked in, trailed by her chief of staff, the rest of the commissioners followed and sat in assigned seats, known only to them.

"Good afternoon, Sheriff. Would you please join us at the table?" Judge Achio pointed to the chair at the end of the conference table. The table, made from a light ash wood, showed evidence of many deliberations. As he sat, Leo realized his eyes would look directly into hers. Thankfully, he didn't have to look at the Commissioners, but he could still see their reflections thanks to the table's highly polished lacquer.

"Sheriff, we've called you here because after much discussion over the resignation of Sheriff-elect Francisco Parasea, we have voted unanimously for you to fill his post for the next four years." The judge leaned back in her well-padded chair and smiled.

The news floated over the table, resting on Leo's shoulders like a butterfly--its wings covered with iridescent scales. It hovered over his wounded shoulder, reminding him of the cartel's bullet which had nearly cost him his life.

"Sheriff, I know this is a surprise to you, but it is not a surprise to us. You have been a wonderful sheriff, and we were all tremendously sad when you lost the election. We knew you were the better man for the job. I hope you will accept this appointment and do so quickly. We need you!"

Leo stood. He now had the courage to look at both sides of the table. Every commissioner, both male and female, was smiling. "Your Honor, I accept!"

Cheers and clapping exploded around the room. Two assistants wheeled in cake and punch.

"It is time to celebrate our victory." The Judge took a cup of punch and toasted the sheriff. "*Salud!* Sheriff Leo Tellez is back!"

Chapter 73

Penny checked the battery on her cell phone. It showed 17 percent. She closed as many applications as she could to save power. She wiped her forehead, which was wet with perspiration. She had not realized how hot it was in the room. There did not seem to be any air ducts, and no windows. How did anyone survive in the Southwestern heat of the summer in here? She was grateful it was November, and not June.

Was the room growing even warmer? Or was it her imagination? She took off her sweater, leaving her bare arms to find any fresh air left in the stifling office. She knew she should remain calm. Johnny was on his way, and he was bringing help. But something wasn't right. She looked up at the light on the ceiling. It appeared to be flickering. Or was it her eyes, growing tired from a week plagued by a torrent of emotions? She stared intently at the light bulbs above her head, waiting for them to flash off and on again. Her vision began to blur. The blinking lights created a crescendo of confusion in her mind. Was that Milly calling out to her? Penny's head fell forward onto the desk.

She heard Milly's whinny before she saw a vision of the mare galloping toward her. Her belly swayed as she picked up speed. Her mane flew backwards creating a sail of certainty. Penny knew Milly was on her way to rescue her from this cage. She jumped on Milly's back and patted her side. The horse nickered with joy. Together they climbed above the rows and rows of barns, filled with horses and trainers and jockeys with dreams. They soared through the night sky, wrapped in the comfort of a billowing cloud. In the distance, Penny could see a barn in flames. Puffs of white vapors rose into the air, followed by gusts of black smoke, choking the air beneath them.

Penny began to cough, waking her from her reverie. Smoke stung her nose. Millie coming to her rescue was only a dream. Something was truly burning. She felt the inside wall, and it was warm. *Not again!* Penny was angry that she had been so stupid to walk right into Whatley's trap. She did not have time to wait for Johnny. He was still 30 minutes away.

Penny had tried the door earlier but knew she could not budge it. Her eyes moved around the room with intensity, searching for a way to escape. She pulled out her cell phone. It was now barely red. It would soon turn off, to save the battery. She shoved it in her pocket. Then Penny opened the middle drawer and grabbed her revolver.

She aimed the gun at the lock on the door and fired. The first bullet missed the lock and landed in the paneling. Her hands were shaking. She closed one eye and pulled the trigger a second time. The lock blew away from the door, along with the doorknob. Penny searched for pistol, and the scissors she had pushed to the back of the drawer. She shoved her pistol in her bag, and with her right hand she pried open the door. The hallway was filled with white clouds of hissing vapors rising from the rubber floor. Horses were whinnying and kicking their hooves against their stalls. She ran back and got her sweater and proceeded down the hall with her sweater halfway over her head. She opened each stall and clicked her tongue coaxing the horses forward. She ran ahead of the herd as they stampeded down the long hall. Penny could hear sirens in the distance.

She stumbled over a man who was lying in the walkway. It was Ken Whatley. Blood was trickling from his nose. Penny felt for a pulse, but there was none.

"It is too late for Mr. Whatley."

Penny jerked her head in the direction of the voice, which floated above the blackening smoke. It was Genevieve March, the woman in the beige suit that Penny had met in the lobby. Now she was standing at the doorway to the barn, with a gun pointed at Penny. "He killed my brother, Sonny. And now, I am paying it forward."

The woman teetered in her high heels, trying to stay vertical on the spongy rubber floor. She grabbed the side of the wall and aimed her gun at Penny.

"Why would Ken kill Sonny?" Penny yelled at her, as if her breath would stop a bullet.

"It's war, baby! The Betas are fighting the New Generation cartel. Everybody wants a piece of the action, including me. Whatley tried to undercut my relationship with the Betas."

A bullet whizzed by Penny's shoulder. She dove into a nearby stall, tumbling onto the straw bedding. Her revolver skittered across the cement. Without her weapon, she was vulnerable to the angry woman who would no doubt come after her. Forgetting she still had her pistol in her bag, she scrambled to her feet, sweeping her revolver into her hands.

The horses still trapped in the stalls were startled by the gunfire. They began shoving their rumps into each other and kicking the walls. They nickered and whinnied so loudly that a window shattered above the door, showering glass upon Genevieve who was still wobbling in her heels. Penny watched in amazement, as Genevieve, bruised and bleeding, struggled to her feet. She threw off her shoes, and ran out of the barn, with the rest of the horses hot on her heels.

A chestnut gelding broke free from the melee and galloped to the exit, knocking the woman on her rear end and flipping the gun from her hand which landed in one of the open stalls. Penny scooped up the woman's firearm, a semiautomatic pistol and charged after her.

Chapter 74

Johnny saw two black and red firetrucks from Sunland Park Fire Department heading into the parking lot of the Rio Grande Racetrack and Casino. He was just behind them, and turned on his bubble lights, in hopes of staying with the stream of emergency vehicles. The Fire Chief barreled around the whole squad and pushed down the road toward the stables.

Johnny knew what that meant. There was a barn fire. Horses, many of them contenders for the Kentucky Derby, were housed there during race days. The hopes and dreams of the race- track were also at risk if any of these horses were injured.

Johnny saw Don waving at him from the front steps of the casino. He pulled over so Don could jump in the patrol car. "I couldn't get back any further. The area was roped off and casino security would not let me through, even with my El Paso Fire Department credentials," Don said.

Johnny blew out a breath in frustration. "Let's inch our way back there and see if we can penetrate it."

Johnny's mobile phone rang. "This is Captain Trejo."

"Captain, this is Judy from Verizon. We have tracked the phone in question. I'm sending you the coordinates."

"My thanks, Judy. You may be saving lives. I'll let your supervisors know you came through for the state police."

"My duty and honor, sir."

The Verizon coordinates showed Penny's phone was located about 200 yards away, due east of the casino parking lot. Johnny pressed on the accelerator, trying to move faster, but there was no rushing the firetrucks, who were lumbering toward the fires as fast as they could. With the parking lot filled with cars, and people running in all directions it was a precarious journey. Johnny flashed his I.D. and he and Don were waved through.

"I could run faster than these trucks are going," Don said.

"Yes, I wondered if it would be better to get out of the car. But I need to stay with the vehicle because I have two patrol cars with officers on their way to Sunland Park."

"I'm going to go ahead. I'll call you with updates." Don jumped out before Johnny could come to a complete stop and took off running.

This was the last thing Johnny wanted, but he was grounded, waiting for his back up team. He pulled over to the side of the roadway. He had learned a long time ago that heroism was about executing a well-made plan, not having just one person trying to save the day. Johnny gripped the steering wheel, causing his fingers to burn against the leather. "Hurry up, you guys! I need to be there for Penny!"

Johnny realized that his words pinpointed his motivation. Of course, there were others in danger, but right now all he could think and worry about was Penny. He loved her, and if she made it through this, he was determined to tell her and ask her to marry him. Was that so tough to confess it? The declaration of love opened the flood gates of hope, Johnny had long suppressed. He was free and he would not let this feeling ever leave. Love wins! He was sure of it.

The bubble lights of two patrol cars pulled behind Johnny. Officer Grenhold knocked on Johnny's window. "We're ready, sir."

"Thank You, Gren. Follow me. We're headed to a GPS position sent to me by Verizon. I'll text it to you now."

Two New Mexico State Police vehicles roared passed the firetrucks. Johnny's GPS confirmed he was headed in the right direction. As the rows of barns came into view, one of the barns was in flames. Johnny's throat tightened. The barn on fire was the location of Penny's cell phone and the phone appeared to be on the move. *Where is she?*

Firefighters were jumping out of their trucks and stepping into their turn-out gear. They pulled on their oxygen backpacks and strapped their masks around their waists. They walked resolutely passed Johnny's car adjusting their gear and slinging their hatchets over their shoulders. Johnny knew from experience that firefighters don't run, they walk. With so much gear, running was a recipe for disaster. He watched them head into danger with much admiration. They were so very skilled, and knowing they might be saving Penny, as well as the horses, he respected them even more.

He searched for Penny among the crowd of firefighters in reflective gear and among onlookers who crowded a little too close to the flames. It was a madhouse. People were screaming. Trainers were chasing after horses with bridles and leads. And the fire chief was shouting out orders and trying to move bystanders out of the way.

A barefooted woman was making tracks away from the barns, with horses running behind her. Johnny thought that was a bit odd, but maybe she was a horse owner who got caught in the barn and was running for her life. Could the scene be any more chaotic?

Johnny ordered his team to pull to the side of the road and to wait for his orders. He would formulate a plan before sending his men into the fray. Automatic weapons, crowds and flames do not mix. And as much as he wanted to storm the barn, he restrained his desire to be the one to find and save the woman he loved.

Chapter 75

Black smoke caused Penny to pull her sweater over her head. She left enough room in her cardigan to find her way forward. She pushed onward. The woman in the beige suit had disappeared and the horses had long ago galloped to freedom. In her pursuit of Sonny March's sister, Penny could no longer see well. The dust was thick, and smoke was billowing passed her face. She stumbled as she rounded the corner of the barn and fell into the arms of a firefighter. He was just pulling on his oxygen mask and lifted it to see who it was. She pressed her hands into her sides, hoping he did not notice she was armed.

"Whoa, young lady. You, okay?"

"I'm okay. Thanks." Sweat poured down her arms and legs, trickling into her tennis shoes. She regretted having worn shorts. Her legs were scratched and bruised.

"You need to get as far away as possible from this building. You hear me?"

"Yes, sir. I will."

"I'm okay. Thanks." Sweat poured down her arms and legs, trickling into her tennis shoes. She regretted having worn shorts. Her legs were scratched and bruised.

"You need to get as far away as possible from this building. You hear me?"

"Yes, sir. I will."

"The best way through this mess is to your left. Keep heading south and you will find a medic who will help you."

Penny moved toward the shouting and the angry voices of owners and trainers, who were looking for their horses. Tears fell from her eyes, inspired by disgust and rage. She had been a fool and though she was free from this burning barn, she was still trapped by the bridle of her aching heart.

She took off running, a gun in each hand, serving as a ballast for her stride. She didn't care about anything anymore. She was a failure at life.

Penny cried out in despair—a long sorrowful cry. "God help me find my way to sobriety!"

Don Tellez grabbed Penny by the arm and pulled her close. "Penny. Thank God you are safe!" When he pulled on her arms, to check to see if she had been injured, he noticed the guns. "Give me those. You are in no shape to fire one."

She handed over the firearms and leaned into his side. "Don, I've got to find the woman who killed Ken Whatley. She is an employee of the casino and claims to be the sister of Sonny March."

"She can't have gone far. The roads are clogged with cars and emergency vehicles."

Don shoved the guns in a shoulder pack he had strapped to his waist and then moved Penny forward.

"Don, thank you for coming for me." Penny couldn't help but cry. Tears were streaming down her face and on to her neck. She was so relieved to be out of the way of the flames and bitter smells of burning straw and wood.

Don took out a handkerchief and handed it to Penny, who wiped her eyes, face and neck. For an instant, she thought of Leo, who always carried a handkerchief, too. "I was such a fool to believe Whatley—that he would help me find trainers who…" Penny stopped in mid-sentence. She had yet to confide in Don about the Argentine Dog Bone Bit and the drugs. She had lied through omission to the one person who had cared to come to her rescue.

"Don, I am so sorry. I haven't been truthful with you. We need to talk before anything else goes wrong."

"Nothing else will go wrong. Right now, you need medical attention before you confess your sins." Don smiled and led Penny to a first aid station where a medic looked her over for injuries and burns. The medic cleaned off the scrapes on Penny's arms and legs with an alcohol swab and bandaged one deep cut on her arm. She took a cup of cocoa from a volunteer and sat at a table, that was filling quickly with coffee urns, and hot pots.

"The casino is sending over some food," the medic told a volunteer. Be ready to serve the firefighters, as they need it."

Penny stuffed Don's handkerchief in the pocket of her shorts and when she did, Ron Becker's AA chip fell into the dirt. She picked it up and rolled it over in the palm of her hand. She had tucked it in her shorts for luck and now she read Shakespeare's quote again, "Unto thine own self be true." When had that ever occurred for her? She had a habit of lying her way through life to survive. It seemed like the best way to keep people from knowing her heart.

Don returned while Penny was still drinking her hot chocolate. "I want you to follow me, Penny. There is something important you need to do."

Penny was puzzled about what could be more important that finding Sonny March's sister. She finished her hot drink and followed him through the maze of people, some in tears, some yelling out angry words to firefighters. "My horse. Why haven't you found him?"

Penny walked arm-in-arm with Don. She felt safe and assured that life would improve now because he had cared enough to find her. "Don, wait a second, will you?" He stopped walking and looked at her and then smiled. Penny leaned up to his face and kissed his cheek. "I have totally misjudged you."

"As have I, Penny. I admire you so much."

"Admire is a pretty strong word!" Penny laughed.

"I care for you, Penny. It is more than admiration for sure, but my feelings started with my respecting what you do. Now I know you are someone with amazing skills. And I am grateful you agreed to work with me." Don took Penny in his arms and rubbed her back. His fingers crossed the place where Penny had taken the brunt of the coat rack, when Whatley shoved her into the wall. She knew this pain would soon disappear. He kissed her on the lips, lightly, and tapped her on the nose. "You are someone special to me. You always have been. Ever since Leo brought you to Thanksgiving dinner, I have cared about you."

Penny looked up at Don in amazement. "What are you saying? You always told Leo you thought I was a fraud."

"I lied to protect myself. I was pretty good at it, no?" He smiled and kissed her on the cheek.

"Yes, you are the master of disguise." Penny chuckled, and rubbed her hands across his face, and lips. "But I am beginning to see the real you, now."

"We'd better keep moving, Penny."

Penny and Don trudged on passed the firetrucks, until they reached three New Mexico State Police vehicles, with their engines running. The lights were whirling and creating a rainbow of colors that radiated against the stars.

Don led Penny to the first car they met. "Here she is, Captain. A little scraped up, but she will heal." Don quickly turned and walked away before Penny could protest. She looked over her shoulder for him, but Don had disappeared into the crowd. She had yet to confess the truth to him.

Johnny jumped out of his car and held Penny tightly. "Thank God, you are okay. I am never going to let you go!"

Chapter 76

Leo was just about home from the County Building when Don's call came. "Leo, I wanted you to know that Penny is okay."

"What are you talking about?"

"Penny was trapped in a barn fire at the racetrack, but she escaped. I found her and left her in good hands."

"Where is she now?'

"She's with Johnny Trejo."

Leo groaned.

"Penny dodged a bullet from Sonny March's sister, Genevieve, who shot and killed a feedstore owner. She is now on March's trail with Captain Trejo, trying to arrest the March woman for murder."

"I would rather you have taken Penny away from all that chaos, when you found her."

"Not a chance! Penny isn't budging. She figured out that Sonny March and Ron Becker's wife Georgia were drugging the Becker's mares to get them to abort their foals. And they were being paid generously by the New Generation Cartel."

"There is no way I could convince her to leave the racetrack, and besides, the roads are clogged because of the barn fire and unbridled horses running wild.

"Damn her. She is so bull-headed." Leo spit his rage into the dust. "Once again, I cannot help her."

"Well, Leo, you introduced her to Ron Becker. So, as you know, once Penny is given a challenge, she won't stop until she has found the people responsible for burning down horse barns."

Chapter 77

Penny pulled away from Johnny's embrace. Her fingers lingered on the sleeve of his uniform. She could tell something was different about him—different about them. But she had no time to weigh what this difference was. And besides, what in the world was happening with Don? Who would have ever expected such a confession of his affection for her? This was such a puzzle in her life, but there was no time to process the likes of it because her urge to chase after Sonny March's sister was pressing on her frontal lobe like a vise.

Johnny had no doubt overreacted to the fact that Penny had been in danger. Holding her so tightly and declaring that he would never let her go, had certainly been a momentary loss of his professional demeanor. She helped him recover it by directing him to the task at hand.

"Johnny, what's the hold up? We've got to catch up with Sonny March's sister!"

"She can't go far in her bare feet." He laughed, and then turned away from Penny, heading toward the officers, who were hanging tight in their patrol cars with the engines running.

"Johnny, if we find this woman, it will lead us to the cartel boss who is responsible for the barn fires," Penny said. She had not previously considered that a woman might play a role in having pregnant mares killed, but why not? Genevieve March worked at the casino, relatively close to the track. And Penny remembered that she had viewed the poker players in the backroom of the casino. Those men looked like they were betting with more than chips. A shiver moved up and down her arms. She had to find Genevieve March as soon as possible. She was key to solving this case.

Penny watched as Johnny and his officers dressed for the hunt, donning bullet proof vests and strapping on gun belts loaded with special gear and extra magazines. Two of the men had automatic weapons slung over their shoulders.

Johnny brought Penny a flak jacket. "Put this on."

Penny didn't fight it. She knew the dangers of chasing after a fleeing suspect. They often panic and do stupid things, like fire a gun at you. Penny had taken Genevieve's gun, but maybe this woman had friends who were armed, such as those cigar-smoking, poker players.

XXXXXX

As they moved toward the casino, Johnny was overwhelmed with anxiety. He tried not to show it, otherwise his men would lose their confidence. And, besides, he did not want Penny to think he was shaken at finding her alive. She was banged up and badly bruised. Her shirt was torn, and she looked as though a black eye might be forming on her beautiful face. He wanted more than anything to be a hero in Penny's life, but he also knew she could take pretty good care of herself. It was a tight rope loving a woman who was capable and intuitive. Heck, she probably could view his thoughts, which were dancing in his eyes like flickering neon lights. If that were the case, then Penny already knew he loved her.

Johnny ordered Officers José Silva and Juan Navarro to split up and make a wide arc around the casino. Silva and Navarro were equipped with automatic weapons, and Johnny wanted to give them a wide berth. "Stay alert, Officers!" Johnny yelled. "If we need you, I'll give you the signals on your radios to move. The orders of the day are 'One-Armed Bandit.' If you hear me calling to you over the radio, you know I need you."

Penny, Johnny and the other two officers, Nick Grenhold (Gren) and Pablo Montoya (Monty), headed straight to the backdoors of the casino. Penny showed them the way she and Whatley had taken. "I remember it was the door leading directly into the paddocks."

"Stay close to me," Johnny said. "Do you have your revolver or your special issue?"

I don't have my revolver. Don took it, but I do have my pistol."

"I still want you to walk right behind me. If you see the woman, then tap me on the shoulder. I'll take it from there."

Johnny wished he could send Penny to some place safe, but he knew better than to tell her she wasn't needed on this hunt. And how else would he know for certain who they were tracking? There would be hundreds of guests playing the slots—and many middle-aged women with brown hair, for that matter. But of course, none would be barefoot, he would wager.

When they tried to enter from the back of the casino, a security officer was guarding the door. "Sorry, sir. No one can come in through the back right now."

Johnny flashed his badge, and the guard said nothing. He opened the door and gave the crew a nod. Johnny knew the man did not want to stir up trouble with the New Mexico State Police. The racetrack and the casino tried hard to maintain a good relationship with law enforcement because gambling establishments always attracted trouble.

"Penny, take us to the last place you saw the woman." Johnny said.

"Sure. It was in the lobby." Penny pointed in the direction of the lobby, trailing back through the noise of the bells signifying a win, and the dropping of coins into plastic buckets. "After talking with Whatley, she exited through those double doors." Penny pointed to the doors that read, "Do Not Enter. Alarm Will Sound."

"Let's test those alarms," Johnny said. He charged through the doors with his officers following, with Penny close behind them. No alarm was triggered.

Chapter 78

Penny felt naked, even with a flak jacket. Why had she let Don take her revolver and Genevieve's pistol? By now he had probably realized that her 38 Smith and Wesson had belonged to his own father. As a gift from Leo, Penny cherished it, knowing that Leo and Don's father had carried this *Chief's Special*, for more than 30 years. And now her only recourse was using her official agency-issue pistol—the firearm she had used to kill two fleeing fugitives. The chicken had come home to roost, and she *was* the chicken.

On the hunt for Genevieve March, Penny would never forget those dark eyes, long lashes, and beautiful beige suit. Certainly, March was part of the casino's management. Why else dress so formally in the Southwest heat, unless you were in charge of something?

The double doors from the lobby led down a long, dark hallway. Johnny and his team, and Penny Larkin crashed through them without repercussions. Gren flipped on his flashlight, which produced an eerie spear of brightness that bounced off the paneled walls. Penny was frustrated. She needed to know what Johnny and his officers were facing. Why didn't anything appear in her mind to help them?

A blast of cold air blew across Penny's legs. She shivered. Were there air conditioning ducts on the floor? The blast of air arrived again. This time Penny realized there must be a lower level. In her mind's eye, Penny thought she saw Genevieve March crouched beneath the floor, hiding under a table.

"Hold-up, Johnny!" Penny said. "I'm getting the feeling that the casino has an underground bunker right beneath us. Maybe this is where our fugitive is hiding."

XXXXX

Johnny dropped to his knees and began feeling the floor. Officer Grenhold pointed his torch at Johnny's hands. He knew that drug cartels were famous for their underground tunnels leading in and out of Mexico, but why would they need one under a casino? And then it dawned on him that the village of Anapra, Mexico was walking distance, just across the border.

"It's too late to get a drug dog in here," Johnny said. "Perhaps they are hiding contraband. It would be handy, since the Mexican border is so close."

The blast of air shot across Penny's legs again. At the end of the hall was a slot machine, the old kind, that took quarters. Penny rushed over to the machine. "Does anyone have a quarter?"

"What the hell?" Johnny looked at Penny and shook his head. He threw her a quarter from his pocket. Penny pushed the coin in the slot and pulled the arm on the machine. A door opened.

Johnny could see a stairway leading downward. "Let's go!" He ordered.

Gren and Monty followed Johnny. Once again, Penny trailed behind as they charged down the stairs. Johnny slowly opened a door at the base of the steps. The room was long, narrow and dark. Gren's flashlight revealed a series of shelves filled with white paper bags.

"What in the world?" Johnny asked. The shelves held a myriad of drugs, each labeled and alphabetized. "This is a regular pharmacy."

At the end of the room, Johnny thought he heard the legs of a chair rubbing against the cement floor. The officers rushed toward the sound, as a woman in house slippers ran to the stairway leading to freedom. "Stop. Now!" Johnny ordered.

"That is Sonny March's sister!" Penny yelled.

Genevieve March groaned as Officer Montoya wrestled her off the steps.

"What is your name?" he asked.

"I am Genevieve March. I am the administrative director of the casino. You have no right to hold me."

"You fired a gun at me!" Penny said. "That's enough for starters."

Chapter 79

Leo's mind was wound tighter than the ball of rubber bands he kept in his office drawer. What had he been thinking? He could not stand by and let Penny fall into the hands of the Betas or the New Generation Cartels. Now that he was officially the El Paso County Sheriff for the next four years, he was emboldened to act but still constrained. Rio Grande Racetrack and Casino was in New Mexico. The casino was so close and yet light years out of his jurisdiction.

Leo punched in Don's number into his cell phone. "Hi, Don."

"I still want to help." Leo said. He could hear loud noises in the background.

"I think everything is in good hands," Don answered.

"I can be there in 30 minutes."

"Unless you can hire a helicopter to transport you into the Sunland Park campus, you aren't going to get too close. Everything is locked down, right now. I'm still near the barns looking over the fire damage, while Penny and Captain Trejo are searching the casino for Genevieve March."

"I have an uneasy feeling about this, Don. Delivering drugs to pregnant mares through a bone bit is one of the worst things I've ever heard."

"What are you talking about?"

"Didn't Penny tell you about the horse bits the cartels are using to deliver cocaine and clenbuterol, and heck knows what other drugs, to pregnant mares trying to get them to abort?"

There was no response on Don's end of the phone.

"Don, are you still with me?"

"Yeah. I'm here." Don kicked the dirt with the toe of his boot.

"Penny found an Argentine Dog Bone horse bit in your burned-out warehouse. She had a reaction to its copper bead, even holding one in the palms of her hands."

"Damnit!" Leo could tell Don was angry. "Why am I the last to have this information? I thought Penny was working for me!"

"I only know it because I ran into Penny at the emergency room. She was there after a bad reaction to a cocaine and clenbuterol combination."

"You checked-out okay?"

"Yes, just a bad case of food poisoning. You've got to find Penny. She may have Johnny with her, but that is not enough cover for the likes of the Betas or even worse, the New Generation boys. They are *bastardos malos!*"

"What do you suggest?" Don asked.

"I'll call on Sheriff Rodriguez in Dona Ana County. He can get me near the casino."

"I'm not waiting for you to show up, Leo."

Don disconnected the call. Leo didn't blame him for being angry. Why hadn't Penny told him about the bone bit? He rang his friend, Sheriff Ted Rodriguez, in Las Cruces.

"Ted, what are you doing for the next couple of hours?"

Chapter 80

Johnny Trejo ordered Officer Montoya to cuff Genevieve March as he and Officer Grenhold examined the shelves of drugs. Each container was marked. There was MDMA, or ecstasy or molly, as it was known by frequent abusers. They also found the shelves of cocaine in various doses and mixtures. On the back side of the shelves were opioids such as oxycodone, hydrocodone, diphenoxylate, clenbuterol, morphine, codeine, fentanyl, propoxyphene and hydromorphone.

It was a storehouse whose street value was unknown to Johnny. He would leave that task to the FBI. He did know this was an unprecedented and dangerous holding. And it was big enough that it would make national news.

"Over here!" Gren was pointing to an opened door, which led to what looked like a tunnel.

Before Johnny could respond, a bullet blistered Gren's shoulder, dropping him to his knees. "Damnit!" Johnny growled under his breath as he and Gren, ducked behind the shelves, their fingers gripping their firearms. Johnny watched as three cartel *sicarios* stomped up the stairs from the tunnel, their own guns sweeping through the basement. They did not fire again.

"*¡Sal de detrás de esos estantes!*" One of the hitmen yelled at Johnny and Gren to come out from their hiding places.

Johnny had been stupid. He had broken a cardinal rule in law enforcement. Overwhelmed by the cache of drugs, he had forgotten about Genevieve March, and for God's sake, he had also left Penny vulnerable. He and Gren walked out from behind the shelves of drugs. Johnny held his hands in the air, but Gren could only hold his bleeding left arm with his right. Johnny looked for help from Monty, but he, too, had his hands in the air.

Johnny located Penny, who was crouched in the corner of the room. Her eyes were darting back and forth. Johnny knew Penny was hoping he had a plan, but he had none. He was letting them both down, and the pain of disappointing her, wrestled with the fear in his gut.

"Suelta tus armas!" Johnny and Gren complied and laid their guns on the floor. Monty sat on the cement floor with his back against the wall.

A shooter standing by Genevieve March, pointed to her handcuffs.

Gren walked over to Monty and pulled his keys off his leather belt and unlocked the woman's cuffs. Genevieve rushed over to the man with his gun on Johnny and Gren and kissed his cheek. *"Gracias, Felipe."*

Felipe ignored her, keeping his eyes on his prey. He wasn't about to be distracted. In a perverse way, Johnny admired him. He would have made a good law officer, focused on the task, and not blinded by passion or the possibility of making a big splash in the evening news. He swallowed hard at the thought of his own misguided aspirations.

Felipe ordered the two other henchmen to move everyone upstairs. *"Marco y Hector, matarlos aquí hace demasiada sangre."* He waved his automatic rifle in an upward motion. *"Llévalos fuera del casino."*

Johnny knew the gunmen would not kill everyone in the storeroom, as it would cause too much of a mess. And besides, it would be tough trying to haul four dead bodies up those narrow stairs, and away from the casino. That was a lucky break, if you could call it one. Johnny hoped there was still time to save their lives, if he could come up with a plan. His mind was shooting blanks.

Hector took the lead, with Johnny, Monty, and Penny following in single file up the narrow staircase. Marco grabbed Gren by his good shoulder and hauled him up, one step at a time.

Chapter 81

The night air stung Penny's eyes. Her face was covered by a suffocating pillow of smoke. Felipe shoved Penny and the rest of his captives into a storage area that served as a receptacle for garbage and recycling. The place was protected by a tall chain link fence woven through with privacy strips, to keep prying eyes out of the dregs of casino life. Penny looked at piles of trash, with stained cocktail napkins, stirring sticks, and cigarette butts. Another barrel held heaps of cracked yellow plastic cups used by gamblers to collect their coins. Penny hoped these gamblers were luckier than she because right now, Penny was on a losing streak. She didn't believe Johnny held a winning hand either.

Penny pulled her phone from her pocket. It was now dead. There was little hope of anyone tracking her location.

"You thought you were so smart!" Penny jerked her head toward Genevieve March, who was standing in between her and a mountain of garbage from the bar. "No one will know you were ever here," she said. "Felipe has his ways of making people disappear." She laughed so hard, she fell against one of the metal cans, knocking the lid against the casino wall.

The stink of lemon slices, cherry pits, and coffee grounds floated passed Penny's nose. It seemed fitting that Penny and Sonny March's sister would have a conversation over bags of garbage. After all, Genevieve and her hitmen were no better than trash.

Genevieve's beige suit did not look all that bad, considering she had murdered Ken Whatley and been kicked by a horse, before running from the paddock in her bare feet.

Her lipstick was fresh. Who was she trying to impress? Certainly, the woman wouldn't be accompanying them out to the field in her house slippers.

"Marcha a través del estacionamiento en un campo!" Felipe was now giving orders, and from what little Penny could understand, he was moving everyone out of the recycling area.

Penny knew the area around the casino was surrounded by open desert. It was set apart from the City of Sunland Park, New Mexico, thanks to sparse development, other than some temporary horse barns which the racetrack opened and closed according to overflow of competing horses.

Horse trainers usually didn't live near the racetrack. They chose to rent stalls before their horses competed. Penny had driven through the area often and had seen these make-shift stables, set up for major races. Were they heading to one of those barns? They would be empty of people and horses now that the races were over for the weekend. And, of course, racetrack security would be focused on the fire in the paddock near the casino. There would be no one to hear gunshots in the lean-to shelters scattered in the surrounding fields. No horse would whinny and pound their hooves against the stable doors.

"¡Vamonos! Come on!" Felipe yelled. Hector and Marco shoved the group forward. Gren was still on his feet, holding his shoulder. Penny noticed that the bleeding had stopped. Perhaps, the bullet had mercifully just grazed him.

"I'll say goodbye here," Genevieve said. "It's been lovely meeting you. *Mucho Gusto!*"

With that, she turned and shuffled her slippers back toward the casino.

The gate to the trash collection area swung wide open, and the motley group moved with deadly ease across the parking lot into the desert like a bed of scorpions on a mission. Penny shivered from fear and the cold night air. The sky was clear, revealing a stunning array of stars. Penny caught a glimpse of Johnny's face. He gave her a half-hearted smile. She knew there was nothing more one could do, short of trying to make a break for it across the parking lot, hiding behind cars. That plan had its merits, but Johnny did not indicate he was about to make a move. No thumbs up. No "one armed bandit" calls of distress. Penny knew Johnny well, however. Something was rolling around in his brain. She was sure of it.

When Hector was closing the gate, Penny thought she saw the shadow of someone creeping up behind one of the dumpsters. Another killer lurking in the debris? If so, why did he not show himself? For an instant, she hoped it was Don, or Leo. But that hope was short-lived, as Marco wrapped his arm around her waist, and pulled her close.

His breath was hot. His body smelled of sweat and salsa. He leaned into her neck and licked her ear. "My beautiful *señorita*. You will be my dessert this evening. I did not have time to finish my dinner. And my meal is never complete without something a little sweet."

Chapter 82

Don's mind was ablaze with anger. Penny had been keeping secrets from him about his arson investigation. Is this how you treat someone you hired to help solve it? He mopped his face with his sleeve and started running toward the casino.

"I'll be damned if I get taken for a fool!"

Winded from a burst of overconfidence, Don slowed his pace. As he got closer to the casino, he noticed two New Mexico State Police cars parked at the back of the building. Had Johnny and Penny and his team entered from the rear? Why? As he crept around the backside of the building, he heard voices coming from a fenced off area.

Don figured it had to be the casino's garbage and waste disposal site. "I'll bet that's a big pile of Maraschino cherries!"

Just as he closed in on the gate that opened into the garbage dump, Don heard a male voice shouting. "Andelez! Let's get going. We will carry these idiots to the overflow stables. No one will hear gunshots from that range."

The door to the waste area swung open, and Don dropped flat on the ground. He hoped the sage bushes growing around the fence line, would keep his presence a secret. He watched as three men led Johnny, Penny, and two police officers out into the desert. One police officer looked like he had been shot in the shoulder.

Don's anger transposed into worry. What had Penny got herself into that was also endangering the New Mexico State Police?

Chapter 83

The Dona Ana Sheriff's Department helicopter hovered over the smoky acres of chaos before choosing to land in a field 75 yards from the burning barn. Leo and Ted waved thanks to the pilot as they jumped off the chopper. The desert underbrush exploded in the air as the helicopter rose from the ground, covering the men in a bushelful of desert caliche. Still carrying a sense of law enforcement humor, they wiped one another's backsides and laughed.

Leo's phone buzzed. "Don, where are you? We've landed and are on our way toward the fire."

"Stop! I need you elsewhere. I had decided to join Penny and Johnny in the hunt for Genevieve March, but when I got to the casino, I found they had been captured by what looks like cartel heavies. Right now, the cartel is marching Johnny and Penny and a couple of New Mexico State troopers toward the temporary stables."

"The cartels have Penny?" Leo couldn't believe it.

"Yes. I heard the cartel boss say they should take the hostages to the stables and kill them."

Leo's anxiety was raging. "We'll head your way."

"I'll stay where I am. Though it stinks out here!"

Leo looked out over the parking lots at the rows of barns and the huge casino, which stood before them like a fortress in a fog of war. From what he could see, the fire had been contained to one barn, but the residue of smoke made it difficult to tell how much damage had been done.

Neither lawman relished trekking toward the casino. Both were wearing bulletproof vests and carrying extra rounds of ammo on their belts. Moving into the desert without lights would also be awkward in the dark.

Leo was driven by his desire to save Penny, and this shoved his feet forward. Ted who was Leo's fiercest friend, followed in Leo's footsteps.

At 60, Ted was not as agile as Leo at 40, but Ted was more surefooted along the rugged trail of life.

Don waved them down from the recesses of the fenced-in trash area. There was enough light for casino employees to empty the bar residue there and for the men to check their firearms, and lock and load.

Leo was grieving over the situation in which he had placed Penny. If he lost her, he would never forgive himself. Losing Alejandra was nothing he could control, but Penny was a different matter. This was all on him. And the graveyard was already full of people he loved.

"Hang in there, my friend. Penny's resourceful. Remember that." Ted placed his hand on Leo's back. "She chose law enforcement, and you should honor her decision just as you asked your family to honor yours."

Ted was right, as usual, but it didn't make it any easier to imagine Penny being subjected once again to a drug cartel. Would these evil bastards ever stop?

In a tandem decision, the men dropped into a crouching position and scoped out the path of this ominous caravan of people. The officers crawled toward the group, angling their trajectory so that they would eventually be able to approach the cartel on all sides.

Chapter 84

The pain in Johnny's body from the confrontation with the International Harvester was nothing compared to the aching in his heart for Penny. He watched in horror as a terrible leach held Penny's body close to his and rubbed his grungy hands all over her. He knew well how much Penny hated human touch. He had tried over the past year to make her feel more comfortable with the passion he had for her, but she rebuffed him each time. Penny had confessed that her experience with her foster father had changed her feelings about intimacy, perhaps forever.

Johnny had concluded they were headed for a certain death, but he never imagined his life ending without a fair fight. His father had valiantly defended his position before the Betas Cartel had gunned him down. Johnny would not even have the dignity of self-defense. Unarmed and overpowered, there did not seem to be a solution to this impending doom.

In his reverie, Johnny must have fallen behind. A hitman slammed the butt of his rifle into Johnny's back, knocking him into a prickly pear cactus. The spines dug into Johnny's hands. He was in pain, but he would not give this thug the satisfaction of knowing it. He wiped the blood from his fingers on the back of his jeans.

"Get up!" The man kicked Johnny in the side. This time, Johnny rolled out of the way of the cactus, landing on top of a yucca. It leaves were like spears, tearing into his flesh, even through his clothes. "Keep up."

Johnny spit blood out of his mouth, and grimaced. He looked around for Penny, who had mysteriously disappeared from the group. *"Donde esta la mujer?"* Johnny asked.

"She is no concern to you. She is in good hands, if you know what I mean."

The man's laugh erupted from the depths of his stomach, causing him to bend over to catch his breath. Johnny delivered a judo chop to the back of the man's neck, which dropped him onto the desert floor like a bag of casino coins. Another blow to the top of the head knocked him unconscious.

Johnny grabbed his rifle and made a sweeping search with his eyes for Penny. He could see the lead hitman, 50 feet ahead, walking in quick strides toward a row of barns. At this point he was outgunned, and Penny was nowhere to be found. But Johnny would find her if it was the last thing he ever did.

Chapter 85

Marco shoved Penny's hips against the foundation of one of the barns, leaving her bruised legs exposed to his healthy appetite for inflicting more pain. He pulled a flask from his hip pocket and leaned over her. "*Bebida*!"

Penny shook her head, but Marco placed his fingers in her mouth and poured whiskey down her throat. Gagging, she wrenched her body forward trying to keep from drowning. She spit the alcohol in Marco's face.

Marco threw his fist against her stomach, blowing the air out of her body. Penny collapsed. She craved air, but there was no oxygen left on the planet.

"You are not dying on me!" Marco cried. He lifted Penny over his shoulder, which miraculously brought air back into her chest. He threw her against the board and batten wall of the barn and began to unzip her jeans. Penny gasped for more air, as Marco groped her body. She could not fight him off while trying to pull air into her lungs which was her first priority.

For once she was grateful for an alcoholic's craving for another drink. Marco stopped his love fest to take a big slug of whiskey from his flask. When he did so, he swayed and staggered forward. As he was unzipping his own jeans, he stumbled toward the corner of the barn. "*Debo excusarma.*" I must excuse myself.

Penny watched as Marco disappeared around the corner to pee. She opened her bag, which Marco had miraculously ignored, as if the purse were an appendage. She fumbled around for the secret compartment. Her hands were shaking, trying to pull out the pepper spray. She'd never used it and could only hope it would work. Using her gun against him was out of the question.

When Penny heard Marco shuffling on his return, she unleashed a shot of pepper spray even before he turned the corner of the barn.

Marco walked right into the mist of hot peppers and capsaicin. He began wheezing and coughing.

"¡No puedo ver! ¡Me has cegado, perra!" I can't see! You blinded me, bitch!

Penny kept squeezing the trigger until there was nothing left in the canister. And then she took off running into the desert. Anywhere was better than in the hands of this bastard!

Chapter 86

Leo's knees were aching from crouching and crawling across the desert floor. He could hear Ted, a dozen feet behind him, panting. Leo waited for Ted, whose legs weren't as agile as they once were. *What in the world were we thinking?*

"I heard some shouting just ahead," Don whispered. "Let's be ready."

Ted gave an affirmative grunt. As sheriffs from bordering counties from different states, they had worked together many times. Leo and Ted had learned that crime doesn't respect state lines, and neither does friendship. And as for his brother, Don, Leo had never worked with him professionally, but he knew Don could overcome these killers. He was reassured by the company he kept.

Chapter 87

As much as Johnny wanted to hunt down the guy who was holding Penny hostage, and wring his neck, he had to save his deputies first. They were in the most danger for their lives. He crept as quietly as he could toward the leader who was cracking Johnny's officers on their shoulders with the butt of his rifle, to keep them moving.

Johnny checked the gun he had taken off his captor. It was loaded with a magazine of 10 rounds. He would be able to hold his own, as least for a while.

Now the *el jefe* was yelling. "*Estúpidos gringos. Puedo tener tu tipo para el almuerzo todos los días*" You stupid gringos. I can have your kind for lunch every day!

Johnny was close enough to realize there was only Felipe guarding his two officers. Gren was still vertical, thank God, although he was holding his arm.

Johnny looked back but saw no one following him. The leader seemed confident that the others in his team were bringing up the rear.

As repugnant as it was to see her being molested, Johnny knew Penny could disable her captor, remembering how much she hated drunks. Thus, Johnny had to be satisfied with his decision to take down the *el jefe* alone.

Johnny turned his head anyway and looked back in hopes that he could see Penny and the leech who was holding her hostage. *Nada*. But things were looking up. He hoped *mano a mano*, he could take on Felipe and win. Felipe would be expecting help from Hector, but Johnny had already de-commissioned him. Armed with the semiautomatic rifle he had commandeered, Johnny checked it over. It was a WASR-10, a rifle made in Romania and quite popular among the drug cartels. Johnny had never fired one, but he had confiscated quite a few. This one had not been modified, so it still held only a magazine capacity of 10.

Chapter 88

Penny ran in a blind panic through the desert, not caring what direction she was taking. It didn't matter as long as her groping guzzler was not following her. She stopped to catch her breath and to assure herself that no one was on her trail. Penny could still see the lights of the firetrucks and the police vehicles in the distance, giving her a bead on a place of safety.

She knew Johnny and his team were still headed with their cartel captors toward the temporary barns, which were due south of the racetrack. She could see the faint glow coming from those barns, which were empty since racing was over for two weeks.

The smart thing, of course, would be for Penny to hike toward the firefighters and get help from the medic tent. She had been there before and knew she would be safe there. But what is safety worth, when the person you love is not safe?

Her conclusion surprised her. *I love Johnny!* Penny had always wanted to experience love first-hand, but her days in foster care with a wayward foster father, had kept her from ever risking it. And yet, here was love arriving unexpectedly, like a feather perching in her soul—just as Emily Dickinson had described it.

Penny had to find Johnny and together go down fighting for their lives.

Chapter 89

Johnny rubbed the barrel of the captured WASR-10 with his shirt tail and checked for any dirt or other obstructions in the barrel. He knew the WASR-10 was a cheap foreign-made gun, but he also had heard it was reliable up to 400 yards. He had to count on it. It was all he had. He looked closer and saw that the barrel was chrome-lined, which eased his concerns about the military surplus ammo, with which the gun was loaded.

Johnny headed toward the dimly lit barns which were nothing more than tilt-up structures designed to house visiting horses and their trainers during racing season. He hoped the cartel hitmen didn't try to kill his officers before he got there. His plan was to pick-off Felipe, and gambled there wasn't any other hitmen waiting at the stables. Johnny would spend his 10 bullets wisely.

As he ran toward his prey, Johnny fell into a gopher hole, slamming his face into the rocky soil and knocking himself unconscious.

XXXXX

Leo and Ted were having a hard time keeping up with Don.

"Come on, you, guys. Keep up!" Don shouted.

Leo and Ted's flak jackets were heavy enough, but they had also stuffed their pants pockets with an overload of ammo. The decision was made to pare back. They dropped several magazines of bullets, much to their chagrin. They knew they would need all the firepower possible when fighting against the cartels.

Once the load was lightened, the three men picked up speed. They were drawing close enough that they could detect dust in the air from where the hitmen and their captives had marched.

Don could hear faint sounds of voices. "Drop down!" he whispered.

They crouched to keep from being detected, while slowly and painfully making forward progress. Don could smell cigarette smoke. He lifted his hand in a cautionary way. "We're close."

XXXXX

Penny's mind was consumed with Johnny's welfare. She had a new appreciation for her mother's longing for the safety of her father, who risked his life in open wheel racing every time he could get a sponsor. Penny had a better understanding of her mother's drinking. It was perhaps her way of coping with something out of her control. *Was this sobriety—learning what you can control and doing something about it, and accepting what you can't control, and letting it go?*

Penny moved forward with new confidence. She didn't know if she would live or die in her confrontation with the cartel hitmen. Most likely she would die. But it would not matter for her to live if she was not sober enough to enjoy it. She began running toward the barns in a desperate attempt to find Johnny.

Chapter 90

When Leo, Ted, and Don were within 25 yards of the barns, they saw a man staggering around, carrying a flask of whiskey and crying. "La he perdido!" I've lost her!

Another man came out from the shadows of the barns and yanked the drunk by the arm.

"Eres un estúpido idiota. No puedo confiarte el seguimiento de una mujer." I can't even trust you to keep track of a woman.

Leo took heart. Perhaps Penny had managed to escape. *But where is she?*

Leo, Ted, and Don decided to split up.

"I'll stay put, "Don offered.

"Then I'll head west," Leo said. "And Ted, how about you go south?"

Ted gave the men a thumbs up.

"The goal, mi amigos, is surprise the cartel. We will circle the barns and ping each other when we are ready to attack." Leo said.

The plan wasn't perfect. Who has time to text during an emergency? But their cell phones were all they had to communicate with each other.

XXXXX

Penny pulled her agency-issued pistol from her bag and wrapped her fingers around the grip. She was now on the clock as a U.S. Marshal, and fully prepared to hunt down these barbarians, and bring back Johnny alive. As she shoved the magazine into the grip, she was prepared for pain, but the magazine slipped in easily—thanks to Ollie's great instructions at the firing range.

The dust was making Penny cough, so she tied her scarf over her nose and mouth. As she closed in on the temporary stables, she could hear angry voices. Her Spanish wasn't good enough to interpret, but she knew there was descension in the mix. Maybe she could use it to her advantage.

Creeping closer, she heard heavy breathing, and figured it was Marco. He was drink, no doubt, after trying to pour his whiskey down her throat and in the end, emptying his flask into his own belly.

She listened intently trying to understand what the men were saying.

"¿Qué pasó con Hector?" What happened to Hector?

"No sé. Él simplemente caminaba detrás de nosotros con el oficial Trejo." I don't know. He was walking behind us with the señor Trejo.

"Marco, te pedí que mantuvieras a todos en línea." Marco, I asked you to keep everyone in line.

Penny looked around the corner of the barn and realized Johnny was not there. But she could see Officers Grenhold and Montoya still being alive. Penny wondered if she should rescue them first before looking for Johnny. She was torn. She knew as a U.S. Marshal she should not prioritize who she saves.

During her quandary, about 200 yards out, she saw lights of a vehicle heading toward them. She had to take out Felipe now. Penny ran toward Felipe, firing her pistol and hitting him in the chest with her first bullet. He fell in the dust. Marco, who had been roused by the sound of the gunfire, remained confused, his gun trembling in his hand. Officer Montoya responded by grabbing Marco's pistol and throwing the drunk against the wall of the barn.

"¡Ponte de rodillas!" Get on your knees!

Montoya threw handcuffs on Marco, while Officer Grenhold, grimaced and zip-tied Felipe's hands and ankles, even though the man appeared gravely injured.

"Is everyone prepared for the trucker?" Penny asked. "My guess is he came alone."

Gren nodded and Monty gave a thumbs up. "Let's do this!"

As if on cue, Ted, Leo, and Don appeared on the scene. Penny, Gren, and Monty all cheered. "Thank you!"

"Now that we have crowd funding, we can certainly take down the truck driver," Penny laughed. But while Penny was smiling, her heart was aching because Johnny was nowhere to be found.

Chapter 91

The A team easily overcame the truck driver, who was unpleasantly surprised by his reception committee. In a quick decision, the cartel members, both surprised, injured, or inebriated, were loaded into the back of the box truck. The *el jefe*, who had been shot, was still breathing but horizontal. His hands and feet were disabled with zip ties and his body was wedged between a couple of tire jacks so he wouldn't roll around during the trip through the desert. Marco's feet were cobbled with someone's belt, and his hands zip tied behind his back.

Don took over the assignment of guarding this motley crew, while Monty and Gren sat on the truck bed, on the look-out for other cartel members who might be on the hunt for their amigos.

Ted and Penny rode in the cab while Leo drove.

"I don't want to spoil our party, but Johnny Trejo is missing," Penny said. "If he's been injured let's make sure this truck doesn't run over him."

Sure enough, the truck passed a wounded cartel member, Hector, whose head wound looked serious. He moaned as the team picked him up and laid him in the back of the truck.

Since the Rio Grande Racetrack and Casino was in Dona Ana County, New Mexico, Sheriff Ted Rodriguez called his headquarters for an ambulance, as well as a patrol car to transport the suspects to the county jail.

As the truck moved toward the casino, Don was yelling, but it was hard to hear what he was saying over the engine roar. "There is another body! Stop! There is someone else lying in the dirt. Stop!"

Leo shoved on the brakes. Everyone piled out of the truck.

XXXXX

Penny recognized Johnny. She ran to him, yelling while trying to assess his injuries. “It’s Johnny!” He appeared unresponsive. “He’s not breathing!”

Leo knelt beside Johnny and turned him on to his side, *the recovery position*, to open his airway. Johnny moaned. “Call 9-11. He’s still alive.”

Chapter 92

Penny sat in the intensive care waiting room with Johnny's mother. They had stayed there all night, after Johnny had been rushed to Mountain View Regional Medical Center in Las Cruces. Leo, Don, and Ted had left at 4 a.m. hoping to catch some breakfast.

"At least the surgeon said there was no brain bleed, "Penny said, trying to reassure Ollie.

"Remember what I told you, Penny, about wasting your time?"

"No. What do you mean?"

"I urged you and Johnny many times to confess to each other what was so painfully obvious to me. Your love for one another brought me a rare joy. It's been keeping me going, actually."

Penny rested her head in her hands. "I'm not sure who is more gun shy, Johnny or me."

Ollie pleaded. "It shouldn't take a near a death experience to bring two people to their senses."

"Ollie, I'm sorry, if I've caused you to worry about us. You know how I feel about your son, but I have a lot of baggage, and I don't want Johnny having to haul it around all our married lives."

'When there's two people holding the load, it doesn't feel so heavy."

"Truth is, I watched my mother drink herself to death worrying about my dad at the racetrack. And I'm not sure how you handled it so long with your husband being in law enforcement."

"Here's the point, Penny. Just like those horses you've been trying to save, we crave a bridle, to help lead us to safe places in our lives. The problem is when the trainer puts a bit in the horse's mouth. It's no fun anymore. It's work."

"But, when a horse is unbridled, they are likely to run wild and injure themselves.

There's got to be a compromise here."

At that moment, Johnny's doctor appeared in the waiting room. "Mrs. Trejo. Your son is asking to see you."

"Praise God. Can she come, too?"

"Yes, but just stay a few minutes. He's still pretty weak."

Chapter 93

Leo, Don, and Ted were grabbing breakfast at Lucy's Coffee Shop on North Mesa. No one spoke for several minutes while the men shoveled eggs and bacon down their throats.

"I don't know when I've been this hungry," Don said.

"I can't stay long. As starved as I am, you know the Feds are going to be breathing down my backside trying to figure out what the cartels are into now."

"I'm sure they hadn't counted on horses being the center of all the intrigue," Leo laughed.

"I'll keep you posted after I make a house call on Genevieve March, Marco Lopez, and the truck driver, Juan Martin. And I'll have to I.D. the dead bodies, for what that's worth.

Leo took a breath and pushed away from the table. "Be prepared for the international spotlight, Ted. This is drug smuggling kicked up a notch. Who suspected the cartels had dug a tunnel from Mexico to New Mexico? You have to give the cartels props for their ingenuity."

Ted chuckled. "I can see the DEA now, rubbing their hands together and salivating over such a broad selection of pharmaceuticals. They will be inspecting the casino's unofficial pharmacy for months."

"And don't forget the preciseness of the FBI. They will be dusting for fingerprints and looking for remnants of DNA." Leo said.

"Ah, yes. I read that the Mexican Biolab has the DNA of more than 1.8 million Mexican citizens right now. Maybe we will get lucky."

"We are in unchartered territory—sharing DNA might be a new frontier worth pursuing especially in arson investigations." Don said. "But I don't have to tell you I'm really miffed at Penny for holding back on me about the dog bone bit. She's taking City of El Paso money, for heaven's sake," Don said.

"Why don't you talk to her first before you break up with her," Leo replied.

"What are you saying?"

"Don, I know you. You try to move in on every woman I've ever cared about."

Ted wiped his chin and took one last slurp of coffee. He swiped the check off the table. "I'm not going to get in between a dispute with brothers, so I'm paying, knowing one of you will soon be collecting unemployment."

"Whoops. I forgot to share the good news. The County Commissioners voted to hire me for four more years."

Ted slapped Leo on the back. "You were with me for hours and never mentioned it. Congratulations."

"Honestly, I wasn't thinking about it just knowing Penny was facing the cartels again. Nothing seemed to matter but her safety."

"Adios!" Ted ambled his way to the cashier and dropped some bills for the breakfast and left the restaurant.

Don looked at Leo in disbelief. "Leo, as I recall you and Penny are not even dating. How is caring about her, moving in on your territory? You aren't even a border state right now."

"I'm just saying, before you dismiss Penny's actions, ask her why she didn't tell you."

"Fair enough. I'll ask, but I'm also going to ask for my money back."

Chapter 94

Penny would never forget the sounds of excessive noise of the hospital as she and Ollie followed Dr. Robert Howard to the ICU. She was struck by the jarring noises emanating from the business of caring for people. Perhaps it was the hard surfaces which were expected to absorb the clatter of food carts rolling down the hallway, or the intercom announcements, or the hustle and bustle of the nurse's station. Penny didn't understand how this kind of environment encouraged healing.

"Right this way, "Dr. Howard said.

Penny and Ollie followed the doctor down a long, seemingly endless hallway of tile walls and linear architecture, that made Penny nauseous. Finally, the doctor pointed to the ICU where several patients were strapped to an endless road of tubes and wires.

"Captain Trejo is in the third bed."

Penny let Ollie lead the way. Ever Since Ollie's husband had been killed in a cartel gun battle, Ollie had held on tighter to her only son. Penny could understand it, and never discouraged their relationship, even when as a couple, they struggled with conflicting hopes and dreams for the future.

Ollie leaned into Johnny, whose eyes were open, though not appearing to be focused on any person or thing. "Honey. I'm here."

Johnny's eyes rolled toward the voice and immediately acknowledged his mother.

"Mama. I wish I had better news. My head is harder than we figured. It's going to take more than a concussion to straighten up my life."

"Johnny, I've brought along someone who wants to give you a piece of her own mind. You already know how I feel about your taking risks."

Johnny looked at Penny and let out a long breath. "You are alive."

"Yeah. I know we both did our best to kill ourselves off, but we are still breathing. This is a victory of sorts."

"Where do we go from here?" Johnny asked.

"Your mother thinks we need to take a closer look at our relationship and make a commitment to each other."

"Mama. Since when do you interfere in my love life?"

"This isn't interference, it is Divine intervention. I've prayed to God for the last year for you and Penny to realize you are perfectly suited for one another. And now, with both of you laying your lives on the line, I think it's time to come clean and confess, you both love one another."

Ollie turned on her heels and left the room

Johnny held out his hand for Penny. "Is there any truth to my mother's wild ideas about love?"

"I have to confess that when I thought you were likely going to be shot by those murdering thugs, I knew that love was going to drive me to do whatever I could to find you and kill those idiots myself."

"I love you, Penny."

"I love you, Johnny. But I must warn you that I've got a long road ahead. I'm planning on taking some time to attend Al-Anon meetings. Just because I don't have an alcohol or drug issue, I've been nursing on my mother's inability to accept things she couldn't change.

Penny pulled Becker's AA coin from her pocket. "If it's okay with you, let us be true to ourselves. And if this turns out to be a relationship that keeps us from being false to each other, or to anyone else, then we have a wonderful chance of living sober and loving with joy."

Johnny reached for Penny's hand. "I promise to be true to you, and to be true to who I am, too." He looked up and saw his mother walking toward them.

"I think this occasion deserves a big plate of green chile enchiladas. I'm heading home to roast the chiles and put on the tea kettle."

#

www.ingramcontent.com/pod-product-compliance
Lightning Source LLC
LaVergne TN
LVHW010309070526
838199LV00065B/5490
9798992603101